# Jack
## *of*
# Spades

*A World War Two Story*

D1452509

DAVID LUCERO

Published 2020 by Your Book Angel
Copyright © David Lucero

Printed in the United States
Edited by Keidi Keating
Layout by Rochelle Mensidor

ISBN: 978-1-7356648-5-9

World War Two readers will find *Jack of Spades* a fast-paced, involving study of men at war. Lucero does a fine job contrasting major character moves, experiences, and struggles. Personal insights and details are part of what make *Jack of Spades* more than a dispassionate series of battle encounters one might expect from usual World War Two stories. The author injects a level of understanding about major players and their motivations and perceptions of the struggle in war. The novel is spiced with psychological, military, and political tension through different characters with different objectives. The major players feel human and understandable as they experience vivid battles. Readers looking for depth and complexity will find this novel a standout choice.

– *Midwest Book Review by D. Donovan,*
*Senior Reviewer*

*"Jack of Spades'* takes place during an unforgettable period in our world history. The novel depicts an array of interesting characters centering on an independent, self-centered American officer, Captain Jack Ruggero. After crash landing on the beaches near the strategic port city of Tobruk, Jack finds himself in the unfortunate position as prisoner of war. After a miraculous escape he learns the location of a secret German fuel depot with enough war material to supply Rommel's panzers in his drive east toward the Suez Canal.

When the newly-formed Special Air Service (SAS) receive news of this base, Jack's assistance is requested. But Jack is no hero. Behind-the-lines operations, firefights, planting bombs on enemy planes are of no interest to him. His priority is to make it through the war in one piece, which means staying as far away from the fighting as possible. "I'm a man of opportunity, not patriotism," he tells SAS leader, Major Lawrence.

This exciting historical novel might well have taken place. The author has written an electrifying novel that keeps the reader glued to its pages."

– K.D. McNiven, author of the
*Decker & Callie Adventure Series* and other novels

"'*Jack of Spades*' is an exciting historical thriller based on real and fictional events during World War Two in North Africa. It celebrates the unquantifiable success of the then-newly-created British SAS (Special Air Service). Their mission: Destroy German planes, fuel depots, and create fear among enemy troops far behind the battlefront. The author's vivid descriptions of SAS attacks against German troops, Rommel's near-capture by British soldiers, and his reference to real-life persons (Rommel, Montgomery, Churchill, Roosevelt, David Stirling and Paddy Mayne to name a few) provide the novel an authentic feel. One will have difficulty finding which parts is fiction.

Jack Ruggero is the central character in this story. He's an American liaison officer and self-proclaimed man-of-opportunity. Add to his skill as an unabashed card shark and womanizer, his anti-hero personality highlights bravery of Axis and Allies suffering common deprivations of hunger, thirst, and the sickening horrors of mechanized warfare. His knowledge of a secret German base loaded with precious petrol needed for Rommel's advance into Alexandria and Cairo have made him all-important to the SAS. Their mission, along with Jack's help, is to locate this base and destroy it before Rommel beats Montgomery to the punch.

But will Jack put his desire to save his own skin aside and do his part in the fight against the powerful Afrika Korps? Or will he resign himself to let others do the fighting for him?"

– Shawn Callon,
author of *The Diplomatic Spy*

# Prologue

## June 21, 1942
North Africa

The strategic port of Tobruk has been under siege nine days and is now on verge of collapse. Defenders of the Libyan port were 35,000 strong, mostly South African troops of the British 8th Army. They were a tough lot, some having been in the fight against the Germans since 1940. This was the second time the dreaded Afrika Korps attempted to take the port city by force.

A year earlier when Colonel-General Erwin Rommel, coined the nickname *Desert Fox* by his English adversaries, ordered his newly-formed desert fighting force to attack the Allied defenders, he had been beaten back by a surprisingly tough British defense.

Rommel desperately needed Tobruk if he were to supply his troops pushing deep into Egypt through Cyrenaica. His lines of supplies were driven overland via Barce, Mechili, and on to Sidi Barrani. At that time, he chose to bypass Tobruk altogether. It proved a perilously long route for his supply trucks to travel and one that remained dangerously susceptible to British air attack. In a battle proving to be one of attrition, neither side could afford to lose a single drop of petrol, which had become as valuable as water.

Rommel knew if he were to continue his push to Cairo he needed a port capable of supplying his troops without having to travel hundreds of miles across open desert. In short, he had to have Tobruk!

…. So he attacked relentlessly.

…. And the defenders wearily fought on.

# Chapter 1

## Alexandria, Egypt
## June 21, 1942

Dawn fell upon the coastal city of Alexandria unnoticed by the group of British soldiers entertaining themselves in the Officers Club tent, and for good reason. Word had it the German Afrika Korps was about to launch another offensive, and this might well be the last opportunity to enjoy off duty time.

In one corner of the club tent a live band played the latest music from a range of American jazz to Egyptian folklore tunes. In another corner a small buffet arrangement displayed a variety of local food. The busiest area was the bar and dance floor where men and women danced comfortably in their taut-fitted uniforms all night and into the wee hours of morning. In another section of the tent, a number of people paid attention to the card game between four British officers and an American liaison officer, whom they referred simply as *Yank*.

Upon arrival to Alexandria, the small contingent of Americans was treated like celebrated heroes by the British. This was inspired by the general feeling with America now in the War; the tide of victory might turn in their favor sooner than later. For more than a year since their arrival, the German Afrika Korps, under leadership of Erwin Rommel, wreaked havoc all across North Africa. Time and again Rommel proved a better general, but with America now supplying the British Army, and more importantly, opening a second front in the east, Rommel and the Afrika Korps' days were numbered—or so they hoped and prayed for.

The yank played poker like he wrote the book, and this created irritation and anger amongst the English gentlemen in uniform. They did not appreciate his self-assured behavior. Not to mention he was the lowest ranking officer at the table sitting across a full colonel, one lieutenant-colonel, and two majors. They glared at the cocky yank in the most arrogant manner they could muster in hopes of intimidating him to back off from his winning streak. Everyone present knew it was never recommended to best senior-ranking officers in a card game.

The yank stared across the table at the highly-decorated colonel, studying him. The colonel held his gaze, knowing full well the yank was trying to *read* him. A flinch, excessive blinking, tapping fingers, heavy breathing, all might give him a feel for what hand he held, and this was the final hand before the card game ended. The other players were tapped out. It was between the colonel and the yank, and the pot held five thousand pounds, winner take all!

The yank looked at his cards, and then lifted his eyes to the colonel. He slid his hand to the stack of bills in front of him and added more to the pot. "I'll raise you two hundred pounds," he said, evenly.

The colonel stared back looking for a sign, but the yank did not perspire, did not flinch, nor did he fidget. He offered nothing in the way of giving away his hand. *Could be bluffing,* he told himself. But he also knew he might well not be. Throughout the entire night the yank's winning streak was nothing short of amazing.

The colonel reached for his stack of bills and tossed in the ante. "Call," he said, with finality.

"After you, sir," the yank offered with a wave of hand.

The colonel hesitated, and then set his cards down on the table. "Three kings, he said, hopeful it would be enough.

The yank paused. He stared a few moments at the colonel before lowering his eyes to the cards on the table. He laid his cards down one at a time. The first was a Seven of Spades. The second was an Eight of Spades. The third was a Nine of Spades. The fourth was a Ten of Spades. He held the last card in his hand, intentionally pausing while observing the colonel's reaction. He saw beads of perspiration forming on his head, and forced himself not to smile. Then he laid his card on the table alongside his other four cards.

It was a Jack of Spades.

"Straight flush," the yank said point of fact.

The group of onlookers looked away, disappointed for their colonel, who sighed in defeat. His shoulders slumped, and he shook his head as if to say, *I might have guessed.*

Ever the gentleman, the colonel managed a weak smile. "Congratulations, yank—Uh, I mean, captain. You play exceptionally well."

The yank reached across the table, scooping his winnings with both hands.

"You mind sharing how you manage to be so lucky?" one of the majors asked. He sounded like he was pleading.

"Luck is a small part of playing," the yank replied, without looking at them. He started counting his money before continuing. "Any one of you has an equal chance in winning," he went on. "The key is *reading* the players sitting across from you."

"How so?" the lieutenant-colonel asked.

Still counting his winnings, the yank explained. "Each person reacts in a special way based on the cards they hold," he began, nonchalantly. "For instance, you major," he looked to the officer sitting on his right, "you tend to raise an eyebrow when dealt a favorable card. When you have a plain hand, you remain expressionless." He looked at the lieutenant-colonel. "You sir, straighten in your chair when your cards are favorable, and slump your shoulders when they aren't." He looked at the major sitting on his left. "You twitch the right side of your face when you don't like your hand, and snort when you do." He turned his attention to the colonel. "And you sir," he paused for effect, "you are the most difficult to read."

The colonel sighed relief. *At least the chap is giving me some benefit,* he told himself.

"In the end," the yank continued, "I found you tend to study your cards too hard when they aren't good enough, and barely glance at them when they are."

The British officers glanced at one another uncomfortably, shrugging as if to say, *who would have guessed?*

A sergeant entered the tent, looked around at the occupants, and focused on the yank sitting at the table with British officers. He marched over and snapped to attention.

"Begging your pardon, sir, but I've orders to escort you to the airfield at once."

"What's this about, sergeant?" asked the colonel.

The sergeant handed the yank a folded piece of paper. "Orders from GHQ, sir."

The yank opened the paper and read in silence.

"Bad news?" asked the major on his right.

The yank looked up at the sergeant. "What's this about?"

The sergeant stared down at the yank. "You've been ordered to accompany one of our pilots for a reconnaissance over Tobruk, sir."

"Why me?" the yank asked, incredulous.

The sergeant appeared perplexed. "I don't question orders, sir, I follow them." He paused, waiting for the yank to speak. When he did not, the sergeant said, "Please come with me, sir. I have a car outside."

"Now?" the yank asked, still in a state of shock.

The sergeant nodded. "Right you are, sir. There's a pilot standing by. He'll be taking you up in one of our Westland Lysander aircraft."

The yank looked in the direction of the colonel, who offered a sympathetic smile. "Appears you might have been too lucky at cards with too many of the wrong people," he said, grinning.

Without further ado, the yank followed the sergeant out of the tent, stuffing his winnings in his uniform coat pockets. A corporal sat in the driver's seat of a car waiting for them. They all got in and the corporal drove them straight to the airfield, a mere fifteen minutes away.

A two-seater Westland Lysander was already on the landing strip, revved and ready for takeoff, its pilot seated in the cockpit. The yank got out of the car and was escorted to the plane by a British major.

"Whose idea is this?" the yank barked. He did not offer a salute.

The major remained unperturbed. "Received an order from your commanding officer," he said, raising his voice so he could be heard over the plane's engine. "You're to join our pilot on today's reconnaissance over Tobruk. Seems *Jerry* is attempting a final push to take the city and our GHQ wants first-hand information how close they are to succeeding."

"Why me?" the yank challenged.

The major shrugged. "Got me there, old man. I only know we received word from your command to have you along. Once you size up the situation, you'll be flown back here and make your report to GHQ."

The yank stood stock still, summing up how he might have been selected for such a mission. *I'm not a fighting soldier,* he reminded himself. *I'm an administrative liaison officer.* Then it came to him. *If my commanding officer selected me for this assignment, it must be payback for having bested him at cards. Damn, that must be it!*

The major motioned for the yank to climb aboard. "Please," he said, motioning him toward the plane.

With no room left for argument, the yank climbed up the ladder and into the rear cockpit seat. He strapped himself in while the pilot looked over his shoulder to verify he had done so correctly. When the yank finished, the pilot nodded, waved to the major, who waved back, and increased engine power. The plane sped down the dirt runway and in a matter of seconds lifted off and headed east toward Tobruk.

# Chapter 2

*"To every man of us, Tobruk was a symbol of British resistance and we were now going to finish with it for good."*

*— June 1942 General Erwin Rommel*

At eight o'clock in the morning the day was already exceptionally hot. The Tobruk garrison defenders looked to the sky not to curse the merciless sun bearing down on them, but to watch for the beginning of what would be endless attacks from the Luftwaffe (German Air Force).

Colonel-General Erwin Rommel made full use of his resources in North Africa, combining attacks against his enemy with air, land, and naval forces. The tactic had the British reeling clear back to Alexandria and Cairo. English commanders had not yet learned the importance of a combined attack, thus suffering its consequences. The problem lay in their chain-of-command. Each branch of the British military had a separate commander for army, air force and navy. Seldom did either commander communicate to their opposites during the course of battle. It proved a major flaw in their fight against Germans both tactically and strategically.

In his bunker headquarters South African Major-General Hendrik Balzazar Klopper (known simply as H.B.), commanding officer of the Tobruk garrison, paced the dirt floor wearily. It had been a long time since he smiled and his exhaustion showed all over.

Klopper had been a proud man all his life. Tall, handsome and always quite sure of himself, the general reminded his troops of a football coach with his muscular bully frame, commanding voice, and the mindset to win.

*Not today,* thought his staff officers.

And with good reason. The burdens of command finally caught up with him. Anyone who knew him would have thought him to be only a shadow of his former self. The bags under his eyes grew more pronounced with each passing night from lack of sleep. His skin grew sickly white from too many hours in the dark confines of his bunker, and the personal knowledge of being unable to do anything about their situation wore out his morale.

His troops faired even less. The British Army was being worn down with each passing day. The Germans had cut off supply routes from land, sea, and air and each man knew they could not keep the German juggernaut at bay indefinitely.

General Klopper stood in front of his desk appearing solemn and grim. "The inevitable outcome is fast approaching," he mumbled in a low voice.

"Begging your pardon, sir?" It was one of his staff officers standing nearby, but not in close enough earshot to have heard.

The general shook his head, gesturing for the young officer not to press him. He looked at his aides standing nearby watching him. They were his responsibility. They all were. And they looked worse than he did. No one had eaten a decent meal in months, having been forced to live on tight rations due to the change of fortunes of war. Everyone lost weight, some to the point of looking deathly ill.

General Klopper thought back to the days when his command was flush with victory after having defeated the Italians in 1940. Those were glorious days for the British 8th Army. They whipped Mussolini's forces across the desert and threatened to knock the Axis forces from that theatre of war altogether.

Everything was plentiful back then, especially food! At this time of morning Klopper would brunch with his staff officers. What a meal that was. Eggs benedict, bacon, biscuits, fruit. There was fresh milk and tea to wash it down, and entertainment provided by the radio which played a variety of music.

.... It seemed like a thousand years ago to the general now.

Klopper cursed the Royal Air Force (RAF) and Navy (RN). They had let him down. They let the Desert Rats of Tobruk down. Even the all-inspiring Prime Minister Winston Churchill had assured him the fighting men of Tobruk would not be forgotten.

For nearly a year they had been living on rations, with a new promise each month that relief was on the way. They would receive new equipment, men, food, and medical supplies. Churchill promised! General Klopper now knew what he should have known then.

Tobruk was lost.

There would be no reinforcements. They would be saved for Field Marshall Sir Claude Auchinleck's defense of Cairo. This city was more vital than Tobruk, and every man knew this, including General Klopper.

Sir Auchinleck (nicknamed the 'Auk' by his men) had orders to prevent the Suez Canal from falling into German hands. This was his primary concern. All available men and material would be kept in reserve to repulse Rommel's push towards Cairo. This was known throughout Klopper's command, which did nothing to help morale.

Klopper sat heavily in his chair. *What more can I do?*

His aides looked on sympathetically towards their commanding officer. They knew he had done all a body could do. He was after all only human, unlike Rommel, who had become a living legend amongst British and Germans alike.

"Don't look so glum, sir," said a young, skinny lieutenant. "The RAF and navy are to blame."

General Klopper slowly lifted his eyes to the young officer, and nodded appreciation for the comment.

For the better part of a year the Royal Navy had fought to maintain its presence in the Mediterranean Sea. However, the Luftwaffe proved too much. They constantly bombed and strafed British ships at will, making it virtually impossible for them to keep a steady flow of supplies to the Tobruk defenders.

Captain Higgins, another of the general's aides, stood across the small command post (CP) looking on curiously at the general. He knew the general still had a job to do and occasionally needed reminding of what that job was, especially when he was overcome with emotion like now.

Higgins started to say something when a sudden high-pitched sound whistling through the air caught everyone's immediate attention.

*Incoming!*

It was an artillery bombardment. Everyone froze, staring up at the ceiling of the bunker, awaiting the inevitable explosion that would follow upon impact. The 155mm shell burst 100 kilometers from the command bunker, with still enough punch to shake the ground beneath their feet. The blast stirred dust in the CP, causing everyone to cough heavily. Their lungs ached for fresh air.

Higgins waved a hand in front of his face to clear dust from his field of vision. He looked for the general, who had lost his balance and fell on his haunches in the most ignominious way unbefitting a man of his rank.

"Sir!" Higgins shouted, running to help his commander to his feet.

Klopper appeared dazed. "What the deuces happened?"

Higgins helped the general to his feet. "It was the concussion of the blast, sir. It knocked you right off your feet." The young captain coughed, adding the obvious, "Jerry is starting up again, sir."

Everyone braced themselves, holding onto anything solid. Any second now they expected to hear the eerie, high-pitched whistling of incoming artillery shells raining down on them. Lamps hanging from the ceiling still swayed from the first blast, casting shadows of the men in queer forms. One of the officers reached out and held the lamp overhead still. The dust began to settle. It was then they realized something odd.

Silence.

The shelling did not continue.

One of the junior officers looked nervously about the room. "They've stopped," he said, practically stuttering the words.

General Klopper regained his senses enough so that he was ashamed of himself for having let the burdens of command overwhelm him. It was a mistake, he knew, a commander could never allow, especially in front of his staff.

*Blazes, H.B.! What the deuces is wrong with you?!* Cursing himself had become no surprise to the general these past months, not with Jerry besting his every move. *Remember what schoolmaster Richardson said. 'When in the face of confusion, stand tall, look sharp; never let anyone know you are unaware of what you must do. Perception is as important as the reality at hand.'*

Those words rang true as Klopper and his battered bastion of Tobruk faced defeat in the face of the German Afrika Korps. He looked at his men and saw how they needed him for leadership, guidance, and hope, despite knowing their situation was clearly hopeless. He prayed members of his staff were a forgiving lot.

*After all, even a general can only do so much.*

"They haven't stopped," Klopper said, clearing his throat and standing as tall as humanly possible. "It's one of Jerry's old tricks." He paused to let his words sink in. "They are telling us with that single shell to get ready for the final push."

Captain Higgins turned to communications officer, Captain Hughes. "Is there any news from our air force?" His question was thick with anxiety.

Hughes sat with earphones to the radio dangling around his neck. He quickly put them to his ears and listened. Then, turning back to Higgins he shook his head. "Nothing," he answered, despondently.

Higgins rolled his eyes as if to say, *great!* He turned to face the general, who nodded his permission. "Well, try them again and keep on reaching out until we hear word from them," Higgins said. Then he mumbled, "We simply must have air support!"

Without saying a word, General Klopper picked up his field glasses and headed up the stairs leading outside the bunker. Higgins and two other officers followed. They were glad to get out of the stuffy room. Even the heat from mid-morning sun was more tolerable than the dungeon serving as command post.

Sergeant-Major Binns stood watch in his trench, observing Jerry (Germans) through his field glasses. Like everyone in the garrison, he awaited the final enemy assault on Tobruk and was not optimistic for their chances. He had been stuck in the port city for more than a year and witnessed first-hand how their defenses dilapidated bit by bit after each attack.

*Surprised Jerry hasn't been able to take us until now,* he thought. Jerry was British slang for German and their most used reference for their sworn enemy.

He believed this for good reason. The RAF and Royal Navy failed to maintain steady supplies. The Luftwaffe bases on Crete harassed British efforts to the breaking point. Too many of His Majesty's ships were being sunk by German JU-87 Stuka dive bombers, and ME-109 fighters prevented the RAF from maintaining a steady line of supply drops by parachute.

*It's only a matter of time,* the sergeant-major knew.

One of his men calling out to him caught his attention. "Hey, Sarg-Major, whad'ya make a that?" The soldier pointed in the direction of the garrison commander's bunker.

Binns turned to see for himself, raising his hand to shield his eyes from the glaring sun. He recognized General Klopper and his aides standing atop the bunker, and turned back to the young private.

"You bleedin' idiot! Don't you recognize the commanding general?" The sergeant-major shook his head, exasperated. *Kids they send me!* What he would have given for a fresh company of seasoned troops. *But no, that would have been too easy,* he swore. *Instead they send all available men to Cairo.*

Sergeant-Major Binns knew why.

The Suez Canal.

If Rommel captured Tobruk the German line of supplies would be shipped to this port city, reducing their line of travel from Benghazi by hundreds of miles and saving them thousands of gallons of precious petrol. This meant Tobruk had to be held at all costs.

*And means we're expendable!*

Binns shook his head, frustrated. He knew each day the *Battling Bastards of the Bastion of Tobruk* held out kept the Afrika Korps from achieving total victory in North Africa. However, that didn't mean the sergeant-major had to like it.

*Because I don't!* Binns pounded his fist in the sand. *Damn desk-jockeys! They must've pulled my name from a hat and selected me to remain. Bastards! If I ever get my hands on those buggers I'll ring their necks.*

The sergeant-major picked up his canteen and put the open end to his mouth.

"Empty!" He was out of water. "Damn!" He drank his rations for the day at breakfast and now regretted it. He knew better, a man of his tenure in the army losing all self-control and discipline. "What kind of example are you?" he asked himself aloud. *You're bloody lucky the men hadn't seen you do that or they might've followed suit.*

Binns reached down and picked up his shovel to help clear the trenches of sand. It was a chore that needed constant work due to sandstorms filling them up. Normally the sergeant-major would supervise troops performing such work, but with so many men injured and not up to par with performing fatigue duty each man now did their part regardless of rank.

Binns suddenly froze. A thought came to him, causing him to shudder. Could someone on the general's staff have recognized his short-comings and chosen him to remain with the doomed defenders? It was not a pleasant thought, but it now crossed his mind. The sergeant-major did have a temper on him, occasionally thumbing his nose at officers. He looked over where the general stood observing the enemy through field glasses.

General Klopper stood atop his bunker staring at the German line of defenses through his powerful field glasses. Ironically, the field glasses were the Dienstglas German-made standard issue for the Wehrmacht (German Army). An army private found them lying in the sand after an enemy assault on Tobruk failed the previous year. The defense of Tobruk was hailed a success due to Klopper's superior leadership, and the men presented him the German field glasses to demonstrate their gratitude and honor him.

Klopper's use of the glasses was meant to snub the Germans. When Rommel defeated the British 2nd Armoured Division, capturing 2,000 prisoners including the division commander, Major-General Michael Gambier-Parry, in the Battle of Mechili, he took Gambier-Parry's desert goggles for a trophy. Photographs of the now-famous *Desert Fox* were shown of him sporting the British-manufactured MK 3 Anti-Gas Goggles on his schirmmutzen (peaked cap) and giving orders to his men. The snub was not viewed lightly by the British, so Klopper using enemy field glasses provided him a form of retribution.

In truth, Major-General Gambier-Parry was invited by Colonel-General Rommel to drink wine and smoke fine cigars after their battle in a gesture of camaraderie between soldiers. When Gambier-Parry mentioned his hat was taken from him by a German soldier, Rommel ordered it returned to him. When Rommel saw the MK 3 goggles belonging to Gambier-Parry he commented how he would like to have a pair for his own. Gambier-Parry then presented them to Rommel as a return gesture of camaraderie between foes.

General Klopper lowered the field glasses and surveyed his own defenses. All around him were his men, known as the *Desert Rats.* They manned artillery and anti-aircraft guns, stood in trenches, and sat atop Matilda tanks, which by now were considered obsolete compared to superior German Panzer Mark III and IV type. All waited the inevitable attack.

Soldiers were equipped with Vickers and Lewis twin-barreled machine guns, and Enfield .303 bolt-action rifles, a weapon used by the British since the Boer War and still effective compared to the German Gewehr 41 Walther self-loading rifle. Both rifles accepted bayonets, and Klopper knew all too well the men would be using them soon enough.

"What a poor sight we are," the general said aloud.

His aides heard him and glanced quizzically at one another. "Excuse me, sir?" Higgins said, asking for clarification from the general.

"A year earlier our defenses were strong enough to repel Jerry," Klopper noted. "Rommel had to bypass this port and continue supplying his troops over fifteen hundred miles, which cost him valuable time, equipment, and most importantly—petrol!" The general sighed exhaustion. "If they breech our tank ditches, trenches, and any line of defense, that'll be the end of Tobruk."

The general's aides lowered their heads as though submitting to a battle already lost.

Captain Hughes was first to speak up. "Surely General Auchinleck will send support, sir?" It was a feeble question, he knew, but all he could think to say.

"One would think so," Klopper replied, "but he won't. He's building up his troops for his own attack against the Afrika Korps. The PM (Prime Minister) has been pressing him to attack Jerry and wither their supplies down to the point they'll be incapable of mounting a future offensive against Cairo."

"That makes sense, sir," Captain Higgins interjected. "The Royal Navy has been performing a standup job in preventing German ships from crossing the Mediterranean with supplies."

"That's true," General Klopper agreed, and then added, "but they haven't done so well at supplying us, have they?"

The aides lowered their heads once more in submission to defeat. The Luftwaffe, they knew, had done a standup job of their own in sinking British supply ships to the point the Royal Navy practically stopped sending any supplies to Tobruk.

Klopper studied the tank-ditches lined up on the outskirts of the city. He could not help notice how many had been filled over with sand during storms they experienced over the past year. Tank-ditches proved most effective against enemy tanks. Once a tank fell in it was doomed. All a British *Tommy* had to do was wait for the tank crew to open their turret to attempt escape and then lob in a hand grenade. The confines of the tank heightened power of the blast, killing all inside. As it was now a tank crew could simply drive over most of the ditches without ever knowing they were designed as traps.

Klopper shook his despairingly. He worked hard not to appear defeated, but it was difficult. Seeing his men did nothing to improve his morale either. They were tired. Bone tired! He could no longer keep them from realizing they had been forgotten by British High Command. No longer did he bother with pep talks for they would have done no good.

*After all, what the hell am I going to tell them which they haven't already heard?*

Klopper turned around and stared out at the Mediterranean Sea. The harbor had not been as damaged by aerial bombardment as he would have thought. *And I can guess why?* It was only a matter of time before the

Afrika Korps took control of this strategic port, and Rommel undoubtedly wanted it intact.

"I've got a surprise for you when you come goose-stepping in Tobruk, Rommel," Klopper said aloud, but to no one in particular.

"Begging your pardon, General?" one of the nearby officers said.

Klopper shook his head. "Never mind. Are the demolitions ready?"

Captain Higgins nodded. "Yes, sir, in most parts of the city, but not all stores are ready to be destroyed."

"And why the bloody hell not?" the general asked, scornfully.

The young captain cleared his throat. "Getting a detail large enough to do the job means pulling men off the line, sir."

"And Jerry is observing our lines with keen interest, sir," Hughes added. "If they detect a weak defense in any of our lines we can be sure that's where they'll hit us hardest."

Klopper nodded. "Yes, I suppose you're right," he said, acquiescingly. He laughed at the irony of the situation. "Under different circumstances I would do precisely that, pull men back from a particular line of defense in order to lure the enemy into a trap." He paused as if to reflect on how desperate their situation was. "But now…." he finished, his voice trailing off.

Hughes thought best to change the subject. "Excuse me, sir, but is there chance of evacuating the wounded by sea?"

"In our dreams!" Higgins declared. "We can't count on the Royal Navy, what with the Kriegsmarine harassing them with those blasted E-Boats."

All agreed. The Kriegsmarine (German Navy) was equipped with *Schnellboots,* or fast-boats more commonly referred to as E-Boats. These attack craft were the fastest of their kind afloat, more so than the British Motor Torpedo Boats (MTB) and the American Patrol Boats (PT Boats). The S-100 E-Boat class was the fastest, capable of exceeding 45 knots (50 mph). They were extremely seaworthy and armed with a single 20mm machine gun, a 37mm anti-aircraft cannon, two torpedo tubes, and had a range of over 650 nautical miles. A crew of three functioned quite efficiently, and the Royal Navy quickly learned to respect these sailors.

Klopper had seen firsthand how effective E-Boats were. He reflected how on one occasion several boldly entered the harbor under cover of darkness. Their boats boasted three Daimler Benz MB 501 Marine diesel engines, capable of operating on special silencers reducing their sound to little more than a dull purr. Once inside they shot 'Very' lights (flares) that lit up the harbor, and opened fire with canon and machine gun fire.

The gunners were either incredibly skilled marksmen, or incredibly lucky, for one of the boats raking the coastline with deadly fire struck a supply bunker. The explosion was great enough to turn the night into day, and the concussion rocked sailors in their boats, some fearing they were going to capsize.

Before the British could mount a coordinated return fire the E-Boats darted out of the harbor and back into cover of darkness in the Mediterranean Sea. It was an embarrassing episode made more so since the British considered the *Med* to be their own little swimming pool what with their navy being the dominant force present.

General Klopper turned around and looked back out to the desert. This was where he would face his most dreaded foe—*Rommel!*

Colonel-General Erwin Rommel had become the British Army's worst nightmare since his arrival in North Africa in February 1941. For an entire year Rommel's by-now world-famous Afrika Korps pounded the Tobruk garrison with a clear strategy of wearing down its defenses. Rommel needed Tobruk not only because of its vital piers that could allow the German navy to supply his army, but to maintain German military prestige.

The Afrika Korps was comprised of three divisions, the 15th and 21st Panzer Divisions, and the 90th Light Mechanized Division. The Italians were put to use where Rommel saw fit, which primarily was support and defense. Although some distinguished units like the Ariete Tank Division fought alongside them throughout the desert campaign.

The British had been able to defeat the Italians early on during first stages of the Desert War when Italian Marshal Rodolfo Graziani was ordered by Dictator Benito Mussolini to invade Egypt. Graziani had a force of 250,000 men at his disposal compared to 35,000 British troops, roughly seven times greater! But the Italian Marshal knew his numbers outweighed the British in problems too. Much of their military equipment was obsolete, especially their tanks, the primary weapon needed for desert victory.

When it became apparent the Italians would lose their African territory, German Dictator Adolf Hitler ordered his military attaché in Rome to inform Mussolini that General Erwin Rommel and the newly formed Afrika Korps would be sent to prevent the British from taking control of Italian controlled Libya, Tunisia, and Ethiopia.

Things changed for the British when the Germans arrived. They managed to route the British at every turn, sending them reeling back in defeat. Even foreign press stated, *"The British Army can manage to take on Italian forces, but turn and run in complete disarray at the sight of the German Afrika Korps."*

Tobruk had been the first British stronghold to keep the Afrika Korps at bay. With it came prestige and pride that the common soldier needed to keep up morale. *"Maybe the Germans were not the Master Race after all,"* quoted one world press correspondent upon witnessing how the garrison repelled everything the Germans threw at them. *"Perhaps we can defeat the Huns!"* cried the Tommies.

General Klopper received a standing order from 8th Army commander General Neil M. Ritchie that he must keep Tobruk in British hands. *"Rommel must not be permitted to have Tobruk,"* Ritchie told him. *"You must defend your post and hold the Germans at all cost!"*

As Klopper put his field glasses to his eyes he thought back when General Sir Claude Auchinleck, Commanding Officer of British Middle East Forces, issued orders to all officers in the field stating that he had no intention of holding Tobruk once the enemy was poised to take over the garrison.

*"We have done our best keeping Jerry at bay,"* he told his staff, *"and the time has now come for us to invest our forces at El Alamein. That is where we shall defeat Rommel."*

But those orders were issued back in February 1942, five months earlier. During that time London decided the 8th Army should hold Tobruk. They could not afford to relinquish the strategic port to the Germans. Another victory in Rommel's hands would further demoralize the troops and enhance the mysticism of the German general as a *bogey-man,* or a *superman.* This had to be where the English proved to the world the German War Machine was not invincible as the press declared.

Captain Higgins put his field glasses to his eyes to view the battlefield alongside the general. He saw their enemy preparing for attack. Their artillery gun crews were getting ready to send their first volley of shells into the city. Panzer crewmen were seen sitting atop their tanks, awaiting orders to advance with infantry close behind, whose main task was to mop up enemy resistance.

"Should be any minute now," Higgins said, despair reeking in his tone. He looked up toward the sky, shielding his eyes from the sun glare with his hand. "I don't see them, sir, but I know they are on their way."

General Klopper nodded, knowing full well the young captain referred to the Luftwaffe. The British laid claim to sea superiority, but the skies belonged to the Germans by day. Their planes attacked unhindered by the RAF at this stage of the war.

"We simply must do the best we can," General Klopper said. It did not go unnoticed by his aides how his mood seemed grimmer than before.

The air raid alarm sounded! Men scrambled for cover as the siren grew louder with each cranking hand turning the wheel that powered the siren. The final assault on Tobruk had begun.

On the German side of the battlefield Colonel-General Erwin Johannes Eugen Rommel got out of his open-topped staff car, followed by his aides. Nearby soldiers snapped to attention in the presence of their leader and saluted smartly. Rommel returned the salute, beaming ear to ear.

Before arriving in North Africa Rommel's reputation had preceded him. British Middle East Commanders were anxious to see how the situation would develop with Germans now facing them in the North African theatre. In 1940 France Rommel commanded the 7th Panzer Division, nicknamed *Ghost Division* by retreating British and French soldiers due to the Germans' ability to turn up where they were least expected.

The British knew Rommel had a knack for battle and was a professional soldier in every sense. Intelligence reports estimated it would be several months before he could launch an offensive. Those reports proved wrong when Rommel attacked with great surprise in a matter of weeks upon his arrival in North Africa. Victory followed victory, and British commanders were left dazed and confused by his unconventional methods. In one month's time the Germans had pushed them all the way back to Alexandria.

In the course of a year his Afrika Korps, although outnumbered by British in men and material, had placed the entire British Middle East Army on the verge of total defeat. His cunning, stealth, guile, and ability to attack when the army least expected it earned him the nickname, *Desert Fox*. The British came to admire this new kind of German general, so much that when any of their own officers performed with exception they were referred to as 'trying to be an English Rommel.'

The Desert Fox reached for his field glasses dangling from his neck. He never seemed to be without them. His entire attention focused on Tobruk. A victory today, he knew, would be the greatest coup of his career. He scanned British defenses carefully, looking for weaknesses. He knew his enemy still had some fight in them. The siege had been continuous for the past eight days and the *Desert Rats* had not received fresh supplies abundant enough to sustain them much longer.

Tobruk was ready to fall!

What bothered Rommel, however, was the amount of material he spent on this battle. With fewer men and resources, Rommel's victories had stunned the world and made his name famous alongside that of the Afrika Korps. If he received the troops and material requested they could be in Alexandria by October and take Cairo before the end of the year, thus knocking the British out of Africa entirely.

However, German High Command had other priorities, Rommel was told. Field Marshal Walther von Brauchitsch, the German Army commander-in-chief, had convinced Hitler the Desert War was nothing more than a sideshow, and sending more troops and supplies would weaken their advance in Russia.

"*I remind you, General,*" Brauchitsch told Rommel on his recent visit to Berlin, "*your original orders were, and still are, to hold Libya. It was never intended for you to take the offensive.*"

Thus Rommel had to make do with what he had, and the attack had spent more supplies than anticipated.

"We'll have to pray we capture British supplies before they blow them to smithereens," he muttered between his teeth.

"I beg your pardon, Herr General?" an aide standing behind him said.

Rommel continued staring in the direction of Tobruk. "If we take Tobruk," he started, "we not only get our hands on a strategic port, but can confiscate their supplies to our advantage." He lowered his glasses. "That'll be enough for us to push on into Alexandria."

"And then Cairo, Herr General!" The aide was beaming as though victory had already been achieved.

"Yes....Cairo." Rommel turned to his intelligence officer Major Freiherr von Mellenthin, a dapper, career-minded man. "Is the Luftwaffe ready?"

Von Mellenthin clicked his heels together. "Jawohl, Herr General," he replied, smartly. "They should be arriving any moment now."

Rommel and his aides turned their eyes skyward. "Good. This will be the final blow."

In the distant sky the humming of engines belonging to 150 German planes reached their ears.

The Luftwaffe had arrived.

# Chapter 3

*'In the desert war, speed is the essence of the plan.'*

Sturmbannfuhrer (major) Wolfgang Klement held the controls of his Junkers JU-87 Stuka Dive Bomber steady at 20,000 feet above the Mediterranean Sea. His squadron left their base in Benghazi and traveled over sea to attack the Tobruk defenses from their rear, a ruse the British would most likely not expect.

Klement looked over his shoulder to his right, then to his left. On both sides of him were his pilots flying in close formation.

*This is it,* he thought. *This is the final attack that will crush the English.*

In the rear seat of the plane sat Gunther, an impressionable Luftwaffe gunner aching for action. He manned the rear 7.9mm machine gun, and scanned the sky carefully for enemy planes. Both he and Klement knew the Stuka was an excellent dive bomber, capable of pinpoint accuracy. However, against fighter planes it was highly vulnerable, lacking speed and agility.

A voice came over the radio. "Herr Sturmbannfuhrer, Tobruk is dead-ahead!"

Klement looked over his shoulder to his wingman, flying just behind him on his left. He nodded and looked straight ahead where he saw the shoreline of Tobruk. Flashes from the shattered city began lighting up all around the outskirts of the city, an indication deadly anti-aircraft batteries opened fire.

The Stukas shook violently as shells (ack-ack) exploded all around them. Puffs of black smoke filled the sky, and shrapnel came from all directions. Klement smiled and shook his head. He had been through this many times before, as far back as 1937 when Hitler authorized his Luftwaffe to aid dictator, Franco, in the Spanish Civil War.

"Stay sharp, everyone," he said, speaking in his radio mouthpiece. "The English are spitting in all directions."

Another pilot's voice came over the radio. "Beautiful weather!" he said, with a laugh.

Other pilots laughed over the radio. Indeed, the ack-ack gunfire was weak compared to what they experienced some months back when the British were better equipped. Every pilot knew this was likely the last battle before the city fell, and this confidence was felt throughout the Afrika Korps, helping lift German spirits.

Klement led the way as the squadron of dive bombers marked their targets into a steep vertical dive once over their objective. Each plane had a siren attached to the underside of the fuselage that let loose a piercing shriek in its dive. The siren was meant to frighten the enemy, which it accomplished with chilling effect.

Klement lined his sights on a row of tanks located along the front lines of the British defenses. When he was just under 1,000 feet altitude he released his 110 lbs. bombs, four of them, and sent them plummeting to their targets. The fins attached to the bombs also made piercing screeching sounds that told defenders what was coming their way.

Klement pulled back the controls of his Stuka and the plane steadily began to climb. His squadron did the same once they released their payloads, and their planes trembled from the explosions their bombs created upon impact.

After levelling his plane at 3,000 feet Klement surveyed their target. "Excellent work, comrades!" he said over the radio. He smiled and waved to the pilots flying to his left. "Let's return to base."

On the German side of the battlefield Major von Mellenthin stood next to Rommel, and lowered his field glasses. He watched as the Heinkel 111 bombers flew over Tobruk and dropped their bombs over British defenses. The air assault was combined with German and Italian artillery, making for an amazing sight.

"Wonderful!" von Mellenthin said, completely mesmerized by the battle scene.

The Afrika Korps and the XX Italian Corps was about to finish off British resistance for good, and every man in Rommel's command was excited. During the past year Tobruk had been the symbol of British pride, and to see it crushed under the mighty German Army meant their Fuhrer's claim of German superiority proved true. Rommel, the Desert Fox, lowered his Zeiss high-powered field glasses and nodded ever so slightly at von Mellenthin. A sly smile pursed his lips. He could feel it in his bones.

"Victory is about to be ours!" he declared.

Inside Tobruk the South African soldiers of the British Army fired back against their enemy. They threw everything they had. Artillery, tanks, machine guns, rifles, mortars, hand grenades—everything but their bayonets, which they kept close for when hand-to-hand combat proved necessary. Despite a valiant effort, their gunfire was less coordinated than the Germans, even sporadic. With so many enemy planes bombing and strafing their positions, combined with enemy artillery fire, they became confused and battle-weary.

To their front the German and Italian tanks advanced at an incredible pace, with fast-moving infantry following in their trail. British troops fired twin-barreled 20mm guns, 37mm guns, and small arms weapons, but it was not enough to stop the Axis juggernaut. Two years of living under constant bombardment had finally taken its toll. Their gunfire was erratic and uncoordinated, whereas the Germans maintained a strong offensive with combined air and artillery bombardments supporting their advance.

The main British tank, the Matilda, a 30-ton hunk of metal armed with a 2-pounder cannon and 78mm thick armor could only reach a maximum of 15 mph. It proved no match for the German Panzer Mark III tank. It was plated with 30mm armor and armed with a 50mm gun. The 22-ton tank was highly maneuverable and much faster than the Matilda, and easily knocked them out of action with precision tank fire.

The success of the German tank gunners over their English enemy was in large part to them having a five man crew in each tank. They had a tank driver, a machine gunner, tank commander, tank gunner and gun loader. British tanks were fitted for only a three-man crew. The British tank gunner had to do his own loading while the German tank commander relied on his gun loader to quickly reload after launching their shells. This allowed Germans a five to seven second firing advantage over the British, and the effect was chilling.

Things grew worse for the British when Germans deployed their 25-ton Panzer Mark IV tanks. This fast-moving tank sported a 75mm turret gun and knocked out of action anything the British had. The Panzer IV faced off enemy antitank weapons, machinegun fire, infantry attacks, and tank-to-tank duels. More often than not, Germans won against the ill-equipped British.

Another German secret weapon was the 88mm anti-aircraft gun. The men of the Afrika Korps turned their sights from enemy planes to enemy tanks with deadly effect. With its long-range firing capability, gunners knocked out enemy tanks long before they came within firing range of their own turret guns. It operated with a crew of six and effectively fired 20 rounds per minute. Rommel considered this weapon the backbone of his anti-tank defense force.

A British sergeant was the first to see another wave of German bombers approach the city from above. *"Cover!"* he shouted.

Tobruk defenders needed no warning to do what had come natural over the past two years. Stuka Dive Bombers roaring in on a strafing run fired their forward 37mm guns, located beneath each wing. Their bullets tore through any armament then in existence. Squadrons of Heinkel-111 H-6 bombers flew overhead and released their payloads of 5,512 lbs. bombs, wreaking havoc and destruction on the already devastated city of Tobruk. Most buildings in the city were shattered and deemed too weak to be used. Now they were reduced to rubble. The British had since lived in air raid shelters. Smoke and dust stirred over the English Tommies and they covered their nose and mouth with handkerchiefs in order to breathe somewhat normally.

Lieutenant William Hudson grabbed the young private standing next to him by the arm and yanked him back into the trench. The private had lost his senses during the first bombing and now stood frozen as enemy planes came in for a strafing run. Were it not for the lieutenant's actions, he most certainly would have been killed.

The private had been one of the few in the city who arrived by accident, the victim of a vehicle breakdown on his way to Alexandria. The outfit he belonged to, a platoon reduced to less than three squads had been ordered to help defend the garrison due to lack of men. His CO was ordered to continue to 'Alex,' and hated leaving his men behind, but orders were orders and in time of war that was that.

The Luftwaffe continued bearing down on Tobruk, their gunfire and bombs destroying the city. British defenses were strafed and bombed beyond belief. HE-111 bombers were equipped with a glass-nosed cockpit for a gunner strategically operating a .50 caliber machine gun. They focused their sites on troops seeking shelter in trenches, ripping them to shreds if they were unlucky enough to be caught in the cross-hairs of their machine guns. Others were buried alive by bombs dropping all around them, or crushed from the falling buildings being shattered to smithereens.

Lieutenant Hudson pulled himself to his feet once the wave of enemy planes flew off. "Come on, man!" he said, scanning the sky for the next wave he was sure would soon follow. "We've got to—"

He never finished his sentence, for when he reached down for the private's collar he immediately pulled back upon seeing the back of the boy's skull missing. A .50 caliber bullet had somehow harmlessly passed Hudson and struck the private, killing him instantly.

"Another life thrown away for nothing," Hudson said, gritting his teeth in disgust. He shook off the shock of the sight and ran for cover in another trench.

On the other side of the city the *Desert Rats* fought fiercely against German E-boats as they whizzed into the harbor at top speed. The *Kriegsmariners* raked the port defenses with surprising accuracy, knocking out coastal gun battery gunners before they had a chance to return fire. E-boats wreaked havoc upon the British to the point they were left to wonder if they stood any chance of surviving this terrible ordeal.

A South African corporal was in command of three privates manning a machine gun post on the beach when another wave of E-boats sped into the harbor, guns ablaze. The German sailors had not seen the gun post and headed for larger ships still left afloat despite intense bombing from the Luftwaffe.

"Mark your targets, lads!" the corporal ordered, as he checked the sights of his Bren MK1 light machine gun.

The E-Boats opened fire at the British ships right when the corporal gave his order to fire. Their bullets slammed into the E-boats squarely, and German sailors found themselves ducking for cover as their boat captains continued toward their targets. When two other British gun posts opened fire on the E-boats the Germans realized it was time to retreat, lest they be killed to the last man.

The corporal was about to rise and cheer at the sight of the retreating Kriegsmariners when one of the E-boats made a 180 degree turn and came speeding back toward them. His smile vanished right when he saw muzzle flashes of enemy guns blazing. He barely had time enough to dive behind sandbags for cover as bullets tore up their post.

Other E-boat captains saw how British gunners failed to return fire and quickly changed course to make good on their original plan of attack. Armed with torpedoes, the E-boat captains had every intention of launching them before returning to their base. British gunners on board the supply ships opened fire with machine guns and 2-pound cannon, but the E-boats were swift and maintaining a line of fire was difficult. Bullets created a stream of water spurting alongside the E-Boats, an occasional round striking armor, but not penetrating it. Their task was made more difficult by Luftwaffe coming in for another attack.

Officers on board two British destroyers assigned to protect the supply ships barked orders for their men to fire smartly at the E-boats with 20mm machine guns while anti-aircraft batteries opened fire on enemy planes. In a matter of seconds the sky was filled with exploding shells and bullets streaking past the Luftwaffe, but failing to knock any plane down.

"Doesn't anything stop Jerry?!" shouted an officer observing the scene.

The sight the British most feared happened when the E-boats launched their torpedoes. The *iron fish* left their silver-lined casings and jumped into the water, speeding at 80 knots toward their targets—the troop supply ships. E-boat captains ordered their helmsmen to get them out of the line of fire while the getting was good, and the boats turned in a wide arc 180 degrees before making a run for open sea.

Deck officers on board the supply ships ordered the collision alarms sounded, and the piercing sirens shrieked throughout the harbor. British sailors looked on in horror as white streaks from the torpedoes sped toward their ships. A deafening explosion rocked the first supply ship. It was quickly followed by another. A second supply ship was struck.

BOOM!

Sailors were thrown to the deck from force of impact. One ship struck by two torpedoes began listing dangerously on its starboard side. It was plain to the crew it would capsize soon enough.

"Abandon ship! Abandon ship!" shouted the captain.

Officers on board the destroyers knew this fight was over. Losing supply ships was a heavy blow, but losing the destroyers would be catastrophic for the British Mediterranean Fleet.

"Captain, they're coming back for another run at us," a young officer warned.

The captain looked up and saw two squadrons of German Stukas lining up for attack. "Make for open sea, full ahead," he ordered the helmsman in a calm, deliberate tone.

The South African corporal slowly rose from behind the sandbags that no doubt saved his life. He saw the enemy boats leaving the harbor and heard their crews laughing and waving goodbye as they sped off.

"Damn you to bloody hell!" the corporal shouted. He waved a defiant fist in return for their arrogance.

Hauptmann (captain) Konrad Diestl, a Luftwaffe pilot, checked his watch. In less than one minute his squadron of Junkers JU-88 Tactical Dive-Torpedo bombers would be over their target—Tobruk!

*There it is!* he said silently, and with excitement. He could see long, dark plumes of smoke billowing toward the sky like multiple tornados sweeping across the port city. He looked at his co-pilot sitting on his right. "Have we heard from Klement?"

The co-pilot nodded, having received news from Sturmbannfuhrer Wolfgang Klement a few moments ago. *"Jawohl.* His bombing run was a success, and they are returning to base."

Diestl looked out the window at one o-clock. In the distance he saw Klements' squadron of Stukas on their way back to base. The two were old friends, having enlisted in the Luftwaffe together and completed flight school with honors in 1936. Little did they know a scant three years later they would be putting their training to work when *Der Fuhrer,* Adolf Hitler, ordered the invasion of Poland, thus marking the beginning of the Second World War.

Since September 1939 both officers took part in the invasion of Poland and later France in 1940, honing their skills as combat pilots. The experience came handy when in February 1941 they were assigned to the *Afrika Korps'* Desert Air Force. Of the two, Wolfgang Klement proved the imaginative one. In fact, it was his ingenuity inspired Diestl to come up with battle plans to harass the enemy in ways they could not easily overcome. One such plan of attack was for Klement to take his squadron of Stukas to bomb and strafe the enemy in short concentrated airstrikes. This did two things. First, surprise and create confusion among the enemy. Second, give the enemy a small taste of things to come, which made your foe nervous and edgy enough so much they could not maintain focus on a concentrated return rate of fire.

The air war in France taught them how much the British dreaded the Luftwaffe, with sirens blaring from the underbelly of each plane's fuselage, causing soldiers and civilians alike to shiver in their boots. The fact Stukas had pinpoint bombing accuracy was another advantage for them. Stukas attacked in a sharp vertical dive made possible with a self-fuel injection engine to prevent stalling. It was the first type of plane capable of performing such a tactical maneuver with great success.

Once Klements' squadron performed their task, Diestls' JU-88s would quickly follow up with a payload of twelve 250 lbs. bombs in each plane. Their mission was to pulverize the enemy into submission with heavier bombing runs, and the JU-88 was precisely the type of bomber up for the task.

The Junkers JU-88 had two advantages. First, it could be utilized as a tactical dive bomber capable of delivering 3,100 lbs. of bombs over enemy targets. Second, it could be a torpedo bomber capable of launching *'explosive fish'* against enemy ships. It required a crew of four, with the bombardier operating as a forward-gunner in a glass-nosed turret, which provided him clear visibility of targets. There was also a rear-gunner, who also performed the task of radio-operator, and a navigator worked as a ventral gunner. A downside to this aerial weapon was its speed. It flew a maximum speed of 269 mph, making it an easy target for fast-flying British Spitfire and Hurricane fighters. Despite this disadvantage, Hauptmann Diestl had every intention of making good on their advantage of air superiority, and his target, Tobruk, was about to receive another pounding!

Anti-aircraft gunfire flashes dotted the ground as British gunners opened fire, and soon puffs of black smoke erupted all over the sky as shells exploded. German planes shook as though an aerial earthquake swept through their fuselages, but none suffered a direct hit.

Diestl knew the British were not up to repelling his attack. The *Abwehr,* German Military Intelligence, learned how Tobruk was on brink of collapse. Supplies had become dangerously low for troops in need of weapons; ammunition, food, and most importantly—water. Defeat for the South African defenders was a matter of time. Had the British been more cautious with their communications, the Germans might not have learned precisely how weak their defenses actually were. In fact, they were amazed how freely their enemy discussed their dire situation, and how their defensive lines had become inadequate.

*So much the better for us,* Diestl thought. He put the mouthpiece to his radio over his face and said, "Maintain attack formation."

"What about enemy planes?" asked a pilot.

"I don't see any," Diestl replied, "so let's make the most of this while we're able."

Diestl was confident the RAF had been kept in check, having been ordered to return to their bases in Cairo and Alexandria where 8th Army Headquarters attempted to rebuild their defenses against Rommel's push to the Suez Canal. Had the sky been filled with *Spitfires* and *Hurricanes* the attitude of the Luftwaffe would have been much different, for their slow-moving bombers were extremely vulnerable to the superior agility of British fighters. This was proved decisively during the *Battle of Britain* in 1940.

When they arrived over the city at an altitude of several thousand feet, Diestl said over the radio, "Bombardier, you are free to drop your load as you see fit."

*"Jawohl, Herr Hauptmann,"* came the enthusiastic reply from the bombardier-nose gunner. He targeted enemy artillery and tank positions through his telescope, careful not to target fuel trucks and remaining enemy ships in the harbor.

Rommel instructed commanders to make every attempt to avoid destroying supplies they might confiscate upon their taking over the city once it fell. With the *Wehrmacht* (German Army) locked in fierce battle in Russia, supplies on all fronts were dreadfully low. Requisitioning captured supplies for their own use had become vital for future offensives.

The bombardier targeted what appeared to be the top of a reinforced bunker. *Perhaps this is the command HQ!*

It only took a moment for him to decide it was worth the gamble of his payload, so he opened the doors in the underbelly of the JU-88's fuselage. Observing the target closely through the cross-hairs of his telescope, he released the safety on the handle of his bomb-release pistol-gripped style lever. A moment later he pushed the red button with his thumb on the back of the lever and the twelve 250 lbs. bombs tumbled out of the plane in no apparent order. In fact, they appeared as though they were wildly tossed out, spinning and tumbling to earth.

German airmen counted the seconds, waiting for flashes from their bombs exploding upon impact. When they appeared, thick plumes of black smoke engulfed the Tobruk garrison. Diestl and his men smiled, but only for a moment. The thought of what those men below experienced was not comforting. Though they were the enemy, they were still men who belonged to families. Unlike the war on the Eastern Front, Geneva Convention's Rules of War were actually followed by both Germans and British fighting in North Africa.

*"Thank God we don't have the Waffen SS fighting alongside us in the desert,"* Rommel once told an aide. *"Otherwise our treatment of each other would be extremely different."*

Germany had not yet declared *Total War* and this type of chivalry between British and Germans existed in the Desert War. Unfortunately, the situation was much different on the Russian Eastern Front where German and Russian soldiers treated each other as beasts. War correspondents reported how soldiers on both sides endured similar privations in the desert. Heat, sand, scorpions, snakes, and lack of water affected everyone regardless of the uniform one wore. The desert made no distinction between them. Perhaps the most dreaded scourge of the desert was the common fly. They were everywhere. They appeared when you ate, drank, slept, and never left you a moment's peace. This shared experience between enemies generated mutual respect. How long the feeling lasted depended how long the war dragged on.

A British Westland Lysander aircraft was flying low over Tobruk when the Luftwaffe's second wave of bombers arrived for their assault. The Lysander was on an aerial reconnaissance mission from Cairo. It had a crew of two, a pilot and observer, and a range of 600 miles. Lightly armed with two forward-firing .303 Browning machine guns and two .303 Lewis guns operated by the observer, its maximum speed of 212 mph made it vulnerable to German ME-109 fighters. The Lysander was comparable to the German Fieseler Fi 156 Storch plane used for aerial reconnaissance, and sometimes mistaken by German pilots as one of their own aircraft. Lysander pilots were grateful for that seeing how the small top-winged plane was no match in aerial combat.

The pilot and observer could not have flown over Tobruk at a worse moment, and he cursed himself for not having turned around for a retreat to Cairo when the opportunity presented itself. He glanced at the man sitting in the observer's seat.

"How you holding up, Yank?" He guessed the American was terrified. *I don't know anything about you, but you're certainly no soldier.*

The pilot had no idea who the American captain was, only that his orders were to fly him over Tobruk for a recce (reconnaissance) and return to Cairo for a report at General Headquarters (GHQ).

*Bloody Intelligence,* the pilot swore. *They should've known about the Jerry air attack and provided me fighter support.*

"Damn Germans are everywhere!" The American screamed.

"Aye, they are at that," replied the pilot.

The only evasive action he could take was to fly low over Tobruk in hopes German fighters would not follow out of fear of being in range of British anti-aircraft gunners.

*I only hope they don't shoot me in place of Jerry,* he prayed.

"Enemy fighter on our tail!" the American shouted.

"Open fire with the Lewis guns!" the pilot demanded. His voice was laced with urgency and impatience.

The American looked quizzically at the twin guns, and it was apparent he knew nothing about weapons. "Can't you get away?" he begged.

With German planes overhead and their bombs dropping all over Tobruk, it was a miracle the small Lysander wasn't hit by a bomb or destroyed by jittery British gunners below. He could not gain altitude for Messerschmitt ME-109s would surely shoot them down.

"Blimey! Release the safety on the guns and shoot!" the pilot growled. *Bloody Yanks! What the hell good are they for in this war?!*

The general feeling among the British was with America on their side the question of men and material would tip in their favor. After all, wars were fought and controlled by the quartermaster of supplies. The side with most men and supplies was the guaranteed winner. But Americans had yet to prove their mettle in battle. Only in the Pacific Theater of war had Yanks proved their worth with victories at Coral Sea and Midway. There the American navy crippled the Japanese Imperial Naval fleet in both battles which subsequently placed Japan on the defense.

A general opinion among British soldiers, especially with their leaders, was that America was dragging their feet about joining the fight against Germany. Prime Minister Winston Churchill negotiated strongly with their new Allies to agree their primary enemy was Germany, and they should focus efforts in the European Theater of war. Africa was viewed by Germany as a sideshow. *Der Fuhrer* only sent the Afrika Korps to the region to keep his ally, Italian Dictator Benito Mussolini, from reeling in defeat. However, every British soldier knew otherwise. Victory in the desert was important for the British Empire's continued existence, and the Suez Canal proved this during the First World War.

The Lysander pilot stared at the Yank through the mirror in the cockpit and saw him working the Lewis guns. The man trembled more than the guns as they fired away at approaching German fighters.

*Perhaps we'd be better off if Yanks stayed home,* he thought.

The Lysander pilot knew their survival chances were slim, and ME-109 pilots reminded them of this by flying past them at breakneck speed without firing a shot.

*They're taunting us,* he said silently.

Their plane rocked violently by exploding bombs from below, making it difficult for him to keep it under control. He thought it a miracle they remained in the air thus far.

The pilot of the ME-109 flew above the squadron observing the scene below, and ordered his pilots not to shoot down the British Lysander spotter aircraft.

*That privilege is for me!*

He had not been in an aerial dogfight since 1940 during the Battle of Britain, and wanted to enjoy this moment of reflection.

During the summer of 1940 the air war over Britain proved a decisive victory—*for Great Britain*. Despite outnumbered, The RAF with 600 planes squaring off against 2,000 Luftwaffe planes prevented Germany from obtaining air superiority. British Spitfire and Hurricane fighters proved too great for ME-109 and ME-110 fighters to overcome. It was the Luftwaffe's failure which prevented an invasion of England, combined with *Der Fuhrer's* obsession of invading the Soviet Union.

Every German pilot who fought the Battle of Britain had a bitter pill to swallow over their defeat, and the pilot setting his sights on the Lysander believed this was to be a day for retribution. It made no difference his fighter outmatched the spotter aircraft.

*War is war,* he told himself, justifiably.

The German pilot followed the Lysander and was reminded of a particular dogfight against a British Spitfire fighter plane. The Spitfires were known to be faster and more maneuverable than the ME-109s, and could fly at higher altitudes. On the occasion he reflected, he had managed to elude an attacking Spitfire and get behind him. It appeared all too easy. The Spitfire came in fast, its guns blasting away. The German pilot quickly pulled back the throttle, gained altitude and then turned into a steep dive. The Spitfire did the same. The German pilot remained in a dive until it appeared he would be unable to pull up in time before crashing in the trees. The Spitfire pilot lost his nerve, fearing he would crash if he followed Jerry, and pulled back immediately. The German pilots' *fingerspitzengefuhl,* the German equivalent of a 'sixth sense,' told him the Englishman in the Spitfire broke off his attack and was regaining altitude. He then pulled back his throttle and did the same.

When he caught sight of the Spitfire he immediately took to pursuit. He figured the Englishman must have spotted him because he was making for higher altitude at maximum speed. It would only be a matter of seconds before he was out of firing range. The German managed to close distance with the Spitfire and opened fire with his two underwing 20mm machine guns. In a matter of seconds the Spitfire was shattered to smithereens.

*Those were the days,* thought the German pilot, still grinning over his reflection of that victorious day when he brought down the superior Spitfire.

He knew the Lysander spotter plane would be nothing close to the type of victory he enjoyed two years earlier. This battle would be viewed as a sort of *David and Goliath.* This meant little to Germans due to their burning desire to bring their English enemy to their knees. Tobruk had been a thorn in the side of the *Afrika Korps,* and they were going to now pay for their resistance.

The German pilot put his thumb on the firing button controlling his machine guns when the Lysander suddenly dropped out of sight. In that split second the German pilot opened fire, missing his mark by a wide margin due to the British pilot's quick-thinking.

"Britische Schwine!" the German swore, angrily gritting his teeth.

His pride was damaged from being outsmarted by a pilot in a plane no match for his. The time for reflection was over. It was now a matter of honor he destroyed the Lysander, and he immediately went in a dive in pursuit. After leveling off at 500 feet he once more had his enemy in his gun sights.

The German grinned. "Not too clever after all," he said aloud, to himself.

Then he realized something was not right. He was coming up too fast on the British plane. A few more seconds and he would collide with it!

*"Mein Gott in Heaven!"* he cried.

He banked to the left of the Lysander, barely missing its tail. It was a near collision that would have destroyed both planes, and there was no doubt the British pilot knew precisely what he was doing. By deliberately slowing his plane, the ME-109 would have to veer off course, thus giving up gunsight on him.

The Lysander pilot saw the ME-109 pass them and thought he saw a surprised look on the pilot's face. It was enough to force him to smile, but not for long.

"He'll be back soon enough," he said, desperately.

"What are you going to do?" the Yank asked. There was no hiding fear tinged in his tone. "I doubt he'll fall for the same trick."

The pilot nodded. *You're too right about that.* "A plane like that is bound to get us sooner than later," he reluctantly confessed.

"Well, I'd rather it be later," cried the Yank. "*Much* later!"

The Lysander jolted violently as its rudder was torn to shreds by 20mm rounds fired from the ME-109. It had circled back as fast as the English pilot knew it could, and now sought vengeance.

"Blimey!" the Englishman shouted. He struggled with the controls, but the plane lost altitude and went into a steep dive.

The Yank shouted, "Pull up!"

"What the bloody hell do you think I'm trying to do?" The Englishman replied quickly.

He wrapped both arms around the controls and pulled with all his might so they might regain altitude, but it was no use. They had been shot to pieces, making all efforts useless.

The Lysander crashed into a sandy beach and bounced across the sand, breaking in two before skidding to a halt. It did not explode, but the fuselage caught fire and sent up a plume of smoke, adding to the many pillars of smoke filling the sky over Tobruk.

The German pilot witnessed his work on the Lysander and a smile creased his lips. It was not a glorious victory, but at least he could say he was not duped by the pilot of an inferior plane. A victory roll, a single air loop, was not called for, but he looked forward to toasting the saving of his honor over a glass of schnapps with his fellow Luftwaffe pilots.

While the port city of Tobruk was bombed and strafed by the Luftwaffe, the Afrika Korps continuously shelled the garrison with artillery fire. Troops of the 6th South African Brigade defending the western sector of the garrison were taking cover when they witnessed the air battle between the Lysander spotter plane and the ME-109.

"Come on, Laddies!" shouted one of the noncoms. "Let's bring down Jerry while we have a chance!"

The anti-aircraft gunners manning 20mm machine guns and anti-aircraft batteries needed no coaxing, and immediately opened fire at the unsuspecting ME-109. Nearby troops opened up with .303 Vickers and Lewis machine guns, all determined to bring it down for taking part in such an unsporting battle against a lesser plane. A victory for them was a long-shot, but their enthusiasm remained undaunted.

Their efforts paid off, for a few seconds after they opened fire, a puff of black smoke emitted from the ME-109's engine, followed by a brilliant orange light. Black smoke billowed from the Daimler-Benz engine and grew dense by the second. Soon the cockpit was engulfed in flames. The familiar whistling sound of a plane out of control and plummeting to earth caused British troops to stop firing. They looked on in disbelief. When the plane crashed in an orange ball of flame and black smoke, the British cheered thunderously.

# Chapter 4

*"The Luftwaffe dived on the Tobruk perimeter in one of the most spectacular attacks I have ever seen. A great cloud of dust and smoke rose from the sector under attack and while our bombs crashed onto the defenses, the entire German and Italian artillery joined in with a tremendous and well-coordinated fire. The combined weight of artillery and bombing was terrific."*

*- Major Freiherr von Mellenthin, Rommel's Intelligence officer*

The American captain crawled from under the wreckage of the Lysander, awakened by a foul stench attacking his nostrils. The smell was intense and he nearly vomited.

*What the hell is that?* he wondered.

The yank stumbled onto the sandy beach and lay face down, trying to collect his senses. He opened his eyes slowly. Everything was a bright blur. He shook his head to clear his vision, and his head ached tremendously. He touched his forehead and could feel a thick, gooey substance.

*Blood! My blood!*

His vision cleared and the ringing in his ears diminished enough for him to hear the ongoing battle for Tobruk. Reaching inside his trouser front pocket, he pulled out a white handkerchief, something he always carried, and tied it around his head to stop the bleeding. He stared at his hands. They were sticky and covered in dark, crimson blood.

He rose to his feet. *What's that smell?*

He turned to face the Lysander wreckage and to his horror saw the English pilot's body smoldering in flames. *Burning flesh!* That was what he smelled.

*"Oh, my God!"* screamed the Yank. He jumped to his feet, but quickly dropped to his knees, unable to maintain balance. The crash rendered

his vision blurred and everything swirled around him. He stared at the burning body of the British pilot and a sudden flow of anger swelled within him.

Forcing himself to his feet, he moved towards the cockpit and reached for the corpse to see if he could do anything. However, the flames were too great and he staggered back on rocks strewn across the beach. The sound of the Mediterranean Sea splashing waves on the beach caught his attention. He would have loved a swim to clear his head and wash away the blood. His uniform was in tatters and he was covered with bruises and scratches.

*I have to do something—fast!*

He had no idea what a lone Yank could do in the middle of a battle he was ill-prepared for. He looked to the west and saw men and tanks moving about.

*Who are they? Afrika Korps? Or are they Italians?*

He could not be sure, but knew it made no difference. Both were members of Axis forces, enemies of the Allies. The Luftwaffe continued buzzing over the port city, dropping bombs and strafing troops. No friendly ships were nearby for him to swim to.

*Looks like I'm heading for Tobruk,* he told himself, much to his chagrin.

Joining a battle-weary city was the last thing he wanted to do, but he had no choice. It made little difference the city was on verge of collapse. If it meant staying alive, then that was where he would go.

*This means I'm going to be a prisoner.* And this was something he never imagined possible. At least not for a man who had gone to extreme lengths of avoiding becoming a fighting soldier. The very thought of life in a prison camp made him shiver.

*Well I'm not a prisoner yet,* he reasoned. He rose to his feet and wearily marched toward the city.

*How far is Tobruk?* he wondered. His best guess was 300 meters. *Shit! That's three football fields.*

That was not far, he knew, only the distance from the beach to the edge of the city was littered with tank ditches, trenches, barbed-wire, and in all likelihood land mines. Regardless, he needed to cross over this area. It was either that or be taken prisoner-of-war, which was not an option. With this in mind, he went about crouching low along the rocks and boulders strewn on the sandy beach, dashing from cover to cover.

Luftwaffe and German-Italian artillery continued their attack on British Army defenders, and it was a magnificent sight from a military point of view. The Yank, however, was in no mood for admiration. His only concern at this point was survival. He had not gone more than 50 meters when he saw a group of men coming his way from the east, and making their way to the wrecked plane, still burning and billowing black smoke high in the sky.

*Damn! They're Krauts! Or Eyeties! Or both!* he figured. Had to be. He reached for his pistol in the holster on his waist. "Careful," the Yank told himself, aloud. "You'll probably shoot yourself in the foot."

He laid low against the rocks as enemy soldiers inspected the wrecked plane. His first assumption was right. They were Krauts (another slang word for Germans). Their baseball-style headgear was unmistakable, and their tropical uniforms were similar to Allied uniforms from a distance. One of them shouted orders loud enough for him to hear.

The Yank did not understand German, but could see by the soldier's gestures, probably a sergeant he guessed, and barking orders that he was instructing his men to conduct a search for survivors. The plane was, after all, capable of carrying two men and only one remained in the wreckage smoldering.

The German *soldat* (soldier) was in fact a sergeant placed in charge of the detail to search the downed *Britische* plane and confirm all persons were dead or take prisoner. The smell of burning flesh was horrible, and the detail covered their noses with handkerchiefs tied around their necks.

"Too bad," the sergeant said. "I would have enjoyed presenting prisoners to *Herr Oberst* (colonel)."

German soldiers took pride in gathering as many prisoners possible. It made for superior propaganda film coverage over how the *Afrika Korps*, though smaller in numbers, proved a higher degree of battle-worthiness than those of the mighty British Empire. It added to *Der Fuhrer's* belief how today's Germans were the true *master race*.

The Yank checked his makeshift bandage wrapped around his head. The bleeding stopped, but he was smeared in blood over his face and uniform, giving the appearance the wound was much worse. His vision cleared, as did his head, and he was ready to move quickly to British lines. He wiped his face with his sleeve, dirtying it with dried blood.

*Too bad I have no second white handkerchief in case I need to surrender,* he noted.

He observed the soldiers until they tired of the scene and began making their way back to their lines of advance. Only then did he continue racing from cover to cover, hiding in small ditches and behind large boulders littered on the beach.

Soldiers of the 6th South African Brigade had suffered all that was humanly possible since the battle began. Axis forces stepped up aerial and artillery bombardment. Then their tank and infantry divisions began their assault. Tanks of the 5th Panzer and Italian *Ariete* divisions engaged what remained of British tank divisions. German and Italian infantry followed the panzers in great numbers and mopped up pockets of enemy troops who were overrun, but had not surrendered. Bitter machine gun battles took place, and neither side appeared to give any quarter.

British tank crews were defiant, but they knew their cause was lost from the start. The 30-ton *Matilda* was superior in class only against Italian M-13 tanks. German panzers were a different story. The British operated captured Italian M-13 tanks from previous battles, and immediately abandoned them when the German-Italian assault began. "No way am I going to be caught inside that *mobile coffin*," was the common statement from crews. Indeed, the M-13 proved as useful in the desert as most other Italian equipment—*Worthless!*

Early in 1941 when Italy invaded Egypt the march had nearly come to a complete halt by ill-equipped troops and vehicles. Traveling over rocky desert terrain was brutal, and solid-rubber tires on their lorries broke to pieces. Tanks fared little better with treads falling off tracks. The Italian Army had no support vehicles to retrieve equipment, and the British used as many M-13 tanks in battle for as long as they could since their own supply of tanks was thin. However, the worthiness of the M-13 proved so unreliable no one thought less of the man choosing to abandon them.

On the northern sector of the Tobruk garrison a South African officer observed the battlefield through a porthole in the sandbags along the trenches. Something moved toward them, but he could not make out what it was through all the smoke and dust kicked up from explosions. He adjusted his field glasses for a better look.

A nearby sergeant also did the same. "No-man's land," he said, grimly. "Can't see a bloody thing, sir. Can you?"

The lieutenant did not answer right away. "Something's moving our way," he said with certainty. He squinted hard to see. "I can't make it out. Too much smoke." Finally the smoke cleared. "Blimey! It's a soldier!"

"How do you mean, sir?"

The lieutenant pointed in the direction he spotted a man making his way toward them. Finally the sergeant saw him, too. A single man jumped, ran, and crawled through barbed-wire and headed straight for the minefield.

"The *Kraut* must be barmy," the sergeant declared. "He's going to get himself blown to Kingdom-Come."

*Agreed.* "Perhaps," the lieutenant replied. "Unless of course he's—" He stopped mid-sentence, staring harder at the man in no-man's land. "My God!"

"What is it, sir?"

"He's not Jerry! He's a bloody Yank!" He turned to the soldiers to his left and right in the trenches. "Give that man covering fire!" he shouted.

Crawling beneath the barbed-wire, getting cut and his uniform torn from sharp metal, the ground all around the Yank suddenly spat up chunks of rock and dirt. He looked over his shoulder and saw enemy infantry charging toward him.

*"Jiminy Cricket!"* he swore. His eyes practically popped from the socket at the sight of Axis troops heading toward him.

The German detail spotted him moments earlier and quickly turned around to either kill or capture him. The captain saw a German soldier barking orders viciously at his men, deducing he did not want to allow him to escape. It was a matter of honor at this point of the war. Wasting no time, he crawled like his life depended on it—which it did!

The ground all around him continued exploding in a fury as bullets ripped apart rocks and sand, practically burying the Yank. The going was rough, but he continued making his way for British lines.

*Don't turn back,* he told himself. *Not this late in the game! Not so long as freedom is so close at hand!*

He came across a large hole, a former anti-tank ditch no longer effective due to the British not being capable of maintaining a proper defense for lack of men and material, and threw himself in. He had no idea he laid in middle of a minefield. All he could think of was making it to safety inside the Tobruk Fortress.

*Once inside, I'll be all right!*

He was unaware of the desperate situation the British were in, thanks to Prime Minister Winston Churchill and the ministers of White Hall keeping a lid on this from the press. "No sense worrying the great people of England any more than necessary," the prime minister told his generals.

Lying on his back, the Yank caught his breath. He looked at his hands, expressing surprise at the sight of them trembling.

*Why be surprised,* he told himself.

After all, who would not be frightened if they were in a similar situation? He sat up and looked over the top of the ditch. Enemy troops were gaining ground, but would have a rough time crawling through barbed-wire with British troops firing on them.

"Okay, Jack," he said aloud. "It's now or never!"

With speed and agility he never dreamed of possessing, the Yank sprang to his feet like a bolt of lightning and made a dash through the last barrier standing between him and the Tobruk defenders—a minefield!

Within seconds enemy soldiers opened fire with machine gun and rifle fire, kicking up sand and rocks all around his path. Bullets whizzed past him, the piercing *snap* causing his ears to ring as the rounds broke the sound barrier. The Yank crouched midway in his sprint, then straightened as he desperately ran in a zig-zag pattern to keep from being an easy target. He had no idea how the strategy came to him. It seemed to come natural as his thoughts warned him how close to death he was.

The German sergeant barked orders at his detail, commanding them to pursue the Yank. They knew about the minefield and the thought of running through it was not appealing. Only when their sergeant threatened to shoot them if they did not follow his orders did they reluctantly tread forward.

Suddenly the air was filled with several explosions, one after the other, followed by screams of agony. The Yank dove for cover, kicking up sand as he did. Desperate seconds passed before he rolled on his side for a look to see what happened. It only took a moment for things to register. The enemy detonated land-mines, setting off a chain of explosions in a pattern designed to decimate troops.

A number of men had been torn to shreds, and laid motionless in the harsh sun beating down on them. The German sergeant had not been touched, but had dove for cover when the first mine sent a shattering explosion that caused the earth beneath them to shudder. When the air cleared enough for his vision to return, he saw the Yank lying on the ground, staring in his direction.

"*Schwein!*" the sergeant muttered, through gritting teeth. He brought his Luger P-08 pistol to bear and squeezed off three rounds in rapid succession.

Knowing what would happen if he remained lying there, the Yank rolled away, oblivious of land mines he might trip. Rising to his feet, he continued his mad dash to friendly lines.

The German sergeant took note of his detail, or what remained of it, and saw only three appeared uninjured. They were, however, dazed and in no condition to fight.

*I'll have to do this myself,* he told himself.

Grabbing his MP-40 submachine gun laying in the sand next to him, he brought the weapon to bear and squeezed the trigger. The ground all around the Yank exploded, spitting up rocks, dirt, and sand like little volcanoes erupting. Fortunately for the Yank, the MP-40 had an effective range of 100 to 200 meters, and he was just beyond that point. Within seconds the 32-round magazine emptied, and the sergeant had no choice other than swear a personal oath to find the man who managed escape, and make him pay for embarrassing him before his men. Of course, he had to wait until the British garrison fell, which every German and Italian soldier awaited with anticipation.

The Yank continued his dash through the minefield in a zig-zag pattern, and amazingly did not set off a single mine. To his front he saw British soldiers cheering him on, and it was enough inspiration for him to find the strength needed to make it to safety. When he reached the trenches he threw himself over sandbags and fell into the arms of soldiers in the 6th South African Brigade.

# Chapter 5

*"The Italians are brave and anxious to fight,
but lack leadership in their officer corps.
They are certainly no good at war."*

— Colonel-General Erwin Rommel

The soldiers caught the Yank and hastily laid him on the ground for rest. One of them handed him a canteen, a gesture the Yank could not fully appreciate seeing how he was unaware how low rations were. He reached for the canteen, but could not find strength to hold it, so the British *Tommy* lifted the Yank's head with one hand, and put the canteen to his mouth with the other.

"Blimey, mate!" the British soldier exclaimed. "It looked like the *Jerries* were going to pick you off like a fish in a barrel."

Another soldier stepped forward, a lieutenant. "You must have fodder for brains," he said coolly, and with a friendly grin. "You ran through the field as though you knew where each mine had been laid."

One of the soldiers, a conscript from India, shouted, "Sir, they're returning to their lines!" He pointed at the enemy patrol.

Without skipping a beat, the lieutenant barked, "Let'em have it, lads!"

British soldiers opened fire with machine gun and rifle fire, giving their enemy a taste of their own. They ran amok and in disarray, but none were hit. They were too far for accuracy. Soldiers of the 6th South African Brigade gained somewhat of a notoriety reputation with the Afrika Korps. Germans considered them particularly vicious in battle, sometimes refusing to take prisoners.

The German sergeant ordered his men to stop, drop to the ground and return fire. They raised their rifles and aimed high, just above heads of British defenders, and fired a volley of rounds meant to force them into cover so they might have time to make a clean escape. Although they were out of rifle fire, they knew English troops still had functioning mortar and artillery weapons which could turn them into mince-meat. His plan worked, and British rate of fire slowed enough for them to make good an escape safely to their lines.

The sergeant was last, and waited for his men to get a head start before he got up and started running. He had not gotten more than a few feet when the ground erupted in a deafening explosion, and was flung through the air a good 10 feet before falling on a pile of dirt and rocks. He landed with a thud. Air drained from his lungs, causing his chest to strain as he desperately inhaled smoke and dust.

British defenders broke into wild cheer at sight of the German soldier going down.

"Poor bastard," said a South African, with very little sympathy. "He should've zigged instead of zagging."

The German sergeant caught his breath before slowly opening his eyes. Dust covered him, and his vision was blurred.

*What happened?* He could not remember.

One moment he was on his feet, the next he sailed through the air. He shook his head to clear the cobwebs, and unwisely sat up. A moment later it all came back to him. With every bit of strength he could muster, he pulled himself to his feet, picked up his MP-40 and ran as best he could back to his lines. His men watched him, anxiously, and cheered him on.

"Will ya look at that," said an astonished Tobruk defender. "He ain't dead!"

In fact it was a stray bullet striking a mine that set it off, not the German stepping on it like they thought he had. British soldiers opened fire again, but it was too late. The German was out of range. He ran into the arms of his *kameraden* (comrades), inspired by his survival and gallant display of courage.

"Herr Feldwebel (sergeant), thank God you are all right," said a private holding him up by the arm.

"Thought you were dead, Herr Feldwebel," said a corporal, who assisted.

The sergeant took a moment to catch his breath before managing to stand without assistance. He turned around for a look at no-man's land, where he nearly lost his life. His face was caked with dust and perspiration, adding to his physical discomfort.

"I will get that English *Schwein* yet," he declared through gritted teeth.

German armor of the 21st Panzer Division and Italian Ariete Armoured Division broke through British lines of defense after two years of bitter fighting and siege. Fast-moving ground troops of the 90th Light Mechanized Division and Italian Trieste Infantry Division followed behind panzers, mopping up what little resistance the British offered.

British Matilda tanks fired dead-on target against Mark III and IV German tanks, but their weak 2-pounder main gun was no match for the heavily-plated and highly-maneuverable panzers. British tank crews could do little other than look on with frustration as their rounds bounced off the panzers, which then turned their guns on them, forcing them to abandon their tanks as they burst into flames from direct hits. Most British troops managed to escape harm, but a few unlucky chaps were torn to shreds from hot metal shrapnel cutting into flesh and bone. Some were killed instantly; others lay dying in agony before a German soldier ran up to him and put him out of misery with a clean shot to the head.

Colonel-General Erwin Rommel observed what was planned to be the final assault on Tobruk through his field glasses when the sound of planes approaching overhead caught his attention. It was the third wave of 150 Luftwaffe bombers making way to targets inside the British garrison. The Desert Fox grinned broadly at the sight.

"Magnificent!" he boasted to his aides, beaming with pride.

A few moments later the whistling sound of bombs falling from the sky erupted like a thunderous volcano upon impact with their targets. Giant plumes of black smoke and orange flame erupted all over the city.

"What it must be to be under that," said a junior lieutenant not far away, and close enough for all to hear him comment.

Rommel brought his glasses to his eyes again, curious over destruction taking place inside the city. *This was not right,* he knew. He paid particular attention to explosions taking place in the harbor and his *fingerspitzengefuhl* told him what he dreaded. "The English are blowing up their supplies," he said in a subdued voice. *"Damnf!"*

The Desert Fox's staff turned to see what upset their kommandant. They were too imperfect in the art of war to see as he did. Rommel, on the other hand, was a *soldat* through and through. He was only himself when in battle. A *kamerad* would one day state him as being "body and soul in war." No one around him possessed qualities of leadership as he did. To his misfortune, this created enemies within the Ober-kommando der Wehrmacht (German Army High Command), jealous over his popularity with the German populace and Der Fuhrer.

Men of the Afrika Korps, however, were loyal right down to their socks, and Rommel knew in time they would learn never to underestimate their enemy. In order to defeat them you had to think as they did.

*They will learn,* he told himself, *even if it must be the hard way.*

Witnessing stores of supplies go up in smoke did little to raise spirits within German ranks. Captured supplies were part of the prize that went to the victor. Besides, with the German Army fighting what appeared a much longer battle in Russia; supplies for the Afrika Korps were limited. Hitler informed Rommel personally no increase in supplies would be sent to Africa. The offensive in Russia swallowed up too much men and material. So far as Berlin was concerned, Egypt would have to wait.

But Rommel saw things differently. He knew the key to defeating England was to deny them access to the Suez Canal and the Mediterranean Sea. Deprive them of that and you took away England's ability to receive resources from colonies abroad that kept their empire alive. Unfortunately for Rommel, no one in Berlin agreed. It was far easier—and safer—to agree with Hitler. For the present, Der Fuhrer was obsessed with conquering the Slavic nation ruled by Josef Stalin.

Still, Rommel had an ace-in-the-hole.

Tobruk!

If he took control of this strategic harbor it was believed Hitler must recognize the importance of controlling North Africa if Germany was to win the war. He simply had to have Tobruk!

The Afrika Korps' general headquarters had been moved not more than 1,000 meters from the front. Rommel's reputation for being a frontline commander was not fiction. He knew the best way to give his men direction was to be where they were. His troops found this inspiring, but Rommel's staff officers and quartermasters found this frustrating. Their reason being was his direction over maps and supply routes was needed, too. His staff constantly searched for him in the heat of battle to keep him informed on other areas of enemy movement, so that he could provide them with orders on how to engage them. As commanding general only Rommel could issue a change in battle plans should the need arise, thus the frustration from his deputies and lieutenants.

Rommel was about to enter an open tent complete with large tables covered with maps when a commotion on the northeastern part of the front caught his attention. "What is the trouble?" he asked a nearby soldier.

The soldier snapped to attention. "I'll find out, Herr General," he said, and rushed off. He returned a few moments later and found Rommel discussing strategy over maps. "Herr General," he said, smartly saluting. Rommel looked up and nodded. "A downed British pilot returned safely behind enemy lines," the soldier said. The embarrassment for giving this news to the general was apparent in the soldier's tone and body language. "Our troops failed to capture him."

Rommel shrugged. "So the enemy has a moment of gaiety," he said, grinning like a fox. "It will not change the outcome of this battle."

The entire staff snapped to attention and clicked their heels. *"Jawohl, Herr General!"* they said in unison.

Everyone believed their commanding general would defeat the British at last.

Rommel removed his peaked cap and set it on the table. He poured himself a glass of precious water and drank it, careful not to spill a drop. He looked over the maps again, studying them carefully. Tobruk was circled in pencil and positions of his Afrika Korps and Italian Ariete and Trieste divisions were also marked for his reference. Staff officers patiently stood by, looking on while he put together his thoughts. Being assigned to Rommel was unlike any post his officers were accustomed to serving. This was largely due to the fact Rommel was unlike any commanding general in the Wehrmacht.

From early stages in his career, Rommel had always been in the thick of the fray. He would be at the frontlines with his troops, "Pacing the lines like a caged lion," as some would say. He displayed character of a man determined to fight by his own rules. His men would adapt if they were to remain in his command.

The general looked at his watch. *Amazing the sand hasn't destroyed it,* he thought. "Let's see how long they hold out this time," he said, focusing on the map marker identifying Tobruk. He turned to Major von Mellenthin. "You are certain they possess two tank battalions, no more?" he challenged.

Von Mellenthin nodded respectively. "Jawohl, Herr General. The English have virtually no effective tank formations worthy of the name. We intercepted enemy radio transmissions there will be no reinforcements from Cairo for at least another week. They have to stand and fight where they are, Herr General."

Rommel grinned like a kid in a theme park. "Well, no one can doubt their courage," he said with respect. His eyes sparkled at the thought of being so close to capturing Tobruk. He turned to face his staff. "Gentlemen," he said, causing them to snap to attention and clicking their heels, "mark this day well in your diaries. This shall prove to be a great moment for us!"

"Jawohl, Herr General!" the staff cried, in unison and grinning confidently at their commander.

German tank Sergeant Heinrich Priess ordered his machine gunner to open fire on enemy troops as they retreated from their foxholes and trenches. The machine gunner, a proud *soldat* having been raised by a father who himself was a veteran of the *Great War,* trained his sites on them. He locked and loaded a fresh belt of 7.92 mm rounds in the MG 34 machine gun, a deadly weapon firing nearly 900 rounds per minute, and touched the trigger gently.

"Jawohl, Herr Feldwebel!" the eager gunner replied, and squeezed the trigger at the same time.

Five British soldiers were cut down in flight. Bullets tore into their back, ripping apart flesh and bones. Two others took rounds in their legs and shouted for help, but the rat-a-tat sound of gunfire drowned their cries.

Sergeant Priess looked through the telescopic sight of his 50mm main turret gun on his Mark III Panzer tank and observed three British Matilda tanks moving toward the oncoming panzers.

"What balls," he said, shaking his head in disgust. "Will these English ever learn?"

The scene brought to mind a coined phrase he heard from captured British soldiers. "Matildas are little more than a *steel coffin!*" he recalled them declaring.

"Fire!" Sergeant Priess commanded.

The tank trembled as the turret gun fired, and Priess witnessed a British tank take a direct hit, blowing its turret clean off.

"That should teach them," he said, laughing jubilantly.

Feldwebel Walther Prien of the Afrika Korps' 90th Light Mechanized Division led his patrol of soldiers closely behind the panzers as they approached enemy trenches, recently refilled with sand from neglect on the British side and the *ghibli* (sandstorms) that turned clear skies into dark, swirling worlds of sand. He witnessed panzers overrun tank ditches with no trouble, and was grateful things were running smooth. He desperately wanted to get inside Tobruk and find the British pilot who narrowly escaped his patrol earlier in the day. The blow to his pride was too great to allow him to forget how he had nearly been killed by an exploding mine triggered by a stray bullet. He swore he would locate the Englishman and set things right.

*After all,* he told himself, *we are the Aryan race!*

Prien and his troops were about to continue their advance when they noticed movement in the trenches. Something was buried in the sand. Prien looked closer and suddenly a hand popped from beneath the sand, groping for something to grab hold of.

*An Englishman! He must have been buried by the panzers during their advance.*

Prien and his troops moved forward when another soldier came up from beneath the sand, and another, and another. They all gasped for air and when they saw Germans standing before them, rifles and machine guns at the ready, they raised their arms in surrender.

Prien was first to fire and his men quickly joined in, cutting them to pieces. Wasting no more time, he ordered his men to continue their advance in the city.

*I want that pilot,* he swore silently.

Major-General H.B. Klopper was in his bunker when another artillery shell exploded close enough to rattle his headquarters. He looked at the calendar hanging on a post. The date was June 21st, 1942, he observed. He looked at his watch. The time was 9:00 am. He shook his head despairingly.

"This will not be a good day for Britain's military history books," he said aloud, and to no one in particular.

Captain Hughes called out to him, "Sir, I've got General Ritchie on the line."

Klopper went over and took the earphones and hand-mike from Hughes. "Hello Neil," he said, in a raised voice so he could be heard over explosions from outside. There was no response. "Neil, are you there, sir?"

A voice crackled over the radio. "Yes, I hear you, H.B. How goes your situation? I understand Jerry is punching his way in the city?"

Klopper ignored his superior officers' casual tone. It was a flaw in the British officer corps, he believed, to maintain composure even when times were desperate. Sometimes it was good to display a sense of urgency during a crisis, he thought. It motivated men to work extra hard.

"I regret to inform you we have nothing to hold back the enemy advance." His words were more of a statement than explanation, and he remained silent a few moments to allow his words to sink in. "We have no serviceable tanks," he continued. "Artillery is at half strength, and my men are exhausted." He paused again. After a few awkward moments of silence from the other end of the line he asked, "Are you planning an offensive to breakthrough?"

The silence was broken by an exploding artillery shell nearby, filling the room with dust. Klopper only heard static on the radio and pressed his question once more. He silently cursed Churchill.

*If only the fool had not boasted Britain's determination to keep the Libyan port in Allied hands, perhaps the Germans would not have persisted in wresting it from us.*

Finally, General Ritchie's voice crackled through the radio. "My staff is finalizing details for our next course of action. Will keep you posted as events develop. This is Ritchie out."

Klopper threw down the earphones in disgust. His staff looked on, despair written on their faces. He turned and faced Captain Higgins, who over the course of night had been wounded, and had his arm in a sling.

"Are the supply stores destroyed yet?" He spoke in a tone of a man who lost hope.

Higgins hesitated. *Why I must always be the one to offer disappointing news,* he wondered. He shook his head slowly. "I'm afraid not, sir. Our communications to the Quartermaster have been cut. All I know is he is doing best he can, but Jerry is moving up too fast. They are bound to capture some of our supplies, sir."

The general nodded twice. Their situation on the front was deteriorating rapidly. The Germans and Italians broke through their defenses and were already inside the garrison. The skies were dominated by German planes, with not a single RAF plane to repel them. British troops were being routed and captured by the hundreds. It was now only a matter of time, he knew.

General Klopper turned to face Hughes. "Make radio contact with the Germans," he ordered, in a somber tone. "I wish to speak with their commanding officer immediately."

As Germans and Italians poured into Tobruk, resistance stiffened from near-spent British Army defenders. Australian units in particular refused to give ground to advancing enemy columns. Captain Higgins had been correct in his report to General Klopper that some units under his command would refuse to surrender, and even continue to fight hand-to-hand if necessary. This was the determination of Australian and South African soldiers in the British Army.

Gunfire echoed throughout the desert for miles, and Bedouin tribes listened with intent, trying to determine the victor. Up to now, Bedouin tribes supported the Germans, but were known to switch sides. Their loyalty had limitations to those only in power.

The Quartermaster had been placed in charge with destroying munitions and fuel which, if captured, would assist the enemy in their fight for control of North Africa. However, German troops advanced with lightning speed, in small mobile units, catching the British by surprise, along with many supplies rigged for destruction.

"Herr Rommel will have the booty he desires after all," a German officer commented upon entering a warehouse full of war material.

Afrika Korps troops entered the city in all directions, and British soldiers began surrendering in the hundreds, and eventually thousands.

Lieutenant William Hudson fought his way back to the harbor in hopes of catching a ride on an MTB, which could then take him to Malta, still under British control. An explosion knocked him and three soldiers off their feet. The blast did not render him unconscious, but his vision blurred and he had difficulty rising. A moment later he felt a pair of hands lift him up from under the shoulders.

"You okay, boy?" the stranger said, in a deep guttural monotone.

Hudson squinted hard to make out the man's face. It was *him!* "You're the man from the downed plane," Hudson said with surprise. "Yessir, Cap'n, I'll be all right."

"What's your name, Lieutenant?" the captain asked.

Hudson was shaking all over and had to fight to control his nerves. "Hudson, sir. William Hudson."

"Well, William, my boy, I suggest we get the hell—"

Their conversation was interrupted by an ME-109 fighter. The Messerschmitt came swooping low, strafing enemy troops making way for escape in the harbor. Its 20mm guns tore up the ground all around them, sending up dirt and rocks. They dove for cover behind a burning tank, and the captain swore he heard Hudson cry out.

When the fighter flew past them the captain grabbed Hudson by the lapel and said, "Come on, William, we've gotta—" Before he finished his sentence he realized the young British officer had been killed by shrapnel.

The grotesque sight made the American react squeamish, and only when a shell exploded nearby did he snap out of his silent trance.

"Come on, Jack," he told himself aloud. "Get off your ass and get movin'!"

Colonel-General Erwin Rommel entered Tobruk in his 'Mammut,' a mammoth-sized captured British armored command vehicle. The top was down and he stood on the front passenger side as he was known to do when on parade. His driver took them along a paved coastal road leading to the harbor, with German and Italian troops marching alongside into the city.

Victorious troops shouted "Sieg Heil!" repeatedly and then began singing their famed 'Panzerlied' German tank song verse after verse. Rommel beamed at the sight of his proud Afrika Korps troops smiling and basking in triumph.

British soldiers, now prisoners-of-war, stood in solemn silence at the sight of Germans and Italians marching into the city. Their defense cost two years of hard fighting, depravation, and a strong feeling of haven been let down by their leaders in England. Thoughts of being forgotten by loved ones back home filled their hearts and mind and did nothing to improve morale.

Despite Rommel being a sworn enemy, British troops could not help looking on in admiration at the man who turned their world upside down. His quick-thinking and fast reflexes in battle wrote a new set of rules for tank warfare and demanded their respect.

Behind Rommel's command vehicle followed panzers, troop carriers, motorcycle units, and infantry marching in triumph. The Luftwaffe flew overhead in tight V-formations, a sight that impressed even defeated British troops.

Rommel's driver stopped in front of General Klopper's HQ. The South African commander of British forces stood at attention with his entire staff ready to offer their official surrender.

A junior German officer shouted, "Achtung!" (Attention), and German soldiers snapped to attention, clicking their heels.

Rommel returned a military salute, not a Nazi salute, as the British were glad to see. He stepped down from his vehicle, flashing a broad smile from ear-to-ear, and walked over to General Klopper, who saluted first as was custom of a POW (Prisoner-of-War). Rommel smartly returned the salute.

All eyes focused on Rommel. This was the mysterious *'bogeyman'* responsible for ruining careers of many able-bodied English officers. This was the Desert Fox whom Prime Minister Winston Churchill praised in the House of Commons as a daring, great general. He was the man who finally broke British resistance in Tobruk.

He appeared smaller in person to many, and somewhat large around the waist. He carried himself with an air of confidence displayed only by Germans, which appeared more in the form of arrogance. There was, however, no underestimating the man as a soldier. Indeed, Churchill had been proven right by how great this man's skill as a fighting general was on this day, June 21st, 1942.

The time was 9:40am.

General Klopper stepped forward and saluted. "General Rommel, I am General H.B. Klopper, commanding officer of the British garrison of Tobruk." He paused to clear his throat. "I have reviewed the situation with my staff," he continued, speaking in a subdued monotone, "and concluded further fighting to be fruitless." He paused again, working hard to maintain a soldierly composure. "I am therefore compelled to surrender this entire garrison to you." He saluted once more, fighting back tears swelling in his eyes.

The Desert Fox returned the salute smartly. "I accept," he replied, in heavily accented English. Turning to junior officers of Klopper's command, he gave a slight nod and said, "Gentlemen, the war is now over for you. All of you. I pay tribute to your gallant defense of Tobruk. You have truly fought like lions." Rommel then turned eyes to Klopper. "It is only by a bad case of luck you were led by jackasses."

Nearby German officers and soldiers snickered at the sleight from their leader, and British POWs did best not to appear wounded by the insult.

A junior officer ran excitedly up to Rommel. "Sir, I have reports of captured supplies and materials you requested," he said, catching his breath.

*Good*, Rommel thought. *Please let the news be good!* "Very well," he said, calmly. "Read them aloud," he ordered. He stood before the junior officer with his hands folded in front of him, patiently listening while the young officer read the reports.

The man cleared his throat, appearing nervous speaking before so many of his kameraden and enemy soldiers present. "We have captured 2,000 vehicles, mostly cars, troop carriers, and lorries. We have also captured

33 operable tanks, 403 artillery pieces, 6,000 tons of food and water, and enough petrol to replenish our panzers and continue our offensive."

Rommel clasped his hands jubilantly. "Well, gentlemen," he said, now facing his staff, which always followed him, "it appears as though Alexandria and Cairo will soon be ours after all."

His staff clicked their heels and saluted. "Jawohl, Herr General!" they said in unison.

And the air was filled with cheering Germans and Italians.

# C h a p t e r   6

*"With the fall of Tobruk, we believed nothing would stop us now!"*

*– from the diary of an unidentified German soldier*

## June 21, 1942 10:00am

S oldiers of the Afrika Korps drove into Tobruk on panzers, lorries, and kubelwagens, and quickly took charge of thousands of British, Australian, South African, and Indian troops to be interned as prisoners-of-war. Surrendering troops were a solemn lot, and did their best to maintain composure before victorious German and Italian soldiers.

Feldwebel Walther Prien stood inside the passenger side of a kubelwagen observing his men instructing prisoners where they would be taken. Prien preferred the top of his car to be down and enjoyed standing up while they drove through streets. It was an arrogant display of authority. In the German army, only officers were afforded the luxury of their own car, but in the Afrika Korps men of all ranks enjoyed perks.

German half-track vehicles passed them, followed by captured lorries, cars and light and heavy armored vehicles. The soldier in the driver seat next to Prien noticed his sergeant did not appear to be in a celebratory mood.

"Anything wrong, Herr Feldwebel?"

Prien did not answer right away. He stared at bombed-out buildings, streets, and the smashed harbor and piers. "Herr Rommel is fortunate enough to have gained important munitions and petrol," he said, finally, "but the *Britische* have handed over to us a destroyed city."

It was a good observation. Although General Klopper's orders to destroy their supplies was not followed through, his men had succeeded in blowing up piers and sinking ships in the harbor, all of which would delay the Germans of being able to make good use of the port.

"Look, Herr Feldwebel," the driver said, excitedly. He pointed at a captured American Wylies Jeep driven by three German soldiers.

The vehicle was popular among Germans whenever they got their hands on the speedy vehicle. The jeep, operated by British Special Air Service (SAS) soldiers, proved to be an effective vehicle for long-range military operations in the desert. With a little creativity, the SAS outfitted their Wylies jeeps with mounts capable of holding .5 inch Browning machine guns and twin .303 Lewis guns. The fast-moving vehicle allowed groups like SAS and Long Range Desert Group (LRDG) to operate hundreds, even thousands of miles behind enemy lines where they gathered intelligence reports on troop movements and engaged in pre-dawn attacks against enemy planes parked in airfields.

A group of German soldiers driving past Prien and his men boasted another popular military vehicle captured from the British, a Light-Armored Car. This speedy car had a top speed of 50 mph, fast over rough terrain, and a range of 180 miles. It boasted a 20mm cannon and one 7.92mm machine gun.

Also among captured vehicles was a Heavy-Armored Car armed with a 7.5 cm L/24 cannon and the same 7.92mm machine gun as the Light-Armored Car. Its range was 372 miles and a top speed of 53 mph. Both vehicles proved highly effective in desert warfare, and the Germans had yet to create comparable vehicles for behind-the-lines operations. This lack of foresight was due to their belief that the main weapon in the desert was the tank. This opinion was correct at this stage of war, but their lack of support vehicles had only just begun to hamper their ability to drive into Alexandria, their next choice city for conquest.

Sergeant Prien waved at vehicle drivers to continue moving through the streets. They had yet to finish searching all the buildings for prisoners and supplies, and he was getting hungry.

"This is going to take some time," he noted to his men.

The buildings were damaged by bombing to the point they could not be used, and reconstruction would have to take place before they could be occupied for offices and supplies.

"I don't like risking a search in these buildings, Herr Feldwebel," one of the privates declared. "They look like they'll fall on top of us."

Prien flashed the soldier an irritated look. "Our orders are to secure important papers the English failed to destroy," he reminded his men. "With such information we could learn more about enemy troop movements, their strength, and location of vital supplies." He paused, staring at the buildings. In truth he agreed with the soldier. Their siege had taken a heavy toll on the port city. However, orders were orders. With reluctance he said, "Proceed."

Prien disembarked the kubelwagen when he noticed a particular POW standing among a small group of others awaiting transport to a prisoner-of-war camp. They were a motley group comprised of South African, Indian, and Australians. They were identifiable by their uniforms, the Indians of course by their dark skin and turban headgear. Another wore the uniform of a British Army captain. His coat and trousers were disheveled, but he appeared healthier than others standing in the ranks, and did not display battle-weary features.

Prien recalled the British soldier he chased through the minefield. He had not gotten a good look at the man's face, nor could he determine his rank, but he guessed him to be an officer in the British Army. He approached the group in typical German arrogance of the day, hands on hips, and grinning from ear to ear.

To the surprise of the Germans, the POWs were equally arrogant, staring back at them in defiance. It was plain to see they would bow to no one, not even the *Aryan Master Race*. They were defeated, but not broken. Indeed, for them to have held out so long against impossible odds had made them known throughout the world as among the toughest fighting men in any army. *The Battling Bastards of the Bastion of Tobruk* would be forever remembered regardless how much the Germans detested them.

A corporal in charge of the POWs said to Prien, "Herr Feldwebel, are you searching for someone among the prisoners?"

Prien did not immediately answer. A moment later he nodded and replied, "Yes, but I'm not sure what he looked like. I know he's an officer, a survivor of the downed enemy aircraft."

"Would you care to interrogate them?" the corporal offered.

Prien would have loved to so that he could be sure he was not passing up the chance of getting his hands on the man who barely escaped him, but he needed to report to his commanding officer (CO) for further instructions. "Later, perhaps," he said, and then turned to leave.

Jack Ruggero stood among the group of prisoners awaiting instructions from his captors. He grew thirsty, and licked his lips, aching for a drink of water. He unbuttoned the dress coat to his captain's uniform, finding the British clothing uncomfortable to that of his American uniform. A

German soldier barked orders at them, and he found himself being lined up along the coastal road, probably to be marched out of the city, he reasoned.

A burly German officer shouted orders none of the POWs understood, so soldiers guarding them shoved the barrels of their weapons into their guts, indicating for them to straighten up and stand at attention. The prisoners did so, but half-heartedly. They were too exhausted from the long battle and lack of food and water to be ready to stand on parade.

"Easy, mate!" one of the South Africans said to the German poking his MP-40 submachine gun into his stomach. "What's the fuss 'bout?"

A moment later everyone understood. Rommel's motorcade approached and the officer in charge wanted a proper display of military respect for their commander. And the newly christened prisoners-of-war were going to do their part whether they agreed to or not!

Rommel stood on the front passenger side of his Mammut in the same manner he had been photographed so long ago and been made famous by the generous world press, and saluted his men. The fact he had a British-made armored vehicle for his personal command car was a slap in the face to the British, not to mention wearing a pair of large British goggles across his peaked cap.

When the general's vehicle neared his group, Jack thought he saw Rommel stare directly at him and offered a salute. Jack froze, failing to return the military gesture. Although he had no way of knowing it, the Desert Fox intended his salute for all POWs present.

"They fought well," Rommel said to one of his aides. "And if there's one thing I admire," he continued, "is a good fighting soldier!"

British officer Lieutenant Anthony Duggan stood beside Jack, watching the motorcade drive until out of sight. He turned to Jack, who appeared more nervous than others waiting to be transferred to a POW camp.

"Blimey, mate," Duggan started, "the man salutes and you don't return the courtesy! You look for trouble with Jerry?"

Jack pulled himself together. "In case you haven't realized, Rommel is the enemy." He paused, staring in the direction of Rommel's command car driving off. He added, "He's a brilliant general, but he's still the enemy."

"At least he's a man of honor," Duggan interjected forcefully. "The man follows rules of war, unlike Hitler's SS. I've heard stories how those bastards fighting in Russia are killing women and children along with soldiers." The lieutenant shook his head at the thought of it. "What kind of man in uniform kills women and children?"

"Well, consider yourself lucky you're not fighting in Russia," Jack shot back.

Duggan stepped back a bit and noticed Jack's head bandage was soaked with blood. It was dirty, too, and he pulled a handkerchief from his pocket. "Here, mate, take this," he said, handing it to him with his left hand. His right hand was incapacitated by shrapnel, and wrapped in a field dressing.

"Thank you." Jack took the handkerchief.

"Got a dressing to go with that?" Jack shook his head, so Duggan reached into his pocket and offered him a fresh one. "Here, I've an extra."

Jack removed the bandage from his head and carefully replaced it with the new dressing, tying a knot at the back of his head. "Thanks!" It was not a threatening injury, more like a cut on the side of his head that would not stop bleeding.

Duggan noticed something odd about the man standing beside him. Jack's accent was off. No way was he English, or Australian. In fact, Duggan swore the bloke was a Yank. "Where you from, mate?"

Jack thought better to answer when he saw a lone kubelwagen drive up to his group. It was occupied by three Germans, but one in particular seemed familiar to him, and his color turned pale at the sight of the man sitting in the front passenger seat.

Feldwebel Walther Prien challenged himself the impossible task of studying each prisoner's face. He was determined to find the pilot of the downed Lysander. "Not so fast!" he growled to the driver.

Standing alongside the road was a man who caught Prien's attention. He wore a head bandage, and recalled the man he sought had a head injury.

*Then again, a lot of these men wear head bandages,* he told himself.

He ordered the driver to halt, and studied the man in the rank and file carefully.

*Could that be him? Among these thousands of prisoners, is it him?*

Certainly there was no way for him to be sure, but he was determined not to miss any opportunity of getting his hands on the man who caused him embarrassment in front of his men. He was about to disembark from the car when he saw two men standing near the soldier in question. They too, wore head bandages. Nearby was another group of prisoners, many of which wore bandages from injuries.

Prien shook his head, disgusted over his rotten luck. *"Scheisse!"* (Shit!)

The driver looked up at him curious. "Herr Feldwebel?"

Reluctantly, Prien ordered his driver to continue down the road. He knew it was a waste of time searching for a single man among these thousands of prisoners. Still, he had a feeling their paths would cross again. His *fingerspitzengefuhl* told him so.

"I'll be a son-of-a-bitch!" Jack Ruggero swore softly.

When he saw the German standing in the kubelwagen, a cold feeling swept through him. Then it came to him! It was the man who led the soldiers after him through the minefield.

*Could he have been looking for me?* Jack wondered. *Impossible! What would he want with me?* He reflected on his mission. *What about my mission? It's only a reconnaissance.*

Jack was new to war, but common sense told him anything was possible in these trying times. *At least he didn't get a good look at my face,* he told himself with relief.

Lieutenant Duggan stepped closer. "I've been meaning to ask," he began, with a touch of reluctance; "You're a Yank in British Army uniform why?"

Jack was not surprised Duggan discovered his ruse for he made no attempt of speaking with an English accent. "I've been called many things," Jack replied, "but I suppose Yank will do."

Duggan studied him carefully. "Your rank real?"

Jack nodded. "Yeah, I'm a captain."

"Whatcha doin' in our man's army, sir?"

The last thing Jack wanted was to disclose information about himself, but he figured he needed a friend seeing how things were about to get rough on their way to a POW camp. "I'll go over that another time," he said with finality. "What happens to us now?"

Duggan snickered. "Don't know. It's my first time being taken prisoner."

Jack let out another sigh. He stared hard at Duggan, studying him with his eyes. *Aw, what the hell?* "I was on a reconnaissance mission from Cairo," he began, in a hushed voice. He saw how Duggan appeared perplexed. "Need-to-know," he quickly added. "What you do know is I'm an American, or *Yank* as you put it."

"How did you get here?" Duggan interjected.

"The plane that crashed on the beach earlier today, you know the one I'm talking about?"

Duggan nodded.

"That was me. The pilot was British, and got killed. I managed to make it inside the city, only to find it a hornet's nest of trouble." He stopped to look over his shoulder, making sure no one listened. "The krauts can't learn I'm an American, you understand?"

"The Yanks are coming, aren't they?" Duggan practically screamed.

Jack struck him with a fist to the gut, and Duggan nearly doubled over. Then he grabbed him by the arms, helping him to his feet.

"The hell's the matter with you?" Jack scolded. "I can't be interrogated! They'll strap me in a chair and make threats what they'll do if I don't cough up what I know. If that happens, I'll sing like the *Andrews Sisters*. I ain't cut out for this hero crap! That's why I'm a liaison officer, not a combat one." Then he added, "Or worse, they can shoot me as a spy for wearing a British uniform."

Duggan pulled himself together. The Yank's confession of not being able to withstand interrogation surprised him. *What you expect from an American,* he told himself. *They've no idea what they're in for.*

"All right, captain," he said, nodding. "I understand what you mean." He paused, looking Jack up and down, studying to see if he was genuine. After all, it wouldn't be the first time the Germans planted a man within ranks to gain information. "How can I help?"

Jack sighed relief. "You're a good man, Duggan," he said, patting him on the shoulder.

# Washington D.C.
# June 21, 1942

President Franklin Delano Roosevelt sat in his wheelchair in the Oval Office at the White House entertaining his guests, British Prime Minister Winston Churchill and General Sir Hastings Lionel Ismay, Churchill's Military Chief of Staff. The three were laughing while discussing non-political issues. Roosevelt looked up when a member of Churchill's staff entered the room. The man was a British officer, a captain assigned to Ismays' staff.

Churchill's ever-present cigar smoke filled the room, but no one seemed to mind. Roosevelt was a heavy smoker too, and clenched the ceramic cigarette holder he was known to use tightly between his teeth, puffing away. All three drank brandy, Churchill's favorite. The prime minister was interested in fly fishing and discussing the sport with much eagerness when the young captain approached General Ismay.

"Sir," the captain started, clearing his throat, "may I have a word, please."

The general was wise enough to know he would not be disturbed unless it was important. He rose from the soft linen sofa, politely excusing himself, which went unnoticed by the president and prime minister, who were still engulfed in their conversation. Ismay followed the captain outside into the next room. Here he faced a group of senior American and British officers with deep concern on their faces.

"What's all this now?" he asked, using the common words of an inquiring British *'Bobby.'* The general was obviously irritated by the untimely interruption.

The officer standing before him was a British colonel, also a member of his staff. He shook his head despondently, and his slowness in providing the general an explanation caused Ismay to be more irritated.

"Get on with it, colonel," the general ordered, in a commanding tone.

The colonel told General Ismay the news they received moments earlier from British Army HQ in London. Ismay looked up to the ceiling and rolled his eyes. "God save us all," he said softly.

He returned to the Oval Office where the president and prime minister remained consumed by their conversation of fly fishing, and wondered how he would break the news to the PM.

*Action this day*, he told himself.

Those were words Churchill famously used when pushing for action against the enemy.

Ismay closed the door behind him, leaving the officers in the adjacent room wondering how things would go. Once inside he remained standing in order to grab attention of the two world leaders. Churchill was first to notice him standing at attention.

"Pardon the interruption," General Ismay said, clearing his throat. He paused before continuing, and then appeared to be at a loss for words.

"Hastings," Churchill said, puffing on his cigar, "have you something to say?"

The smoke from his cigar and Roosevelt's cigarettes filled the room with a soft cloud and strong incense. Ismay could not help bringing a hand to his nostrils.

"What is it?" the PM asked, impatiently.

General Ismay drew a deep breath. "Tobruk has surrendered to the Germans, sir."

President Roosevelt removed the cigarette holder from his mouth. "When?" he asked, with unmistakable surprise.

"9:40 this morning, Mr. President, their time."

An uneasy silence filled the room. Churchill took a swig from his glass and puffed slowly on his cigar. He did a good job maintaining composure, but his eyes widening over this news expressed the shock coursing through his veins, and for good reason. He knew survival of his country depended on keeping the Suez Canal in British hands. The Battle of North Africa could not be lost. If it were, then the war was lost for England.

Churchill removed the cigar from his mouth and nodded twice. "Rather disconcerting news," he said, laconically.

Roosevelt put his cigarette holder between his lips and said, "I'd say this changes things dramatically, Winston." He tried sounding compassionate as possible.

Churchill shook his head and said in a hoarse voice, "This changes nothing!" He took a drink of brandy from his glass, nervously set it down on the table, and turned to face Roosevelt. "This proves how important the Battle for North Africa is," he explained in as calm a voice he could muster. "The *Suez Canal* must not fall to the hands of Nazi Germany. The War would be tipped in Adolf Hitler's favor if it did." He paused, determined to press his point. "We fight for freedom of the entire world, and yet there are men in the *House of Commons* bickering over my conduct."

This was a moot point. It was widely known how Churchill's political enemies within his government opposed his hiring-and-firing of so many generals over so short a time. His pestering military commanders for quick victories on the battlefield were seen as desperate attempts to defeat a superior commander, Erwin Rommel, and this embarrassed the government. This proved especially true when Churchill all but praised the German field commander publicly.

"If my political brethren provided me support versus constant criticism," he continued, "these shattering and grievous losses might never have come to pass!"

Roosevelt empathized with Churchill. All during the years before America entered the War, the president battled with a pacifist mindset among Americans. He had gone to great lengths to get the United States' military up to par and was fought at every turn by politicians on all sides. These were people who wanted nothing to do with Europe's problems, and it took the Japanese sneak attack at Pearl Harbor to change America's way of thinking.

Despite a common enemy shared, politicians in Great Britain sought personal gain and influence, and questioned Churchill's way of handling the military. "Had it been up to me," cried Churchill, "I would have bolstered troops in Tobruk so that a defeat could have been avoided altogether."

General Ismay thought otherwise about that, but wisely kept his opinion to himself. He knew with Japan taking over Singapore, much of Southeast Asia, along with a number of strategic islands in the Pacific, troops destined to beef up forces in North Africa had to be placed on hold. Churchill knew this to be the case, but the loss of Tobruk was a blow to English pride, seeing how the beleaguered garrison had become a symbol of British resistance.

*My opponents in Whitehall must be gloating over this,* Churchill thought.

He was certain, though Germany was poised with a knife at England's throat; there were still people in government more concerned about removing him as PM than defeating their true enemy, Adolf Hitler. The loss of Tobruk would be placed solely on his leadership and underestimation of the enemy.

Churchill puffed on his cigar. "I must communicate with Auchinleck," he declared. Then he turned to Ismay and said, "Send this wire to him immediately..."

Ismay wrote the message dictated by the PM on a notepad, rose to attention, nodded respectfully to the two world leaders, and left to have the telegraph office send the message.

Churchill looked at Roosevelt, searching for his response over his actions, and the president nodded approval.

"That's all one can do, Winston," the president chimed. "Even generals need a kick in the trousers to remind them they've got a job to get done."

Churchill was grateful for his support. "It will have to do for now," he confessed, gritting his teeth. His skin turned beet red over anger rising in him. "That bastard Rommel!" he blurted. "He really has turned my world upside down!"

The president puffed his cigarette and wheeled himself to the window of the Oval Office. "That's putting it mildly," he said, grimly.

# C h a p t e r   7

*"Rommel! Rommel! Rommel! What else matters than defeating Rommel?"*

*– Winston Churchill*

## Cairo, Egypt
## June 21, 1942

G eneral Sir Claude Auchinleck took his seat at the head of the conference table in the briefing room with a number of aides discussing developing situations on the battlefront when there was a knock on the door. It was opened by a corporal who hadn't waited for permission to enter, but as a member of the general's office staff needed none on certain occasions such as now. He walked straight to the general, whose attention was focused on his chief of staff, Brigadier John Whiteley, who read aloud a report of men and material losses with the fall of Tobruk.

Auchinleck observed the corporal standing next to him from his peripheral view and lifted a hand, signaling for the young non-commissioned officer to be patient a moment longer. When his chief of staff saw the corporal anxiously standing beside the general, he paused.

Auchinleck turned to the corporal and said, "Yes, corporal?"

The corporal exhaled as if to say, *here goes,* and said, "Sir, message from the prime minister." He handed a single sheet of folded paper to the general, who took it and opened it carefully.

Auchinleck put his spectacles on and read the note in silence. When finished, he looked up at his staff, and then read the note in silence once more.

Brigadier Whiteley felt uneasy. News from the PM was usually tense considering how Churchill continuously pressed army generals to attack even when the consensus was to wait until their forces were beefed up.

"Don't tell me he's sacked another commander," Whiteley blurted, breaking the silence.

Auchinleck slowly lifted his eyes from the message he held in both hands. He then set it down and reached for his cup of tea and took a drink. He recalled how Churchill had sacked General Sir Archibald Wavell, his predecessor, as a way of nudging his generals to get their house in order and push on against Jerry.

Auchinleck faced his staff and said in a most tense tone, "Appears as though the PM believes action this day is most urgent and suggests we restructure our command."

The brigadier shook his head. "How would he know about that?" Whiteley challenged. "Our conditions in the field cannot be understood by a politician busy conferring with Roosevelt in Washington. Besides, is he unaware how too many changes can delay operations and create confusion among troops?"

Auchinleck shrugged and exhaled deeply. He had been a good choice to take over command of British Middle East Forces from General Wavell, who defeated the Italians in 1940 when they advanced into Egypt. But when the Germans came to Mussolini's aid things turned sour quickly, and with fewer men and resources the Afrika Korps recaptured all lost territory to the British and began their advance into Egypt.

As Churchill declared, "Rommel has torn the newly-won laurels off Wavell's uniform and tossed them in the sand!"

When Wavell had been informed he was being relieved he was shaving in his private washroom. A messenger knocked on his door stating he had an urgent message from the PM. "Enter," Wavell permitted, and instructed the young soldier to read the message while he continued shaving.

The soldier, a private straight from the farm thirty miles outside of London paused, his pink-white face turning a beet-red. He had a, *why-do-I-get-all-the-tough-job,* expressions, and cleared his throat before reading the message.

"General Wavell, due to changes on the front which are not favorable STOP—It is my decision a new commander should lead Middle East Forces with immediate effect—STOP."

The private lowered his hands and remained standing at rigid attention.

General Wavell stared at his half-shaven face in the mirror, holding the razor in one hand. Nodding, he said, "The Prime Minister is quite right. There ought to be a new eye and a new hand in this theatre."

Thus began a new command with *The Auk*, as General Auchinleck was affectionately referred to by his men, of all British forces in the Middle East. His reputation of self-discipline had been an inspiration to soldiers throughout his career. An example of his skill in leadership occurred when he left his wife behind in India when he learned lower-rank officers were not permitted to bring their wives to Egypt. The move was well-received among his men.

The Auk also had strong loyalty for subordinates chosen to lead divisions in his army. Relieving one of his commanders had never been easy for Auchinleck, and this situation proved no different in the case of Major-General Neil M. Ritchie, Commanding General of the Eighth Army. What Auchinleck had not realized was the plain simple fact many generals he chose for command were unprepared for the job at hand. In fact, his decisions had been so poor that those close to him on his staff considered him to be incapable of choosing anyone worthy of command.

General Auchinleck rose from his chair.

His staff shot glances at each other, confusion dwelling among everyone. *What was the general going to do?* This was the question swimming through their minds. When it appeared the Auk had reached a decision they looked on with much anticipation.

"Appears I'll have to visit Neil in Mersa Matruh," he said, regret seething in his tone and expression. Mersa Matruh was a historical seaport which saw its share of battle dating back to the reign of *Alexander the Great*. General Ritchie's headquarters was located there.

Brigadier Whiteley nodded empathetically. It was the Auk's responsibility as Commander of British Forces in the Middle East to post men in charge of his armies and divisions. It was also his responsibility to relieve them when the situation called for it. General Ritchie had no way of knowing at this point he was about to be out of a job.

"My chief of staff will make preparations for our journey to Mersa Matruh," the brigadier offered, rising from his chair. He and the others got up from their chairs and started to leave with the brigadier following up the rear. He was about to exit the room when something about the Auks' silence caught his attention.

Auchinleck was going over Churchill's letter once more. It read:

*To: Commanding Officer of British Middle East Forces*
*From: Prime Minister Winston Churchill*

*I am disappointed about fall of Tobruk. This creates much worse situation than anticipated—STOP—Your choice of Ritchie for command is a miscalculation—STOP—Suggest you take a more personal approach to matters at hand—STOP—Action this day—STOP*

Auchinleck shook his head forlornly. This was a part of command he disliked most of all.

# Chapter 8

*From beginning of the desert war, both Axis and Allies realized the terrain made it ideal for tank warfare. The tank became the war-horse in the Battle for North Africa. Thus, fuel became as precious as water. When prisoners of war came into the fold, the need to conserve became more desperate, and supply chains were strained to the point where each man was permitted only one canteen cup of water per day.*

No one existed in the desert more naturally than nomadic Bedouins. They travelled across vast sand dunes freely, undeterred by grand-scale war fought between Germans, Italians, British, South Africans, Australians, and Indians. Bedouins trekked across the desert without compasses and maps, yet knew where they were going without such modern tools. They accomplished this with their instincts and followed the stars. Even when giant sandstorms shifted great seas of dunes from one pattern to next, Bedouins managed to conquer all obstacles and found their way to the next precious waterhole. This was not the case for Axis and Allied forces. They required a steady supply of rations in order to sustain themselves.

Germans and Italians received supplies from air bases in Sicily to Benghazi, but mostly by ships traveling across the Mediterranean. Trucks then transported food and war material from Benghazi to the frontlines. However, British Desert Air Force routinely bombed and strafed these convoys with harrowing effect. Now that the vital port of Tobruk was in German hands the distance between shipping supplies to the front had been reduced hundreds of miles, saving time and precious fuel.

Their current problem was that British garrison forces scuttled most of the harbor right before its capitulation. Piers were blown to smithereens; ships had been sunk in their moorings and entrance to the harbor, making it impossible to put the port to effective use. It would in fact be some time before Germans could make full use of Tobruk's harbor.

And time was not on Rommel's side if he was to continue his push to Alexandria and Cairo. This meant he must continue using the overland route to receive supplies from Benghazi, risking aerial attacks. At this point of the campaign, supplies were utmost importance for his offensive to continue.

"The last we need are tens of thousands of prisoners to deal with," the Desert Fox confided in a subordinate.

Prisoners of War consumed manpower, time, equipment, and even more important,—*food and water*. Geneva Convention rules of war concerning treatment of POWs clearly stated how the victor had responsibility to see prisoners were properly cared for. They were to be removed far from the battlefield and harm's way, and given sustainable food and water for survival.

It was fortunate for Allied prisoners of war that General Erwin Rommel had been a traditional German soldier and not a member of the *Waffen-SS*, Hitler's military arm organized by the Nazi Party to fight alongside the German Wehrmacht, police, and other organizations within German society.

Rommel was a man of integrity and staunch military discipline. He led by example and earned respect of his men wherever he served as commanding general. When food and water became scarce, he instructed his orderly to serve him and other top commanders the same rations his men received. This move earned him respect from soldiers unwilling to share vital supplies with prisoners, and thus prevented brutal acts against them.

Soldiers of the British Army, now classified prisoners-of-war, were herded into a large encampment fenced in with barbed-wire. German and Italian guards were everywhere, armed with automatic weapons and ready to prevent any escape attempts. German and Italian cooks arrived and prepared POWs their first meal of the day inside the encampment where prisoners lined up in single file to receive their meal. Their expressions were of astonishment over hospitality from their captors, and they remained suspicious due to having been briefed over how Germans treated prisoners in Russia.

"Britische Schwein!" shouted Oberst Otto Krieger. "Schnell! Schnell!"

He appeared suddenly and struck POWs with his horsewhip to hurry them along through the food line. Even guards were taken aback by his brutish behavior and made certain not to get in the way of his whip.

Sturmbannfuhrer Hans Mueller was in charge of the prisoners and was surprised by Krieger's appearance as much as the POWs were. He stood at front of the line as the oberst strode arrogantly toward him.

"Herr Oberst, what is the meaning of this?" he asked, standing at rigid attention and offering a military salute, not the Nazi Party salute.

Krieger returned the salute, touching the visor of his Afrika Korps cap with the tip of his horsewhip in typical aristocratic-style.

*Not another one of these sorts,* Mueller prayed.

The military was full of high-ranking officers from the *old school*, where money bought rank and privilege, along with extremely poor behavior. Mueller found it odd how the aristocrat society of Germany bowed to their Fuhrer, a man who held a rank no higher than corporal and received no formal military training in waging war. It was ironic how this part of Hitler's past helped his popularity through ranks of the common soldier.

"What is the meaning of providing these pigs with such luxury?" Krieger demanded. "They are eating and drinking better than men in my command." His contempt was obvious in tone and stance.

Mueller remained standing at attention, unphased by the bully-boy behavior from his superior-ranking officer. *You simply stand your ground and respectfully inform him of your duty to follow orders,* he reminded himself.

"I beg your pardon, Herr Oberst," Mueller replied, calmly, "but General-Oberst Rommel was quite specific how we handle prisoners of war."

Krieger stiffened. The mention of Rommel's name appeared to humble him enough to embolden Mueller.

"If you prefer, Herr Oberst, I will inform you of those instructions?"

Krieger nodded permission for Mueller to continue.

"All POWs shall be treated in accordance to rules of war described by the Geneva Convention," Mueller began, speaking smart and without pause. "Equal rations of food and water shall be distributed to each man regardless of rank and uniform. There will be no exceptions." He paused for effect. "Those are my orders, Herr Oberst."

Krieger snorted. "Are you certain your interpretation of Herr General Rommel's orders is not exaggerated?" he asked.

A smirk materialized on Mueller's face. "We can contact Herr General's adjutant for verification if you prefer, Herr Oberst," he suggested.

Krieger eyed Mueller cautiously. He recognized the smirk on Mueller's face for what it was, but knew there was nothing he could do to retaliate. With support of the commanding general, the sturmbannfuhrer was untouchable.

Mueller knew this too, and his grin grew wider. *Too bad for this high-minded snob,* he said silently. *Now he will have to scurry off to the hole he crawled out from.*

Krieger rubbed a gloved hand over his dusty face. His desert goggles were wrapped over his tropical field cap with officer's designated *Soutche* insignia in orange-red, the official color of the military police. Mueller figured this added to his aggressive behavior. They tended to bully regular troops the same way the *Schutzstaffel* (SS) did against civilians. It was all part of their plan to show who was in charge.

After a few awkward moments Krieger said, "I sometimes wonder if General Rommel is aware how preferential treatment to prisoners appears in the eyes of our troops."

Mueller tilted his head to the side curiously. "I do not understand what you mean, Herr Oberst."

"These men are the enemy," Krieger spat. "Rules or no rules, they should not be fed as equals among our soldiers."

Mueller nodded understandingly. "Hmmm, that is quite an observation, Herr Oberst. Shall I ask General Rommel his thoughts?" His grin was replaced with the seriousness of a schoolteacher asking a disruptive student a challenging question, and Krieger did not appreciate being upstaged.

The oberst stiffened. He recognized insubordination when he saw it, and knew there was little he could do. He did an about face and headed for his staff car. "That will be all, sturmbannfuhrer," he said through gritted teeth.

Mueller saluted despite Krieger showing him his back. "Danke, Herr Oberst."

Many POWs witnessed the scene between the two German officers and were confused over what they argued about. A few among them fluent in German explained the exchange between them, and were surprised how the sturmbannfuhrer defended them. Reports on how the German Army conducted itself on the Russian front were well-known to the British Army, even in North Africa. Never in their wildest dreams would they have imagined a junior officer standing up to a colonel over prisoners' right to equal rations in a time of war.

Jack Ruggero and Lieutenant Anthony Duggan observed the exchange between the German officers, and were also taken aback by the sturmbannfuhrer standing up for them.

"Blimey!" Duggan exclaimed, not too loud so the guards would not hear. "Who'd have guessed a *Jerry* defending us get'n our fair share of rations?"

Jack shrugged idly.

A British major standing nearby chimed, "Nothing surprises me in this war." He pulled out a gold cigarette case and waved it before them. "See this?" he said, flashing it like a prize. "I was with General Gambier-Parry at Mechili when we surrendered back in April of '41. The *Fox* himself went over to the old man's command car whilst Jerry was busy unloading his personal belongings. Rommel saw one of his officers remove this cigarette case from me, but ordered him to hand it back, stating how looting was not permitted in his ranks." The major shook his head, astonished over the memory of his experience. "All this surprised me because I recalled how some Germans are known to take no prisoners due to supply shortages and no facilities to receive them." He paused again. "One doesn't expect chivalry from soldiers fighting for a madman like Hitler."

Jack's eyebrows lifted in surprise. "War does that," he said carefully. "It brings out the best and worst in people." He stared longingly at the gold cigarette case the major held.

The major sensed what he wanted and shook his head. "Sorry, old man. They returned my case, but helped themselves to my cigarettes." He snorted before adding, "Looks like you're right about this war bringing out the best and worst in us all."

Jack motioned with a nod for the major to step back with him out of ear-shot from the guards. The major mentioned how he'd been captured earlier in the year in April, which meant he escaped in time to be caught once more in Tobruk.

*But if he escaped once before....*

"How did you manage it?" Jack asked, curious.

The major laughed. "Jerry had taken so many prisoners they needed help from their *Eytie* friends, which played in our favor." He eagerly explained. "As you may be aware, Italians aren't a thorough lot, especially when it comes to soldiering. Back in 'Forty we'd showed them up good, pushing them out of Egypt despite our being outnumbered six to one. We did such a job of it; *Der Fuhrer* found it necessary to send Rommel and his Afrika Korps. *Il Duce* was grateful, but it only proved Italy wasn't up to par to do its part in this war. Anyways, the *Eyties* proved a bit slack watching over us, so one night I slipped past guards and escaped." The major reflected on his ordeal, wondering how he could have been so fortunate. "I doubt Italians ever much liked the desert," he continued, somberly, "which is why I doubt they sent a search party for me. Eventually I made my way to Tobruk with help from a Bedouin tribe."

Jack nodded appreciatively. "Interesting story."

The major turned his head and faced him. "Where's my manners?" he said, regretfully. "The name's Lawrence, Thomas Lawrence." He extended a hand.

Jack shook it, and both he and Duggan introduced themselves. Jack suggested they move away from the larger group of POWs for a private conversation, and before long they were discussing plans for escape.

Jack saw why Germany had been the more successful partner of the Axis. They possessed spirit and desire to wage war.

*Or perhaps their inspiration comes from their sense of history,* Jack thought, curious.

He thought how England had the uncanny habit of losing battles here and there, but coming through in the end and winning wars.

*Maybe Germany knows they have to keep on the ball or suffer a repeat of their surrender in the forest of Compiegne on the 11th hour of the 11th day of the 11th month in 1918,* he thought to himself.

In any case, his observation formulated Italy being an unfavorable ally for Germany. They were unenthusiastic about everything. Italian soldiers did not properly maintain vehicles and equipment. They performed duties in a lackadaisical manner. They lounged about whenever the opportunity presented itself, especially while on guard duty. German soldiers complained about their Italian allies whining about how much they missed home and did not favor the war. In fact, Italian complaints were so intense even the British POWs hated listening to them.

However, for Jack this was music to his ears. Once the Italians took over responsibility for the POWs their chance of a successful escape increased tenfold. Jack paced back and forth behind the barbed-wire fence like a caged lion. There were over thirty-five thousand POWs on their way to a prison camp, and somewhere along the way, Jack committed to himself he would manage an escape.

Major Lawrence calmly stood nearby, puffing a cigarette he shared with Duggan. "Take it easy, old boy," the major said. "Our time will be soon enough."

Jack stopped in his tracks at the sight of a cigarette. "Got another of those?" he asked with a touch of desperation. He looked like a drunk in need of a stiff drink.

Major Lawrence reached in his uniform coat pocket and pulled out his gold cigarette case. He opened it and to their surprise found it full.

"Gee-wiz! I thought you said you were out?" Jack asked, sincerely astounded.

"English ingenuity, old boy," Lawrence answered with pride. "I traded a chocolate bar with a German officer in exchange for them," he explained, offering him one.

Jack lit his cigarette and inhaled a long drag, savoring it. "Thank you! I needed this."

Major Lawrence looked out into the desert through the barbed fence. "With luck, we'll have plenty more when we reach our lines at El Alamein."

Jack took another drag and Duggan asked, "What do we do now?"

Jack and the major looked at each other, then to Duggan. "We wait," they said together.

## Rommel's Headquarters
## Tobruk – 7am June 22, 1942

The man known worldwide as the Desert Fox sat at his desk whilst his staff hurried about cleaning up their new headquarters. Most buildings in the port were destroyed by the Luftwaffe, not leaving much left for the conquerors to utilize. Rommel, however, was no stranger to toughing out the elements with his men, and sat comfortably at the worm-eaten desk writing another letter to his beloved wife, Lucie.

*Dearest Lu, you may recall I once wrote you how I could not sleep for happiness over the dazzling success we enjoyed over the defeat of the English forces at Benghazi. It seems long ago, what with the many victories we have won since our arrival in North Afrika almost two years ago. By the time you receive this letter you will have already learned we have Tobruk! Yes, my love! We have finally removed the Union Jack and hoisted up our flag in its place. I suppose I should be upset over my extensive efforts needed to achieve this. The cost was heavy in regards of men, time, material, and most importantly—petrol.*

*Our HQ is setup in the only suitable building left due to our bombers making good on their experience. Appears they were able to do here what they failed during the Battle of Britain. On another note, my dear, I've received a telegram from the Fuhrer. Appears I've been promoted Field Marshal. Yes, Field Marshal! Apparently our victory was enough to compel our Fuhrer to award me this honor despite those in High Command suggesting another Ritterkreuz (Knight's Cross) more appropriate. You see, Lu, with this new rank is the distinct gratification of having direct-access to the Fuhrer. This means I no longer go through Kesselring first.*

*Please understand, dear, I do not wish to appear ungrateful, but I would much rather receive another division. Although we have taken Tobruk and received much in the way of spoils, there is still much to do and I require more men and supplies if I am to push ahead to Cairo. Our Italian allies are unable to prevent enemy air and naval forces from sinking my supply ships and the strain is great on my men. The consolation I have with being promoted is now I may address these issues directly with the Fuhrer and not be side-stepped. With luck things will continue to turn for the better. Time will tell.*

Rommel looked up from his desk and saw Sturmbannfuhrer Freiherr von Mellenthin enter his office and snap to attention. "I have more good news, Herr Field Marshal," the major said, beaming. He held out a piece of paper and Rommel took it. While he read the note, von Mellenthin explained its contents. "Your presence is requested in Berlin immediately for the Fuhrer to present you your field marshal's baton."

Rommel read the telegram and sighed heavily when he finished. "With so much to be done this comes at a difficult time," he said with regret.

Von Mellenthin appeared genuinely shocked. "I do not understand, Herr Field Marshal? You have been awarded the highest rank in our army. Is this not a time for celebration?"

Rommel lifted his eyes to meet his intelligence officer. "Have you read our supply situation reports lately?" he asked, challengingly.

"Jawohl, Herr Field Marshal. With English supplies, we've requisitioned another two thousand vehicles, thirty tanks, four hundred artillery pieces, and enough fuel for—"

"It's not enough!" Rommel blurted, slamming his palm down hard on his desk for emphasis.

Everyone stopped what they were doing and the entire floor fell silent.

Rommel got up from his chair and paced the floor back and forth, hands folded behind his back. The sound of his boots tapped the floor loudly, breaking the silence. He stopped in front of his desk, staring at his men.

"We need a steady supply of material," he said, speaking urgently. "We cannot continue foraging for it like we have been doing. Relying on captured enemy supplies is not the answer. Captured supplies are enough for an advance on Alexandria, yes, but unforeseen delays and flanking maneuvers will use up precious time, men, and most importantly—petrol."

He stared ahead, not expecting answers from his men, who in turn waited for him to speak. Rommel slowly turned to the side and stared out the window of his office. There was no glass in the frame, as many of the windows throughout the city had been broken due to the heavy bombing. Below in the streets he saw soldiers directing prisoners cleaning the streets and removing rubble. Vehicles drove through the city and the sound was deafening, but welcome. It indicated the Afrika Korps was well-equipped for the upcoming campaign. However, Rommel knew any advance east toward Alexandria and Cairo was doomed failure unless he received a steady supply of war materials.

He continued his silent stare out the window with his *fingerspitzengefuhl* hard at work. Then it came to him! He turned to face his intelligence officer.

"Prepare my plane for flight to Berlin at once," he ordered.

Von Mellenthin snapped to attention, clicking his heels like all German soldiers did when addressing a superior officer. "It is being done as we speak, Herr Field Marshal. As I mentioned earlier, your presence is requested in Berlin at once."

Rommel strode to his desk, scooped up the letter he had yet to finish writing for his beloved wife, put on his peaked cap, picked up his riding cane and nodded. "Very well," he said in high spirit.

At that moment elsewhere in the desert, Italians moved their POWs along the road. The wounded and high-ranking officers had the luxury of traveling in transport vehicles while the rest marched in the grueling sun. Italians were ordered to take them from Tobruk to Benghazi, through Tripoli, and finally Tunis. They did not accept this assignment with much eagerness for they too suffered similar elements of a hard-beating sun, heat, and the ever-present scourge of the desert—the common flies.

Snakes and scorpions were also a common threat to soldiers on all sides. They were behind every rock, beneath the sand, crawled into tents, boots, and their bites were painful and sometimes deadly. Flies, however, were the worst. They appeared anywhere and everywhere you went. One could not enjoy a meal without being pestered by them. Head nets, mosquito biers (bed nets), and improvised table nets placed over entire groups of soldiers while eating at a table helped some, but one way or the other, flies found their way into making life miserable for everyone.

During the march east along the coast road it was obvious to prisoners something made the Italians nervous. They kept looking skyward, searching for something. Jack knew it wasn't the sun they were looking at, and became curious.

"What're they searching for?" he asked, quizzically.

"Our Desert Air Force," Duggan answered with pride.

Being new to the war, Jack had no idea how dangerous a threat the British Royal Air Force had become. Spitfire and Hurricane fighters gave the British air superiority, and prisoners knew they were subject to being killed by their own planes if they suddenly appeared, strafing and bombing enemy vehicles at will.

*That would be perfect!* Jack thought. *A distraction would allow me to escape.*

He knew he could not make it alone and needed help, and turned to Duggan and Lawrence, grinning. They studied their captors' behavior and believed they were bored, showing little concern over the POWs. He figured they had their belly full of Africa seeing how the war took them far from home to a desolate desert not worth the rocks and sand that covered it. They had the long, sojourn expressions of men longing for home.

After nearly three years of desert fighting, troops were acclimated to changing seasons, but in the latter half of June walking or driving along coast roads became intolerable for even the most toughened breed. Sun and heat beat down on them like a hammer on an anvil.

So far as Jack Ruggero was concerned he was experiencing hell on earth. Far from being a toughened man, he lacked endurance and will to push himself to the limit. Although Jack appeared fit and healthy, he was used to soft living. He stood six feet tall with a lean frame. His thick, dark wavy hair parted on the right complemented his brown eyes and slightly-tanned complexion. He had high cheekbones and rugged facial features topped off with a standout smile emphasizing a neat row of gleaming white teeth. Considered a handsome man with never a lack of female companionship, at least not until the day he went off to war, some sighed relief when Jack learned he had been drafted. Back home in Pasadena, California he had become something of a nuisance for married men and those with girlfriends. Growing up, Jack had been a selfish boy, looking after himself over others. He had grown quite comfortable using people to get what he wanted at their expense, and was unconcerned for consequences that fell on their shoulders.

*Better them than me,* he often told himself.

How he became an officer in the United States Army was a miracle in its own right. But then again, never before in the history of the United States Army had the need for men to be inducted for military service been more urgent. In quick time many officer candidates came to be known as *Ninety Day Wonders.* Such things happened when a nation's military became neglected during times of peace.

While the POWs marched on the dusty road, an Italian car rode alongside them with an officer standing on the passenger side of the car waving them to make way for a tank convoy coming towards them. The Italian officer looked somewhat comical, or so Jack thought, shouting at the top of his lungs in his native tongue as though the British, South African, Australian, and Indian troops understood a word.

Lieutenant Duggan walked behind Jack and Major Lawrence when the small car drove past them creating a dust cloud in its wake, filling their nostrils and eyes with sand.

"Blimey!" he shouted, coughing up sand and waving his hands in front of his face to clear up the air. "Where'd that idiot come from and where'd he learn to drive?"

The POWs needed little coercion to get out of the way of the oncoming tanks and supply trucks. Their powerful diesel engines created a cacophony of noise heard miles throughout the desert. Tank commanders stood arrogantly atop the hull, their heads adorned with brown desert tank cap and earphones. It was an incredible show of force and the prisoners' hearts sank at the sight of how strong their sworn enemy was and how their fellow soldiers would have to face them soon enough in the heat of battle.

Jack recalled the little town name. *El Alamein, I think?*

In spite Jack being a newcomer to the desert war, he formed a reasonable opinion as to why the Germans appeared to be winning. Their tanks were faster and more maneuverable. To date, the British had nothing to match them on the battlefield. He also noted how Germans were better equipped with salvaging equipment, enabling them to remove disabled tanks and vehicles from the field for repair and refitting, something the British had yet to improvise. This advantage allowed the Afrika Korps to become experts in mechanics and make the most from all their equipment, whereas the British left their knocked out equipment to rot in the field.

However, for Jack it was more than equipment and ingenuity that demonstrated their invincibility. Jack was among the chosen few who possessed a very perceptive point of view and understood what he saw. And what he saw more so than tanks and trucks operated by the enemy were the faces behind the driving sticks and steering wheels.

*The Krauts are confident! Damned confident!* Jack thought.

He was not far from wrong. You could see the look in their eyes, not so much in the Italians, but most definitely in the Germans. It was in the way they grinned, displaying bright white teeth. Their laughter and arrogance, all of which left Jack an impression they had no conception of defeat. They were winning this war precisely as Hitler swore they would. The Germans were going to push the British out of Libya and Egypt, driving them into the sea, and take control of the Suez Canal. Victory was in their sight, and they knew it!

"ATTENCION! ATTENCION!" shouted an Italian guard marching along the column. He pointed skyward. "AEROPLANES!"

All eyes looked up. At first all anyone saw was a bright sun and clear blue sky. Moments later the sound of propellers reached their ears. The prisoners strained their eyes, but still could not see any planes. As the sound grew nearer the sky displayed tiny black specks flying toward them.

"AIR RAID!"

An Italian soldier in the back of a lorry turned the crank handle to an air raid siren and its loud, screeching sound reached the ears of tank drivers who couldn't hear the planes over their own diesel engines. Tanks and trucks immediately pulled off the road, dispersing in a wide formation, careful not to bunch up and make a more inviting target for enemy fighters and bombers. A thick heavy cloud of dust kicked up by their speeding engines made visibility poor, and with luck, enemy pilots would have trouble focusing on targets.

Prisoners scattered in all directions. There was no semblance of organization whatsoever. No one took the chance pilots might recognize the convoy for that of British prisoners. After all, Germans were masters of trickery, masquerading as British soldiers to prevent their own convoys from being bombed and strafed. Most prisoners steered clear of enemy tanks and supply trucks. Those vehicles were priority targets for Allied pilots. The war favored the side with the most tanks, and the Germans could not afford to lose any.

Prisoners stumbled over one another still searching for cover. The sound of planes screeching a high-pitched tune as they dove in for attack was ear-piercing. Lieutenant Duggan fell face-first in the sand and struggled to get back on his feet, which was impossible as fellow prisoners trampled over him in search of cover.

*How in hell am I gonna get outta this fix?* he wondered.

A moment later he felt a pair of hands reach under his armpits and pull him to his feet.

"Stay close to me!" the stranger shouted.

Duggan's vision was blurred, so he intended to do precisely as ordered.

British Spitfire and Hurricane fighters opened up with 20mm and 50mm machine guns. The constant *rat-a-tat-tat* from their weapons sounded like a rumbling cacophony of an orchestra desperate to create a worthwhile tune. Rocks and sand erupted as large caliber rounds tore into the earth. A supply truck was hit and exploded in an orange-black ball of flames and smoke. The earth shook like an erupting earthquake. German and Italian soldiers opened up with anti-aircraft machine guns with little effect, but they continued doing their best to shoot down their enemy.

Then came a squadron of British Avro Lancaster bombers (affectionately called *Lanc* by pilots), flying just above several thousand feet. This aircraft had been introduced to the war in February 1942 and in this short time gained respect and fear for its capabilities. The belly of the planes opened up and out came multiple numbers of 500 lbs. bombs. One by one they erupted on the convoy, blowing tanks, trucks, and cars to smithereens. Men were shattered like matchsticks. The sight was incredible and sheer chaos. The ground was being torn to shreds. Thick, black plumes of smoke billowed from destroyed supply and transport vehicles carrying barrels of fuel. Bombs rained endlessly all around them.

Duggan grew dizzy after having been knocked senseless from the explosions. Each time he fell he was lifted to his feet by the faceless man who continued to order him to, "Stay close to me!" He desperately wanted to know who his savior was, thinking him to be his guardian angel.

Not far away an Italian officer standing in the back of his open car shouted frantically at his driver, ordering him to drive like mad and get them both the hell out of the area. Although the soldier could not hear his commander through all the bombing and machine gun fire, he knew precisely what he shouted—"Let's get the hell out of here before we're both blown to hell!"

The driver could not risk traveling on the road, so he drove like mad off to the side parallel with it. Bomb after bomb sent shockwaves on either side of them. At times they thought they were about to be blown over, but miraculously they survived. Soon the explosions subsided as the bombers spent their payloads and withdrew.

The Italian officer ordered the driver to halt when he believed they were safe, and turned to look back at what was left of his troops. Carnage was everywhere. Smoke and fire from vehicles burned heavily. A few mighty tanks had been destroyed, and men laid everywhere. Slowly, one by one, men began to get to their feet. In fact, so many men had survived the bombing that the Italian officer looked to the sky, thanked God for sparing their lives, and made the sign of the Crucifix.

"Grazie a Dio."

He tapped the driver on the shoulder with his riding stick. "Turn around and let's get to sorting out this mess," he said. He could not help sounding like he knew it would be an impossible task.

The driver turned the car around and got on the road. They failed to notice a single Hurricane fighter high in the sky begin a dive towards them. When they heard its propeller screeching towards them, the driver floored the pedal.

"Hurry, get us out of here!" the officer said desperately.

The British plane came nearer and nearer. Its high-pitched sound from its propeller sent a spine-tingling feeling coursing through their veins.

*This is no good*, they thought.

After coming all this way from fighting in Ethiopia against under-equipped troops and murdering entire villages with mustard gas, forcing the Ethiopian king into exile, it looked as though their fate was finally sealed. The officer momentarily thought of his early victory against the British in 1940 when they invaded Egypt and attacked Sidi Barrani. Then the British counter-attacked, forcing the Italians to withdraw. Germany came to their aid and before long Italy was on the offensive once more. To have come this far and not see the war through to its end seemed ironically unfair to the Italian officer.

*Then again, when is war ever fair?* he thought.

It mattered little to the soldier driving the car how close Italy had come to winning the war with Germany on its side. He had never been a soldier in the fighting sense. No, he was much too smart for that. He had no desire to fight and die for *Il Duce*. He had a wife and two children to return home to. They barely survived on his grocer's pay, but at least they were happy. So long as he survived he would be victorious. And at this moment this was all that mattered to him—surviving.

The final thing they saw was the look of fear in each other's eyes when they realized they were not going to escape the enemy planes' bullets tearing into their car, followed by a tremendous explosion when the fuel tank was hit.

Lieutenant Duggan witnessed the disintegration of the car from afar whilst he still followed the shadow-faced man. "Poor buggers," he said, in a remorseless tone.

"Just be glad it wasn't you," replied Jack Ruggero.

Duggan quickly turned and faced him. His vision was still blurred, but he recognized the familiar voice and realized it was Jack who saved him. "Captain Ruggero, it's you!"

"Of course it's me. Who the hell did you think I was?"

"Christ Almighty, sir! I had no idea, what with me being half blinded. Thank God you're all right, sir!"

Jack patted him on the shoulder. "Yeah, well now we gotta get our bearings straight and see if we can make way to friendly lines." He looked all around them, searching for which direction to take. "The Krauts will be coming for us soon enough," he reasoned. "I have no intention spending the war as a prisoner. I hear the food is terrible and the lack of female attention will drive me crazy."

Duggan saw a sand dune half a mile from where they stood among the wreckage. Nearby German and Italian soldiers began rising to their feet. They were shaking their uniforms of dirt and gathering their weapons. They soon went about collecting prisoners, but lacked coordination, still suffering from the effects of having been bombed and strafed.

"What about Major Lawrence, sir?" asked Duggan.

Jack shrugged. "What about him?"

Duggan stared disbelievingly. "Well—we're not going to leave without him are we, sir?"

Jack looked back at the prisoners being rounded up and thought about the possibilities. "Chances are he's with that sorry lot," he said, finally.

Duggan looked in the direction of the POWs being rounded up by their captors, then back to Jack. "Aren't we going to help them, sir?"

Jack waited. *The kid's not joking!* "I'm only going to say this once," he began, curtly. "We're here," he continued, emphasizing their position by pointing to the ground. He grabbed Duggan by the shoulders and turned him around facing the POWs. "Lawrence is there." He turned Duggan so that he faced southeast toward the open desert. "That's our direction to freedom. Lawrence is out of the picture as far as I'm concerned. He just plain didn't make it. You and me—we're still in the ballgame." He paused, gauging Duggan's behavior before adding, "Are you up for this?"

Duggan hesitated for what seemed an interminably long time. "Right sir, I'm with you," he said finally, and with reluctance.

Jack nodded approvingly. "Okay. Stay close to me."

They picked up any supplies they could from fellow prisoners lying about, dead from the bombing and strafing. They pulled off shirts to ward off the frigid night cold, cigarettes, chocolate bars, matches, and found a canteen half full. When an Italian soldier shouted for them to halt, Jack and Duggan bolted toward the open desert.

Rifle shots whizzed past them, but failed to hit their mark.

After making it out of sight over a rocky hillside littered with dried shrub, Jack motioned for Duggan to stop. "We need to catch our breath," he said, huffing and puffing from their all-out sprint. "We're going to need our strength if we're going to make it back to friendly lines."

Duggan dropped to his knees, grateful they made it out of firing range unharmed. He stared in the direction of the desert they had to cross. There were dunes of rocks, sand, shrubs, all of which looked desolate. "You certain we have to cross all of that?" he asked, deeply concerned.

Jack looked wearily in the same direction. "Yes," he said in a subdued voice. "If we're going to reach friendly lines, we have to cross that."

Duggan wiped the perspiration from his brow, and got to his feet. "Any idea how much of that there is?"

Jack looked at him sharply. "No, but we're going to find out."

Duggan bobbed his head twice. "This ought to be interesting," he said, mechanically.

# Chapter 9

*"A risk is a chance you take; if it fails you can recover.*
*A gamble is a chance taken; if it fails, recovery is impossible."*

*– Erwin Rommel*

J ack Ruggero and Lieutenant Anthony Duggan marched on and on and on. It seemed a lifetime crossing over dunes, rocky hills covered with dried shrub. Not a tree was in sight, and Jack longed for one for its shade. They slept during the day beneath boulders or an occasional cave they found along a ridge not far from the main road crossing the coastline, but not too close so that they would not be spotted by the enemy.

Two days of marching passed quickly, then four, and six. Duggan recalled an oasis his outfit had camped at during a recce some time ago, and managed to steer them in the right direction. Jack was reluctant to trust the young man's instincts, and did not prefer marching away from the coastline. However, both knew the half-filled canteen would not sustain them, so he acquiesced and was grateful for doing so when he saw palm trees and water, glistening in the sun upon arrival.

Unfortunately the oasis was occupied by an Italian rifle company. Jack was impressed the young Duggan had been able to remember his way through the desert, what with few land markers other than sand dunes and rocky hills. Duggan had been in North Africa since 1939 and since acquired local attributes such as a good sense of direction. He even showed Jack how to utilize his wristwatch to work as a compass and use the stars for navigating at night.

Duggan looked up at the sun, shielding the bright rays with his hand. "I'd say it's the right time of day," he said, enthusiastically.

He removed his wristwatch and laid it on the palm of his hand face-up, horizontal with the ground. Next he turned his body so that the hour hand pointed at the sun. Then he sought the mid-mark between noon and the hour hand, which was 4:00 o'clock in the afternoon. "There!" he said, excitedly. "South is in that direction, two o'clock." He pointed in the direction he mentioned, and then turned to face opposite. "North is in that direction, eight o'clock."

Jack looked in both directions, and then up at the sun. "I'm no boy scout, but I'll take your word for it," he said, shrugging.

Duggan looked perplexed. "What's a boy scout?"

Jack laughed. "That's a story for another time."

So far as Jack was concerned he could not decide which the worst discomfort they faced was; heat of the desert during the day, or the biting cold of night. Neither compared for their insuppressible thirst, and when they reached the oasis it was only the Italian soldiers preventing them from making a headlong run for the water surrounded by palm trees.

"We wait until they leave," Jack ordered.

They observed them from a rocky hilltop. The Italian company consisted of seven lorries and close to a hundred troops. It amazed Duggan how lackadaisical they conducted themselves. Sentries were not posted even at night. The men lolled about as though they were on an outing, listening to German and Italian music on the radio loud enough to be heard for miles. They cooked rations of beef stew over a large fire pit, and drank enough wine until they fell into drunken stupor. Even officers participated side by side with enlisted men. Eventually they quieted down for the evening.

Jack found their behavior amusing. "How can such a ragtag group go to war?" he asked, incredulous.

Duggan scoffed. "It's not the Italians we have to worry about in this war," he said, with disgust. "It's the Germans. Before they arrived we whipped over a quarter of a million Italians, kicking them out of Egypt and driving them all the way back to Benghazi. Things changed when Jerry showed up. Had they remained in Europe, we'd have taken Tripoli, and eventually kicked them out of Tunisia and all of North Africa."

Jack agreed. "Yeah, the krauts seem to be good at fighting."

Duggan tilted his head to the side as if to say, *I'd rather not say what I really think.* Finally he said, "There's no mistaken they know their business when it comes to war. Their tanks are superior to anything we have. Despite our having superior numbers of men and equipment, the *Desert*

*Fox* is a kind of bogeyman. Right when you believe you have him bested, he counters with a one-two punch, knocking you clear back to where your battle lines began."

Jack nodded understandingly. "Let me ask you, Anthony," he began, referring to Duggan by his first name for the first time, "Do you believe we can win this war?"

Duggan perked up. "With you Yanks now in the picture, you bet we will! We stopped Jerry in the Battle of Britain, and made friends with Stalin. With the war material you chaps are bringing onto the battlefield, there's no way Jerry can win. They simply don't have the resources."

Jack thought the young lieutenant sounded most certain. "So why would they take on the entire world?"

The question seemed to leave Duggan perplexed. "Don't know," he said, bleakly, "but I don't see what kind of miracle could help them defeat so many of us fighting them from all sides." He added what his commanding officer told him. "Hitler thinks he knows better than his generals, is most likely why. Had he focused on defeating England first, not invaded the Soviet Union, and not declare war on America, Germany would be sitting quite comfortably now."

Jack nodded, thinking hard about Duggan's points of view on the war.

The next morning the Italians ate a small breakfast, gathered their things, and left the oasis. Jack and Duggan ran down the hill and dove into the water, gulping down enough water to fill a camel. Luck was on their side, for the Italians had left a couple of empty canteens at the base of a palm tree. A small rucksack full of tinned beef and biscuits was there too!

"Can you believe it?!" Duggan shouted with glee. "What bloke leaves their rations behind?"

Jack could not appreciate their luck as much as Duggan. The Germans were more disciplined and would not have left anything behind. Duggan had seen the difference between the two after nearly three years of fighting them.

After drinking and eating, they rested at the oasis the remainder of day. Duggan protested, believing they should rest back atop the hill in case an enemy patrol arrived, but Jack quickly fell into a deep sleep after eating two tin cans of beef, dates from the trees surrounding the oasis, and drinking a bucket load of water.

"I can't move an inch," he declared, and fell asleep beneath the shade of a palm tree.

Sometime later, Jack woke and looked over at Duggan and was reminded how surprised he was over how Duggan handled himself. He hadn't complained at all about their predicament despite his youth. In fact he behaved like an experienced soldier. Jack thought a person his age would have whined throughout their journey to friendly lines, but then Jack had no way of knowing that Duggan had been in the war since it began in September 1939.

Jack looked up at the night sky and was amazed by its serene beauty. The nights were clear, the sky bright with moonlit stars illuminating the territory. Sand dunes snaked across the terrain and looked majestic in their natural form. Had he not been in the middle of a war fighting for his very survival he might have appreciated the scene more. However, all he could think of was making it to the next waterhole and then to friendly lines.

Before long Jack laid back to back with Duggan, trying to stay warm, wishing they could start a fire for warmth. It would be a long, cold night, they knew.

*But at least we're free,* he reminded himself.

The next morning they walked at a snail's pace over sand dunes heading east. The road was out of view, as was the coast. They could not risk walking too close to it for fear of being spotted by an enemy patrol.

Jack looked at his watch. *Four AM. It's a couple more hours of dark before sunrise,* he told himself, exhausted over their march.

They would have to find cover for the day, he knew. The sound of explosions awakened them from their walking stupor. In the distance northeast from their position, flashes and thunder illuminated the horizon.

"What do you make of it?" Duggan asked. The past several months he'd been holed up in the Tobruk garrison with little contact from the outside world except the occasional letter from home. He had no way of learning what went on outside the port city.

Jack did not answer right away. He knew what they were witnessing. Somewhere north a battle raged between German and British soldiers.

Sturmbannfuhrer Hans Mueller stood on the passenger side of his command vehicle, shouting orders into his hand radio. His column of tanks and trucks had been ambushed by the British, who were making some sort of last stand against them to try and prevent them from pushing further east into Egypt.

Mueller had been forewarned the enemy may attack him thanks to Sturmbannfuhrer von Mellenthin's intelligence reports. They believed some British units might be sacrificed in hopes of slowing down their advance in order for General Auchinleck to rebuild his forces. Although the British took beating after beating, time appeared to be on their side.

British Intelligence reports learned the Germans were having difficulty receiving fresh supplies from their bases in Italy and Sicily. Only one in four supply ships reached ports under German control in North Africa while British forces enjoyed unlimited supplies of war material, thus enabling them to dig in and make the German advance difficult. For the first time in North Africa it appeared the unstoppable Afrika Korps would be prevented from achieving an all-out victory.

There still was, however, a price for the British to be paid. Troops lost faith in their commanders' inability to defeat the Desert Fox in battle. Time and again Rommel proved the better field commander as he turned the tide of battle back in favor of his troops. The one thing the British Army had going for them was time and material. Every battle fought meant depleting petrol for the panzers. More often than not, the German advance came to a halt for lack of petrol needed to fill the thirsting panzers. This reason alone was enough to inspire British troops to continue the fight and win by attrition.

Tank Sergeant Heinrich Priess received orders from Sturmbannfuhrer Hans Mueller and ordered his driver to make a hard left so they could meet the British counter-attack head-on.

*"Schnell!"* (Hurry!) Priess shouted excitedly into his radio headset.

The 75mm cannon let loose its fire on the badly outnumbered Tommies struggling to get the upper hand. Other panzers followed suit, and one by one a column of five 30-ton Matilda tanks were stopped in their tracks as more powerful German panzers made mince-meat out of them.

It was plain to Priess, the British attempted to swing around and hit them from behind, where panzers were most vulnerable. Had they succeeded in positioning the Afrika Korps in crossfire it was possible to turn the tide of battle in their favor. The psychological victory for the British would be immeasurable.

"Right turn quickly!" he ordered to the tank driver.

The driver shifted throttles and the powerful Panzer IV sped toward the oncoming Matilda tanks.

British tank drivers saw panzers, four total, heading in their direction, and coordinated a volley of fire. The next five Matilda tanks fired their 2-pounder tanks simultaneously for greater effect. However, the 30mm armor plating on the Panzer IVs were too great, and the shells bounced off the panzers like tennis balls.

The driver in the lead Matilda turned to the tank commander. "Blimey, they're coming right for us!" His voice trembled and the look of fear on his face was plain.

"Reload," the tank sergeant ordered.

"We should get the bloody hell outta here," the driver cried.

"What for, so we can surrender?" the sergeant replied. "Get hold of yourself." He remained calm, a seasoned soldier from three years of fighting.

The other two crew members became excited. "I say we turn round and make for Alexandria right quick before we wind up dead," one of them said.

"I give the orders here," the sergeant reminded them. "Now hurry on with your jobs!"

One of the crew closed the breech to the cannon and locked it. "Reload complete!"

The tank sergeant looked through the targeting scope, its crosshairs aimed directly on a panzer. The gun stabilizing system improved his aim capability despite heavy vibration from the hull during travel. He squeezed the trigger and their tank shuddered as the cannon fired.

Sergeant Priess and his men heard the *thud* and felt the vibration in the hull of their panzer when the British Matilda tank's 2-pounder shell struck them. It bounced harmlessly away. This sort of thing happened to them in previous battles like the ones at Sidi Barrani and Benghazi, but the persistence of the Britische surprised the Germans, fighting with such inferior weapons.

"Your orders, Herr Feldwebel?" asked one of the men behind Priess.

Priess thought for a moment. He looked through the tank telescope, gauging the enemy approaching them. "Take out the lead tank first," he answered.

The tank gunner watched as his gun loaders thrust the 75mm shell in the breech, locked it, and said in unison, "Loaded!"

The tank gunner looked through his telescope and aligned the British enemy tank in the crosshairs. "Fire!"

Less than two seconds later the German tank crew witnessed the British tank lighting up like a roman candle, its turret popping off like a cork from a champagne bottle opened during a New Year's ball.

Priess backed away from the gunsights of his telescope, closing his eyes so they could readjust from the explosion's brightness. A moment later he looked through the telescope and reviewed the scene.

How many times had he witnessed this? How many tanks did his crew destroy? When Priess first arrived in North Africa he already was a battle-hardened veteran from their invasions of Poland and France. He displayed such bravery and enthusiasm he was awarded the German Iron Cross First Class, the same award Adolf Hitler earned during the *Great War*, and seldom presented to enlisted soldiers.

During his first battles he winced at sight of enemy tanks they destroyed. Men jumping off their burning tanks trying to flee were mowed down by German machine gunners. Priess told himself it was justified putting them out of their misery, as some men had caught fire. But he knew better. He knew much better. It was, however, his way of dealing with killing his fellow man. British and French were enemy of the Fatherland, but Priess was Catholic and a firm believer of the Commandment, *Thou Shalt Not Murder.*

Like many Germans, Priess was caught up in the fervor of the New Germany. After the Great Depression devastated the modern world, no other country in Europe suffered more than Germany. With the Rise of Hitler things changed. His rearmament program provided work for millions. Yes, their work was for war preparations, but after years of living hand-to-mouth in poverty, no jobs available, no future, most Germans did not think about how their work was leading them to a path of another war—a war most Germans did not want—not at first anyway.

When war broke out in Europe, Priess like many Germans, even though he was in the army, did not know what to think. Their elation over war was not great, and for good reason. Germans still recalled the 1.8 million men lost in the *Great War.* Although all anyone had to do was read *Mein Kampf* to understand the Fuhrer's intentions from the start, many Germans did not believe war to be inevitable.

Then came German victories!

Poland fell in six weeks. After a seven month lull, the battle turned to France, also falling in a matter of weeks. The Battle of Britain was a failure for Germany, but the German Army was not led to believe so. Denmark fell, as did many of the Baltic States. Soon Priess believed the war to be necessary for Germany's future.

*Perhaps Der Fuhrer's Lebensraum (living space) plan was for the good of the Fatherland after all,* Priess told himself. Soon the killing of men did not affect him and he became jubilant when the enemy fell from his guns.

Priess looked through the telescope of his gunsights and grinned. "Excellent shooting!" he blurted, and slapped his knee with the palm of his hand for effect.

British soldiers could be seen climbing out of their tanks, desperate to escape death from fire. Most were gunned down by machine gunners.

Priess observed the scene, grinned, and said softly, "I like that. It's a sign we're going to win this war."

One by one, the four remaining British tanks were picked off by the panzers. The staccato of machine gun and rifle fire reached a cacophony, mixed in with the sound of tank fire. The Germans seemed to dominate the battlefield, and English troops following behind their tanks soon found themselves running in full retreat.

Sturmbannfuhrer Hans Mueller oversaw the battle from his command vehicle, a *Puma Schwere Panzerspahwagen* armoured car, a fast multi-wheeled vehicle with a crew of four and capable of traveling 80 kilometers per hour. Its armament was rather light, sporting a single 7.92 mm MG 42 machine gun and one 5 cm caliber gun capable of firing 13 rounds per minute from its maneuverable gun turret. This vehicle allowed Mueller the mobility a commander needed to oversee tactics.

Mueller spoke into his headset, ordering his company commanders to advance their infantry units so they could mop up enemy resistance. As he expected, the British fought from makeshift positions not easy to hold, and without heavy artillery they stood no chance of resisting the German advance. In the end the British retreated in wild disorder.

Mueller lifted his field glasses dangling around his neck and looked through them. He scanned the battlefield carefully, missing nothing. Enemy tanks, armoured carriers, and troop transports billowed thick, black pillars of smoke. An occasional vehicle would erupt in a thunderous explosion resulting from unexploded tank shells and fuel tanks. No matter how many times he witnessed the enemy in retreat it always brought a smile to his face.

"Look carefully, korporal (corporal)," Priess said to the soldat standing behind him.

"Yes, Herr Sturmbannfuhrer?"

Mueller lowered his field glasses and turned to face the corporal, who straightened to attention. "*There* is the sign of victory," he said, beaming with pride, and pointing at the sea of destruction in the desert.

A British Army lieutenant with the impossible task of holding the infantry line while the main body of the British 8th Army retreated fired a flare from the Verey pistol he held. The flare hissed as it sailed high in the sky, leaving in its wake a bright white trail of smoke. The single-shot breech-loaded snub-nosed pistol was named after its American creator, Edward Wilson Verey, and used widely in the Great War as a signal for troops to advance or retreat. In this case it was the signal for British soldiers to retreat.

When the lieutenant witnessed men stumbling over one another out of their foxholes, dropping their weapons and packs in the process, the officer cringed. "DON'T LEAVE YOUR RIFLES, YOU BLOODY IDIOTS!" he barked, ferociously. "GATHER YOUR WEAPONS AND PACKS! WHAT THE BLOODY HELL DO YOU EXPECT TO FIGHT WITH?!"

Some men snapped to their senses and did as ordered; others out of earshot did not. German tank and machine gunfire was so great they could not hear their officer, and emotions were high in fright at the sight of the oncoming German war machine.

Miles away from the battle, Jack Ruggero and Anthony Duggan listened to the explosions and gunfire echoing across the desert. They were too far to see actual fighting, but flashes indicated a major battle took place.

Duggan wondered who was on the winning side. After so many battles resulting in British Army retreats, he winced at the thought of learning his fellow soldiers being defeated piecemeal—*again.*

"I know I told you we'd beat Jerry in the end, what with you Yanks now in the picture, but at what cost?" he asked with a touch of desperation in his tone.

Jack glanced at him, then back in direction of battle. He had no idea what British soldiers went through over the past two years of desert fighting.

"War's not over yet," Jack reminded him. He pretended not to notice tears rolling down Duggan's face. Tapping him on the shoulder, he said, "Come on, let's get moving."

And off they went heading east toward Alexandria.

# Chapter 10

*"I swear to God this sacred oath that to the Leader of the German Empire and people, Adolf Hitler, supreme commander of the armed forces, I shall render unconditional obedience and that as a brave soldier I shall at all times be prepared to give my life for this oath."*

*– The Wehrmacht Oath of Loyalty to Adolf Hitler, August 2, 1934*

## Berlin, Germany
## September 1942

The Fuhrer addressed the group of high-ranking officials and members of the world press in his usual robust manner from the podium in one of the reception rooms in the Reichstag. The event promised to be another opportunity to prove once more to the world how the Aryan Race was indeed master above all others. In fact, the Fuhrer had been anxious to preside over the ceremony and personally oversaw the staff decorating furniture placements, food and drinks, and music.

From wall to wall there were long scarlet red curtains hanging from ceiling to floor. In the center of each curtain a bold black-and-white swastika loomed eerily over the VIP's and guests. Cushioned chairs were in straight rows and refreshments placed on long tables along the side of the room. Tall, lean, blonde-haired men with blue eyes and pink-white skin worked as servers. They dressed in deep black trousers and white dress coats with black bow tie. They stood at rigid attention with one arm half raised above their waist, a white cloth draped over their forearm indicating their role as servers. Personally selected by the Fuhrer for their Aryan heritage, the men epitomized the appearance of the German master race.

Hitler pounded his fist on the podium grinning broadly while declaring victory on all war fronts. German victories flowed their way since the fall of Poland in 1939. France fell in 1940. Britain had been under siege since Dunkirk. German troops occupied Norway and Denmark. The Balkans, Greece, and Crete had been overrun, too. And in the east the Germans drove into Russia on a five thousand mile front toward Moscow and Stalingrad. And today, he told them, the German Army was one battle away from defeating the British in North Africa.

The world press found Hitler's ranting and raves familiar. The little man in dark trousers and beige uniform jacket and tie, with his black hair parted on the side, and his face displaying a small, trimmed mustache, spoke in an overblown tone how superior the German Army was.

"Global domination will belong to the Fatherland!" he bellowed. "And every German will continue the fight until we have achieved our destiny as decided by Providence."

Members of the press recalled listening to Hitler before the war began when few took him serious, paying him little mind. His words appeared to be empty threats back then. Hitler was viewed by many as a pouting child complaining over those not willing to play games he chose. However, Hitler was no child and the games he played were deadly. Only after it became too late did the world wish they acted before he had the opportunity to start war.

After what seemed an eternity, the Fuhrer stopped his tirade long enough to turn and introduce the person responsible for this event. "I introduce to you," he started, beaming from ear to ear, "Colonel-General Erwin Johannes Eugen Rommel, newly promoted to the rank of Field Marshal."

German officers and high-ranking civilians applauded with a standing ovation, while the foreign press snapped photographs, wrote details of the event on notepads, applauding very little, but taken in by the extent of the event. Flash bulbs popped continuously as photographers took shots from every angle.

Rommel strode forward, standing beside the Fuhrer in a seemingly impossible erect posture. He looked grand in his best uniform, his knee-high jackboots glistening like mirrors. His uniform jacket was adorned with some of the highest military awards in the German Army. Around his neck he wore the *Pour le Merit*, the highest military honor for soldiers having fought in the First World War for bravery in action on the battlefield. Also around his neck was the *Ritterkreuz* with Oak Leaves for his success against the French during his attack that drove French and British troops to the English Channel at Dunkirk. Now he was promoted to the highest rank in the German Army—Field Marshal!

Rommel turned and faced the Fuhrer, took two steps back and thrust his right arm out, palm facing down—the stern Nazi salute adopted and modified from how Romans saluted their *Caesar*. Der Fuhrer returned the salute rather half-heartedly. He was after all, leader of the Fatherland and not required to salute so stern when he deemed it unnecessary. Hitler then faced a nearby soldier holding the field marshal's baton in a diamond-encrusted case, and gently lifted it from the red-felt interior box.

Turning to face Rommel, Hitler said, "For your military brilliance on the field of battle, I hereby promote you rank of Field Marshal." He handed the baton with both hands over to Rommel.

Rommel grasped the baton and bowed slightly, but ever so generous. "Danke, Mein Fuhrer," (Thank you, my Leader) he graciously replied.

"No, Herr Field Marshal," Hitler said, quickly, "It is I who thanks *you*."

The Fuhrer stepped aside so Rommel could address the group in his own words. No questions were permitted from the press, which disappointed them. This indicated whatever the new field marshal said was likely what the Fuhrer wanted them to hear.

"I accept this honor humbly and with gratitude," he began in a clear, pronounced tone. "I wish to thank each soldier in the Wehrmacht for their contribution to the Fatherland, and in particular the men of the Afrika Korps, whom without I would have been unable to stand before you here today. Thus far our victories have been steady, and with the recent fall of Tobruk, British resistance is collapsing across the entire front. Alexandria will soon be ours, as will Cairo, and the Suez Canal. In fact, I expect to be standing atop the Pyramids before year's end."

With that said, Rommel stepped back, inhaling applause from the crowd of onlookers with a beaming smile. No one clapped more enthusiastically than Minister of Propaganda and Popular Enlightenment, Josef Goebbels, who orchestrated the gathering. He intended this ceremony to be grand more so for Der Fuhrer than Rommel, for he owed his success in politics to Hitler.

For much of his life, Goebbels had been a tormented soul. He excelled in school, earning a PHD in Philosophy, but when he went to enlist in the army at the start of the Great War, he had been laughed at and turned away when recruiters saw his grotesquely clubbed foot, which was a birth defect. Not to mention a thin, weakened physique from his battle with polio, he was nicknamed, *Poison Dwarf,* by his rivals. Goebbels saw Hitler as his way out, and the man who would one day become leader of the Fatherland appreciated Goebbels for his public speaking skills, and more importantly, loyalty.

When the Fuhrer excused himself all of a sudden from the gathering, Goebbels appeared distressed.

"Is anything wrong, Herr Reichs Minister?" It was Rommel who stood beside him and noticed the tightening in Goebbels' face. He had to bend at the waist to whisper in the ear of the short Reichs Minister (state minister), who was barely over five foot tall. "You appear disturbed," he observed. "Is there anything I can do?"

"Nein, Herr Field Marshal," Goebbels replied, never taking his eyes off the Fuhrer as he left the room. "I simply did not expect Der Fuhrer to leave so suddenly."

Rommel straightened his frame. "I beg your pardon, Herr Reich's Minister; I must speak with him before I return to Afrika. It is a matter of utmost importance." His tone and tightened expression left no doubt of that.

Goebbels glanced at Rommel nonchalantly. "And so you shall, my friend," he said, with his usual touch of arrogance. "So you shall."

When festivities ended the new field marshal was escorted by the limping Goebbels and two SS guards dressed in all-black Nazi uniforms. Rommel had not been told where he was being led. Goebbels met him in his study and said simply, "Come." It was not a request.

Der Fuhrer's study in the Reich Chancellery was a grand room to say the least. Each wall was adorned with magnificent paintings of German military victories, priceless tapestries, and tables overflowed with refreshments. Hitler was not a drinking man, nor did he eat meat. In fact he was a vegetarian and very much aware how this inconvenienced guests who preferred their own favorable dishes. On this day cooks preparing meals were instructed to deliver delicate dishes of all types, including wine for those who preferred, or needed, a drink. This indicated to those close to the Fuhrer his mood was most favorable.

"The War must be going well for the Fatherland," was the most spoken words this evening.

Rommel entered the immense study and immediately recognized Reich Marshal Herman Goering, second in command of the Third Reich.

The pompous Goering came from an aristocratic family with extreme wealth. During World War 1 he served in the German Air Korps as a fighter pilot in Baron von Rictofen's celebrated *Flying Circus*, as they were called in part for their exquisitely colored biplanes as well as their many victories against the Allies. When the *Red Baron* had been shot down and killed—after his 80-plus victories—Goering took command of the squadron, earning himself the *Pour le Merit*.

To look at the man now one would scarcely believe him to have been a war hero. Years of soft life and indulgence caused him to balloon well over 300 lbs. Even German newspapers nicknamed him *Der Fetthaltig* (fatty), which failed to offend Goering. "Their remarks only help my popularity," he exclaimed to those looking to punish offenders.

As the number two man in the Third Reich, Goering had fallen a bit out of favor with Der Fuhrer for failing to win the air war during the Battle of Britain. However, failure of his Luftwaffe did not discount its importance, for there was still much work to be done and Germany still boasted the largest military air force to date.

Also in attendance was Heinrich Himmler, Reichsfuhrer of the SS (State Police). A one-time chicken farmer who now oversaw Death Camps where millions of Jews, intellectuals, political enemies, school teachers, homosexuals, priests, and anyone posing a threat to the Third Reich faced torture and death, this little man had become the most feared man in Germany.

Generals Walther von Brauchitsch, Commander-in-Chief of the German Army, Alfred Jodl, Chief of the Operations Staff of the Armed Forces High Command, and Field Marshal Albert Kesselring, Commander of South Mediterranean Forces and Rommel's direct superior also were in attendance.

Relations between Kesselring and Rommel had not been well, everyone knew. Kesselring was from the 'old school' of strict, military discipline. There were no *mavericks* in his days. So far as he was concerned, a soldier's primary duty was to follow orders to the letter.

"Wars are won by soldiers obediently following orders!" he declared on more than one occasion to his staffers.

Rommel, however, was a maverick Kesselring had come to loathe. He took far too many risks on the battlefield and his methods were unorthodox. From the outset, Kesselring believed Rommel in contempt of disobeying orders. The Afrika Korps' primary mission was maintaining a defensive position against the British 8th Army—Period! Rommel received no orders to take the offensive.

However, one of the perks Rommel enjoyed was his command being located so far from the *Wolf's Lair*, Hitler's field headquarters in East Prussia near the small town of Rastenburg. He practically had freedom to do as he pleased. Hitler had been so obsessed with defeating Russia that the African Campaign was of little interest to him. And so, Rommel's actions went unchecked, allowing him to do as he thought best.

Rommel learned from experiences in Poland at the start of the war, and again in France that initiative was all important to winning battles. The desert offered a wide range of opportunities for a commander willing to take full advantage of the battle tank. The English had been fighting the desert war with caution and indecision, failing to make use of their tanks on the battlefield. Rommel knew he could not sit idly and wait for orders. He had to take action before things turned worse for his Afrika Korps.

And so he attacked!

In spite the unorthodox methods with which Rommel deployed on the battlefield earning the Afrika Korps victory after victory, his pompous, cocksure manner highly irritated Kesselring and others in the German High Command. Kesselring thought Rommel a showoff, always having plenty of cameras nearby to take a photograph of him standing atop *Mammut*, looking out across the desert in search of the enemy. His now-famous British goggles placed perfectly on his peaked cap and his plaid scarf wrapped tightly around his neck to ward off the cold became a trademark look. Everything Rommel did was news. He had become world renowned, respected—and feared. But he was despised by those in Hitler's closest circles. The newspapers in Germany claimed him to be Hitler's favorite general, which made others contempt with envy and jealousy.

Kesselring was further irritated with Rommel's promotion to field marshal, for now the Desert Fox would have direct access to Hitler, and no longer need go through him first. And he knew Rommel would do precisely that. It was this sort of reputation which infuriated men like Kesselring. The German Army was victorious because it was capable of maintaining iron discipline and followed orders! Orders were meant to be obeyed, pure and simple. Only Rommel knew from the start he would disobey his orders and take the offensive, thus placing an even greater strain on supplying his troops while the German Army was on the offensive in Russia.

Standing in the room at the table with Hitler, Kesselring noticed Rommel waiting for his turn to speak. The Fuhrer's speech about how things went on the Eastern Front must have rubbed Rommel wrong, for he seemed irritated.

*He probably realizes the battle in Russia is precedent to the war in the desert,* thought Kesselring.

Those present were privy to classified information, and they were fully aware of the situation in Russia, which was not well. The German 6th Army had in fact managed to make considerable gains against the Russian Army, but their supply lines were stretched beyond its limits. Like the forces at Leningrad, the proud German Army was forced to fight a stalemate for which they were ill-equipped at Stalingrad.

Der Fuhrer was oblivious of facts. All he saw were dreams of glory which made no sense to generals who saw how the situation was. And Hitler listened to no one. *He* knew what was best for Germany. It was *he* who ordered the army to march into the Rhineland in 1936, a direct and clear violation of the Treaty of Versailles, prohibiting German troops to occupy the industrial Ruhr Valley. It was *he* whom the British Prime Minister visited in 1938 to negotiate peace in our time. It was *he* who defeated France, the Crimea, Crete, Greece, and the Balkans. Indeed, Hitler had proven his generals wrong time and again.

But that was then, and this was now.

With war being waged on so many fronts, the German Army was stretched well beyond its capability of fighting sustained battles. Few in High Command had the stomach to discuss this with Hitler, which many saw as a career-ending move.

After listening to Der Fuhrer rant on about the battle on the Eastern Front, Rommel realized he would never be heard unless he interrupted his Leader. The moment came when Hitler paused for a drink of water (he never drank alcohol, much to the disappointment of those in his circle who did), and so Rommel took two steps forward, clicked his heels and smartly stood at rigid attention.

"Mein Fuhrer, may I have a word, please."

The silence followed was dreadful, and onlookers' faces turned white. No one dared interrupt the Fuhrer whilst he spoke. The world was his stage and his alone. However, this time was different. Rommel had provided Germany unexpected victories in North Africa, and had become world-renowned as a brilliant military strategist. Even the *gangster* Winston

Churchill praised Rommel as a daring and great general in the House of Commons. This meant if anyone could interrupt Hitler during one of his speeches and not face harsh reprimands; it was Field Marshal Erwin Rommel—at least for now.

Momentarily, Hitler was taken aback by the interruption. To the astonishment of everyone present, Hitler smiled quite evilly and extended his arms to Rommel. "Certainly, Herr Field Marshal," he said, gleefully. "Today you are the most privileged man in Germany. You have provided us with this momentous occasion, showing the world how invincible the German Army is."

"Danke, Mein Fuhrer," Rommel replied, bowing slightly at the waist.

The newly-promoted field marshal then went on about requesting troops, tanks, supplies, and above all petrol. It was a most common request the Fuhrer heard from his generals on all fronts. The demand for men and material was overwhelming. Without supplies the German Army could advance no further, and in truth, there were no additional supplies available for distribution. The oil fields of Ploesti in Rumania produced oil at its maximum, but still this was not enough. This was why Hitler demanded they capture Russian oil fields in the Ukraine and British-controlled oil fields in the Middle East. The German Army needed them if they were to continue their advance to Moscow.

In regards to the question of receiving fresh troops, those closest to the Fuhrer knew this to be a ridiculous request. Germany had none left to offer. The occupation of France swallowed forty divisions alone. Then there was Scandinavia, Denmark, Norway, Greece, and Crete. They simply were stretched too thin! The armies on the front had to make do with what they had, pure and simple. Troops of the Afrika Korps took no leave from the battlefield for if they had there was a strong possibility they would be snatched up by recruiters and shipped off to the battlefield in Russia.

Determined to have his way, Rommel continued with his requests though he could see by the Fuhrer's behavior he had lost his interest over the topic. Had he taken a moment to look at his fellow officers observing the scene he would have seen them rolling their eyes, exasperated over his pressing the matter.

*Here we go again,* they must have thought, *another schoolboy asking for the chance to choose more teammates.*

Then the Fuhrer did something Rommel had not expected.

"How can you stand there making such demands knowing full well I need every man available for our push in the east!" he shot back. He motioned to the large map on the table before them. It was marked with German and enemy troop dispositions all over the continent. "We're pushing the enemy back along a five thousand miles front—Five thousand! Another winter is about to set in and if we do not take Stalingrad before the year is out, *my* victory will be delayed yet again!"

Rommel displayed a confidence rarely seen by other generals. He yet again interrupted Hitler. "Mein Fuhrer," he began, his voice unwavering, "victory in the desert will mean controlling the Suez Canal. With Egypt in our hands a clear path to the oil fields in the Caucasus will make total victory within our grasp. My army could join forces with those already in Russia by approaching from south, thus offering the necessary relief."

Rommel stepped forward to the map table, fully intending to show his plan to the Fuhrer, but Hitler raised a halting hand. He was about to demonstrate how hypocritical he could be. Earlier he spoke of glorious victories, never mentioning the serious matter of how strained supply lines had become. If broken, it would mean defeat for Germany. Then he did what those closest knew he would do—He lashed out at them!

"There is never enough for any of you!" he spat. "You generals always ask for more and in return deliver nothing! You, Goering," he lashed out, pointing in the Reich Marshal's direction, "your Luftwaffe has proven not to be worthy of its name! You, Brauchitsch, with your choice of Manstein commanding our forces in Russia after haven proven he could not defeat the enemy in Leningrad; leaves me doubting your judgment. Now we have Von Paulus in command at Stalingrad, and proving to be equally inept!"

Hitler paused to catch his breath before turning to face Rommel. "And now here you are Field Marshal Rommel, standing before me asking for more after I have awarded you the highest rank you can achieve in the army. It is never enough for any of you! What more must I do before you give me victory?"

By this time Hitler's face had turned red with anger. His large, black eyes looked as though they were about to pop from the sockets. Veins on his forehead bulged to the point of exploding. "All of you present have betrayed me!" he said, accusingly. "You should be disgraced as failures to Germany for this outrage! What is the Fatherland without *me*? What is life itself without me? You, Rommel, Go back to Afrika and fight with what you have! If you cannot give me victory, then you will give me death for you and your men! No one will return to the Fatherland lest they be victorious! Do I make myself clear?!"

Indeed, Der Fuhrer had been abundantly clear.

A few moments of silence passed and Hitler calmed down somewhat. Rommel flushed with embarrassment. Still standing in rigid attention, he clicked the heels of his knee-high jackboots, bowed slightly at the waist, did an about-face, and left the gala. Although none close to him would have realized it, Rommel could not recall a time in his life when he had been so disappointed in a person he held in such high esteem. Like many Germans he trusted Der Fuhrer. He approached him with what he believed to be reasonable requests. With what he delivered over the past year one would have thought the German High Command would have been all too happy to supply him with men and materials so that he could achieve final victory in the North Afrika.

Rommel walked down the long halls of the Reichstag in short strides before being joined by Field Marshal Albert Kesselring. "Congratulations on your promotion," Kesselring said, flashing an evil grin which displayed his crooked teeth. "I suppose you believed with your new rank you could speak freely to Der Fuhrer. I now presume you know otherwise." Kesselring appeared to gloat over Rommel's dressing down.

Rommel recognized the glee in Kesselring's smile and was reminded how he despised the man. He considered him a pitiful-looking man, standing over 6 feet tall with a large paunch and round face. He spoke in a loud monotone and displayed few manners among others. His reputation for thinking more of himself and laughing harder over his own jokes was embarrassing enough, and Rommel could not believe such a man was his direct superior.

Kesselring was an officer of the Luftwaffe and fought on both fronts during the *Great War*. Considered a skillful tactical leader, he was posted to the general staff without having graduated from Germany's War Academy. After the war he maintained a commission in the army and in 1933 helped establish its new Luftwaffe. When World War II began Kesselring commanded Luftwaffe forces and played an instrumental part in the invasions of Poland, France, the Battle of Britain, and Russia. As commander of the Mediterranean sector, North Afrika was included under his command, but like many senior officers, Kesselring believed the campaign to be little more than a sideshow.

Rommel stopped and turned to face Kesselring. Looking more stern-faced than usual, he looked Kesselring up and down as though measuring him. "I hope you present Der Fuhrer our supply requests with the same fervor you have for other areas under your command," he said, somewhat condescending.

Kesselring stiffened. "What do you mean?" he asked, pretending not to know.

A smile pursed Rommel's lips. "I have understood from the beginning how High Command believes North Afrika to be unimportant," Rommel began, talking like a professor addressing a student. "The mere fact England has dispatched over forty divisions to the desert should be an indication how important this theater of war is."

Kesselring flashed the same evil grin as before. "I hope you are not naïve and believe the propaganda Goebbels has been feeding the Fatherland. Your position allows you to be familiar with our current situation in Russia. Last year's winter took the starch from our trousers. Our push to Moscow failed, and the situation has failed to brighten." Kesselring paused and stood holding his peaked-cap, cupped under his arm. Still holding his field marshal's baton in one hand, he managed to light a cigarette. He took a long drag, exhaling away from Rommel.

"No one will admit it," Kesselring continued, "but we are still unprepared for a sustained advance on the Eastern Front." He paused, lowering his eyes while in deep thought. "This is September. By late October if our gains in Russia are not substantial enough to encourage Stalin to surrender, we will be right back where we were last year, freezing our pink-white skin in the harsh winter at the gates of Moscow."

Rommel nodded understandingly. "I presume you are willing to admit this truth to Der Fuhrer, yes?" he asked, curiously.

Kesselring looked up at Rommel. He was unaccustomed to challenges. He smiled again, displaying those crooked teeth once more. "Why would I do such a queer thing?" he replied, coldly. "I do not have the privilege of being Der Fuhrer's *favorite* general. Besides, I am a firm believer in the Fatherland and have no doubt Providence will turn things in our favor."

The sound of footsteps approaching caught their attention, but they did not turn their gazes from each other until the sound of a familiar voice broke the silence between them.

"Ah, there you are, Erwin!" It was Hitler. "I was hoping to find you," he said, beaming. He embraced Rommel like they were best friends. "You wait and see, Erwin, I will send you supplies needed to defeat the English and together we will send Churchill and his cronies running with their tail between their legs. As always, victory will be ours!"

While Hitler spoke of his grandiose plans and promises of supplies, Rommel found himself being escorted down the hallway arm in arm with the Fuhrer. Hitler waved his free hand in the air emphasizing confidence in his plans for world conquest, and Rommel tried to interrupt.

"But Mein Fuhrer," he started, almost desperately, "the Britische have a new field commander in the Middle East and are receiving large supplies of tanks and material from Amerika. Their buildup is enormous and if we do not act immediately—"

"Yes, yes, I know of these false reports," Hitler said, cutting Rommel short. "It's propaganda, all propaganda!"

*Sure, and you and your clan wrote the book on that subject,* Rommel wanted to say.

"Our armies will be victorious on the Eastern Front as well as the Middle East," Hitler continued. "You wait and see! Providence has delivered me leadership of the Fatherland, and I need men like you to share in our glory. You wait and see, Erwin."

Rommel thought the Fuhrer sounded like a broken record.

The Fuhrer turned and left, walking in great strides to the door from which he came. Rommel and Kesselring remained standing in silence, watching the Fuhrer until he entered the room and closed the door behind him.

Rommel turned to face Kesselring. "Did you notice how the Fuhrer failed to mention who will receive much needed supplies first?" he asked, disappointedly and annoyed. "Is he going to send supplies to our armies in Russia first or mine in Afrika?"

Kesselring shook his head and offered a half smile. "My dear, Field Marshal," he began in a fatherly tone, "the answer to that is a forgone conclusion."

# Chapter 11

*When the idea of behind-the-lines action against the German Afrika Korps came to fruition it was believed parachute drops would achieve best results. That idea was soon replaced by jeep attacks, which could deliver men and supplies to great distances in the desert, allowing British soldiers to strike in the heart of German bases and leave without a trace. Soon, the British Special Air Service would be feared by German and Italian troops alike.*

The German aerodrome (airfield) located southeast of Benghazi laid a hundred miles from the nearest village. The field was handpicked by Rommel, who found its remote location while flying on reconnaissance. Himself an unlicensed amateur pilot, Rommel was known for flying many such recces in his Fieseler Fi 156C Storch two-man scout plane. Being so far from the coast road and prying eyes left Britische intelligence in the dark as to how many planes the Desert Fox had at his disposal.

Rommel knew the Britische employed Arabs to spy on German troop movements. His English enemy trained Bedouin tribesmen on how to operate cameras for first-hand photographs of German aircraft, tanks, troops and shipping. In addition, the Bedouin were provided radio equipment to send messages on troop movements. Rommel knew he needed to keep the Britische on edge, and employed many tactics to outwit them.

It was well-known the bulk of German soldiers were in Tripoli, Benghazi, Sidi Barrani, and in Tunis, all of which were coastal cities and vital to the German-Italian alliance. To draw enemy spies from these cities, Rommel ordered construction of airfields and fuel depots throughout the desert, knowing the British Long Range Desert Group and Bedouin searched for location of such bases. Many were empty of actual troops and war material. They were replaced with trucks and tanks made of wood, balloons and other material, and all fuel drums were empty. Soldiers' uniforms were stuffed with material to give appearance of men standing guard. The idea was to fool the enemy into thinking Rommel's force was much stronger than first believed.

Men of the Afrika Korps lost eagerness working on such tasks because it meant spending weeks in the desert, away from port cities where they could entertain themselves in brothels. Instead, all they had for comfort was playing football and listening to *'Lili Marlene,'* the most popular song of the war on radio. Rommel remained persistent and knew from experience such ruses proved highly invaluable in fooling the enemy.

His best attempts at fooling enemy intelligence came upon his arrival in Africa in 1941. He ordered a mass parade of men, tanks, and planes to participate down the main boulevard in Tripoli, with the majority of the city viewing from the streets, from windows, shops, hotels, anywhere to draw attention. German and Italian troops marched rank and file, singing military songs in unison. Rommel and his staff, along with top Italian commanders stood on the viewing stand, saluting as they marched past them.

High above them in the sky flew Junkers-88 bombers, Junkers-52 Transports (affectionately called *Auntie Ju* by German troops), Junkers-87 Stuka Dive bombers, and Me-109 Messerschmitt Fighters, all of which cast shadows over the entire parade of tanks and soldiers. It was an amazing display of power and a proud moment for German and Italian civilians in attendance.

It was the panzers which really pulled off the greatest ruse. Columns of tanks drove down Main Boulevard, passing Rommel and spectators on the viewing stand. Each tank commander stood atop the turret saluting their commanding general, and Rommel smartly held his own salute in return. Once the tanks reached the end of the street they drove around the block and back to the starting line using back streets behind the buildings, out of view from spectators and British spies. Then they entered the main boulevard and drove down the street for another passing review.

The ruse worked! British spies reported to their intelligence liaison officers the Germans were supplied with a far greater number of tanks than they actually had. It was important information which helped them gain a psychological advantage over the Britische, who were keenly aware how in the desert the tank was the main battle weapon needed for victories.

Now the Desert Fox was hoping to fool the Britische into believing he had a larger number of planes than they had by setting up phony airfields all over the desert. Rommel did this because he learned over the past year and a half that with superior air support they could smash enemy tanks and machine gun troops with greater ease. After more than two years of desert fighting both Axis and Allies learned in the desert it was the fighter-bombers that had become the main battle weapon which decided victory.

The airfield in question today had been located so far from Benghazi and was by no means a 'phony' one. In fact it was Rommel's largest airfield in North Afrika, and he went to great lengths ensuring its security and operational value. The runway was paved unlike other fields operating on a dirt path. Guard towers were setup on all corners of the field and a barb-wired fence had been put up to protect numerous planes lining the field. Guards patrolled with dogs trained to sniff out the enemy. There was an aerodrome, machine shops, troop barracks, everything needed to sustain the base.

The Germans were so confident of the base's secrecy they permitted desert nomad Bedouin to move their flocks of goats across the airfield unhindered, which they were known to do on many fields occupied by both British and Germans. Such was the case with a particular nomad of average height, a bit overweight around the waist, who stumbled upon the field after being told its existence from a beggar who passed on the information for the price of a bottle of whisky.

The fat shepherd and a male companion moved their goats over the runway past a pair of German soldiers on guard. The soldiers wore their new desert brown uniforms and scuffed boots and were in deep discussion when the nomads approached them. Such occurrences were common in the desert and both British and German soldiers paid them little attention. In fact, guards never unslung their rifles from their shoulders, oblivious to any danger they might face.

From one of the barracks a phonograph played a slow version of the now-famous song adopted by both sides of the war, *'Lili Marlene.'* A loud-speaker amplified the music so that everyone on the base could enjoy it.

The music blared loud enough for men on a hill five hundred kilometers away to enjoy. From their vantage point they had a bird's-eye view of the airfield, observing guards and normal activity. Like the Germans, they admired the song *'Lili Marlene,'* often listening to both the German and English versions.

"Lovely song," said the large man, lying prone and observing the Germans below through a pair of field glasses. The man next to him nodded, but said nothing. He too, was busy making mental notes of German activity on the airfield.

Men of the SAS were not easily identifiable for they did not wear standard uniforms while operating in the field. Sometimes they wore trousers without shirts, or shorts without shirts. Sometimes they wore boots, or sometimes sandals with puttees wrapped up their ankles for protection against thorn shrubs. Their official headgear was a beret, but in the field they sometimes chose to wear Arab headdress, or an Australian field hat, or sometimes no headgear at all. They were unshaven, for water was precious and could not be wasted on body washing.

The pair of SAS men lay prone on the hilltop keeping their silhouettes in the dark from watch towers on the airfield. The moon was full, illuminating the desert without need of searchlights. This was good for the Germans, for they did not approve of using too many lights in the evening so as not to give away their position to enemy planes. Even at this late stage of the desert war the Germans still did not appreciate the danger the Special Air Service posed. They viewed them as gangsters and bandits, not soldiers.

The bigger man lying on the right stood over six feet tall and had a rugged look about him, like he belonged in war. His beard had grown nearly three inches, but he managed to keep his hair trimmed short enough for during the day when it became unbearably hot long hair posed a nuisance. His frame was lean, but sturdy, and he possessed a certain air of authority like it was natural for him. As far as looks went, he was considered a bit average. But his self-confidence made him stand out over those much handsomer. Having been one of the first to join the SAS, this mission proved to be, "Just another walk in the park," as he was known to call such sorties in the desert.

The other man lying beside him was his second-in-command. He was fairly new at this sort of business, having only recently transferred from 7th Infantry Division. He had seen combat since the Italians invaded Egypt in 1940, but after two years of fighting he realized the regular army was not for him. He had difficulty following orders from officers he believed inept. His then commanding officer sought to make him pay for disobedience by transferring him to what many longtime army officers believed to be a career-stopper unit known as *L Detachment*.

*L Detachment* was the derivative designation for 'Layforce,' what GHQ called their commandos. The name came from Major Robert Laycock, who was commanding officer of all five commando units in North Africa. It was not until then Major David Stirling took command of the brigade when they became referred to as Special Air Service due to his then-plans for dropping paratroopers behind enemy lines to strike against the Germans, and then be picked up by the Long Range Desert Group for the ride back to base.

At the time the young officer had no way of knowing it, but the transfer to SAS proved a blessing in disguise. It did not take him long to believe fate intervened at a time when he needed it most. He looked at his CO curious, trying to gauge his thoughts.

The man was hand-picked by Lieutenant Colonel David Stirling himself, founder of Special Air Service. Stirling proved extremely different from Laycock, and saw the genius and possibilities of an elite outfit operating behind enemy lines. The CO volunteered on the spot to join SAS and trained alongside Stirling and others for months. They went through parachute training, hand-to-hand combat training, weapons training, land navigation courses, machinist training, explosive training, and anything else needed to be fully operational and independent while operating on special operations against Germans and Italians. Each man in SAS had to be an expert specialist in order to make full use of necessary skills needed to mount missions behind the lines.

"There's the signal, Major," the junior officer said, excitedly. He pointed at the shepherd moving his herd across the runway.

The major lowered his glasses. He grinned broadly, and glanced at the captain beside him. "Yeah, that's the signal all right." He nodded and added, "See the men are ready to move."

"Yes sir."

The captain crawled away from their post keeping his belly close to the ground. Only when he was safely behind the hill did he get to his feet and jog down the remaining distance to their vehicles camouflaged at the bottom of a ravine. He was met by a score of friendly faces, some standing beside their American-made Wylies Jeeps, converted for desert warfare, others sitting inside them raring to go.

"The mission's a go!" he exclaimed, much to their delight.

It was a statement the men hoped for—in fact prayed for! The captain recognized the look on their faces and could not help grin himself. It was all they could do to keep from cheering out loud.

Back on the hill, the major peered through his field glasses, studying the shepherd moving his flock off and away from the runway. The Germans continued walking their posts here and there along the runway, but gave no indication they were aware of enemy presence.

*Good,* he thought. *We'll give them a nice surprise.* He lowered his glasses and smiled. Then he shook his head at the incredible luck of Lieutenant Colonel John Haseldon, who had once again donned Bedouin clothing and masqueraded as a nomad moving his herd from field to field.

Colonel Haseldon reached the dry riverbed five hundred kilometers from the airfield, far enough for him to be out of sight of German sentries. Taking in his surroundings, once certain no enemy soldiers were about he reached for one of the nearby lambs in his herd and opened a satchel bag he had strapped on its back. Pulling out the American-made SCR-536 Walkie-Talkie hand radio receiver-transmitter, he pulled out the antennae fully extended, which automatically turned on the radio, and off when the antenna was retracted. It was the most marvelous radio the colonel thought anyone created, and the smallest, easiest to conceal for its time. Designed for US Army Signal Corps, large shipments of the popular hand radio-transmitter were shipped off to Egypt from America in support of England's fight against the Germans in North Africa.

Colonel Haseldon brought the Walkie-Talkie to his hear, depressed the 'talk' button and spoke into the mouthpiece. "Taras Bulba, this is Ali Kazam," he said, softly, "the goods are ready to be received. How copy, over?"

To receive transmitted messages the operator had to release the 'talk' button. A few seconds later the colonel received a response. *"Ali Kazam, this is Taras Bulba, read you loud and clear."*

Haseldon pursed his lips in a slight smile and pressed the 'talk' button. "Jerry has a good eighty planes lined up on the runway," he said, trying hard to contain excitement. "Perhaps more if you count those in the aerodrome. The fuel depot is located on right of the drome on far left of the airfield. I believe them to have battalion strength. That's several hundred men, but most appear to be laid out in barracks enjoying music. How copy, over?"

The Walkie-Talkie crackled when Taras Bulba acknowledged his message. *"Roger that, Ali Kazam, thank you and see you back at the nest, over and out."*

Colonel Haseldon placed an open palm on top of the antennae and pushed down on it, retracting the short silver rod. Looking in direction of the airfield, he just made out the silhouettes of the German planes.

*Such a splendid sight,* he thought.

The major handed his Walkie-Talkie to a nearby soldier standing near one of the jeeps, and reached in the back of the vehicle and donned his gear consisting of ammunition belt, clips of ammunition, pistol, and grenades.

"Where'd you come up with the name *Taras Bulba* and *Ali Kazam*?" asked one of the soldiers.

The major smiled. It was a sort of joke between Haseldon and the major to utilize colorful codenames. He looked over at the captain standing beside his own jeep and donning his gear as well. Both officers reached for their Sten submachine guns, a most popular weapon among commando units. Known as the *Sturdy Sten*, it was simple in design and lightweight with a low-cost production. It fired a 9x19mm Parabellum cartridge, open-bolt action operated, had effective range of 100 kilometers, and a 32-round box magazine fed from its side.

The officers pulled back the firing bolts quietly as possible and chambered rounds. The major looked at the row of jeeps and soldiers in his command. There were seventeen jeeps in all with three men to each jeep. The man sitting in the rear was armed with a Bren light machine gun. It proved highly reliable, weighed 23 lbs., usually required a crew of two, but the commandos operated it single-handedly. It fired a .303 cartridge up to 500 rounds per minute with a 600 kilometer effective firing range, in 20 and 30-round detachable magazines.

However, their main weapon for the evening was the twin-mounted Vickers K machine guns. This rapid-fire weapon was designed for gunners in planes for effective defense against enemy fighters. SAS soldiers believed it perfect for desert warfare and mounted the twin-barreled weapons on the front of jeeps. It fired a .303 cartridge, was gas-operated and had a rate of fire of nearly 1,200 rounds per minute. Its feed system was a round drum of nearly 100 rounds a drum for each barrel. These were weapons desert raiders relied most against their enemy, and they had every intention of putting them to good use on this night.

The major signaled his men to mount their jeeps. He climbed into his lead jeep on the passenger side. Jeeps were loaded with equipment, mostly *Jerricans* of petrol and water, and at times men seldom knew which was more important—petrol needed for return to base, or water needed for survival. The *Jerrican* was a German-designed container for transporting water and petrol. It proved far more reliable than British containers, and was quickly adopted by the British Army too. Jerricans were strapped on top of the hoods, rear, and sides of jeeps. Inside were spare ammunition, food, and clothing.

The major felt a certain excitement he had difficult containing. This would be the largest raid he conducted thus far in the war and was confident things would go right. *After all, Jerry suspects nothing,* he reasoned.

His confidence was due to experience. When Colonel David Stirling came up with the idea of destroying German planes by jeep attack, British GHQ had not been keen on such a daring venture. In fact they believed sending men behind enemy lines across hundreds of miles of open desert in jeeps and lorries quite delusional.

"Sounds though you're having a bout of over-imagination rather than logic," declared Stirling's commander upon presentation of his idea.

Stirling managed to receive approval for some 'limited' action behind enemy lines, and immediately went to work putting his first night assaults into action at once. Night assaults against Germans consisted of small groups of men in jeeps and lorries. Drivers were recruited from the Long Range Desert Group. This outfit's main orders were to gather intelligence on enemy movements, not engage in battle. Their knowledge of the desert and experience in traveling over long distances in open desert made them the perfect choice to take Stirling and his men to their targets.

During the major's first night assaults, he and his men, sometimes teaming with LRDG, would sneak up to an enemy airfield in the middle of the night on foot, after having been dropped off a safe distance so as to keep vehicles out of danger. However, this took more time than they desired, belly-crawling through barbed-wire, dodging guards, dashing to planes parked on side of the runway where they then placed their demolition charges. Depending on time not on their side, sometimes they placed their demolitions on landing gear of the craft, or on engines or cockpit. It all depended on time before German guards walking their rounds approached them.

Their first results were less than encouraging. Demolition charges used by SAS were newly-made Composition C. This plastic-type explosive charge was 88% RDX and 12% plasticizer. It was soft and could be molded by hand in a solid form. The men called it *plastique* for short, and found it to be quite lethal, capable of destroying a tank when placed in the right area.

However problems besetting desert raiders from the outset were blasting caps required for detonating demolition charges. All too often, blasting caps failed to work properly and even timers were found to be deficient, sometimes ticking away without so much as ringing a bell. Dynamite had to be ruled out since it would have required a fuse, which made a loud hissing noise and flash when lit.

On several missions Stirling and his men failed to destroy a score of enemy planes all due to faulty timers and blasting caps. Hundreds of enemy planes could have been knocked out of the war on a single night. Stirling knew he must rethink his plan of attack, and this was when he came up with the idea of jeep assaults.

His plan was to form an arrow-shaped column of twos with a lead jeep driving center of formation. Directly behind him was a navigator giving commands to drivers of each column via radio. Once they approached the airfield the lead jeep guided the columns onto the smooth tarmac and gunners in each jeep opened fire with twin Vickers and Lewis machine guns, considered the deadliest type of guns in early stages of the desert war. Adding those machineguns totaled sixty-eight barrels letting loose a lethal barrage of firepower.

The major looked at his watch, angling it in the brilliant silver moonlight so he might read the time. *Half past one a.m., good—it's time!* He raised a hand in the air with index finger pointing skyward, and made a circular motion.

Drivers in each jeep started their engines and moved forward into position in a ravine not far from the airfield. The major stood up on the passenger side of his jeep. Peering through his field glasses, he scanned the airfield one final time. Everything was perfect! The Germans on the towers and the guards marching patrol were no more the wiser to their presence. He lowered the glasses and turned to face the men in their vehicles behind him. Clenching his left hand in a fist, he pumped his arm up and down several times furiously.

The Go-signal given, jeeps moved out following the major in first gear, then worked speed up to second gear, then third, and finally fourth. Driving was rough over uneven terrain, but jeeps were specially outfitted for such work. Their wheels dug in deep in the soft sand, but worked their way out as the ground hardened. Things got bumpy coming across a stretch of hard ground with rocks strewn everywhere. Drivers could not avoid this for they relied on keen vision and moonlight. Headlights were not permitted so as not to give their presence away.

The major kept an eye on the guards in case they suddenly became aware of their approach. They reached two hundred kilometers from the tarmac and the major pumped his fist up and down again, the signal for all jeeps to let loose. Gaining speed, they reached the tarmac in less than sixty seconds.

# Chapter 12

*The SAS came up with the idea of striking enemy bases in fast-moving, heavily-armed American-made Wylies Jeeps. This combat strategy proved not only effective, but struck both fear and anger in the Afrika Korps.*

The sentry posted on a guard tower arrived in North Afrika two weeks earlier. He hoped to be assigned to 15th Panzer Division or 90th Light Infantry Division, the units he read so much about back home. Much to his chagrin he found himself assigned to a Luftwaffe detachment to provide air cover for Rommel's forces. It was something of a disappointment for the young soldier. His father raised him believing a soldier the proudest profession for a man. He dreamt of returning home a decorated hero, christened after receiving his first taste of battle. This would have been the greatest achievement in his young life, or so he believed.

And yet from the moment Privat Karl Mohr stepped off the German freighter in Tunis he seemed bound for anything other than glory. Battle-tested sergeants took delight in teasing young soldiers, and Privat Mohr was no exception. Karl Mohr had a boyish look of twelve years old, and was puny. His pink-white skin stood out among others with bronzed-skin from having spent more than a year in North Afrika. They teased Karl about his age too, questioning if he lied to join the army before turning eighteen.

"Your father change the date on your birth certificate?" a burly feldwebel barked. He flashed a challenging grin and said, "Fathers do that, you know, especially veterans from the Great War. They want their sons to finish for them the fight they failed to win."

Young Karl, ever determined, assured the feldwebels his age was nineteen, and pleaded to remain in North Afrika. He answered the correct date of his birth, the year he graduated school, and anything else to convince them he belonged there. Then a curious feldwebel got the idea of questioning whether or not Karl actually received military training.

"Probably they used him to clean lavatories," the feldwebel blurted. Those nearby broke into a hearty laugh.

Then something incredible happened to Karl. It proved to be the most fascinating experience in all his young life. A kubelwagen drove up to their group standing on the pier and out stepped a man whom up to that moment Karl had only seen on newsreels in the cinema and in newspapers.

"Stand at ease, soldat," commanded the field marshal.

But Karl could not. He remained petrified with shock in the presence of such a man.

"You are new to our Korps, yes?" asked the field marshal in a fatherly tone.

Karl swallowed the lump in his throat before nodding. "Jawohl, Herr Field Marshal," he managed to say, finally.

Rommel stepped forward and placed a hand on Karl's shoulder. "I was about your age when I joined the Wehrmacht," he began. "I recall those around me believing me to be too young to fight. I was eighteen years old when I enlisted in 1909. When the Great War began I was twenty-three. Those five years of training before the War certainly helped me survive, let me tell you."

Rommel paused and pulled out a flask of brandy, handing it to the young soldat. Karl hesitated, but calmed after seeing the Desert Fox wink.

"Danke, Herr Field Marshal." Karl took the flask, opened the top, and took a quick drink. He glanced up at Rommel, surprised by what he tasted.

Rommel laughed at the sight of him. "What is the matter?" he asked, grinning broadly. "Do you not enjoy the taste of water?"

Karl took another drink from the flask to be sure. "Jawohl, Herr Field Marshal." He replaced the cap on the flask and handed it back.

"You will find in the desert water is not a commodity to be taken for granted," Rommel reminded him. "Learn to appreciate every drop."

"Jawohl, Herr Field Marshal."

Rommel started to leave, and then turned to Karl. "Do not allow this episode from the feldwebels to upset you too much, soldat. During my first year in the army I had the buttons to my dress tunic removed at our parade ceremony before the Kaiser began as a sort of joke. You cannot imagine the humiliation I experienced at the time." Rommel was in deep reflection as he continued. "There I was sitting atop my horse with the front of my dress tunic held together by safety pins. I prayed each second for them to hold as I rode past the Kaiser."

Karl managed a smile. He understood the message and felt a sense of pride over a man of Rommel's importance making time to reveal something so personal with him.

Rommel straightened. "I must be off he said," tapping the tip of his peaked cap with the handle of his field marshal's baton. "Glad to have you in our Korps, Privat Mohr. I'm certain you'll make us proud."

Karl reflected that day while he stood watch on the guard tower. *Some chance to serve the Fatherland,* he thought, pacing the tower. *Doesn't appear I'll be able to do my part so long as I'm here on this wretched airfield in the middle of nowhere.*

His attitude brightened somewhat after recalling his meeting with Rommel. It's what kept him going, the knowledge that their highest ranking officer believed in him. An assignment to protect Luftwaffe airfields was the last thing Karl would have preferred. Guard duty in every army was the most dreadful duty. However, Karl knew there would be plenty of fighting in the future and somehow he knew he would be a part of it.

The SAS jeeps reached a small dune preceding the tarmac and the major in lead zoomed over it as though it were a ramp. His jeep sailed in the air a good five feet before landing on the blacktop with a loud *clang*. The men seated in his jeep prepared for impact by having slightly raised themselves off their seats, and bounced hard once tires touched down.

The major looked over his shoulder for the rest of his jeep raiders and found the scene exhilarating. Two-by-two, the jeeps flew through the air same as he had, landing hard on the tarmac, but managing to keep up momentum.

*Would've made a nice photograph,* he thought.

Then something incredible happened!

Landing lights to the airfield switched on, illuminating them as they approached parked planes on the side of the runway.

*My God! They've spotted us,* thought the major.

He quickly reached for the radio microphone and gave orders to his crews. "Keep tight formation!" he commanded. "We're going to see this mission through. When Jerry opens up I want the rear guard to focus on taking out their gun posts. The rest of us will maintain gunfire on the planes."

The rumbling sound of engines overhead reached their ears and all eyes turned skyward. The outline of a JU-52 transport plane approached the landing strip, and they realized the lights were on for the plane, not because they had been seen.

*Thank God, we still have element of surprise!*

When the JU-52 flew directly over them the major shouted to the gunner behind him. "Knock it down!"

The soldier whirled his twin-barreled Lewis .303 machine guns on its special-designed mount allowing the gunner to swivel his weapon 360 degrees, and took aim skyward. When the plane was less than 100 feet above them he opened fire.

The pilot and co-pilot were caught completely off guard. Bullets smacked into the engine mounted on the nose of the plane, spraying oil over the windshield, effectively blinding their view.

"My God!" screamed the pilot. "Who is firing at us?"

The SAS jeep gunner kept a steady staccato of gunfire for ten seconds, ceasing fire only after the plane's engine caught fire. Its pilot desperately attempted to stabilize the plane and bring it level over the airfield. Instead, he lost control and the plane took a nosedive, crashing into a group of ME-109 fighter aircraft parked alongside the runway. A huge flame of orange and yellow fire erupted, rocking the jeep raiders violently as they drove past the wreckage. A moment later they were upon the parked planes and the sight was incredible.

Every conceivable type of German plane was here! There were ME-109 and ME-110 fighters, Stuka Dive Bombers, JU-88 bombers, Storch recce planes, and most important of all aircraft—the JU-52 Transport planes. The workhorse of the Luftwaffe was their main target for they were the planes capable of bringing in troops and supplies.

The major led his jeep convoy down the middle of the runway in two tight formations. The gunners of each jeep aimed their guns outside the formation and when the major shot a Verey light pistol in the air all gunners opened fire. Their gunfire was enormous and deafening, echoing clear across the desert and into the valleys beyond. Each enemy plane took hits in its canvas and sheet-metal frame causing it to disintegrate and crumble to the ground. Spilled petrol from aircraft tanks caught fire from sparks created by ricocheting bullets off the tarmac. Fire spread to other planes, which caught fire and ignited fuel tanks. In a matter of seconds each plane exploded one after the other.

SAS jeeps continued driving down the runway firing indiscriminately until they reached the opposite end of the tarmac. By this time the Germans, who at first believed the disaster was due to a crashed plane, realized they were under enemy attack. However, it was the sort of attack new to a conventional army, and they were confused over how to fight a fast-moving jeep attack. At this stage of the war an enemy deploying hit-and-run tactics was new and counter-attack on such an enemy had yet to be designed. The result was German soldiers firing sporadically without any coordination whatsoever.

When the jeep raiders reached opposite end of runway the major raised his right arm high, the signal for them to come to a halt. Illuminated by the glow of burning planes, German soldiers were seen running from their tents and barracks, scrambling to their gun posts. They were in complete disarray.

The SAS second-in-command jumped out of his jeep and ran over to the major. "What gives, sir?"

The major surveyed the carnage. Dull thuds of exploding fuel tanks from planes went off one after the other. Not a single plane escaped unscathed. Although they were successful, the major had little time to pat himself on the back. He was concerned about the hangars and repair shops still intact.

"We've got to make another run," he ordered, still staring across the field at potential targets.

The captain was taken aback. "Sir, the element of surprise is over," he pointed out. "Jerry is regrouping. We've got to make good our escape."

The major made his decision and was not listening to objections. "We're not leaving until those hangars and repair shops are destroyed," he barked. "Get back to your jeep and follow my lead."

The captain knew better than to argue at a time like this, and returned to his jeep. As the jeep raiders turned their vehicles around for another run toward new targets, a German soldier opened fire with an MG-34 heavy machine gun. Then a German mortar crew whipped into action and fired two shells in their direction. Bullets from the machine gun raked the area around the raiders, but hit no one. The mortar shells fared better, one exploding in front of the major's jeep, knocking him and the driver out of their seats and to the ground.

"You all right, sir?" asked the gunner in the rear of their jeep. He leapt out and helped his CO to his feet.

"That was too close for comfort," the major said, climbing back in their jeep as the driver did same.

The rear gunner jumped back in his seat and manned his Lewis guns. The driver, a sergeant, turned the ignition, but the engine failed to start. He tried again and again, but the engine failed to turn over. The sergeant got out and lifted the hood to see if there was engine damage when he suddenly stiffened before falling face forward.

"Be quick about it!" the major shouted. "We don't have time to waste?"

Only when the sergeant failed to rise did the major realize something was wrong. He hopped out of his jeep and ran to the sergeant, rolling him over on his back. That's when he saw bullet holes in the man's back, three of them, victim of the MG-34 machine gunner. The major lifted the hood of the jeep for a quick inspection and saw the engine had been damaged by shrapnel from the mortar round.

"This jeep's finished," he declared, disgusted. "Get everything out and pile in the first two jeeps. Be quick!"

The raiders did as ordered, but not without first lifting their dead sergeant and placing his body in back of a jeep. No man was ever left behind if it could be helped. Other raiders fired machine guns at German soldiers regrouping and counter-attacking with coordinated gunfire while the major planted a small time-bomb inside his jeep to make it completely unusable by the Germans.

"Okay, let's move!" he ordered when done.

The major directed the driver of the jeep he commandeered to make way for the hangars and tool sheds. As before, they drove in two-by-two formation, gunners making good use of targets by opening up with everything they had. Their steady staccato of gunfire was effective same as before. Like the planes they destroyed, the framework of light sheet metal and canvas material broke apart under a hail of bullets. Fuel and other ignitable material caught fire, and soon the insides of the hangars and tool sheds glowed orange. Some of the hangars blew to smithereens from stored fuel drums.

When they reached the opposite end of the German base the major ordered the raiders to a halt. "Everyone all right?" he asked into the radio. All drivers checked in. Their only casualty was the sergeant from the major's jeep. "Right, now listen carefully," he continued, all the while struggling to keep calm amidst the excitement, "We're going to make another run down the runway for good measure. How's our ammo?"

The reply from everyone was they were running low. With all the excitement of battle, ammunition conservation was furthest from their mind. The major shook his head disappointedly. "You all know better than not to watch your supply!" He scolded them like they were schoolboys.

A mortar round exploded nearby, rocking the raiders in their jeeps. The captain shouted, "Sir, can we get the bloody hell outta here?!" He practically begged.

"Keep your trousers on," the major answered, calmly. He shook his head, disappointed by the prospect of leaving without making a final run. "Follow my lead," he ordered over the radio. And the raiders followed his command jeep as they left the German base.

Privat Karl Mohr heard the JU-52 as it approached the airfield, straining to watch the plane land in darkness. As a boy he always had been amazed by the sight of flying machines, and grew up dreaming of one day becoming a pilot. However, Germany was a class-oriented society even after the Great War, and luxury of flying remained reserved for those with financial means. Karl caught sight of the JU-52 as lights to the runway were switched on. The sudden sound of automatic gunfire erupted, causing him to jump. He saw flashes on the runway and realized they were from muzzles of machine guns fired from moving vehicles.

Karl reached for the phone and was nearly knocked off his feet from the concussion of the JU-52 when it exploded and crashed on the runway. A battle whistle blew and soldiers from the billets and tents scrambled out and to their posts. Some had been fast asleep and only had time enough to don trousers and jackboots. Karl started climbing down the lookout tower he manned when he thought best to remain in his position and fire at their attackers from an elevated position.

*At least here I've a bird's-eye view,* he told himself.

The 8mm Breda was an Italian-made heavy machine gun highly regarded by German and British soldiers alike. In fact, whenever desert raiders had the good fortune of capturing the weapon and ammunition intact they preferred using it in place of their own. A single man was capable of operating the gun, but moving it to a different location required two.

On the lookout tower the Breda had been mounted on a tripod and Karl quickly grabbed hold of the gun, pulling back the firing bolt to load the tray-fed ammunition. He took careful aim at the enemy below, and squeezed the trigger. Explosions from burning fuel tanks caused Karl to jump, but it was the cacophony of automatic gunfire from enemy jeeps that frayed his nerves more than anything else. It was so synchronized and rhythmic one could not help be mesmerized.

*Snap out of it!* Karl ordered himself to regain self-control. *"Britische Schwine!"* Mohr swore aloud.

When the first tray of ammunition emptied he reloaded with another, took aim, and squeezed the trigger. The gun kicked violently in Mohr's hands and he strained to keep track of his line of fire, but with confusion engulfing the airfield it was difficult. He prayed silently to hit his mark.

The major in the raiders' lead jeep looked over his shoulder and for the first time that morning managed a smile. Planes were burning and crumbling all over the runway. Hangars and tool shops were also in flames. It would be a long time and lots of work before this base was operational.

"How we doing, Major?" the driver asked. His eyes remained focus on the terrain. One simple distraction could have caused their jeep to overturn and crash over rough terrain.

"Appears we made a top job of it," the major gleefully replied.

He turned forward in his seat and was visibly shaken at the sight of a second group of planes outlined against the night sky. They numbered seven JU-52 transports in all.

The driver and rear gunner saw the planes too, and stiffened. "Blimey, we can't leave those birds lying peaceful like that," said the driver. He looked at the major. "Can we sir?"

The major paused, reflecting how much time they had before the Germans managed to regroup and effectively fight back. "We have to—"

Bullets slammed into the front of their jeep, ricocheting off its hood and into the Vickers gun attached to its mounting pod. Sparks caused the major and driver to jump. Jerricans filled with petrol strapped to the hood were punctured and spilled fuel all over the hood. Sparks ignited the fuel and the major and driver jumped clear of the jeep with speed they never knew they had. A tremendous explosion erupted and the rear gunner, having failed to react as quickly was blown from his seat. He somersaulted twice before landing face down on the ground. A raider from the jeep behind them jumped down and ran to him. He rolled him over to inspect his condition. Of course the man was dead.

He looked over at the major. "Sir, you all right?" he ran over and helped him to his feet.

"What the—" The major was unable to manage words, still shaken from the blast.

"You took one right in the kisser, sir," the raider explained. "Blimey! Your hair and face are soaked in blood."

The raider dragged the major to his jeep where the crew helped him climb in back. "Let's get moving before the same happens to us," one of them said. He turned to face the rear jeep gunner. "Take out the Jerry in that tower!" He shouted, pointing at the observation tower where they were taking gunfire from.

The raider let loose a barrage of fire from his twin-barreled Vickers gun. In a matter of seconds the wooden tower was shred to pieces as bullets tore into it. The raiders next whirled their turrets around and took aim at the remaining JU-52 transports that had been missed from their first attack. As if on cue, all gunners opened fire simultaneously. German soldiers returned fire with intention of distracting the raiders, but the British guns overpowered them. After sixty seconds of steady gunfire, the second-in-command ordered a cease fire.

"What now, Captain?" asked a raider. His voice was tense with excitement.

The captain strained to see how much damage they inflicted on the remaining planes. "How's our ammo?" he asked. He knew they were dangerously low, and dreaded their responses.

Everyone shook heads, indicating they had no extra ammunition. What little they had they needed to keep for protection on the drive back to base. The precaution was necessary in case they were attacked by enemy planes in the open desert.

"I still see two planes!" shouted an excited raider.

"Should we tear into them, Captain?" asked another.

The captain shook his head. "No, we can't afford the ammo. Use plasitque and timers."

The raiders assigned for precisely this type action jumped from their jeeps and raced across the field to the remaining JU-52s. When they reached the planes they placed the plasitque explosives at the base of the wings where it connected with the fuselage. The timers were preset for 20 seconds, and tied around the explosives with black tape. By removing the safety pin on the timer the explosive was armed. The raiders then made a beeline back for their jeeps in time to witness the remaining enemy planes blown to smithereens one by one.

"Nice job," one of the gunners praised.

Without being told what to do, everyone climbed on board their jeeps and they drove off putting as much distance between them and the German airfield in double quick time. After driving roughly six kilometers over rugged terrain they reached open desert and came to a halt. The captain now in charge ordered all team leaders to account for all men.

"Four are dead, sir," said one of the team leaders. He sounded calm, almost as though it was expected.

The captain nodded and walked to the jeep where the major was resting in back with the rear gunner. "Feeling better, sir?" He sounded sincere, and disliked having to be the bearer of bad news. *Don't beat yourself up,* he reminded himself. *You wanted the rank, and with it come the distasteful job of making such reports.*

The major shook his head to clear the cobwebs. "Never mind about that," he said, uneasily. "Report—what's our condition?"

"We lost four," answered the captain. He swallowed the growing lump in his throat. "We have their bodies in back of the jeeps. No one will be left behind."

Major Lawrence's composure changed drastically upon hearing the news, and Captain James Guinness, who had been with him ever since joining SAS, could not recall a time when he witnessed him wince. But then, they had never lost so many in a single raid that although dangerous, odds were on side of the raiders over the Germans.

Captain Guinness thought Major Thomas Lawrence a reliable officer, hand-picked by David Stirling himself. And Guinness was proud to serve with him. The SAS founder once boasted of the major, "Tom Lawrence is tough as nails! He doesn't flinch in a fight, which is comforting when one considers how resourceful Jerry can be when the going gets rough." It was a statement Guinness learned to be true after having served on many raids against the enemy in behind-the-line action.

Some likened Major Lawrence's luck as one of a kind, and his most daring escapade was his recent escape from being held prisoner inside Tobruk. Rumor had it he volunteered to go to Tobruk for a first-hand look how close the city was to surrender, which proved false. He was, however, captured as prisoner along with thousands of other British soldiers, and soon managed escape by sheer luck.

One of the more amazing feats carried out by the SAS was their overall low casualty record. This was accomplished in spite the fact their operations took them well behind enemy lines to destroy German planes, fuel depots, ammunition dumps, and anything else coveted by the enemy.

Although this achievement was of the greatest magnitude in the war, many high-rank officers in British HQ objected to formation of SAS. This was due in large part that such a small unit did not function in the way general staff envisioned how war should be waged. However, results the SAS offered could not be ignored.

In three separate raids on German airfields conducted simultaneous, SAS raiders destroyed ninety planes on the ground *before* Operation Battleaxe took place. It was a bold attempt designed to deprive the enemy maximum use of their desert air force, and the raids were accomplished without loss of a single man. In fact, in many of their raids the SAS never lost anyone killed in combat. There were wounded, yes, but not KIA (Killed in Action).

Major Lawrence had not seen a member of his unit killed in action for some time, and was visibly shaken.

Captain Guinness placed a comforting hand on his shoulder. "Could've been much worse, sir," he said, trying to be as empathetic as possible. "You nearly bought it, too."

Major Lawrence looked back at the airfield they raided. The orange glow of fires from their handiwork could be seen for miles. "At least they didn't die in vain," he said, with pride. He turned and faced the men. "We've got to make our run for the Jalo Oasis before sunrise in order to avoid enemy scout planes. They'll no doubt be searching for us first light."

That said drivers started up their engines. Captain Guinness climbed in his jeep, raised his arm, and pumped it several times, the signal for them to get moving. In a matter of moments the jeep raiders disappeared in the night. Although saddened by loss of comrades, a certain pride swept over each raider. Once more they proved their importance in combat. In the back of Major Lawrence's mind he knew their victory would not be so welcome by jealous GHQ officers, but Colonel Stirling's influence was quickly growing among higher staff officers. His influence meant SAS would continue to flourish in the Desert War.

# Chapter 13

*The threat of a German victory in the Battle of North Africa was so great that England dispatched nearly half its military operational strength to defeat the German Afrika Korps and their Italian allies.*

## September 1942

The Fieseler-Storch Fi 156C reconnaissance plane circled the German airfield, surveying the damage. Field Marshal Rommel peered from the passenger window, observing the carnage below. Wrecked planes were strewn about, and barrels of precious fuel still billowed thick black smoke high in the sky. A lookout tower had been knocked down, and everywhere soldats were busy cleaning up the wreckage.

Rommel shook his head at the sight below.

The pilot requested permission to land and circled the airfield once more before landing smoothly on the recently cleared blacktop. He brought the plane to a stop in front of an aerodrome lightly damaged from the night raid. A row of officers and soldiers stood at attention awaiting their commander to address them and discuss their situation in a nearby command tent.

They had much to discuss with the Desert Fox for in recent months soldiers of the Afrika Korps had grown despondent over their inability to protect themselves from this elusive enemy unit which seemed capable of striking whenever and wherever they wished. Rommel too, had been disappointed over how things developed with these desert raiders, and cursed himself for not having the army take control of security instead of the Luftwaffe.

Field Marshal Albert Kesselring prevented Rommel from taking such action because Kesselring, a Luftwaffe officer, insisted all airfields placed under control of their own officers and men, not the army. Rommel thought this line of action to be irresponsible, and was familiar with the discord between each military branch. They behaved as though no trust existed among them. Ever the tactician, Rommel knew the importance of having forward air cover. His lightning victories in France two years earlier proved their value, and he insisted since before his arrival how all members of Afrika Korps remain under single command, and not allow petty squabbles divide them.

Total victory, Rommel knew, relied on their ability to work together. However, big egos intervened, and it was no surprise Kesselring did not share his enthusiasm and demanded Luftwaffe units remain independent from the army. This meant any offensive Rommel took with air support must first be cleared by Kesselring's staff, and the Desert Fox did not appreciate sharing his attack plans.

"Another stupid act!" declared Rommel.

He exited the plane and approached the staff of officers, addressing them candidly; unafraid of consequences should his words get back to Kesselring. Everyone snapped to attention and Rommel returned their action with a salute with his field marshal's baton. He stood in front of a Luftwaffe colonel assigned to the base. It was plain by the colonel's behavior how nervous he was in the face of Rommel.

"How many planes have we lost?" Rommel's expression was as grim as his question.

The oberst stood at rigid attention. Any straighter and his spine would have snapped. He swallowed hard before answering. "Eighty-eight planes, Herr Field Marshal." He barely managed to squeak the words.

Rommel glared at the oberst. It was a look that could have turned even a hardened man to stone. The oberst did not look away from Rommel, but it was plain how frightened he was over a possible dressing down in front of his staff. Rommel was known for having a quick temper and embarrassing poor performing officers in front of junior staff.

"How many men lost?" Rommel dreadfully asked.

Again the oberst swallowed before answering. "Thirteen killed and twenty-two wounded, Herr Field Marshal." His perspiration building on his forehead was enough to show how uncomfortable he was giving his commander this news.

Rommel shook his head and looked at the airfield. Men were hard at work while officers and sergeants barked orders about the cleanup strategy on the base. He turned to his staff. "And what of the enemy?" he asked. "What casualties did they suffer?"

One of the lower-ranking officers stepped forward. "Herr Field Marshal, we destroyed one of their attack vehicles and are sure to have killed and wounded a number of them," he said, trying to sound positive. He stopped long enough to clear his throat. "However, they took their wounded and dead, so we do not have an accurate number."

Rommel nodded, finding the answer acceptable. "What sort of vehicle was it they used?"

Another officer looking to be ingratiated with the Desert Fox said, "It's called a *Jeep*, Herr Field Marshal." He had trouble pronouncing the name, but managed to spit it out. "It is an American-made vehicle, and they attacked with at least a dozen of them, all armed with light and heavy machine guns. They are from the command of the man called *Phantom Major.*"

"Him again?" Rommel had heard the nickname before, and grown to respect the man's capability.

"Yes, Herr Field Marshal," the officer continued. "We are not certain he himself led the raid, but we know they fall under his command. The technique used here is similar with other raids they've conducted."

"Only now they are becoming more brazen," Rommel quickly pointed out. "In our bases at Agebadia and Agheila they infiltrated our security defenses and placed bombs on our planes by simply walking onto our airfields right under the noses of our guards." His face grew distorted over memory of the damage report. "They deployed the same tactic at Mersa Matruh and other stations. This *Phantom Major* is creating more damage on us than the whole Britische Eighth Army."

Another officer stepped forward. "The English have little regard for rules of war, Herr Field Marshal. Perhaps we should organize a similar unit to combat this force?"

Rommel had his back facing his staff while he continued staring blankly at the airfield and destroyed planes. "The English have little regard for rules of war, you say. I am quite certain the English have similar opinion of the *SS*," Rommel scoffed.

With his back turned to his staff Rommel could not see the uneasiness they felt upon hearing his criticism of the *Schutzstaffel Polizei*. That branch of service gained worldwide notoriety when reports of German treatment against Soviets during *Operation Barbarossa*, the invasion of the Soviet Union which began on June 22, 1941, were made public. No one dared speak out against the *SS* for fear of reprisals.

However, Rommel's rank and stature were extremely popular, allowing him the rare position of a man able to speak freely. He knew how Hitler held Germany under lock and key, and secretly despised him for it. Thus, whenever an opportunity presented itself he made certain to speak openly of opinions differing with mainstream thoughts.

*What a fool I have been not to do what needed to be done.* Rommel chastised himself over not acting like the commander he knew himself to be.

He could have ordered his troops to take command over security on airfields despite Kesselring's opposition. However, he had rubbed so many high-ranking commanders the wrong way by doing things *his* way that he did not want to press his luck. He needed support in order to receive supplies and knew no one would stand by him unless he followed military doctrine.

Rommel woke himself from his reverie and turned to face his staff. They snapped back to attention, clicking their heels. "This senseless waste of men and material cannot continue," he said, harshly. "We are not receiving much-needed supplies due to the Fuhrer's obsession with defeating Russia. Every man, piece of equipment, each round of ammunition is too precious to lose in such a disgraceful manner. We must change this."

"Jawohl, Herr Field Marshal," they replied in unison as if on cue.

Rommel looked over both shoulders as if to be certain no one was within earshot outside of his staff. "Gentlemen," he began, quite formally, "I speak with you in confidence over this subject. For some time now I have ordered reserves of men and material to be positioned on special bases at key points within the vast barren desert. This is necessary to replenish our panzers as we press forward on Alexandria, Cairo, and finally Suez." He paused, gauging their expressions. *Good, I have their attention.* He saw they had no idea on his mention of the subject. *They are in for a surprise!* "We will need Luftwaffe support if we are to succeed, and make no mistake we will!" He paused for effect once more. "This airfield must be returned to full operational status immediately, is that clear?"

"Jawohl, Herr Field Marshal," they replied in unison, clicking their jackboots smartly.

"We need to move forward at the earliest possible moment," Rommel told them. "My sources inform me the Britische are strengthening forces for counter-attack, and I want Alexandria in our hands before they are in position to do so. Tobruk is now in our hands and supplies our troops, thus saving much needed petrol and time from having to be driven overland from bases in Benghazi. Unfortunately we cannot celebrate due to much of our supplies being sent to the bottom of the Mediterranean Sea by enemy planes sinking transport ships."

This fact reminded Rommel on the importance of air superiority. With Britain's air bases on the strategic island of Malta, the RAF bombed and strafed many German and Italian ships enroute to North Africa. A mere trickle of supplies reached the Afrika Korps, bringing the German offensive literally to a standstill. If they were to push eastward it remained critical for them to have petrol and munitions readily available along lines of advance. Thus Rommel had taken steps his staff had yet to be made aware.

He paced back and forth like a caged leopard explaining in detail his intentions, and his staff looked on, listening with great surprise. Rommel's mere presence always commanded respect. He spoke with sheer confidence and appeared splendid and fit in his light-brown desert uniform, adorned with red and gold lapels. His peaked cap sported the same English goggles given to him by a captured general, a fact still unknown to the public.

Rommel continued explaining his plans in the open. "The English have a new commander. Not much is known of him other than his record in the *Great War*. He is not without experience, but his knowledge on desert warfare is limited."

Rommel saw the uneasiness among his staff upon news of a new enemy field commander. In spite of their confidence in their own leader and cocksure attitude they were the *master race*, German soldiers were fully aware of England's long history of winning the final battle which gained them total victory. With this in mind Rommel thought best to remind them of their own record up to now.

"Never lose confidence in our ability," he said with a smile. "After all, I think it speaks volumes over how many times the English have replaced leader after leader."

The men broke into hearty laughter.

He went about his future plans for conquering North Africa, all the while his troops continued with the cleanup duties on the airfield and buildings damaged in the raid. Although it was midday and the sun grew hotter by the minute, Rommel continued briefing them in the open sun instead of seeking refuge in the nearby command tent. His men reasoned he was most likely too excited to realize their discomfort.

"We cannot allow disasters such as this to continue." It was not a reminder, it was a demand. "Additional precautions must be made. Increase guards on duty, have more roving patrols on outskirts of our bases, be creative. You must think beyond the realm of what you were taught in military school." That part would not be easy, he knew, for the Wehrmacht was filled with officers incapable of breaking from protocol.

When he finished with his briefing he raised his baton to his peaked cap, offering salute. They returned the military gesture, clicking their heels smartly. Rommel returned to his Storch, climbed aboard, and the staff watched as the pilot started the engine, drove the plane onto the runway, and lift off. They did not return to the shade of the tent until his plane disappeared in the clear blue sky.

Twenty minutes in flight Rommel spotted a convoy of medium tanks and lorries traveling along the coast road. "Long range reconnaissance patrol in force," Rommel said aloud, while looking through a pair of field glasses. "Probably from the 90th Light Division." He studied the scene a bit longer and then saw something unusual about the vehicles. "Hold on, I am not so certain," he said, bemused.

"I beg your pardon, Herr Field Marshal?" said the pilot. He was busy piloting the Storch and could not hear him over the loud single engine.

"Take us down a bit closer," Rommel ordered. He never took his eyes away from the field glasses.

The pilot followed his orders and began a slow descent. They noticed the convoy come to a halt and a group of soldiers disembarked their vehicles and unfold a large tarpaulin across a stretch of sand and rocks.

"Look, Herr Field Marshal," the pilot said, excited. "Do you see what they are doing?"

Rommel nodded. He saw soldiers unfold the tarpaulin with the white emblem of the German Iron Cross emblazoned across it. The soldiers' action was meant to identify themselves with friendly aircraft.

"They're inviting us to land," Rommel pointed out. He thought about it for a moment and said, "Why not? Let's meet with them for lunch."

The pilot brought the plane about and came in for a landing on the desert road. The tanks and lorries pulled over to the side, giving the Storch plenty of clearance. When the wheels touched down Rommel saw something about the soldiers that made him curious and uneasy.

*"My God, they are English soldiers!"*

The pilot thought he misunderstood the field marshal. It sounded like he said there were English soldiers about. When he looked out the window at them he recognized the familiar Mark I *Tommy* helmets worn by British soldiers. He instantly knew what was happening.

"They've lured us in a trap," the pilot said, calmly.

He immediately revved the engine right before they opened fire with small arm machine guns. The staccato of rat-a-tat-tat weapons fire reached their ears over the single engine, and both Rommel and pilot felt the plane shudder as bullets tore into its frame.

"Get us out of here quickly!" Rommel ordered.

The pilot needed no encouragement. He had no desire to spend the remainder of the war in a prisoner-of-war camp. The Storch gained altitude in an amazing short period, and seconds later they were outside of enemy shooting range.

Rommel exhaled a sigh of relief. *What an elaborate trap. Unsuspecting German aircraft land and fall into their hands, thus depriving us knowledge of their movements.* He shook his head over the ingenuity of such a simple plan. He knew some of their Storch scout planes disappeared without a trace, leaving him to wonder if this was what happened to them.

The pilot checked his controls and was relieved to see mechanics had not been damaged. The aircraft's skin had been riddled with bullets and hot air from outside filled the cockpit.

"Are you alright, Herr Field Marshal?" The pilot's concern was genuine. Rommel had become the most beloved general in the modern German Army, and he did not wish to be known as the man responsible for getting him killed while in flight.

Rommel turned to face the young pilot and flashed that famous grin of his. "I doubt I'll be eating solid foods for some time," he said, jovially.

They arrived right before dusk at Rommel's HQ thirty miles south of Mersa Matruh. Rommel had been a firm believer in leading his men from the frontlines, which often drew criticism from senior officers as well as peers still using conventional methods on the battlefield. However, this was exactly what set Rommel apart from comrades and enemy leaders alike.

Rommel was a tactician willing to take chances in order to gain new ground against the enemy. He knew well and good he could not continue fighting a sustained war against the English, not with their superior lines of supplies remaining consistent. He needed to break their morale and will to fight in order to defeat them and the best way to do that, he knew, was to defeat them on the battlefield with lightning strikes.

As the Fieseler-Storch taxied off the runway a group of officers gathered nearby to greet their commander, but Rommel was in no mood for conversation. His recent near-miss with death caused him to grow sick in the stomach and with his mind running circles on how to resolve his supply problems what he desired most at this moment was a good night's rest.

"Achtung!" (Attention) shouted the colonel, who stood before a group of staff officers.

They eagerly awaited their commander to disembark the plane and acknowledge their salutes. In spite Minister of Propaganda Josef Goebbels' declaration of Rommel being a devout Nazi, he preferred military salute over the stiff-armed Nazi salute. Rommel raised his arm to return the gesture before stopping himself halfway, remembering his newly acquired field marshal's baton he left on the seat of the Storch. He retrieved the baton and the pilot, still seated in the plane, pretended not to notice him leaving it unceremoniously behind.

Rommel faced the group of officers and raised the tip of his baton to the brim of his peaked-cap. His superiors requested he remove the goggles stating how they were not standard army issue, but Rommel did as he pleased, stating how English desert goggles were better than their own dust-goggle issue.

The colonel stepped forward. "Welcome back, Herr Field Marshal! Congratulations on your well-deserved promotion."

The group of officers clapped briefly before the colonel motioned with a shake of the head to quiet down. "We have prepared a bath for you in your tent, Herr Field Marshal. If you prefer we can discuss the briefing in the morning."

Rommel's eyes practically lit up. For months his adjutant played role of 'office maid', showering him with reports and driving him mad with what he considered to be an office clerk's duties. The Desert Fox preferred driving along front lines with his troops, and rarely spent long periods in headquarters. It was not until Rommel's military intelligence officer, Freiherr von Mellenthin, informed the colonel of Rommel's distaste for paperwork when they realized it was up to staff to perform the drudgery of shuffling such work while their commander rode in his command car all along the front lines.

"Thank you," Rommel said, nodding in gratitude. "That will do nicely."

Once inside his tent Rommel removed his uniform from his exhausted body and wasted no time climbing inside the bathtub his staff provided him. Bathing in the desert had become a luxury, and rarely taken even by Rommel due to water shortages. Thus, he enjoyed every moment of this bath. He reflected how as Korps commander he did not get much leisure time seeing how the war came closer to climax. His early victories against the enemy now came at heavy cost, more than he could afford due to supply issues. Each counter-attack by the British was thwarted by a gathering of German forces which attacked them on their flank, sending the British in disarray. Rommel repeated this tactic time and again and was surprised how slow the English were at catching on to his scheme.

Rommel learned early on how desert warfare presented a host of opportunities which achieved results beyond imagination. However, to be successful required a commander to set aside conventional-thinking and take on new tactics one could not learn in a war college. Speed in the desert was essential and quite available to a commander with steel nerves to use it. Most military commanders were trained in World War 1 tactics that took on heated, head-on battles draining an army's forces. After a hard-fought battle it was customary for both sides to retire and recover long enough to replenish strength. This was where Rommel employed his ace-in-the-hole!

While enemy forces disengaged from battle, Rommel put together remnants of his battlefield force which included Italian units, and struck the enemy on their flank and rear guards. The tactic was designed to split their forces in two, and weaken their ability to defend themselves. This ingenious move wrested each victory from the British and allowed Rommel to maintain tactical advantages over them. His ability to adapt in desert warfare earned him worldwide reputation as a dangerous, brilliant general.

Contrary to their intentions, the British assisted in promoting that image of Rommel by relieving commander after commander who had proven not to be up to the challenge of facing off with the Desert Fox. However, time was of essence, and in war there was no on-the-job-training for commanders unable to live up to expectations.

Rommel took a cup of soapy water, lifted it over his near-bald head and poured it over himself. *How good this feels,* he told himself.

He relished the relaxation he seldom enjoyed, and believed in experiencing similar privations his men endured. It was another example why his men admired him as a leader. He did not dwell on this moment for he was a military man right down to his socks. No sooner had he poured another cup of water over himself was his mind back on the war.

*What else will the English do?* he wondered.

Indeed, they had done much to tip fortunes of war in their favor. The British even attempted killing him right before a battle because they knew his absence would have a profound effect on German morale. Most field commanders were out of reach and were not too close to the front as a matter of security for top leaders, but Rommel did the opposite. He was known to be as close to the frontlines of battle as possible. It helped him make on-the-spot decisions which tipped battles in his favor on many occasions. More than once, English soldiers reported having seen the Desert Fox standing alongside his men during the heat of battle. Such reports fueled ideas about assassinating the war's most famous general.

Ironically, had the British remained patient, Rommel in all likelihood would have gotten himself killed by continuously, and unnecessarily pressing his luck. A perfect example was the time he visited field hospitals checking on wounded soldiers. He rode in his command car from camp to camp, greeting soldiers while driving past them. When his driver felt they were lost, Rommel spotted a group of tents and instructed his driver to head for them so they could ask directions and learn their whereabouts.

Guards manning the gate saw the staff vehicle approach and lifted the wooden barrier, waving them through without even checking identity papers. Rommel noticed they wore no headgear when they walked outside the wooden guardhouse, but this break in military dress protocol was sometimes overlooked due to excess desert heat. When they stopped the car, Rommel and his staff disembarked and walked to one of the larger tents housing wounded. Soldiers lying on cots were German, Italian, and British. Nothing strange about that, Rommel knew. In a field hospital wounded enemy soldiers were treated alongside Germans and Italians. Rommel did, however, notice the surprised expressions on his men's faces upon them seeing him enter the tent with his staff.

"How are you coming along?" Rommel asked, walking up alongside cots lining the recovery tent.

German soldiers struggled to sit upright on their beds, but some were too badly wounded to do so. One attempted to speak, but kept looking at doctors and soldiers standing guard, knowing that if he spoke they would most certainly hear him.

"Can I help you, sir?" A young field doctor approached, offering an appraising smile over such a high-ranking officer's visit.

"I'm merely visiting my men," Rommel said, nodding courteously. Then he remembered why they stopped here in the first place. "Wait, perhaps there is something you can do."

"And what is that, sir?" The doctor appeared to genuinely want to offer assistance.

"We seem to have lost our way. Perhaps you can have my driver given directions from one of your men, please." Rommel pointed to his driver standing outside the tent next to their car.

His aide, Hauptmann (captain) Radl, standing next to Rommel then noticed what they failed to recognize from the start. "Herr Field Marshal," he whispered into Rommel's ear, "Look!" he pointed to a group of armed soldiers standing right outside the tent. Both of them were surprised when they saw soldiers in British uniforms!

Rommel and Radl suddenly realized why wounded German soldiers lying on cots stared strangely at them. They were surprised to find them in a British field hospital.

Rommel leaned over to Radl and whispered, "Time to leave," he said, calmly.

Radl swallowed the lump in his throat and nodded.

When they returned to their command car they noticed the driver's expression. He too, now realized where they were and was more than anxious to leave before British soldiers were aware of their special guests visiting the field hospital.

"Keep calm," Rommel murmured, while climbing in the car.

The driver took the same road they entered. Guards raised the gate as they approached and saluted. Rommel and Radl returned the salute, all the while holding their breath.

*That had been a close call*, Rommel reflected, waking up from his light sleep.

He sat up straighter in the tub, shaking his head to clear the cobwebs, and sighed heavily. He was exhausted and enjoyed this bath, but needed sleep. He leaned back in the tub, resting his head on the edge and closed his eyes, reflecting on his military escapades and near-death experiences.

There was the time in Italy he had nearly been killed while assaulting an enemy hilltop during the Great War. Then there was the time in France 1940 he had gone too far ahead of his columns and been machine gunned by retreating French troops. There were too many near-misses with death for him to count. Had he known the extreme lengths with which the British attempted to rid themselves of the Desert Fox-threat, Rommel may not have been so hard-pressed to observing rules of war.

Less than a year after he arrived in North Africa, they launched their most daring raid to kill him.

# Chapter 14

*Rommel's skill as a military tactician proved superior to the British. Time and again he managed to wrest control of the battlefield from them right when things seemed to be going their way. It is without doubt his leadership was a great threat in the Battle of North Africa. So much in fact that a detachment of commandos were dispatched with a single mission: Kill the Desert Fox!*

## November 13, 1941
## Mediterranean Sea

British submarines *Torbay* and *Talisman* surfaced in the dark night off the coast of Libya, well behind German lines during this stage of war. The captains of the subs were the first to climb through the hatch on the conning towers, followed by two others who assisted in scanning the horizon with long-range field glasses. Upon verifying no signs of the enemy, the captains issued orders for the commandos on board to begin their phase of the operation.

Hatches forward and aft of the submarines popped open and Lieutenant-Colonel Geoffrey Keyes and twenty-four men climbed onto the decks. Their faces were covered with black camouflage paint, and they wore full-body, black smocks with no military insignia. Each man was armed to the teeth with automatic submachine guns, revolvers, grenades, and knives. They needed no orders on what to do once on deck. They had been briefed on their mission and tasks several times enough so that when the time came to act they went through the numbers in record speed. Time was, after all, of the essence.

While they worked on inflating rubber dinghies, Keyes noticed a strong wind blowing across deck. Earlier in the evening the sub captain read him a weather report predicting high seas and wind, all of which might hamper their mission. But Keyes was insistent they move forward and reach their objective.

"You do your part, Captain," Keyes said with confidence, "and I'll do mine."

The captain flashed an enthusiastic grin. "You chaps simply won't quit, will you?" It was not a question. The captain was well aware the importance commandos played in the war, disrupting enemy chain of command, communications, and lines of supply. Not to forget how their activity sowed confusion and low morale among the Germans. "I suspect with blokes like you we might win the war after all."

The joking lifted their spirits and belied their true feelings on the nature of their mission. From the onset, general opinion was the outcome would be nothing less than failure along with the death of a score of commandos. Only Keyes maintained enthusiasm, which was the main reason the mission had not been scrubbed altogether. Even when he went to brief HQ with his second-in-command, Lieutenant Colonel Robert Laycock, it was Laycock who doubted their objective stood any real chance for success.

"Kill the Fox!" exclaimed Laycock. "We must be barmy to believe a mission of this sort can be pulled off."

Keyes, however, was not one to give up. In spite his physical appearance he proved a determined man. His perseverance belied a person's first impression upon seeing him. Keyes was tall with large ears, a weak mustache, and a dull expression leaving more than one senior officer to question his ability to lead. But looks proved deceiving, and in Keyes' place this was all the more true. His strong ambition and courage in battle was beyond question, and were it not for Keyes' forceful representation at HQ there was high probability no one would have stood on the decks of the *Torbay* and *Talisman* this evening.

Keyes watched his men struggling to inflate the dinghies so they could be on their way, and as minutes passed his nerves grew more and more tense. The wind washed waves over them, making it difficult to inflate their dinghies, and with the way the submarines rolled in the sea it was impossible to maintain steady footing.

Growing evermore impatient, Keyes took over the foot pump from the man nearest him, but as he began pumping a sudden wave came over them, sweeping Keyes and a number of his men into the murky waters. One of the men on the *Torbay* who had not lost his grip on the rope strung across the forward and aft decks tossed Keyes a line and pulled him back to the sub.

*Thank God we took time to secure a rope on deck for this very reason,* the commando said silently.

Keyes climbed on deck fuming. "I don't believe this is happening!" he growled.

His men maintained focus and retrieved enough dinghies to take his group to shore. During this time Keyes wondered how Laycock, who was aboard the *Talisman*, fared under similar circumstances. The better part of six hours passed before Keyes' party reached shore.

Laycock arrived a few hours earlier and joked how his friend lagged in departing from the sub. "Never received training for that particular situation, eh, Geoffrey?"

Keyes was in no mood. In reality he was embarrassed over the mishap causing such a delay. "Never mind that," he said, sternly. "What's the time?"

"Just past four," Laycock answered, calmly.

*"Four a.m.!"* Keyes was incredulous. "You mean we spent six damn hours getting off the boats?" He shook his head disappointedly. "This is one helluva way to begin a mission."

"Let's not dwell on that," Laycock suggested. "Better to decide how this affects our job."

Keyes agreed. "Right, let's move inland before we go over that."

The commandos moved to an area with suitable foliage for cover. Some of the men managed a few minutes of sleep while Keyes and Laycock went over their plan once more. Despite having discussed details many times before, each knew the importance of going over the mission whenever an opportunity arose. This proved especially true when alterations to their original plan interrupted them, such as their delay disembarking from the submarines. They sat huddled in the dark with only the faint half-moonlight illuminating the ground where they drew a map of the coast for their review.

"We should give up the idea of raiding Cyrene and Apollonia," Laycock suggested. He knew the final decision was Keyes', but also knew Keyes trusted his opinion.

"I agree," Keyes replied, quickly. "Diversionary attacks are off the table." Keyes thought in silence a few moments, and then said, "Let's move on to Beda Littoria. We've still two and a half hours before sunrise. We can be at our target in half an hour."

Laycock got the men up and off they went, stealthily trudging along the coast. Precisely twenty-five minutes later they reached outskirts of town. It began raining hard, and Keyes and Laycock knew it would be good cover for them. The commandos closed the distance between themselves and a dilapidated house. Keyes kicked over a tin can he had not seen in his path, waking up a nearby dog. The animal barked ferociously and a light inside the house switched on. A man wearing a disheveled Italian uniform opened the door. It was plain he had been sleeping for he did not have his boots or coat on, and his plain white shirt was open at the collar.

"Who is there?" he called out.

Keyes stood a mere five feet from the unsuspecting soldier when he saw the little Italian squinting hard to see who, or what disturbed the dog. Right when the Italian noticed the shape of a man standing before him, Keyes charged out of the darkness and thrusted his double-edged commando blade deep into the man's chest. The Italian grunted hard and his body fell limp, crumbling to Keyes' feet.

"Shut the dog up!" growled Keyes, to the man closest to the animal. It was all he could do to keep from shouting.

The group moved on a block further into town, which appeared as similar coastal towns. Brick homes with wood-thatched roofs aligned streets. The windows were small, and most lights inside were out. All the homes and buildings looked aged with weather, beaten down by the elements. The smell of cooking reached their nostrils at one point, and some had to fight the bile rising in their throat, for Libyan cooking did not sit well with many Englishmen.

In the middle of the street Keyes raised his hand, signaling them to halt. The group stood half on one side of the street, the other on opposite side. Some had their sturdy Sten guns at the ready; others had their Smith-Wesson revolvers. Keyes signaled Laycock to join him up front. They both dropped to a kneeling position.

"Look there," Keyes said, pointing forward.

Laycock squinted and saw the white house they searched for. He turned facing Keyes, who grinned with success, and nodded.

Keyes next signaled his men to move closer. "Alright, boys," he started, beaming with enthusiasm, "this is it! Our objective is that house. We're going to cut a hole through the barb-wired fence and low-crawl toward the building. The sentry on duty will have to be taken out."

Several of his men looked on with eagerness, each wanting to take on that part of the job at hand.

"I only spotted one sentry," Keyes continued, keeping his voice barely above a whisper. "I don't believe they're expecting trouble. We're going to have to move through the grove of trees in the main yard before reaching the gated entrance, so be quick and mind your stealth." Keyes leaned forward to emphasize his next choice of words. "Remember, we're not here to take him alive. We're here to *kill* him. The success of *Operation: Crusader* relies on our success here this morning. Our depriving Jerry of their best field commander at the time of our offensive will take away their best chance of beating Auchinleck's plan." He paused for effect. "No one returns before we have killed Rommel. Agreed?" It was not meant to be a question.

Everyone nodded in unison. The question need not have been asked, for it was generally considered this to be a one-way mission to begin with. Such was the passion each commando had for carrying out what they believed to be the highest important mission assigned them.

Keyes led the way and it was he who cut the hole in the fence with wire-cutters. Each man low-crawled through the gap, and he worked his way behind cover of a small shed near the German sentry's line of march. The commandos watched in silence and observed their colonel, who waited for the sentry to walk past him. When the unsuspecting man turned and marched toward opposite end of his post, this was the moment Keyes waited for. He had his back to him.

The German's eyes widened with surprise as he felt a hand cover his mouth from behind. Before he could react, a sharp pain erupted in his throat. Keyes thrust the blade of his double-edged commando knife to the hilt in the side of the man's throat. He held the unsuspecting soldier tight until he felt his body go limp. The sentry made a low, gurgling sound before falling silent, and Keyes let the body fall unceremoniously to the ground. He turned facing his men and waved them forward.

A number of trees provided cover for the commandos as they moved forward one by one, inching slowly, stealthily toward the white-washed two-story home. It was Rommel's headquarters, and the largest home occupied by Germans in this town. When Keyes reached the front steps of the home he looked for Laycock. Each nodded to the other and dashed for the door.

Laycock tried the door handle. It was locked.

*Of course it would be,* he noted.

He reached in his pack and pulled out a small piece of plastique, and pressed it tightly on the door. Next, he inserted a timing-pencil, and snapped the end with pliers. Both he and Keyes moved slightly away from the line of explosion. Five seconds later the charge detonated.

*Boom!*

Keyes entered the house first, followed by Laycock and the rest of the commando group. They did not open fire right away, instead utilizing precious seconds to note their surroundings. When a German corporal appeared in the doorway of an office, Keyes fired a short three-round burst. The man fell backwards hard, slamming his head on the edge of a desk he had been sitting at. He was dead before hitting the floor.

Footsteps were heard coming downstairs from the second floor and Laycock with two commandos moved forward around the corner, firing as three Germans came running down the steps. The first two were killed, but the third managed to return fire with his MP-40 submachine gun. The Germans favored this weapon, which had similar traits to the British Sten. Both fired a 9 x 19mm Parabellum cartridge and had effective range of 100 to 200 meters. When fired in close confines of a building, the cacophony was deafening and part of the commandos' intended effect.

The commandos sought cover, giving the German soldier time enough to climb back up the stairs for cover.

Keyes appeared then and said, "Right! You blokes know what to do. Fan out and search room to room."

They dispersed in groups of two. One group went down the hallway to the right and another on the left. Another group searched the dining room and library while Keyes and Laycock climbed the stairs with the majority of their force. The machine gun fire was piercing, and the smell of gunpowder filled their noses. Germans returned fire, but the commandos threw grenades their way, forcing them to retreat into rooms that had been turned into quarters for the field marshal's staff.

Grenades blew apart furniture in the hallway and the absence of enemy soldiers allowed the commandos to reach the second floor. Once there they approached each room with caution. One man would kick the door open; the other would toss in a grenade.

*Boom!*

They open fired short bursts with their submachine guns, killing anyone left alive in the rooms.

Another pair came across a room full of enemy soldiers, all of whom took cover behind turned over tables and chairs. Unfortunately for them they were cut down by a commando's steady rate of fire and another's grenade.

Meanwhile, Keyes, Laycock and their group were bursting into each room, spraying it with submachine gunfire and tossing in grenades. As the seconds ticked, Keyes became despondent by the fact they had not yet found their main target. Nonetheless they continued their search, killing all Germans in sight.

*Is Rommel even here,* he wondered.

All enemy soldiers on the second floor were quickly neutralized within two minutes of their assault. Two commandos had been killed when Germans opened fire through walls of their rooms rather than wait for the commandos to kick in their doors. A single grenade took care of them. The last room which had yet to be cleared had its door closed. A light shone from underneath the door indicated someone could be in there.

"He must be in there!" Keyes declared. It sounded more like a prayer than a statement.

With lightning speed, Keyes kicked open the door and was surprised to find several Germans fully armed with MP-40 submachine guns. They let loose a barrage of deafening gunfire, riddling Keyes' body from chest to stomach. The impact pushed him back into the hallway. Laycock and another commando fired a burst inside, but were forced to retreat from intense enemy return fire. They managed to toss two grenades inside which blew apart the room and silenced the Germans. Laycock ran to where Keyes laid still, spread-eagled in the hallway.

"Geoffrey!" he called at the top of his lungs. He dropped to one knee and lifted Keyes' head. The lifeless return stare from him verified his worst fear.

Keyes was dead.

A young commando named Lieutenant Roberts came over and knelt beside Laycock. "Sir, we must carry on," the young man said. He looked as tense as his tone sounded. This was expected during the heat of battle still carrying on in the home.

Laycock was about to answer when a German soldier appeared in the hallway from one of the rooms they cleared. He bled from a wound on his head and arm and leaned on the wall for support. His vision must have been blurred because he squinted hard to focus. In his free hand he held an MP-40 by the pistol-grip, barrel pointed down. He saw figures in the hallway, one man lying down with two kneeling beside him. He did not know whether they were German or English, but raised his weapon with difficulty, and squeezed the trigger, letting loose a wild burst of gunfire.

The shots went wild over the commandos' heads. Laycock and Roberts instinctively dove to the floor. Roberts cut down the soldat with three quick shots from his revolver. He turned to Laycock, who still laid face down on the floor.

"Are you all right, Sir?" Roberts quickly asked.

Laycock rose to his feet. "Yeah," he answered, relieved. "Nice shooting, lieutenant."

"It's what I do best," Roberts bragged, and flashed a child-like grin. "Do we bring the colonel with us?" he asked, referring to Keyes' body.

Laycock caught the sentiment in the lieutenant's tone, and shook his head. "No," he answered, flatly and with regret. "Too dangerous and we must move fast." He looked up and down the hallway. "Come on, let's keep moving."

Another commando ran up to them. He breathed heavily from all the excitement. "Sir," he said, facing Laycock, "I don't believe he's here."

"Have we searched the entire headquarters?" asked a desperate Roberts. He and the others were anxious to succeed.

The commando nodded. "Yes sir, we'd have found him by now were he here."

Laycock thought their situation a few moments in silence. Shots could be heard from his men still clearing the home. He hated to admit defeat, but Rommel was nowhere to be found in his own headquarters. In fact, the entire building seemed understaffed for the headquarters of a field marshal.

"I agree," he said, finally. "Let's leave this place before reinforcements arrive."

The commandos assembled in the rear of the building as originally planned. When Laycock informed them of Keyes' death they took the news as he expected—with shock!

"Colonel Keyes is dead?!" one of the men said. He sounded flabbergasted.

It seemed impossible to believe, but his absence was proof. All commando units trained closely and for long periods of time. The nature of their fighting created a bond unlike other regular army units experienced, but now was not the time for remorse. They remained behind enemy lines and had to make their way to the rendezvous where they were scheduled for pickup and return to base.

Laycock led his men through what appeared to be the motor pool. Cars, lorries, and armoured personnel carriers littered the area, and they found it odd so many to be here considering the need for vehicles on the front. A sudden burst of automatic gunfire caught them by surprise. They took cover behind the vehicles and returned fire as they moved from vehicle to vehicle in their retreat. Laycock knew from how poorly they fought they were rear-echelon soldiers, the kind who pushed papers across a desk versus trained fighting men. And yet they chased the commandos with fierce intent on killing their attackers.

*These Jerries are suicidal,* Laycock told himself.

Fortunately for the commandos the town had not been heavily occupied by Germans. The location was so far from the frontline fighting there was no need for a large force here. However, Laycock knew reinforcements were sure to arrive, so they had to make haste in their escape.

One of the commandos dropped to a knee and removed a grenade from his pack. A few others did same. As if on cue, they tossed them simultaneously and then took cover. The Germans failed to see what the commandos had been up to and ran head on into the open when the grenades detonated. In an instant the brave German force were torn to shreds by shrapnel. After a few precious seconds passed, Laycock checked the area. With the coast clear and the shooting stopped, he and his men rose to their feet and out of the motor pool, disappearing into the night.

# Chapter 15

*As it turned out, Rommel seldom used his coastal headquarters in Libya.
He preferred being at the front where the action was, even directing troops
from command tents. This caused resentment from officers who believed their
commander should have been in the rear commanding overall battle plans, and
leave small direct action to them. However, Rommel's in-the-field style most
likely saved his life from the assassination attempt at Beda Littoria.*

## September 21, 1942
## Alexandria, Egypt

Major Thomas Lawrence stared in deep thought out the window
in his office at *L Detachment's* HQ and training facility. His view
of the Mediterranean Sea was magnificent, and much preferred over the
desert ocean he operated in. It was mid-morning and the sound of waves
lapping ashore was soothing. For a time he was able to forget the War, but
only momentarily. Admiring *The Med*, their reference for Mediterranean
Sea, helped set aside memories of the numerous hardships endured whilst
fighting a desert war.

A mission against Jerry was tough enough, but waving off hungry flies
proved more detestable. Those pests cropped up wherever you stopped and
made camp. It had become an irony their worst enemies in the desert were
not Germans. Rather, it was flies, scorpions, and snakes which created
much irritation for soldiers on both sides.

However, this morning Major Lawrence had little time for reflecting
on anything other than his mission at hand. In fact, today's morning news
had been grim. Rommel had pulled another of his lightning strokes and
wrested Mersa Matruh from 8th Army. It had been the 8th's task to setup

defense perimeters in order to buy time and strengthen their forces for a coming offensive. But with the city now fully in enemy hands they needed to focus effort on defending Alexandria. Every British soldier knew the key to Egypt was the Suez Canal. Whoever possessed the canal had access to the Indian and Pacific Oceans. The key to the canal was Port Said, and the key to Port Said was Cairo, and the key to Cairo was Alexandria, a mere sixty miles away.

A knock on the door awakened Major Lawrence from his reverie. He turned and saw the door open without his permission, and in walked none other than Lieutenant Colonel David Stirling, commanding officer of L Detachment.

"Ah, there you are, Thomas," Stirling said, in his usual upbeat tone. "I've been searching for you all morning."

David Stirling had come up with the idea of his special unit while on convalescence leave in a hospital after a failed commando raid. Up to then in 1941, commandos had been used largely as an amphibious assault force, hitting the enemy with large ground forces from sea. Stirling realized correctly how using large forces of commandos as such lost them their most treasured weapon—element of surprise!

When Stirling learned of stories how British soldiers had been cut off behind their lines and how some who spoke German had donned enemy uniforms and walked freely amongst them while making their way back to friendly lines, he realized something of utmost importance. The Germans had not thought about protecting their rear against small, highly efficient units of fighting men. If British commandos parachuted behind enemy lines and destroyed fuel depots, ammunition dumps, tanks, vehicles and such it would prove a devastating blow to the Afrika Korps.

A major difficulty in this plan was getting commandos back to friendly lines after parachuting far behind enemy territory. At first it was believed somewhere in the desert they would be able to land a plane and pick them up. However, an extreme shortage of planes due to the front widening in all theaters of the war made this impossible. But Stirling was not the sort to give up on an idea he believed in. His enthusiasm for finding answers to complicated problems of extraction from the field inspired his close friend, Lieutenant Paddy Mayne, to come up with the idea of using the Long Range Desert Group.

The LRDG was a unit which had been in action since the start of the Desert War in 1940. Their primary assignment was reconnaissance. Unless the situation dictated otherwise they were under strict orders *not* to engage in combat. After all, what good was their recon if they were discovered by the enemy? When LRDG had been approached on the idea of transporting L Detachment from their field of operations back to friendly lines, they jumped at the chance of seeing more action than they had been subject to. With the challenge of transportation resolved, the remaining blessing needed was from British Middle East Headquarters.

It had been a creative idea which received much welcome from General Sir Claude Auchinlech, then the Middle East Commander, and General Neil Ritchie, 8th Army's commander. Up to then the Desert War had not been going favorable for the British Empire, and they understood the need for a diversion to keep Jerry busy while they strengthened reserves for new offensives. The idea of hitting them hard and fast behind their own lines seemed best. Thus, with the blessing of British HQ, L Detachment commenced operations against Afrika Korps.

Stirling had done all a body could think of so nothing was left for chance. For their first course of action he planned a number of simultaneous attacks against enemy airfields which resulted in destruction of more than eighty enemy planes. Needless to say, British HQ was ecstatic.

"Someone finally has created a way of attack which left them completely flustered," was the hot topic of discussion with military and political leaders.

As the War dragged on, L Detachment grew ever larger, what with no shortage of volunteers. Men in the Regular Army were more than willing to transfer to the smaller L Detachment where standard military doctrine was not as strict. Not to mention how their victories against the enemy became more popular beyond Stirling's dreams. German radio referred to then Major David Stirling as *Phantom Major*, and Stirling, emboldened by L Detachment's recognition, pushed to have the unit renamed Special Air Service, which later became referred simply as SAS. The unit's assigned headgear was the usual brown peaked-cap, but with a single difference. On the cap was the badge of a winged dagger with the words, *Who Dares Wins*. It was a badge men in SAS wore with pride.

Thomas Lawrence had been with Stirling from the start. He was there when he had been promoted Major, and shortly thereafter to Lieutenant-Colonel. He commanded many four-man patrols in American-made Wylies Jeeps which more recently were added to collection of special equipment for fighting against the enemy. Nearly everything SAS operated with was referred to as *special* because nearly all their equipment had been requisitioned on the sly rather than acquired through normal channels.

Stirling deemed this tactic necessary due to troublesome supply officers who proved less than enthusiastic to sign over anything to smaller units while shortage of war material was so great.

Lawrence had history with the best in SAS. Early on he was teamed with Fitzroy MacLean, a former Member of Parliament who signed up shortly after war broke out in 1939. There was also Paddy Mayne, Stirling's right-hand man responsible for training new recruits at their main base in Kabrit near the Gulf of Suez. Also in the unit was Peter Stirling, a former diplomat, and Mike Sadler, the best land navigator in all of SAS. Lawrence also worked closely with Jock Lewis, the man who invented the bomb used for planting on enemy planes with a delayed timer. The men affectionately referred to it as the *Lewis Bomb*, after its maker. There were Lieutenants Morris and Gus Holliman of the LRDG, Corporals Cooper and Seekings, who usually went out with Stirling himself, but on occasion worked with Lawrence.

Indeed, Lawrence had worked with all veterans of SAS. In fact he was the most successful patrol leader in the field, even over Stirling, who himself had not consistently been a success in the field against Jerry. There were occasions when Stirling's raids had gone awry and usually over the worst kind of events.

Before the Lewis bomb, which was a combination of plastic and thermite (half-explosive, half-incendiary) had been invented; Stirling had the misfortune of being supplied with faulty timing-pencils. These were required to set a delayed fuse on the explosives in order for men to get far away from enemy airfields before the charges detonated. This was their only chance for marginal escape, and it was unfortunate for Stirling that the first batches of timing-pencils were defective, and even more so that he received the majority of the defects.

Before SAS were supplied with Wylies Jeeps, their usual plan for attack had been to drive through the desert in large Chevrolet 30 cwt lorries specially outfitted for rough travel. When they neared German airfields they disembarked their vehicles and infiltrated enemy bases on foot under cover of darkness. It proved relatively simple to slip past unwary sentries and plant explosives on each plane lining the runway. Since commandos moved with great stealth this took hours for them to complete. Once all explosives were planted they returned to their vehicles and rendezvous far from the enemy airfields where they waited for their explosives to detonate. It was how they confirmed their mission a success. Although many SAS units attacking different airfields were successful, Stirling had been a failure.

Once the problem with timing-pencils had been corrected, Stirling proved successful and 'bagged' his share of enemy planes enough for him to hold his head high among Lawrence, Mayne, MacLean, and the rest of his men. Even more so, once the Wylies Jeep arrived, Stirling thought it prudent for them to change tactics against the enemy. In fact it was Stirling who came up with the idea of driving his jeeps onto enemy airfields and attacking parked planes with massive machine gunfire. The tactic proved time-saving and permitted SAS commandos to attack the enemy faster than they ever dreamed, and retreat to friendly lines before Jerry regrouped.

No one knew this better than Thomas Lawrence. Rumor sprang up a second SAS regiment was to be formed in East Africa where they could assault Germans on another front, and the man considered top candidate for command of the regiment was Lawrence. After ten years' service, Lawrence learned never believe anything until it came to fruition. Besides, he was content doing his best while under command of Stirling.

"I've been here all morning, sir," Lawrence said, cheerfully, and rose from his chair. "What can I do for you?"

A thin smile pursed Stirling's lips. "You can start by calling me David." Stirling maintained his usual calm demeanor. "It's been more than a year since we've worked together. As I told you when we first met, military formality is not a must with me. We only have to put on a show whilst in front of brass."

Lawrence sat back down while Stirling sat in the chair in front of his desk. Despite him being senior rank, Stirling always respected the offices belonging to his subordinates. Throughout his career he never felt need to prove he was in command. His results in the field were enough to demonstrate that.

"Very well, David," Lawrence began, nodding with a smile. "You must forgive me. It's a form of habit, I suppose."

Stirling understood. He knew Lawrence was a career-soldier, whereas Stirling enlisted only after war broke out with Germany. Military protocol was a way of life for men like Lawrence. "Right," Stirling said with an understanding nod of the head. He noticed a framed portrait of the late Lieutenant-Colonel Geoffrey Keyes hanging on the wall by the window. The curtains blew against it by the sea breeze coming in. "Been meaning to ask you," he said, getting off subject. "Where did you get the portrait of Keyes?"

Lawrence swiveled in his chair to face the portrait. It was indeed a handsome one. Keyes posed in full dress uniform and wore the *Victoria Cross* he had been posthumously awarded for his action the year before in his attempt to assassinate Rommel. Lawrence took a moment reflecting before answering.

"A friend of his gave it to me while I was in Cairo. Chap was there for a meeting in GHQ and looking to leave it with persons who knew Keyes. It was Geoffrey's best friend for that matter. Ahh—rather his former best friend."

"Why former?" Stirling asked, with great interest.

Lawrence shook his head as he recalled past events.

"Apparently this best friend fell in love with Geoffrey's girlfriend while he was away and up and married her. He had the portrait commissioned upon learning of Keyes' death, but could not keep it in good conscious, and gave it to me when he learned I was assigned with SAS. Guess the poor sod thought our group would appreciate it more seeing how we worked with him."

Stirling smiled. "Good for you."

Lawrence shrugged.

"Yes, well if it wasn't for Keyes' actions and men like him, the days of the commando might well have been put out of action for the War's duration," Stirling admitted. He alluded to how back in early days of the War how more than a few senior officers protested formation of commando units. They preferred to use those scores of men in units for large-scale battles against the enemy. Fortunately, that was not how things turned out.

Lawrence got back to the issue at hand. "Yes, well I know you didn't stop by to admire my taste of art, David. What can I do for you?"

Stirling liked how Lawrence had no problem knowing when to get down to business. "First thing is first, old man," he said, beaming. "Want to congratulate you on your more recent operation against Jerry."

Lawrence smiled and nodded twice. He had always been easily embarrassed upon receiving recognition for his achievements. So far as he was concerned a good performance was simply part of the job. No need to receive a pat on the shoulder for what should be expected of every man and woman in uniform.

Stirling, however, was not the kind to pass up opportunity of praise for one of his men. Recognition, he knew, was a good way to prove to top brass the importance of their work. In fact, commando units received such recognition and military decorations more so than units in the regular army that high-ranking officers complained over the difference in equal awards not being distributed to their men versus those serving in commando units.

"I understand you bagged quite a number of enemy planes on your raid," Stirling continued. He then added, "Do tell."

Lawrence nodded. "All in a night's work," he replied, failing to sound complacent.

Stirling adjusted himself in his seat to get more comfortable, which was a sign to Lawrence he meant to be here for some time. "This is really our first time we've had a chance to catch up since your escape from Tobruk, is it not?"

Lawrence thought about it. *He's right.* It was the sort of thing he did not like discussing, seeing how to explain one's escape meant explaining how one had been captured in first place. Regardless of the situation, no soldier enjoyed time spent as prisoner of war. It was the sort of thing you simply did not want to discuss, and avoided the subject whenever possible.

Stirling knew this too, and sensed Lawrence's discomfort. "Care to discuss it?" he asked. It was not meant to be taken as a question. Although Stirling developed friendships with many of his officers and men, he was still the man in charge and expected to be treated as such.

Lawrence leaned forward, resting his elbows on his desk. "It all came rather sudden," he began, somewhat sullen. "I haven't pieced together the string of events leading to my capture and—"

"—And the deaths of your men," Stirling offered, finishing Lawrence's sentence for him.

That struck home hard for Lawrence, and he fell silent. He leaned back in his chair, exhaling slowly. Stirling looked on as if to say, Please continue. And so Lawrence did. "We'd completed reconnoitering the road to Derna when the *Stukas* came…." he began.

It was June 15, 1942 on the coastal road between Derna and Tobruk where Major Lawrence and his jeep patrol traveled full speed attempting to make good their escape, but it was no use. Ever since attacking the German airfield at Benghazi the Luftwaffe relentlessly hunted them.

The raid had been nothing from the norm, and they managed to plant thirty-seven Lewis bombs on Stuka Dive Bombers and ME-109 fighters, but mostly the *Auntie-Ju* transports, which were primary targets. All planes went up in smoke and the Germans scrambled in disarray. The raiders had little problem escaping unnoticed on foot while the enemy worked to put out fires and salvage what they could. However, it was not long before the sky was filled with German planes from other bases searching for the raiders. Lawrence and his patrol had much further to travel before reaching friendly lines, and the chance of making it grew much slimmer when their stash of fuel had been located by a group of Bedouins who promptly contacted the Germans in exchange for money, guns, and horses.

In order to prevent being cut off from safety of British lines, Lawrence risked driving down the coast road to Derna seeing how it was the fastest route eastward available. He also considered several intercepted radio reports indicating German forces conducted an extensive air and ground search for jeep raiders in open desert. With this in mind, Lawrence reasoned Jerry would not expect them to be bold enough to take the open coastal road.

He was wrong.

"There they are!" Sturmbannfuhrer Wolfgang Klement said over radio in his cockpit.

His wingman, Hauptmann Konrad Diestl, looked out the window of his own Stuka and saw vehicles Klement referred to. "Yes, I see them," Diestl replied, excited.

Klement looked to his right where Diestl kept tight formation with his plane. "Ready?" he asked. Of course he knew the answer.

"Ja!" Diestl answered. His voice was laced with excitement at the idea of exacting revenge on their enemy.

That said, Klement took his Stuka into a steep dive aimed directly at the group of jeeps speeding east on the coastal road. Diestl followed suit, and the combination of the sirens located on the belly of the Stukas' fuselage screamed its horrific howl echoing miles throughout the desert.

Major Lawrence and his men looked skyward and recognized the piercing screech. They heard them before when in France in 1940. It was not the sort of sound one forgot. Jeep gunners swiveled their turret-mounted twin-Lewis machine guns around, took aim skyward at the enemy planes, and opened fire. But the Stukas had the sun behind them, forcing them to fire with glare in their eyes, making their efforts fruitless.

The Stukas, with superior firepower, dove fast, firing their 37mm cannons and tearing up the road, which exploded under the jeeps' tires, showering the raiders with asphalt and dirt. They did not stand a chance of escape from such an air attack.

Lawrence was in the lead jeep and managed to make it through the barrage of gunfire having only been shaken up a bit. But Lieutenant Williams in the second jeep took hits dead-on, and his vehicle shattered into a million pieces, exploding in an earth-shattering ball of orange and black flame. Another driver attempted to swerve out of the destroyed jeep's path, but lost control. In the blink of an eye, the jeep raiders found themselves tossing and turning as the jeeps rolled over and over across rocks and sand. Men and equipment were tossed from their vehicles like broken matchsticks. Drivers were the unluckiest, being crushed by their vehicles as they rolled in an endless spin.

Lawrence looked back in time to witness the tragedy. It was a scene he would never forget—and a scene he would regret having escaped from. *Why not me?* he asked himself, wondering why he remained unscathed.

Corporal Jennings continued firing his Lewis guns at the Stukas until their jeep came to a sudden stop. He looked at the carnage of what was left of their group. The road behind them was now destroyed. Their jeeps were smashed beyond repair, and the majority of the commandos were strewn among the wreckage—dead!

The Stukas were not finished unleashing their wrath and came in for another attack. With sirens blaring and guns spitting out a cacophony of death, Lawrence had no choice other than to order a full retreat without making time to search for survivors. It was the sort of decision a commander detested, but knew it to be correct considering their situation.

"Let's get the hell outta here right quick!" Lawrence shouted.

The driver needed no further encouragement. He pressed the pedal to the floor and their jeep shot forward like a bolt of lightning.

Sergeant Harris sat in the front passenger side with Major Lawrence driving. The sergeant manned the twin-Lewis guns on the front turret, but could not swivel around to face the rear. He remained at the ready to open fire once the Stukas passed over them.

"I suggest we zigzag, sir!" he said, shouting over the sound of the sirens and steady staccato of automatic gunfire.

The road provided little room for maneuver and Lawrence managed as best he could. The coastal road had once been a marvel for its time in such a desolate place. However, it remained only a two-lane road in much need of repairs which the Italians never made efforts to perform.

Sturmbannfuhrer Klement radioed to Hauptmann Diestl. "What's your ammunition level?" His voice crackled over the radio.

"Not good," Diestl replied, squinting to read the figures. "Perhaps enough for one more pass, but no more."

Klement shook his head disappointedly. Although their 37mm cannons were highly effective, they spat rounds far too quickly, forcing pilots to break off engagement so they could rearm. The only other armament they had were two fixed 7.9mm machineguns in the front and one of the same for the rear-gunner to operate. Klement was pleased they found the desert raiders and took out three of four vehicles. However, he had hoped to bag them all so he could report a complete victory.

"Very well," he said, with reluctance. "Refrain from using cannons and switch to machineguns."

Suddenly Klement's rear-gunner's excited voice came over the radio. "Sir, I see enemy planes at twelve o'clock!"

Klement looked up and spotted a pair of British Hurricane Fighters. He could not have dreamt a more ferocious enemy plane other than the Spitfire. So far as Klement was concerned it made little difference what type of plane he was up against, for the Stuka was a bomber, not a fighter. Its design did not allow pilots to maneuver well against fast-moving fighters, nor could it outfly them. This made Stukas highly vulnerable, and they usually disengaged aerial combat in order to avoid being shot down.

This was precisely what Klement decided to do—and fast!

Major Lawrence brought his jeep to a screeching halt, kicking up dust in its wake. "They're not going to attack," he observed. He waved his hand in front of his face to clear the air from dust. "Looks like our boys are going after them."

Lawrence and his crew looked back at their fallen comrades. The wreckage of the other three jeeps, its crews laid strewn over the desert road, told them what they already knew. But Lawrence insisted they check for survivors anyway. They found Private Johnson, a gunner in one of the jeeps, had not been killed outright. He lay on the side of the road, bleeding profusely from his chest and legs. Lawrence and another soldier gently rolled the critically-injured man onto his back and watched as Johnson spat out blood while attempting to speak.

"Don't talk," Lawrence advised the young man. "We'll get you to Kabrit in one piece, but keep still. It won't do you any good to engage conversation in this condition." He had to fight his eyes from growing misty.

Johnson knew better despite his commanding officer's advice. He was touched by Lawrence's words of encouragement, and flashed him a look as if to say, "Not your fault, sir, but thanks for saying that anyway." He managed a slight, calm smile before he died in Lawrence's arms.

Sergeant Harris completed his search for survivors. "They all bought it, sir." He breathed heavily from running to each wrecked jeep for inspection and he perspired profusely. He looked westward. "We best leave, sir," he suggested, desperately. "We still have to worry about mobile enemy ground troops."

Lawrence rose from his knelt position. "No time to bury them," he said, flatly. "No doubt the Stukas reported our position and will send a motorized unit after us soon enough."

"Doesn't leave us much choice, sir," Corporal Jennings added. He looked about, taking in their surroundings as if he expected the enemy to appear any moment. "Rommel's still on the offensive and threatening Alexandria. So long as he's pushing east we run risk of being cut off from our lines. That only leaves one base for us to seek refuge."

"I know," Lawrence conceded. "Tobruk!"

Major Lawrence continued describing to Colonel Stirling how he and what was left of his patrol found themselves trapped inside the embattled port city of Tobruk. They unexpectedly found themselves fighting Germans as regular infantry versus their unorthodox commando-style. Although everyone put their best foot forward their efforts proved fruitless. The German juggernaut attacked the garrison with a ferocity the British had not seen since Dunkirk. Churchill had ordered the strategic port city be held at all costs with similar defiance they fought a year earlier, only this time there was no stopping Rommel.

"What happened to your men?" Stirling asked. "I believe you had Sergeant Harris and Corporal Jennings with you?"

Lawrence drew a breath before answering. It was plain to Stirling the subject was a touchy one for the major, but he wanted to know. "They were killed when Jerry broke past our tank ditches," he explained. "They moved in so fast we barely had time to high-tail it out of there. You wouldn't believe the score of men crushed in trenches by the panzers."

"And you were taken prisoner along with everyone else," Stirling concluded.

Lawrence nodded. "That's right, sir. They transferred us to the Italians, whom we all know aren't the most ideal soldiers to have on one's side of war. During an air raid they got careless and a number of us managed escape whilst others searched for cover. I tagged along with a junior officer and....as I recall there was a *Yank* among us." Lawrence leaned forward, resting his elbows on his desk and chin on hands while reflecting his experience. Then it came to him! "Yes, that's right!" he exclaimed. "A Lysander aircraft had been brought down by the Luftwaffe and he wound up captured inside Tobruk same as rest of us. Chap was some sort of liaison officer if I'm not mistaken."

"Do you recall his name?" Stirling asked, testing Lawrence's memory.

The major nodded. "His Christian name was Jack," he noted, and scratched his head.

"Any idea what became of him?"

Lawrence became aware how Stirling was going somewhere with this and his curiosity was aroused. "For all I know, sir, he was recaptured or killed while attempting escape. And judging by his lack of experience, if he did escape he likely died in the desert." He watched as Stirling shook his head.

Stirling reached inside his brown leather briefcase sitting on his lap and withdrew a manila file, which he handed over to Lawrence.

The major opened it and flipped through its pages, studying the picture of an American officer and his background. He stopped long enough to glance at Colonel Stirling, and then returned his attention back to the file.

"Jack Ruggero," he said, mildly and with little interest. "His rank is captain, and he's part of the American Army's Expeditionary Force." He looked up at Stirling and said, "It's him."

"I know," Stirling admitted.

"How did you come by this?"

Stirling motioned to the file. "It's all in there," he explained. "It's rather a fascinating story, too. Like yourself, Ruggero and a junior officer managed escape and wandered in the desert quite some time before reaching friendly lines. They lived off minimal rations and drank water from streams in the hills to keep strength. They even walked within a hundred meters of one of our observation posts, but were so delirious and fearful of recapture they dared not take a chance on running into German hands once more. They marched on and reported coming across a rather large German-Italian base. He stated he never saw more barrels of petrol, ammunition boxes, Jerricans, and lorries in his entire life."

Lawrence grew interested at the mention of a secret base deep in the Saharan desert. "The report doesn't mention its location," he noted.

"And that's a pity," Stirling admitted. "Our boys are nowhere in the vicinity of where they saw this mysterious depot, and I've no doubt Jerry is stashing this cache of supplies for their next offensive."

"Alexandria," Lawrence stated.

Stirling nodded. "That's right! Now what I'm about to tell you next is highly classified. No one other than the PM, Monty, you, and I have studied the contents of the file in your hands."

"I understand, sir," Lawrence said, reassuringly.

Stirling shifted in his chair. He had a lot to go over, and this was going to take time. "In his report, this chap, Ruggero, stated he witnessed a group of Arabs enter into the presumed German camp and were greeted by a high-ranking German officer. We showed the Yank a number of photographs of Germans in command in North Africa and he identified the man on the next page of the file you have as being present at this base."

Lawrence flipped to the page with an 8 x 10 black-and-white photograph of a German officer in full military dress uniform. "Von Mellenthin!" he exclaimed, practically shouting the name.

Stirling nodded. "In the flesh. Sturmbannfuhrer Freiherr von Mellenthin is Rommel's intelligence officer, and quite good at his chosen profession. In fact, he's too damn good. We've wanted to get our hands on him some time now in order to deprive the Fox first-class information he obtains for him. The man's leadership skills and abilities are second to none so far as we can see. Rommel's given him a free hand, which has made him dangerous."

Lawrence laid the file down on his desk. "Then our assumption of what Jerry is planning with the Wogs is correct, sir?"

Stirling nodded. "Afraid so," he confirmed. "The PM and Monty are none too happy by the prospect of taking on the entire Arab population in another of their trumped-up Holy wars which would only benefit the Germans."

Lawrence remained unconvinced over the gravity this meant, especially when one took into account the history of Arab loyalty to foreigners. "This sort of thing has come up before," he began, and attempting to sound reassuring. "Arabs have changed side's dozens of times, providing loyalty to those as long as they're winning. Every British soldier treats Wogs as friend and foe alike because of this."

"And so does Jerry," Stirling added.

Lawrence scratched his head uncharacteristically. "Are we expected to take this report seriously?" he asked, a bit incredulous. "Especially from a Yank who was half-witted after finding himself lost in the desert?"

Stirling raised an eyebrow. It was a good question, and one which needed to be taken into serious consideration. "Considering our position," he started, quite carefully, "I don't see how we have an alternative. After each victory we achieve, Rommel manages to pull a rabbit from his cap and turn the tables. Bletchley Park in London has deciphered the German code with what they call *Enigma Decoder.* This enables the RAF and Navy to intercept Rommel's supplies from Italy before they can do him much good. However, Rommel's ingenuity never fails him. His entire Afrika Korps is becoming quite efficient in foraging supplies needed to maintain a serious threat in this theater of the War. Just look at the booty he obtained when Tobruk capitulated." He paused for effect. "Monty doesn't want to begin his offensive until mid-October. He'll need this much time to obtain superiority in men and material. The PM is pressing him to make his move now on threat of being replaced should he continue delaying our offensive."

"Great Scott!" Lawrence blurted. "Not another commander being sacked at this dire moment! Troop morale has yet recovered from Auchinleck's dismissal."

This was true. Commander after commander had been 'sacked' by Churchill for failing to defeat Rommel. This action led troops to believe they were up against a 'bogeyman' that they had yet to find a man on their side capable of turning tables for good on German fortunes.

Stirling raised a calming hand. "Let's keep our wits," he said. "Monty put to rest that possibility by telling the PM if he wanted to take the offensive before he was ready he'd be doing it without him in command."

"You're joking of course?" Lawrence balked.

Stirling shook his head. "Not at all. Seems Monty knew no one was in line to replace him and he called the PM's bluff."

Lawrence let out a laugh. "Good for Monty!" he exclaimed. Lawrence had no ill feeling toward Churchill. Like many Brits, he believed him perfect in the job of prime minister during this most crucial time for England's survival. However, like many military professionals, Lawrence did not appreciate his interference in military matters. He believed politicians should handle politics and let the military handle the war.

Stirling continued. "We cannot afford Jerry the opportunity to go on the offensive before Monty's ready. Ever since *Operation Agreement* failed, our existence as a fighting unit has come into question once more."

News of this angered Lawrence and he demonstrated this by pounding his desk with a closed fist. "How can that be?" he exploded. "The plan was Haselden's, not SAS. Besides, you told him the plan most likely would fail, but GHQ instructed us to press ahead. Surely they're not holding us accountable for their bad call?"

Lawrence's reference to the operation was well known among SAS. Lieutenant Colonel John Haselden had put together the plan to assassinate Rommel at his headquarters the year before after he claimed to have seen the famous general's car at a German headquarters located in Beda Littoria. Turns out the car had been driven by an officer under Rommel's command, but the Fox was not there. Haselden also put together *Operation Agreement* in which a score of commandos traveled through enemy lines disguised as German soldiers transporting British POWs. German Jews in the ultra-secret unit, Special Interrogation Group (SIG), posed as guards while British commandos played the role of prisoner.

Haselden entered Tobruk determined to destroy German fuel bunkers, and actually reached their objective. With the bunkers in clear sight and few armed guards about, they could have blown them up with little resistance. However, he had a time-table to follow and under orders to wait for a coordinated British seaborne force. The delay cost the initiative and their mission ended in complete failure. Haselden and dozens of his team were killed.

"Ever since that failure," Stirling continued, "GHQ has been discussing if SAS should be used to replace men lost on the battlefield." His face then contorted to one of sheer displeasure. "In short, they want us to fight alongside regular army troops in regular army fashion."

"That's outrageous," Lawrence exploded. "To place highly-trained commandos in the field as regular troops not only fails to utilize them for what they do best, but will cost us dearly if any are killed in action seeing how long it takes to train them in special warfare tactics."

Stirling could not have agreed more. "Sometimes I fear GHQ more than Jerry," he confessed. "Our problem is too many in GHQ simply don't like us being self-run. They despise what they cannot control."

It was the same old argument. SAS had proven time and again how highly-trained commandos operating behind enemy lines in small numbers were capable of exacting insurmountable damage on the enemy at low cost of men and material. However, their success may have been their own undoing, as high-ranking officers failed to appreciate the laurels they were awarded over their own larger units in regular army.

Lawrence and Stirling were not known for giving up the fight, even if it meant taking on their own superiors. "What have you in mind?" Lawrence asked. He was more than willing to carry the mantle if it meant keeping SAS out of regular army control.

"Visit this Yank and bring him on our team," Stirling replied, evenly. "He's the only person we know who's seen this secret German fuel depot. RAF has had no luck spotting it on aerial reconnaissance and cannot afford sending more planes to assist. They're busy enough against the Luftwaffe buzzing about in the skies over Malta and the Med, so we've got to hope this Yank can provide us the card needed to beat Jerry in this game."

Lawrence looked surprised. "He's an American," he quickly pointed out. "He's got no reason to join us."

Stirling shrugged. "Use that old half-Irish charm you acquired from your father's side of the family and convince him it's in his best interest to join SAS."

Lawrence smiled and bobbed his head. "Of course, sir," he said, rising from his chair as Stirling did same. "Have you any idea where I might find him?"

Stirling flashed a sly grin. "You're going to love this," he said, mischievously. "He's right here in Alexandria. The Yanks have landed and sent us a group of liaison officers for coordinating troop deployments to Sicily once we've defeated Jerry. This man, Ruggero, is assigned to them."

Lawrence thought it odd for Americans to plan an invasion of Sicily when they had yet to enter the war in North Africa themselves. "Don't they realize we've yet to soundly defeat Rommel? They could at least make their landing in Morocco *before* making such plans, don't you think?"

Stirling shrugged again. "I don't think the Americans believe there's nothing they aren't capable of accomplishing." As he headed for the door he turned and added with a wave of the hand, "Happy hunting!" He was about to leave before half turning around and said, "Oh, by the way, there's a rumor going about that you went to Tobruk on assignment to size up how dire the situation was for our chaps." He paused, observing Lawrence's reaction. "Have you any idea how this started?"

Lawrence lowered his eyes a bit and coughed, holding a hand to cover his mouth. "Wish I could help, but…." He shrugged, signaling he preferred the matter dropped.

Stirling smiled. "Too bad. Whoever dreamt it up is a genius." He left, closing the door behind him.

# Chapter 16

*"Now is the time for all good men to come to the aid of their country!"* –
*Charles E. Weller, who originally wrote, "Now is the time for all good men*
*to come to the aid of the party." For motivational purposes words were changed*
*to inspire national pride.*

## Alexandria, Egypt
## September 22, 1942

Captain Jack Ruggero awakened in his bed to the sound of waves
splashing on the beach from his coast side cottage with a strong
aroma of freshly-brewed coffee reaching his nostrils. He did not get out
of bed right away, instead choosing to enjoy the serene moment of a quiet
morning. He heard someone in the kitchen and the clatter of plates being
placed on his dining table.

*She's probably making breakfast*, he told himself, and this made him smile.

She switched on the radio and Jack heard the popular army song, *'Don't sit
under the apple tree with anyone else but me, anyone else but me, anyone else but me!'*

He sat up in bed, stretched and yawned loudly without caring if she
heard him.

*Confidence in who you are wins them over, not bedside manners,* he had
always said.

He looked out the window and saw ships of all sorts heading west.
Battleships, freighters, destroyers, minesweepers, a sizable convoy, he
thought. They were too far to see which flag they displayed, but he
figured them to be British Royal Navy seeing how they ruled the Med.
This changed, however, at nightfall when the Luftwaffe commanded the
sky with vast numbers of fighter and bomber aircraft.

Jack got out of bed and threw on a white bathrobe covering his nakedness. He slid his feet into a pair of slippers and walked out and into the kitchen. He saw her standing before him by the stove, striking a false pose as though she were modeling for an agency, holding out a cup of coffee for him to take. She wore only a bathrobe too; only shorter and showing a bit more of her wonderfully shaped legs.

"Your coffee is served, my *man* of the house," she said, flashing a seductive smile.

Jack had grown to admire the sound of her voice, especially when she was playful. It had been two weeks since they met at the Officer's Club in Cairo and they hit it off great. Her voice was a natural soft tone, the kind most found seductive. Her body was slender, quite athletic-looking. She wore her blonde hair like a teenage Shirley Temple, but it was her lovely face which attracted him most of all. Jack found her bright blue eyes captivating, the kind commanding one's full attention. When she smiled her dimples reminded him of a childhood friend's younger sister, his first crush, and this had Jack treating her like the princess she appeared to be to most people infatuated with her.

He stood in the doorway; hand on chin, studying her pose. "There's only one thing wrong here," he said, trying to sound serious while moving closer.

She looked at him curious while he took the cup from her hand and placed it on the table. Then he reached down with both hands and slowly untied the knot holding her robe together. She observed his hands moving inside and around her waist before lifting her eyes to meet his.

"You look better holding out my coffee wearing nothing at all," he confessed with a sly grin flashing across his face.

The woman smiled, but the moment vanished when they heard a knock at the front door. She jumped, startled, and pushed Jack away, quickly tying her robe to cover herself. The kitchenette had an open counter adjacent with the dining room, allowing anyone at the front door to see them. When she saw a tall man in British uniform observing them through the screen door she regretted opening the front door earlier that morning to allow fresh air to circulate inside.

"Sorry to intrude on your morning," the Englishman said, jovially. He removed his peaked cap, bowing slightly out of respect for the lady. "I'm looking for Captain Ruggero," he continued. "I understand he resides here."

The woman dashed out of the kitchen to their bedroom, flushed with embarrassment. Jack remained still, staring curiously at the Englishman.

He recognized something familiar about the man, but could not place a name to his face.

"I'm Jack Ruggero," he told him, omitting his military title. He stepped out of the kitchen and motioned for the Englishman to enter his living quarters.

"Thank you," he said, entering. Then he introduced himself. "I'm Major Thomas Lawrence."

Jack suddenly recalled how he knew the Englishman. "My God, I couldn't place a name to your face, but knew I'd seen you from somewhere!" he exclaimed. He offered his hand and they shook hands excitedly.

"It has been a few months since our last meeting," Lawrence reminded him. "Besides, we were both a bit thinner back then, too." His reference was to their living on prison rations, which consisted of one canteen cup of water, a tin of beef, and biscuits per day. All prisoners lost incredible amount of weight during internment. Their lack of a balanced diet caused some to lose vision, hair, and loosened their teeth. But that was then, and here they were now in much better health.

"Sit down," Jack said, inviting Lawrence to a seat on the living room sofa. "Care for some coffee?"

Lawrence shook his head. "Not much of a coffee man, I must confess, but if you have any tea?"

Jack did, and went about heating a pot of water on the stove. "I'd given you up for dead," he said, taking a seat in the chair opposite Lawrence. He sipped his coffee while it remained hot.

"I figured you for same," Lawrence replied in kind. He took in the surroundings of Jack's bungalow. "How'd you manage acquiring a colonel's cottage?"

Jack laughed. "Won it in a card game from one of your army regulars who thought he was the best poker player in all of North Africa," he told him. "Inside twenty minutes I had him five thousand pounds in my debt. Naturally he could not afford to pay, so he offered me his place in exchange."

Lawrence looked on dumbfounded. "Why in blazes would he have done such a thing?"

Jack shrugged. "Chap was shipping off to the front, so what did it matter? Especially if he gets himself killed."

Jack's female companion entered the living room after having changed into her Women's Army Corps (WAC) uniform, bearing rank of lieutenant. "Ahh, there you, my love," he said, rising to his feet and kissing her softly on the cheek. He turned to face Lawrence and introduced her. "This is Valerie," he said, offering nothing more than her first name.

Lawrence rose and bowed slightly at the waist, taking her hand in his. "A pleasure, Valerie," he said, smiling politely and flashing a perfect row of gleaming white teeth. He saw no reason to address her by rank seeing how he wanted this meeting to be more of a courtesy call versus an official one.

"Pleased to meet you, Major," she replied, also returning a vibrant smile.

"Please, call me Thomas," he insisted.

Valerie nodded. "Very well, Thomas."

Jack suggested she make them breakfast, and Valerie took this as signal for what it meant. They needed a moment between themselves. She took on the task with much delight and went into the kitchen whistling the British tune, *Lili Marlene.*

Jack offered Lawrence to join him on the patio facing the beach where the veranda shaded them from the rising heat from the sun. Lawrence followed and took a cup of hot tea offered by Valerie as they walked past the kitchen.

"We had quite an affair in Tobruk," Jack reflected. He sipped his coffee and took a seat on one of the chairs while Lawrence did same. "The Krauts took a beating from your boys before the port finally fell to them."

Lawrence sighed heavily. "Yes, and we'll return soon enough," he said, hopeful. "They have quite the leader with this Rommel," he admitted with a touch of admiration professional soldiers had toward their common enemy. "He's a fine officer who knows tactics." He took another sip of tea and added, "I don't believe we have anyone who can measure up to him at the moment."

"What about this new chap of yours, the man named Montgomery?" Jack blurted. "I heard Alexander took over command from Auchinleck as commander of Middle East Forces and appointed Montgomery commander of your 8th Army."

Lawrence shrugged. "We've had scores of commanders, but there's only been *one* Rommel. Our replacing commander after commander has sapped regular army morale, leaving troops believing Rommel to be more of a *bogeyman* rather than an ordinary man who can be beaten on the battlefield." He paused, looking out at the sea before continuing. "I think this man nicknamed Monty has a rough job ahead of him, and a lot going for him, too."

Jack raised his brow in surprise. "That's quite a statement. How do you figure?"

Lawrence explained. "Hitler's obsessed with defeating Russia, and he cannot accomplish this before winning here in North Africa. The quarter of a million men under Rommel's command could help turn things quickly for them on the Eastern Front, but not while they're tied up here in the desert. Then there's the question of Germany's resources being depleted to the point Hitler cannot supply forces on all fronts. Evidence shows Rommel is reduced to foraging for petrol and his supplies are too low for sustained battles."

"So all you have to do is bleed him dry of supplies," Jack interjected. His tone challenged Lawrence as if this were easier said than done.

"It would appear so," Lawrence agreed. "The fact of the matter is Montgomery does not have to be a better general to defeat Rommel." He saw the bemused look on Jack's face. "All he need do is prevent Rommel from receiving supplies necessary to wage war. Our navy and air force are doing what they can to send as much German shipping to the bottom of the sea, but we've learned Rommel has been storing enough petrol and supplies for an advance on Alexandria." He paused, allowing a heavy silence to stand between them before adding, "If he takes Alexandria, he takes Cairo along with it. And with Cairo goes the Suez Canal."

Jack sipped his coffee. The look on his face indicated to Lawrence he had no interest in this discussion, which was no surprise seeing how he'd studied the Yank's personnel file and concluded him to be anything but a soldierly fellow. In fact, Lawrence was curious what motivated a man like Jack to have enlisted in the first place, and how he became an officer at that.

Jack put down his cup and sat back comfortably in his chair. "Let's hope you boys keep the *Fox* out of Alexandria," he said, hopefully. "I doubt I'd find as nice a place as this anywhere else in North Africa."

Lawrence decided it was time to get down to business. "With the right help I'm sure we can prevent that," he said, in a matter-of-fact tone. When Jack looked at him Lawrence continued. "A strange thing happened to me at my office yesterday," he began, sounding all business. "I read a report by a former POW stating he came across a German supply depot somewhere in the desert between El Daba and El Alamein after his escape as prisoner. Based on his report we believe the depot is located north of the Qattara Depression, and hidden by mountains and sand seas making up much of the terrain. I've traveled across this territory and confirm with certainty it's God-forsaken and extremely rough-going in every sense."

Up to this point Jack had casually listened to Lawrence almost like the war seemed unimportant to him. Now he became curious, especially when Lawrence mentioned the supply depot.

"His report stated quite a bit activity at this desert base, including him witnessing a tribe of Arabs meeting with a group of German officers. He did not learn what was discussed, but the meeting raised concerns." Lawrence stopped when Valerie joined them carrying a tray of eggs, bacon, and toast.

"Hope you both have an appetite," she said, cheerfully.

They did, and Lawrence put off his conversation while they ate. No need to disclose details to the woman, he thought. Besides, this was classified and he had yet to remind Jack not to discuss their subject with anyone. During breakfast Lawrence learned Valerie was a radio operator stationed here in Alexandria. She enlisted at war's outbreak like many other women whose job was to handle tasks not requiring men so they could go off and fight on battlefields. Britain's need for men was acute seeing how the war raged on all corners of the world.

Lawrence thought Valerie beautiful and her personality quite upbeat. In fact, he thought she and Jack made a handsome couple. Both were full of personality, enjoying a good joke versus serious conversation. Throughout breakfast Jack joked how he wormed his way into Officer Candidate School (OCS) back in the States. Turned out he was such a dandy playing cards he'd earned himself a reputation for a card-shark. This brought him to the attention of many influential officers who desired having a man on their side of the table when playing against others whom they held a grudge. Jack's talent won hefty cash and closed more than a few bets for officers, who in return paved his way through OCS without a hitch. They also allowed him to choose any command he wished to serve.

Lawrence noticed how easily Valerie laughed over Jack's description on how he became an officer, and duping the system to get where he was today. This did not surprise Lawrence seeing how he knew most men she knew were English, who were by nature a serious breed. Americans, he believed, possessed a more relaxed attitude, taking things in stride and enjoying themselves in the process. They enjoyed good music, wine, dance, and basked over the mere thought of having fun.

Once finished with breakfast, Lawrence was ready to get back to business. "Your meal was impeccably delicious," he said in his most charming tone. "However, I'm afraid I must continue speaking with our mutual friend, Jack here, in private. Will you excuse us, please?"

"Certainly, sir," she understandingly replied. "I'll take our plates."

Once Valerie left, Jack turned to Lawrence. "Okay, what's this all about?" he asked, lighting a cigarette with an American-made *Zippo* lighter. He held out his pack of *Lucky Strikes* offering one to the major.

Lawrence was momentarily quiet as he stared at the lighter. Like many soldiers in the British Army, they admired the simple design of *Zippo* cigarette lighters and he right then realized how much he longed for one of his own. He looked back at Jack, all business now.

*Is he playing dumb, or is he really simple-minded?* He could not be certain and decided to be more frank.

"The information I've been divulging is from your report you provided Special Intelligence Services in your debriefing after you'd been picked up by an LRDG patrol." He noted the look on Jack's face indicated he knew what he was talking about. *Probably did the whole time,* he thought. "You recall the chaps who found you wandering in the desert after your brave escape?" he added. Jack did not miss the sarcasm laced in Lawrence's tone.

"Don't give your boys too much credit," Jack retorted. "I made most the way back on my own, and had practically reached friendly lines when they came upon me."

Lawrence did not press the issue. "Do you recall the name of the officer with you? I believe his name Duggan, a Regular Army lieutenant. His statement corroborated yours."

Jack had an expression of someone losing interest in the subject discussed. "Yes, that was quite a time for Duggan and me," he said, reflecting on that difficult journey. "Now life goes on," he added, with delightful resignation.

Lawrence nodded. "For some, yes."

Jack thought the major sounded like he challenged him, and his interest snapped back to present. "Excuse me?"

Lawrence explained his meaning. "Lieutenant Duggan recovered from your journey and returned to his unit. Unfortunately he was killed in action at Mersa Matruh. So you see life does *not* go on for everyone."

Jack leaned back in his chair, taking a long drag from his cigarette and holding his breath longer than normal before exhaling a slow trail of smoke. "I appreciate your sentiment," he said, finally, "but I was not close with Duggan. You didn't have to come all the way here to inform me of his death."

"I'm afraid I have more to tell," Lawrence replied quickly. He needed Jack to pay attention, and now he seemed to.

Jack shrugged nonchalantly. "Okay, I'm all ears."

"Yes," Lawrence said, with a nod and slight smile pursing his lips. Instead of telling Jack what was on his mind, he chose to allow a hard silence fall between them.

"Well, what is it?" Jack demanded.

"You've heard of SAS, haven't you?"

Jack had, but forgot its meaning. "What about it?" he said, sounding as though he didn't give a damn.

"Special Air Service is a new outfit, officially designated as *L Detachment*," he explained. "SAS is our preferential name. We operate behind enemy lines using all possible and near-impossible tactics. We originally dreamt up the idea of parachuting behind enemy lines, getting on with our mission, and returning by vehicles driven by LRDG. Now we command our own vehicles to and from the enemy. It's much more feasible than a parachute drop."

"What of it?" Jack blurted, still not the least bit curious why Lawrence was telling him all this.

"We destroy enemy aircraft on the ground," Lawrence continued, as though Jack hadn't chimed in. "We blow up fuel depots, ammunition dumps, vehicles, just about anything before disappearing in the desert." He reached over for a cigarette from Jack, drew one, and lit it with the Zippo lighter. "Nice," he commented about the Zippo before handing it back to Jack. "We've been quite successful, too."

Lawrence paused when Valerie returned. "I must report for duty," she told them, displaying a regretful smile.

Jack looked up at her, admiring her beauty. "Leaving me again," he said, playfully accusing her. He rose from his chair, put his arms around her waist and kissed her gently.

Valerie pulled back despite the kiss not being too frank. "Walk me to the door," she said to Jack. She looked at Lawrence before leaving. "Nice to have met you, sir."

Lawrence was already standing when she said it. "The pleasure is mine," he said, reaching out to shake hands versus accepting her salute.

Jack walked her out and stopped her at the front door. "We must do this again soon," he suggested.

Valerie stared back, smiling like a smitten teen. "We've enjoyed breakfast together for the past two days," she reminded him, sounding as though that was enough for most men. She pecked him with a quick kiss on the lips.

Jack watched her walk out and said, "Yes, but I believe it's my turn to do the cooking."

"First time you tried cooking, we never made it to the kitchen," she shot back. She walked down the sidewalk to a bus stop. Then she added, "I'll see you tonight!"

Jack returned to the patio where Lawrence sat patiently waiting. "She's a nice girl," he admitted, taking a drag from his cigarette.

"Englishwomen usually are," Jack agreed, taking his seat.

Lawrence studied Jack carefully. "Tell me," he started, somewhat cautious, "what's your feeling on the War?"

Jack stared back bemused. "How do you mean?"

Lawrence shrugged as if to say, *it's a simple enough question.* "I don't know many Americans and thus haven't the privilege discussing this matter. Took you Yanks long enough to get in the War, and now that you're here I'd like knowing how you feel about it."

Jack looked out at the sea reflectively. "I'm the last person you should ask that sort of question," he said, unashamedly. "You see, I'm a man of opportunity, not patriotism."

Lawrence grinned. "Yes, I see the opportunity side of you. I believe she served our breakfast this morning."

Jack appreciated the humor and laughed along with Lawrence. "As far as I'm concerned," Jack explained, "this war is your affair. You've got a beef with the *Huns*, not us Yanks, as you like to call us. Our fight is against Japs! They're the ones dragging us in this war with their sneak attack at Pearl Harbor."

"Then why not volunteer for the Pacific Theatre so you can do your part?" Lawrence asked, challenging Jack's point of view.

Jack laughed some more. "You're forgetting I'm a man of *opportunity*, not patriotism."

Lawrence found it difficult figuring out what made this man spin, but he pressed on with more questions. "How'd you manage assignment here as liaison officer?"

This was not a difficult question for Jack, and he let out another laugh, annoying Lawrence with the sarcasm laced in his behavior. "I was actually assigned to the Pacific arena of the War, which I wasn't all enthusiastic about. So I joined a card game with a divisional commander who'd heard of my skills at the table and wanted to best me. Played cards all night, and he was good, but in the end my straight flush bested him. He was ten thousand in the hole, and that amount is a lot even for a general."

"So what happened?" Lawrence asked, amazed by Jack's story-telling.

"I agreed to let go what he owed in exchange for assignment as liaison to the British. You see, in the Pacific there aren't many women like you limey's have serving in your army so close to the front."

Now it was Lawrence who laughed. "You're a man of opportunity all right!" he exclaimed.

Jack had enough of this small talk and decided to get down to heart of the matter. "Why'd you search me out?" he asked accusingly.

Lawrence too, had grown exhausted of this pointless conversation and looked him straight in the eyes. "I've come to offer you an *opportunity*," he said, beaming.

Jack was not amused. "Really?" He remained dubious. "What sort of opportunity? Is it a poker game you have in mind? You catch wind of my card games we play each night at the Officer's Club and want me to play against someone you have a grudge with? Want me to leave them sitting there wearing nothing but their undershorts, is that it?"

Lawrence paused. He preferred wording what he was about to say in such a manner Jack might appreciate. "In a sense it is a game of poker," he said, leaning forward and resting his elbows on the table between them. "And the persons sitting opposite you are Germans."

Jack sat up straight. "What?"

Lawrence continued. "My assignment is to locate the German base you reported and destroy it before Rommel launches an attack against Alexandria. His weakness is lack of supplies for sustained battle. Without reserves he can only conduct lightning attacks before being forced to withdraw. The base you stumbled across is undoubtedly their refueling point. We destroy it and we prevent Rommel from pushing east."

"And you expect me to do what?" Jack demanded, feigning naiveté.

"We need you to help us locate that enemy base," Lawrence said quickly.

Jack sat frozen. His complexion literally turned white. "That's the craziest thing I've heard!" he managed to say.

Lawrence was both amused and astonished how genuine the Yank appeared. *Chap should've been an actor.* "The RAF has had no luck spotting its location, and the German Luftwaffe is keeping them busy elsewhere. We've pinpointed a few spots in the desert where they are likely to have a base setup, and we want you along for recognition of familiar terrain you came across during your escape."

Jack pulled himself together and took a long drag from his cigarette. "I don't soldier," he confessed. "I plan on making it through this war in one piece, and joining you on a ride through the desert doesn't fit in with my plans. Sorry, but you'll have to find your *ace-in-the-hole* someplace else."

"Ace-in-the-hole?" Lawrence queried.

Jack rolled his eyes expressing impatience. "The winning card," he explained, shaking his head.

Lawrence grinned. "Ahh, very good!" He reached inside his uniform coat pocket and withdrew an envelope. He placed it on the table and slid it across to Jack.

"What's that?" Jack wanted to know, without opening it.

"It's my *ace-in-the-hole*!" Lawrence told him, beaming.

Jack took the envelope and opened it. Its contents had a U.S. Army letterhead with orders stating Captain Jack Ruggero temporarily assigned to L Detachment for action deemed necessary for the war effort. Jack turned his eyes to Lawrence.

"How did you manage this?" he demanded lamely.

Lawrence shrugged. "Wasn't all difficult," he admitted freely. "You see, your poker games are something of a legend now. One of the players on the losing side is in hock to you for about three thousand pounds, a tidy sum he doesn't have. Chap is a Yank too, assigned to our GHQ, which is currently working with your people on plans for your entry in this theatre of war. This places him in an invaluable position."

"What do you mean?" Jack persisted.

Lawrence was having fun. "Well, seems as though this person in hock to you has approved assigning you to us with best wishes from your group. Also seems he's hoping to rid himself of a three thousand pound debt should you be killed in action." Lawrence saw the discomfort in Jack's expression and followed up with, "Naturally your people are thrilled to have one of their own in the fight to defeat our common enemy."

"You sound like I'm being taken on a suicide mission," Jack blurted. He looked thoroughly terrified by the thought of fighting.

"Relax, old man," Lawrence told him, with a raised hand to suggest slowing down before jumping to conclusions. "You should feel proud. We've turned down hundreds, even thousands of applicants looking to join our merry group."

"Yeah, well they can have it because this line of work is *not* for me!" Jack cried, angrily. He crumpled up the letter and threw it across the table.

*This is going to be fun,* Lawrence thought.

# Chapter 17

*Rommel's success in the Desert War was such that had Hitler authorized greater reinforcements at start of the War there is little doubt how things would have developed over the course of the Battle for North Africa.*

## SAS Training Camp near Kabrit, Egypt
## October 13, 1942

Major Lawrence gathered his personal belongings in his tent when he heard a knock on one of the wooden support poles.

"Good day to you, Major! How have you been?" It was his close friend, Captain Paddy Mayne.

Mayne was one of the original officers chosen for the formation of L Detachment. He also served as former camp trainer for all personnel assigned to the unit. His responsibility was to ensure each recruit successfully completed the grueling course required before soldiers were accepted in SAS. This gave him certain respect from all officers and men regardless of rank, for they looked up to him as a private would their drill instructor while undergoing boot camp training.

"Paddy, it's good to see you!" Lawrence said, happy by the surprise visit. Like most officers in SAS they were on first name basis, even with most enlisted men.

"I heard you returned from Alexandria and thought I'd drop by and see how things went," Paddy told him.

"Let's have a drink," Lawrence suggested, and motioned him to sit down in the chair by a small table in the corner of his tent.

Paddy accepted his offer, tossing his peaked cap on the table and taking a moment to admire the major's large tent. "Ah, privileges of rank," he said with a hint of jealousy. He took the glass of *schnapps* Lawrence offered him and waited for the major to fill his own.

Lawrence took the chair on opposite side of the table and they raised glasses in toast, gently tapping them. "To SAS," Lawrence said, praising their beloved unit.

"And its founder, Colonel David Stirling," Paddy added, with equal praise.

Paddy looked around the spacious tent provided officers with rank of major on up to full colonel. "One could have a dance party in your living quarters, Thomas," he noted, laughing.

"Don't make fun, old boy," Lawrence replied defiantly. "I've heard about the large bed you customized while David was out hunting Jerry."

Paddy raised a halting hand. "Please, don't remind me," he said, taking another drink. "I did that out of boredom, and a bit of resentment. David never lets me live that down, but I remind him had he not assigned me job as camp trainer I never would have found time to do such a thing."

This was true. Stirling needed a top man with experience to train recruits for the expanding SAS, and believed no man was better than Paddy Mayne. However, Mayne had no desire sitting out the war as a trainer while others took lion's share of glory. In protest he built an over-sized bed for his tent with intention of being as comfortable as possible in a job he considered a waist of his time.

"Was the idea supervising recruits so repulsive to you?" Lawrence asked, curious about this episode that created an uncommon row between Stirling and Mayne.

"What do you think?" Mayne snarled. "We're at war and it's not going to last forever. Like Stirling, I want to fight!"

Lawrence appreciated Paddy's point of view. "What'd you make the bed out of?" he persisted.

"My design would impress even you, my friend," he said, and spread his arms out wide as if accepting applause for his creation. "I made it six feet wide and used discarded barrels for its base. The mattress was made from old mats we used for parachute practice falls." He grinned broadly as he continued. "It was the most comfortable bed in all of North Africa, I assure you."

"Fit for a king," Lawrence offered.

"One could say so," Paddy agreed. "David was a bit teed for me having done that," he added. "Told me he'd expected me to concentrate on training, but I simply didn't have it in me. I spent most of my time either in bed or at the bar. When he returned from Benghazi we'd had a bit of a row over the matter, with him insisting I never disobey his orders again, and in return he knew better than to have me working as a behind-the-lines administrator."

"I'm glad things worked out well in the end," Lawrence told him. "Seems Sergeant-Major Riley has taken over job as recruit trainer rather well, wouldn't you agree?"

"You bet he has! Chap was born for that sort of thing." Paddy downed the remaining contents of his drink and set the glass down on the table. "Anyway, I heard you are about to be off on another hunt."

Lawrence finished his drink and refilled their glasses. "That's right," he said, nodding. "We'll be leaving this afternoon once our guide arrives from Alexandria."

"And this man is?"

"The Yank I came across in Tobruk. Remember my mentioning him to you before?"

"Oh yes, the card shark! I hear he's also a bit of a ladies' man."

Lawrence recalled his meeting Valerie. "Yes, he's doing quite nicely for himself."

"Too bad about Colonel Haselden, eh?" Paddy said, changing subject.

Lawrence lowered his head in reflection. "I didn't know the man well, but from what I've heard he was a decent man."

"He was one of the best!" Paddy said quickly. "He simply should have stuck to reconnaissance and left raiding to us. His plan against Tobruk was sound enough, but once GHQ broadened the attack into a sea, land, and air assault operation things went cockeyed. Too many loose ends in their plan, and Jerry awaited them in force."

Lawrence nodded. "David warned GHQ, but…." His voice trailed off while looking back at the operation that cost so much and so many lives.

"Too many of us are gone," Paddy said, somberly. "McGonigal's group disappeared without a trace. Your outfit got shot to pieces on the open road. Seems like each time we have a victory, Rommel manages to turn tables on us."

"That will change once we locate this secret fuel depot of his," Lawrence said, eagerly.

Paddy leaned forward, resting his elbows on the table. "Do you really believe the Fox has such a base?" he asked, dubious. "I mean, no one has been able to find a trace of its existence. Not the RAF, the LRDG, or any of our own patrols. Not even Bedouin informants have anything to offer about such a base."

Lawrence took another drink. "It's a sound plan for Rommel to have a forward base hidden from view in order for his tanks to be refueled. Foraging for petrol isn't a long term plan, and their supplies from Italy and Sicily aren't reaching them before being sent to the bottom of the Med." He paused, scratching his head in thought. "Makes sense for Rommel to have a base somewhere along the route to Alexandria and Cairo, and we simply must find it."

"But you're taking word of a Yank," Paddy reminded him. "He was lost in the desert and half out of his mind. Aren't you asking for trouble?"

Lawrence thought about this. After all it was not uncommon for persons to hallucinate in the desert, especially from lack of food and water. "I wouldn't be going through all this if I did not believe his story had merit," he declared.

"Does the Yank have any combat experience?"

Lawrence shrugged. "Aside from being shot down and taken prisoner? No. He did manage to escape and survive in the desert. I suppose that counts for something."

"I wish you luck, my friend," Paddy offered, and raised his glass in toast. "Who's going with you on this joy ride?"

"Captain Hawkins and Lieutenant Wilson are my group of officers."

Paddy nodded approvingly. "At least they're veterans."

A sergeant approached the major's tent and knocked on the pole. "Major Lawrence," he said, standing at attention and offering salute, "the Yank has arrived, sir."

Lawrence returned the salute. "Thank you, sergeant. You're dismissed."

Paddy finished the contents of his glass, stood up and reached for his cap. "I must be off," he said, sounding a bit regretful. "You take care and return in one piece." He shook hands with his longtime friend and patted him on the shoulder.

"I'll do my best," Lawrence assured him.

Captain Jack Ruggero had been picked up in Alexandria by a British soldier driving the popular *Wylies* all-purpose terrain vehicle and taken straight to Kabrit. During the drive Jack mulled over how things could have gone so wrong for him. Never in his life did he believe he would be recruited for a dangerous behind-the-lines mission, and the very thought of engaging the enemy frightened him right down to his socks.

When they reached Kabrit the driver took him straight to SAS training camp and came to a screeching halt at the main security gate, kicking up a cloud of dust in the process. Jack slowly exited the vehicle and reached for his bag in the back. He followed the sergeant to Major Lawrence's quarters.

"Ah, there you are, Jack!" Lawrence acknowledged with a beaming grin. "Glad you will be joining us."

Jack stiffened as he turned to face the major. "How jolly wonderful of you to have me," he replied, sardonically.

He took a look around the camp and saw all sorts of activity. In the northern part of the camp a group of recruits maneuvered an assault course under direction of a sergeant. In the southern part of camp others practiced parachute landing falls by jumping off the back of jeeps traveling 30 miles per hour. In the nearby Nile River other recruits took swimming lessons.

"I doubt that sort of training will be any use for us in the desert," Jack noted.

"In SAS we train for all sorts of scenarios," Lawrence told him. "Some of our missions include amphibious activity against enemy shipping and ports. Good swimmers are needed for such work."

Jack shook his head over all he saw. *Why anyone would want to do this sort of work,* he wondered. "I need a drink," he blurted.

"Follow me," Lawrence said, and motioned with his hand for Jack to join him inside his tent. He told his guest to have a seat in the same chair Paddy had occupied and poured a drink.

Jack drank the full contents in one swig, and held his glass out for another. "I still don't know why you want me along on this joyride," he said, acidly. "I was delirious and out of my mind out there." He took another drink before adding, "I probably hallucinated that base you all are so anxious to find."

"I disagree," Lawrence said, reassured he was correct in his assessment. "Your report was too detailed. Besides, we have learned Jerry has been making desperate attempts to stash supplies in forward areas so they can replenish their tanks with enough petrol to keep their advance on Alexandria and Cairo rolling."

Jack took another drink. "And you think this action on our part will help your new commander beat Rommel?" He remained skeptical.

"If any man can beat the Rommel, Montgomery can. Not so much because of his ingenuity, but rather from superiority in men and material. That is what is going to defeat the Afrika Korps, their inability to maintain steady supplies for sustained battle."

Jack leaned back in his chair, drifting into deep thought. "I said it before, and I'll say it again," he blurted. "I don't like any of this. I'm not a soldier." He looked and sounded adamant. "I never have been, and never will be." He studied Lawrence before continuing. "Don't count on me to pull heroics, let alone the trigger of a machine gun. I plan on playing it safe." He shook his head and ran a hand through his dark hair. "I have no idea where to begin looking for this German base. After all, I was trying to keep from falling back in enemy hands and didn't have time to take notes."

He shook his head, contemplating his predicament. "My plan was to stay close to the coast road heading east," he continued, reflecting on his painful experience. "The krauts and eyeties had too many planes scouting the area, so we travelled south a bit in search of water. Found some, too, but got lost and grew delirious when we ran out of water. The heat was so unbearable there were times I thought my brain would fry." He looked apologetically at the major. "You boys hailed me a hero for my escape and journey, and to be frank, it was far from it." He paused searching for words. "I don't have any idea where to tell you we should begin a search for a base I hardly remember."

Lawrence nodded understandingly. "We have an idea about that," he said, spreading open a map on the table before them.

"I just want you to know not to count on me to do your fighting!" Jack snapped back.

Lawrence calmly stared back and said, "You behave as though Germans are not your enemy, too. Why is that?"

"I know we're at war, *old boy*," he explained, referring to Lawrence in English style. "I also know when the shooting stops we'll all be friends again. I'm simply not making enemies along the way is all."

Lawrence studied Jack, trying to figure the man out. He thought back in Alexandria he understood his kind, but now he was not so certain. "Okay," he began, acquiescingly, "enough said in regard for your lack of spirit to fight. What we're going to do now is go over this map so you have an idea what we're up against." He leaned forward and began briefing Jack over the map of the surrounding desert, and Jack's lack of interest did not go unnoticed.

# Chapter 18

*With the need for men and supplies growing, the Germans sought to utilize local Bedouin tribes to fight on their side. This threat concerned the British greatly, and they had yet to devise a plan to prevent Bedouin from fighting with their enemy.*

## October 13, 1942
## Somewhere in the desert

The Fieseler-Storch aircraft flew 500 feet over the great sand sea, approaching a group of mountains which the pilot used as a marker on his map to verify they were on course. His two passengers had flown with him before and were quite comfortable with his flying skills. Despite their being at war, they found it difficult not to admire the beauty of the natural desert, and would have loved to have cameras available for private photographs to send home. When they neared the mountains the pilot took the plane to an altitude of 3,000 feet in order to safely clear them. Once over them they saw what they were searching for.

The desert base located miles away from the nearest German troop concentration at Mersah Matruh carried the distinction of being their most forward base south of El Alamein near the Qattara Depression. To some degree the Germans were surprised its location had remained secret from the British for so long. Their lack of air superiority and mobile units like the LRDG and SAS made the chance of being spotted highly probable. Even the troublesome *Phantom Major* and his jeep-raiding teams which had become legendary amongst German troops failed to locate the base. This reason alone was enough to believe good fortunes of war was on their side and victory imminent.

The Storch flew over the base, dropping to 500 feet before leveling off and circling the makeshift runway, ingeniously disguised as a dried river bed, with deadwood and shrubs off to each side giving the impression of where water ran off the mountainside. When the plane landed it bounced twice and the pilot followed instructions of ground personnel who guided them to a halt near several JU-52s and three Messerschmitt 109s. A large group of officers and men awaited them to disembark and their eagerness was obvious by excitement coursing through their veins.

At first sight of two high-ranking officers disembarking the plane, a Sturmbannfuhrer turned to face the group of soldiers and barked, *"Achtung!"* (Attention). Everyone clicked their jackboots in unison and stood even straighter, as if it were humanly possible.

Field Marshal Rommel casually returned their salute. "Good morning," he said, jovially. Not surprising, he offered his hand to the Sturmbannfuhrer standing before him.

Sturmbannfuhrer Hans Mueller shook Rommel's hand and bowed his head respectfully. "Good morning, Herr Field Marshal, and welcome to our base. We have prepared refreshments for you after your tour is complete. In the meantime we can use my staff car to escort you."

"Thank you," Rommel replied. His smile stretched ear to ear as he was known for enjoying inspecting his commands and talking with men face-to-face. Unlike many career officers of the *old school*, Rommel believed in getting to know men in his command which helped build *kameradshaft* (comradeship). He motioned to the officer who flew with him in the Storch. "Allow me to introduce Oberst Otto Krieger, my new Quartermaster Chief of Staff."

Mueller bowed slightly at the waist, but never took his eyes away from Krieger. "Yes, I believe we've met, Herr Oberst," Mueller said in a challenging manner. He could see by his expression the oberst recognized him too, and also noted his discomfort.

"I do not immediately recall where we met, Herr Sturmbannfuhrer," Krieger replied, trying to hide his irritation.

Mueller relaxed and crossed his arms; touching his chin with one hand to emphasize he was in deep thought. "If memory serves me, Herr Oberst, right after the fall of Tobruk along the coast road to Gazala is where it was. I was escorting prisoners of war and we had a conversation regarding their treatment."

Krieger's face reddened, clearly from embarrassment. "Oh yes, I do recall our meeting." He paused, searching for words. His eyes darted from Mueller to Rommel, and back to Mueller. "Your performance was commendable," he said, bitterly.

Mueller grinned, satisfied with his minor triumph over the snobbish aristocrat. He turned to Rommel. "Would you care to begin the tour, Herr Field Marshal?"

Rommel nodded. "Yes, but first introduce me to your staff." Rommel saw by their expressions how officers and men in formation looked forward to meeting their famous leader in person, and he always made a point of doing so on a personal basis. It was another method of his which endeared him to his troops.

Mueller led his high-ranking guests down the line of formation, introducing each man to Rommel as they passed them. The field marshal took special notice of the Luftwaffe officer standing further down the line, looking splendid in uniform.

"This is Sturmbannfuhrer Wolfgang Klement, commander of the Luftwaffe here," Mueller told him.

"Pleased to meet you, Herr Klement," Rommel said, shaking hands with him. "With good fortunes of war on our side, soon you'll be flying over Cairo by year's end."

"Jawohl, Herr Field Marshal," replied Klement, beaming with pride.

The man beside him was Hauptmann Konrad Diestl. Rommel engaged in small talk with him before continuing the inspection. By the time he finished meeting all of them he saw how his efforts paid off. They were proud and inspired to be fighting in his army. Rommel felt as though he was the most fortunate man on earth, let alone Germany.

Next Mueller took them to his kubelwagen where he acted as driver and escort, taking them all over the base. Rommel and Krieger sat in back, listening as Mueller explained the purpose of each building and men occupying them and their responsibilities. Rommel took special note of the camouflage netting over everything. Buildings, fuel barrels, gun emplacements, everything had been ingeniously concealed.

*No wonder the RAF has been unable to locate this base,* he thought. *They've done a superb job at camouflage.*

This was true! The Germans left nothing to chance. Nothing in the open was without some sort of concealment whether it be camouflage netting, shrubs, dead wood, trees, or rocks. In fact, the RAF had flown over them several times, Mueller mentioned, and failed to spot the base. This was all due to their diligence in maintaining concealment from the air.

Tank Sergeant Heinrich Priess worked on his Panzer Mark IV when he saw Mueller driving with his esteem guests in back of the kubelwagen. He and his crew stopped work long enough to snap to attention as they drove by, and Rommel tapped the tip of his peaked cap with his marshal's baton in return. Priess and his men looked on, beaming with pride for being able to serve with whom many believed to be the Fatherland's greatest modern general.

From the lookout tower north of the base, Privat Karl Mohr observed the base commander driving his guests through field glasses. His position provided him a bird's-eye view and he watched with keen interest as they stopped at key areas like the fuel depot, munitions buildings, and workshops. From the expression on Rommel's face he believed him to be pleased with their accomplishments on base. This did not surprise Mohr for every man here worked hard for Mueller, believing him to be a first-rate officer and leader.

"I'm pleased with what you have done here, Sturmbannfuhrer," Rommel said, congratulating him when the vehicle came to a stop in front of the officer's club. "Keeping this base secret is a miracle indeed."

"Thank you, Herr Field Marshal," Mueller quickly replied. "Each man here is privileged to be part of your command, and we look forward to a swift victory."

Rommel nodded. "I still cannot believe we managed to keep this base secret for so long," he said, incredulous over their good fortune. "One would have thought the Arabs would have sold us out for a small sum of gold and rifles."

"There may be some good news about the Arab issue, sir," Mueller added. Before explaining he led them inside the Officer's Club tent where a group of junior officers snapped to attention upon them entering.

Rommel stepped forward, touched the tip of his peaked cap with his baton and said, "Stand at ease, gentlemen."

A bar had been set up and music played from a radio and phonograph. A long table had been placed in center of the tent with seating available and refreshments loaded to the brim.

*They don't seem to be lacking much here,* Rommel thought, amusingly.

Sturmbannfuhrer Freiherr von Mellenthin was present and stepped forward, clicking his heels. "Herr Field Marshal, welcome to your most important base to date, *Lili Marlene!*" With that said, von Mellenthin turned to face a soldier and nodded.

The soldier then turned on the phonograph box and the War's most popular song played *Lili Marlene*, sung by Marlene Dietrich, the famous German actress who defected at war's outbreak. The men cheered and clapped.

Rommel stepped closer to von Mellenthin and told him, "The base's name seems most appropriate."

"I quite agree, sir," von Mellenthin replied quickly. "I quite agree."

Rommel took his seat at the head of the long table and everyone took theirs only after he sat first.

"I am surprised you were not there to meet me upon my arrival, Freiherr," Rommel noted. "I hope it is not because you are growing tired of my company," he added, jovially.

The group of officers and men laughed. Von Mellenthin shook his head. "Not at all, Herr Field Marshal, I was busy gathering last-minute information on the Arab issue which only now reached us via telegram."

Rommel seemed to brighten upon this news. "Yes, yes, I'm intrigued by all that. When you first put it to me I did not think much of it. Now that we have learned how the Britische are worried over this matter I would like to move forward, if for no other reason than to make them jittery before our push to Alexandria."

"Oh, I believe they will be more than jittery, Herr Field Marshal," von Mellenthin quickly replied. "The man we will be dealing with is known as, El Karum, a Bedouin chief by birthright. His father had been the most powerful tribal leader for the past quarter century until his death. After which the tribe was divided into factions due to elders not believing in Karum's experience for leading such a prosperous tribe."

"How old is this man, Karum?" Rommel asked, taking a sip of water from the tall glass before him. During other times their drinks would have been wine, but in the desert all welcomed fresh drinking water.

"Early twenties is our best guess, Herr Field Marshal. In spite of the breakup of his tribe, Karum was able to gather thousands of followers, enough to make the Britische believe him to be a viable threat. They've been paying Karum twenty-five thousand pounds a month to keep him out of the war, but he's now in a position where he may have to declare an *Intifada,* what they call a holy war."

"What makes you believe this?" Rommel asked, intrigued by this prospect of local tribes turning against their enemy.

"Tribal elders don't believe Britische are any better than their former Italian masters," von Mellenthin explained. "With the English failing to wrest initiative from us on the battlefield, they believe time is ripe for them to attack and be rid of them."

Rommel flashed a curious smile. "And what do they believe they will gain after our victory?"

Von Mellenthin paused, clearing his throat. "Intelligence reports indicate they believe once victory is ours we will return to European mainland."

Rommel and the group of officers burst into laughter. "Such imbeciles!" Rommel blurted.

"When is the meeting with this man, Karum, scheduled?" Krieger quickly asked.

"Next week. We are to receive word twenty-four hours prior to actual date."

"Excellent!" Rommel declared, taking another drink. "This Arab uprising will create a perfect ruse for the Britische. Our troops will push on toward Alexandria and have enough petrol and supplies for our tanks thanks to this base. Our common enemy will be tied up fighting and rounding up many of the locals, which will take much-needed men from the battlefield, thus allowing our troops a freer hand in our drive eastward. With this in mind, it is my belief by mid-November all of North Afrika will be ours."

Everyone burst into immediate applause and rose to their feet in honor of Rommel. A moment later they sang in unison the popular song, *'Panzerlied'* (Song of the Armoured Troops).

# Chapter 19

*The Qattara Depression rests in Northwest Egypt near Matruh. It has a maximum depth of 133 meters below sea level, 135 kilometers wide, and 300 kilometers long. It is full of salt marshes, sand dunes, and incredibly hot. Considered one of the more inhospitable places in North Africa, this area was often traveled by SAS and LRDG soldiers traveling behind German lines to conduct warfare in rear areas.*

## October 14, 1942

The soldier on guard looked at his wristwatch. It read 5:30 a.m. *Where's my relief*, he wondered irritably.

The sun rose lazily over the dunes and the chill of night gave way to heat. The SAS camp began to stir, and the designated cook for the day lighted a fire for boiling water for their morning tea. He had to be cautious due to strict rations, and water was their most precious commodity in the desert. Depending how much they carried in supplies, each man sometimes received little more than a quart each day. Food consisted of burly beef and tinned biscuits, not a favorite among troops. On this planned trip however, Major Lawrence requested from the quartermaster a supply of ham and chocolate, which surprised the men and lifted their spirits.

Captain Hawkins awakened Jack Ruggero, who had made his bed beneath one of the three Chevrolet 30 cwt. lorries specially-fitted for long range desert operations. In fact, SAS requisitioned their vehicles from the LRDG, which had been equipped with these vehicle types at war's outbreak, using them to conduct vital reconnaissance operations against the enemy. The lorries were capable of traveling over 1,000 miles and carried supplies enough for up to three weeks in the desert. They proved highly reliable and were armed with Browning, Lewis, and Vickers machine guns mounted on special turrets.

Jack rolled over in his blanket and stared up at Hawkins. "What the hell do you want?" he asked, groggy with sleep.

"Time to get up, old man," Hawkins told him, cheerfully. "Don't want to waste daylight if we can help it, do we?"

Jack got out from under the lorry and looked at the slow-rising sun. "It's not even six yet," he declared, clearly irritated from having been awakened.

"Come along, Captain Ruggero," Major Lawrence said, walking up to him, "we officers must set a good example before the regulars."

"Yeah, what would they do without us role models," Jack replied with sarcasm laced in his tone. He picked up his blanket and shook the dust off. "Haven't you anything more to keep warm at night? I damn near froze last night."

Lawrence laughed. "You'll get used to it," he said, with a touch of humor. He motioned for Jack to follow him.

They walked over to the campfire where tea was being served. Jack looked around before turning to Major Lawrence. "Aren't you afraid Germans will spot this fire?"

"No worries, sir," the corporal said, intervening while squatting near the fire. "We're two days travel time from the front, and our lookout on guard will warn us if enemy planes approach." He handed Jack a tin cup.

Jack took the cup and sniffed its contents. "Good ole-fashioned tea, huh?"

Major Lawrence took a cup of tea for himself. "Even in time of war it's important we behave like civilized men," he joked.

Everyone nearby broke into laughter except for Jack. He stood stock-still with a blank expression, holding the cup, but not drinking it. He looked at Major Lawrence, who nodded as a way of encouraging him to try the tea. Jack nodded as if to say, "Okay," and took a small sip.

"Well?" Major Lawrence asked, curious.

Jack raised an eyebrow. "Not bad. But it's still not like a steaming cup of coffee."

"*ENEMY PLANES!*" shouted one of the men on guard duty.

The camp instantly burst alive and into action. Jack was shoved back under the vehicle he slept before he could spot the planes. Everyone took cover. Some manned the Lewis and Vickers machine guns, but no one fired. They stopped and held their breath, searching the skies. Jack also looked for planes, but saw nothing other than clear skies.

"There they are!" Major Lawrence shouted. He pointed west.

Jack squinted hard, failing to see any planes. A moment later he heard their engines, and a few seconds afterwards he spotted them. They were five CR-42 bi-planes, very fast and *very* German. Luftwaffe pilots flew them for desert reconnaissance and strafing convoys, and were quite successful with the tiny aircraft. Its undercarriage was fitted for carrying incendiary bombs and was armed with two 7.62 mm forward machine guns.

Jack had no idea how deadly those planes were, but Major Lawrence did. He had been spotted on an earlier mission by an unarmed Fieseler-Storch, its pilot then radioing their location. Half an hour later came the CR-42 planes, a full squadron. Major Lawrence lost three vehicles that day and learned an important lesson: planes against men on the ground stood a better chance of victory.

"How'd the *krauts* find us?" Jack shouted, puzzled.

The major kept his attention on the approaching planes. "If there's one thing I've learned in this war, it's to expect the unexpected," he replied, tersely.

Suddenly the CR-42s went into a dive, their engines screeching in a high-pitch. They were headed straight for the raiders' camp.

Lawrence looked on in full shock. *Damn, they've spotted us!*

"Anything else you learned you'd care to share?" Jack asked, bitterly as the planes were nearly on top of them.

Bright flashes lit up from the CR-42s as the pilots opened fire with their machine guns. Bullets sprayed the raiders' camp, kicking up dirt and sand everywhere, but missing the men and vehicles on their first pass.

Jack turned to face Major Lawrence. "We haven't a chance in hell!" he spat.

Two pilots were veteran Luftwaffe, haven flown combat missions since the Spanish Civil War when Hitler sent his Condor Legion to assist Spanish Dictator Franco in 1937. The experience was welcome to many and helped them immensely during the Battle of Britain in 1940. Back then they flew ME-109 fighters and racked up an impressionable twenty-five enemy planes shot down between them both. In the end, the Luftwaffe failed to defeat the British RAF and Hitler next chose to invade the Soviet Union in *Operation: Barbarossa,* thus depriving the Luftwaffe opportunity to redeem their damaged pride.

Being sent to Afrika was not their preference, however, they welcomed the chance to serve under Rommel, and before long their opinion of the

Desert War changed to something of national pride. Through Rommel's personal leadership, the German Army was on the verge of defeating the English, and they were proud to support Afrika Korps from the air.

This morning's flight was to have been routine, but when a Fieseler Storch reported a camp fire north of the Qattara Depression, they reasoned the *Phantom Major* had sent a group of raiders, *bandits* and *gangsters* they often called them, to have a go at another of their airfields. Thus, the CR-42 squadron was ordered to take action. Ordinarily, pilots preferred the far more effective Stuka Dive Bombers, but none were close enough to take immediate action.

"That fire must be them," Hauptmann Maximillian Kruger, commanding officer, said over the radio.

"Jawohl, Herr Hauptmann," Leutnant Gunther Kleist agreed.

"Rather careless of them," Kruger pointed out. "We'll make them pay for it now."

Kruger led the way, going into a steep dive, with Kleist and the other pilots following one after the other in tight formation. After switching off the safety to their forward-firing machine guns, each pilot let loose a 10-second burst of gunfire. Flying directly over the enemy ground force, Kruger cursed himself and his men for having missed the carefully concealed vehicles draped with desert netting.

"Damn!" Kruger shouted, more so to himself. "How could we miss their transports?" He quickly ordered his squadron to prepare for another run.

Major Lawrence and his men had no choice other than do what each knew had little chance for success. They could not outrun the planes in the open desert, and reasoned a gunfight to be their only opportunity for survival against the fast-moving CR-42s.

"OPEN FIRE!" the major ordered, shouting at the top of his lungs.

He set sights of his twin-barreled Lewis guns on the CR-42s as they banked for another run, and squeezed the trigger. His weapon spat out a blaze of orange fire, and the rat-a-tat-tat cacophony of his guns shook in his hands as he held his line of fire trained on the enemy planes. The rest of the raiders joined in with everything they had. Even those armed with MP-40 Schmeisser submachine guns joined in, although their weapons were ill-suited for defense against armed aircraft.

Jack Ruggero was the only man not firing back. He remained cowering under the Chevrolet lorry, praying for this madness to end quickly. He had no desire to join in on the fighting.

When the CR-42s opened fire a second time their aim was more precise. Their bullets tore into the vehicles, destroying precious equipment. The raiders dove out of harm's way right in time and avoided injury and death, but they still faced the threat of another strafing run.

Sergeant Davenport manning the .5 inch Browning machine gun looked for the major. Finding him he asked, "Do we make a run for it, sir?" It was plain from his tone he was convinced they should.

"Keep firing!" the major demanded. "Those planes can't have enough ammunition for a prolonged gunfight."

Hauptmann Kruger had argued having the CR-42s stripped of ordnance to a bare minimum so they might extend their cruising range was ill-advised. At best he could afford one more pass on the raiders before returning to base, but not before radioing request of a squadron of ME-109s to pick up the fight where they left off.

"We have two incendiary bombs each, Herr Hauptmann," Kleist reported. "Shall we prepare to use them?"

Kruger looked to his right and left, taking note of the damage the raiders inflicted on his plane. Bullets had torn through the thin sheet metal all over his wings and fuselage, and he was amazed over how nothing vital had been hit. He noted how he had difficulty controlling the ailerons and stabilizers, and was uncertain if he could make another run without seriously damaging his aircraft.

"Herr Hauptmann," Kleist called over the radio, "do we make a bombing run?"

Kruger paused, mulling their position. Finally, he scornfully said, "No. Each of you report damage to your planes."

Each pilot reported similar damage, and Kruger determined the squadron may be unable to return to base if they risked another run. He looked down below at the enemy camp, noting how they ceased firing.

*No wonder, we're out of range.* Kruger cursed himself. *We should have wiped out the gangsters on our first strafing run,* he told himself, with scorn.

"How soon before the ME-109s arrive?" Kruger asked, anxious.

"They have only now left base?" Kleist reported, disappointed over the loss of time.

Kruger checked his watch and fuel gauge. *Twenty minutes of flying time. Our fighters will need forty minutes to arrive at high speed. By that time the Britische will be gone.*

"Herr Hauptmann, what are your orders?" Kleist sounded desperate.

Kruger sighed. "We haven't the fuel to continue a sustained fight," he said, with regret. "Our planes are heavily damaged. We must return to base and leave them in care of our fighter pilots."

After a brief pause, Kleist replied, "Jawohl, Herr Hauptmann."

"Why aren't they coming?" Corporal Hemmings, who manned a 37mm Bofors gun, asked. He was certain he had direct hits on at least two planes, and his heart sank when none appeared to fall to an explosive end in the desert sands.

The Bofors gun was the most powerful anti-aircraft weapon in the raiders' arsenal, and more than capable of destroying enemy planes. For a few precious seconds his gun jammed, but Hemmings cleared it and was now ready to take on the CR-42s.

The raiders noted how the German biplanes circled their camp from safe distance, out of gunfire range. It was baffling. Jack was confused by the lull in the battle, too, and crawled out from under the lorry. Seeing Major Lawrence, he ran over to where he stood on his jeep, still manning the Lewis guns.

"What the hell's going on?" he demanded.

The major shook his head. "Either they're short on ammo or their planes got shot up bad enough so they can't afford risking another run," he surmised. He kept his eyes trained on the planes flying in tight formation.

"You can bet they've radioed our position," Captain Hawkins pointed out. "Their Stukas will be on us before we know it." He turned to the major and asked, "Shall we make a run for it, sir?"

Major Lawrence nodded. "Too bloody right we well," he replied quickly.

The raiders scrambled, breaking down camp equipment and throwing their supplies in their vehicles. They discarded whatever equipment they deemed irreparable. Lieutenant Wilson reported their radio had been destroyed. Everyone knew this was a big blow to them for now they would be unable to radio coordinates of the secret enemy base once found. Now the RAF could not be called in for a bombing run should the opportunity present itself. They would have to rely on their own capabilities to destroy the fuel depot. Although attacking German bases was their forte, Lawrence preferred having higher odds in their favor considering how so much depended on preventing the enemy from having a steady supply of petrol.

In a short while the men finished gathering supplies and boarded their vehicles. Despite a few scars on some, none had been knocked out of action.

*Thank God for that,* Lawrence prayed.

Their line of travel skirted the east side of the Qattara Depression and the German planes followed for about 15 minutes before being forced to break contact and return to their base. Once they were out of sight Major Lawrence ordered the raiders to turn northwest.

The going was rough and challenging. The Qattara Depression was believed to have once been a huge inland sea and considered impassable, or so the Germans believed. SAS and LRDG took advantage of their enemy's skepticism and travelled through this terrain on many missions. However, it was not without difficulties and at great cost.

Firstly, the Qattara Depression's bottom was soft and marshy, full of salt. The layer of crust was so thin it cracked when vehicles rolled over it, some sinking in its abyss, forcing crews to abandon their transports like men jumping off a sinking ocean liner. Then there were limestone cliffs hundreds of feet high, molded by wind and erosion into demon-like statues, making any traveler uncomfortable.

Rough-going terrain allowed vehicle average speeds no more than a few miles an hour, and day travel made situations worse for the sun mercilessly beat down on anyone bold enough to make the journey. Heat was so intolerable it became difficult even to speak. Engine fumes made men dizzy, generating strong headaches which made it a challenge to concentrate. Whenever a vehicle had engine trouble or a punctured tire, everyone groaned in despair, for any physical work during daytime sapped one's strength.

"Why in hell aren't we making this run at night?" Jack snapped angrily.

"Can't risk it, sir," Corporal Davis answered, coolly. "The *Kaneitra Crossing* is often travelled by the bloody Wogs. They see us, one can be certain they'll report it to Jerry."

Jack turned and faced him. "Why do you Limey's call them that?" he asked, curious.

"*Wogs,* you mean, sir?" The corporal shrugged. "Dunno. Someone thought it up and suppose the name stuck. It's common enough now we don't think twice about it." He turned and faced Jack. "Why do you Yanks call us Limey's, sir?"

Jack got the point and let it go at that. "What's so dangerous about our running into a tribe of Bedouin—I mean Wogs?"

The corporal shook his head. "You never can tell about them. They can be friend or foe, or both. They side with whoever they believe is winning. Right now winning this war isn't a given, sir. Germans are good fighting men and have able leaders. Rommel is probably the best either side has to offer. Each time we win a battle and take initiative he pulls off a counter-attack leaving our commanders standing in the wind with tails between legs. He's done such a job with fewer men and resources our troops have been sapped of morale."

Jack was impressed with the corporal's understanding of their situation against the Germans. "You talk as if you've already lost the war," he said, regarding him with keen interest."

Davis laughed. "No, sir," he retorted, adamantly. "We'll win this war in the end because *Der Fuhrer* can't supply his most famous general with enough supplies. He's tossing all his resources in Russia. With you Americans now in the fight it'll only be a matter of time before we wear down the Afrika Korps." The corporal laughed. "You'd have thought Hitler learned his lesson from the Great War."

"What lesson is that?" Jack inquired.

"Never fight an enemy on two fronts. It's impossible to win against those odds."

Jack shook his head and sighed exasperated.

"What's wrong, sir?"

Jack turned to face him, and then looked back to their front. "What you say makes me wonder."

"About what, sir?"

Jack paused. "You seem well informed about your position in this war." He paused again, thinking for a moment. "Let's say you're right, and it's only a matter of time before you wear down the Krauts. If you're right, why go to all the risk we're doing on this mission? Why not sit back and let the inevitable happen? If the war is a foregone conclusion as you put it, why take this risk?"

Corporal Davis looked at Jack, studying him while keeping an eye on his driving. "It's not that simple, sir."

"Isn't it?" Jack probed. "I mean, we could be risking our lives for nothing."

Corporal Davis returned his full attention to his driving. "We can't sit things out and allow events to happen as they come, sir," he answered, carefully. "It's up to us to control what we can. Sitting back and doing nothing invites trouble. That's how this war started. We sat back hoping no, praying—for *peace in our time.*"

Jack thought the corporal sounded as though he were preaching.

"Events don't take shape by themselves," Davis continued. "People create them. Hitler rose to power because no one wanted to take a stand against him. Sitting back and waiting for things to go our way is inviting defeat."

Jack suppressed a laugh. "You simply don't get it, do you?" he protested.

"How's that, sir?"

Jack turned his head to face him. "What you're doing is insane!" he argued. "We know Germany can't fight a sustained war. This entire mission isn't worth the risk, but we're doing it anyway because men like your Major Lawrence want to tell their children stories about what they did during the war in hopes kids will grow up wanting to follow in his footsteps." He laughed bitterly. "We're working to breed a future of warriors instead of peacemakers."

Corporal Davis stared at Jack, not knowing what to make of him. "Excuse me for saying, sir," he began, choosing careful words, "but you don't talk like any officer I've met. In fact, you don't talk like a soldier."

Jack flashed a crooked smile. "Oh, I'm an officer all right, corporal, "but I ain't a fighting soldier. I've got me a life to return to when this chaos is over, and I'm not about to throw it away for medals that'll eventually end up gathering dust in a closet. I even have a number of women I plan to court when I get back home. If you boys want to die for a cause, be my guest. Don't expect Jack Ruggero to follow you to glory, though. You can bet your Limey-ass I'm going to survive this war."

Corporal Davis stared intently at Jack, turning his head to face direction of his driving back and forth in order to maintain control. "You know something, sir," he began, sourly; "I believe you will survive this war." He practically hissed the words with distaste.

*CRACK!*

The Jolting snap was followed by a loud hissing of air from the right front tire of the vehicle. The caravan of raiders came to a halt and everyone except the men manning the anti-aircraft guns disembarked. Major Lawrence was first to reach the lorry.

"Tire puncture," he said, wearily. "That's all we need this time of day."

Jack breathed heavily. "Do we camp here while we fix it?" he asked, hopeful.

"No," Major Lawrence replied. "We fix it and move on."

"In this heat?" Jack challenged.

The men slowly went about getting the equipment required to replace the flat tire, taking care not to over-exert themselves and fall victim to heat exhaustion. Jack removed the Arab headdress he wore same as the raiders, wiping the perspiration off his face with it. At first he declined wearing the headpiece, but quickly recognized its practicality for shielding head and back from the hard-hitting sun.

"What do you think you're doing?" Captain Hawkins demanded.

Jack looked to his right and left before realizing the captain was speaking to him. "Wetting my headdress," Jack answered, dipping it in a tin of water.

"Don't do that," the captain ordered. "The cloth will steam and burn your scalp."

But Jack had already done so and put back on the headdress.

A short time later everyone took turns drinking water rations. They experienced difficulty standing straight due to excess heat sapping their strength. Their eyes strained in the bright sunlight and they constantly wiped their forehead to keep beads of sweat from stinging their eyes. Jack proved little help, sitting in the lorry, trying to keep his mind off the unbearable heat. It mattered little to the raiders, for they had not expected much of him seeing how he wasn't a member of SAS. They recognized the Yank for not being in the mold of a soldier, and this was fine with them because they knew heroes had tendency to get themselves and others killed. Corporal Davis, however, took a moment to mention to Major Lawrence his interesting conversation with Jack, and during this lull in their journey, the major took time to have words with him.

Major Lawrence walked over to Jack, handing him a tin of water. "Drink this slow," he said, in a sharp tone. "In this heat you'll cough it up otherwise."

Jack took the tin cup and drank its contents in one fast gulp regardless.

The major shook his head like a teacher keeping patient with an unruly school child. "I believe I have a pretty good idea about you," he confessed.

Jack raised an eyebrow. "How so?" He really was not interested, but felt obligated to ask.

Major Lawrence nodded. "You're what we call a, *man of opportunity*," he explained, sounding certain. "You're about personal gain. Patriotism is allowing others to do your fighting, and you don't lose a moment's sleep over it." He recognized the bewilderment on Jack's face. "I know a lot of Americans," he continued. "Most are good men and women. Don't get me wrong. We have similar types in our army, too. Fact is, when you come right down to it, people are the same everywhere. After all, what sensible person wants to fight a bloody war?"

Jack wiped the sweat from his brow with his sleeve. He adjusted his Arab headdress for a better fit and turned his attention back to the major. "What are you getting at?" he grunted.

Major Lawrence looked down at the ground, and then lifted his eyes back to Jack. "Cut the naïveté act," he demanded. "You know bloody well what I'm talking about."

Jack snorted. "That so?"

"Yes. I mentioned how you're a man of opportunity, and yet you fail to see the importance of what you're involved in right now." He saw how Jack looked on confused and further explained. "Do you not realize our importance in this war? Hitler is this close to winning." He emphasized his point by bringing his thumb and forefinger together. "In less than six months he accomplished what Kaiser Wilhelm failed in four years. Right now he's the most powerful man in Europe. Even now, Russia is close to folding due to a lack of war materials."

"So you admit you're fighting a lost cause?" Jack cut in.

Major Lawrence was not deterred. He shook his head, dismayed over Jack's point of view. "It's only a lost cause if we give up," he shot back, keeping his temper in check. With his foot, he drew a line in the sand. "On this side are the Germans, on this side our boys. Their plan is to seize Cairo, and with it the Suez Canal, our only link to our forces in the east. From there they move into Arabia, up the Caucasus and link with their forces here in Russia." He made an indentation in the sand indicating Russia's location on his hastily made sand-map. "If they manage this, they control all oil fields in the Middle East, and win the war."

Jack followed the major's words and descriptions of how events might possibly develop closely. It was the first time he appeared to take things serious so far as Lawrence was concerned.

"We are all that is left standing in Rommel's way of winning this war," Major Lawrence concluded with passion and determination.

Jack nodded, acquiescingly. "What do you want from me?"

Major Lawrence believed Jack already knew, but told him anyway. "Keep your personal feelings in check," he warned. "Your points of view are detrimental to our mission, morale, and profession." He started to walk away. Before walking out of earshot, he turned and added, "Besides, I wouldn't want one of my men to take your words personal. Might lead them to fail and watch your back when you need them most."

Jack believed him.

# Chapter 20

*SAS proved troublesome enough to the German Army in Afrika that Rommel wrote in his diary how this small unit created more damage to the Afrika Korps than any other unit of equal and greater strength. Ironically, British General Bernard Montgomery and other high-ranking Allied officers formerly complained how smaller clandestine combat units like SAS received more medals for bravery in the field than regular army troops.*

## October 16, 1942
## German Desert Base *'Lili Marlene'*

Stuka pilots Sturmbannfuhrer Wolfgang Klement and Hauptmann Konrad Diestl landed their planes side by side simultaneous on the airstrip and parked their borrowed ME-109 fighters on the end of the runway. Hauptmann Maximillian Kruger and Leutnant Gunther Kleist greeted them.

"Any sign of them, Herr Sturmbannfuhrer?" Kruger asked, anxiously.

Klement climbed out of the cockpit and hopped to the ground. "No," he replied, disappointed in their misfortune. He returned Kruger's salute half-heartedly. "Are you certain what you saw, a patrol belonging to that *Phantom Major?*"

"Jawohl, Herr Sturmbannfuhrer. Our squadron made a strafing run on them, but they got away, driving us off with heavy anti-aircraft fire."

Klement shook his head. "We found nothing," he said, hoarsely. "No tracks, no vehicles, no sign of life. If what you say is true they may be traveling south and avoid the Qattara Depression. Only a fool would dare attempt crossing that hell-hole."

"We must assume they will do precisely that, Herr Sturmbannfuhrer," Kruger protested. "It's all too obvious he is searching for this base and if he manages to locate it, they'll turn it into a fiery quagmire."

"No, Kruger, you are wrong!" Klement bellowed. "It is too dangerous to cross the Qattara. The Phantom Major would never dare venture through there. Even so, this base remains on full alert until the field marshal orders a stand down." He paused before adding, "And he will not issue that order until after he has made his push into Alexandria."

"But, Herr Sturmbannfuhrer, those English criminals *have* travelled across the—"

"Drop the matter, Kruger! You have wasted enough of our time."

Klement stormed off with Diestl in tow, leaving Kruger fuming.

"Why do our superiors insist on underestimating our enemy despite them haven proven they can pull off the impossible time and again," he grumbled in a low tone to Kleist. "I'm convinced that group of soldiers we attacked are making way to this base." He paused long enough to wipe beads of sweat from his brow. "Perhaps I should go directly to the field marshal on this matter."

Kleist stiffened. "No, Herr Hauptmann. Such action will make things worse for you."

Kruger was not one to break rank, but on this occasion he was tempted. Uncertain what he should do, he led Kleist to the field tent for a meal.

In the HQ tent Freiherr von Mellenthin attended conference with the base commander and his staff. Also present was the Libyan Desert chieftain, El Karum, along with two tribal advisors. They went to great lengths to assure their guests' comfort. Delicious foods and sweets laid on a table as well as fine wine. The meeting had gone well and von Mellenthin was certain El Karum would provide full support with local tribes. In fact, the Germans' manner of speech insinuated their belief victory would be theirs soon enough. During a lull in the meeting El Karum turned in his chair to face von Mellenthin.

"Tell me, Major," he said, in a low, soft tone so as not to arouse attention from others, "what makes you certain you will defeat the English by end of month?" Before von Mellenthin answered, El Karum added, "I ask this question because the desert has been handed over from one side to the other on numerous occasions. Neither side has managed to maintain victory long enough for a permanent celebration."

Von Mellenthin leaned back in his seat and thought carefully. The frankness of El Karum's question impressed him. Then again, everything about the Arab impressed others. Unlike images Europeans had of Bedouin tribesmen, El Karum proved opposite those images. Standing nearly 6'-2" with a lean frame covered in long, splendid colorful robes, he carried himself in a well-mannered behavior and with confidence displayed by a victorious leader. His head was adorned with familiar headdress local men wore, and he had a handsome face, emphasized by dark brown piercing eyes. To their astonishment, he spoke fluent German and English!

Von Mellenthin made a mental note to ask where he received his education, curious how a nomad could be so intelligent. For now he contented himself with answering the Arab's inquiry.

"The Britische have proven over their long history they have a strong will to endure hardship so that they may achieve their goals," he said, speaking like he was talking to a man in similar standing with high-class German folk. "Their weakness," he continued, "has always been over-confidence. One might say we Germans suffer that same quality, but our failure to win the Great War and the embarrassing Treaty of Versailles which choked the Fatherland of its dignity taught us something."

El Karum recognized the need for von Mellenthin's pause and asked, "And this is?"

"To be victorious one must claim victory or death," von Mellenthin stated, with the firmness of a true believer. "Victory must be total, not simply in the desert, but across the globe."

El Karum flashed a slight smile. "We are not naïve as Europeans may believe," he began, carefully and coolly. "Your Fatherland failed to defeat the English over their skies and is now engaged in heavy fighting in Russia. Global domination, I'm certain you are learning, is easier said than achieved." He saw von Mellenthin stiffen along with nearby officers overhearing them. "However, that is irrelevant," he continued. "So long as Berlin recognizes us to be an *independent* kingdom at war's end, not a German protectorate, our alliance remains firm." He stared at von Mellenthin, silently waiting for his response.

The German aristocrat did not expect such a blunt statement, especially from a Bedouin. Unlike average Nazis who had habit of speaking in riddles, von Mellenthin had been highly educated and blessed with having common sense and knowing when to use it. He knew well and good Berlin had no intention of allowing an Arab state to flourish. Afrika was not a priority so far as Hitler was concerned, and once the tribes served their purpose, El Karum would likely be setup to lead a puppet regime, nothing more.

However, this educated Bedouin sitting beside him pointed out he knew well and good what his superiors had in mind once the war was over. Von Mellenthin was fully aware he needed to be careful in how he answered El Karum. The last thing he wanted was to jeopardize their delicate relationship. Like the Britische, the Germans knew how desert tribes were one moment friend, the next your foe.

"I assure you," he started, warmly, "my superiors in Berlin do not desire a confrontation with your people. Our agreement will be honored at war's end."

Realizing he could expect no more of an assurance, El Karum raised his glass of wine, something many Bedouins refrained drinking for religious reasons, and toasted gratitude to his German ally. Von Mellenthin tapped his glass with El Karum's, all the while curious how he could have underestimated this young Arab.

"Where did you receive your education?" von Mellenthin blurted. It was a question out of curiosity rather than arrogance.

El Karum wondered when someone might ask, and flashed a mischievous grin. "I am the scion of powerful desert chieftains," he replied, proudly. "I studied in Damascus and learned much about European politics before travelling to Europe where I learned to speak your languages, but my major was economics."

"Economics!" von Mellenthin exclaimed, raising an eyebrow. "That should come handy when you take over head of government in Libya, yes?"

"Yes," El Karum answered, nodding thrice. What he did not include in his background was his skill as a Bedouin warrior. His father and uncles were skilled in horseback riding, sword fighting, and rifle sharpshooting, and were more than pleased passing on their attributes to the next leader of their tribes.

Von Mellenthin drank from his glass and became convinced they were fortunate having the Bedouin on their side. *Too bad Berlin has other plans for North Afrika,* he told himself.

# Qattara Depression
# October 16, 1942

*Another tire puncture!* It was the third time this same afternoon and Major Lawrence cursed their misfortune. The strain was unbearable for the raiders and the only thing they had to look forward to was the time passed

3:00 o'clock, which meant the hottest part of day was behind them. Cooler temperatures allowed them to regain senses.

To everyone's surprise, Jack Ruggero pitched in and helped replace the punctured tire. "I never knew it could be this hot any place on earth," he complained, whilst unscrewing bolts on the rim.

"Being so far below sea level doesn't help much," Corporal Hemmings added. He assisted Jack, eager to complete the job so they could get moving again. "The heat sits in the valley with no wind to push it along, making air stale and difficult to breathe." Hemmings choked the words out, making a sour face. "I've been through this route four times now and believe me when I tell you it doesn't get any better."

Jack managed to pull the tire off the rim. "Thanks for the input," he said, with sincerity.

Major Lawrence stood nearby viewing a map sprawled on top of a jeep's hood. Captain Guinness joined him. "In half an hour's time we should be on the move," the major said with certainty. "Rough terrain isn't going to be any better for some time."

Guinness smiled. "We'll manage, sir," he said, confidently.

Twenty-four hours later the raiders drove within thirty miles of the desert flats. Due to numerous tire punctures they suffered, Major Lawrence decided they bivouac the night in the Kaneitra Crossing. However, they managed little sleep for the desert seemed to come to life with the sound of Bedouins travelling nearby. Guards were posted on rotating shifts and remained alert. The next morning the raiders drove fifty miles, making good time on the desert flats. With nothing between them and the Germans other than hard sand, Major Lawrence ordered all drivers to punch the accelerators full speed and they drove over terrain more than 96 kilometers per hour (60 mph). This part of desert was barren for as far the eye saw with nothing but hard sand everywhere, which made for smooth traveling.

After remaining silent most of the duration on this part of their journey, Jack turned to Corporal Hemmings. "When do we stop?" he asked, agitated. "We've been on the move for hours!"

"In 'bout another ten miles, sir," the corporal replied, not taking his eyes off his direction of travel, "when we reach the *Bir*."

Jack made a face. "What in hell's a *Bir*?"

Hemmings glanced at Jack, forgetting he was new to North Africa. "Means a well, sir, or one might call it a watering hole."

"Thank God for that!" Jack said, relieved. "I can do with a wash."

Hemmings managed a sly grin.

Major Lawrence sat in the lead jeep and signaled the caravan to slow before coming to a halt. He stepped out of the vehicle and lifted a pair of Zeiss long-range glasses to his eyes. Black smoke billowed in the distance.

*Five miles away,* he reasoned. "What do you think?" he asked, addressing Lieutenant Roberts, who walked up beside him.

Roberts was a tall lanky man, reed-thin with a head adorned with thick, wavy black hair. His ears stood out and the men jokingly called him *Dumbo* behind his back. His average looks belied his capabilities as a soldier, for since his arrival in North Africa in 1940 he had proven himself on the battlefield time and again. The men respected him, and Lawrence was glad to have him on this trip.

"That type smoke can only be made from burning petrol, sir," he replied, looking through his own pair of Zeiss glasses. "Must be a Jerry patrol. None of our blokes are in this area other than us."

"No," Lawrence agreed. He paused, contemplating their next move. "Whatever happened took place at the Bir. We'll proceed with caution, stop a few kilometers away and approach on foot for closer inspection."

That said, the raiders pushed on toward their destination at a reduced speed of 30 km per hour. Everyone remained alert. When the caravan halted, Major Lawrence observed the scene through his glasses.

*Nothing.*

He still did not like it. Using hand signals, Lawrence, Jack Ruggero, and five raiders disembarked their vehicles and stealthily approached the Bir.

*What the hell does he expect me to do?* Jack wondered.

Low-crawling was a form of training all armies utilized. It consisted of soldiers lying on their belly and crawling their way forward, rifles cradled in their arms. The tactic was designed to keep one's self from being seen by the enemy you approached, and then springing to action, weapon in hand.

When Lawrence peered over a ridge near the Bir, he saw several disfigured shapes of smashed vehicles.

*British vehicles!*

Scanning the area, he saw nothing and ordered his men to rise and move forward.

They approached the scene and smelled burnt flesh and metal combined with petrol. This caused them to make a distasteful expression and cover their noses with handkerchiefs. Even so the arid stench of death filled their nostrils causing some to fight off the need to vomit.

Jack had seen this before, *but where?* he wondered. *Oh, yes, it was in Tobruk!* Somehow it seemed ages ago.

Major Lawrence noted the vehicles were same fitted for SAS. Jeeps, lorries and equipment were strewn everywhere. Bodies laid in grotesque positions, some split wide open in their mid-section. Flies buzzed angrily over them.

*They don't refer to them as the scourge of the desert for nothing,* Major Lawrence told himself.

Other bodies were riddled with bullets, leaving their shirts soaked in dark crimson stain. He approached one of the dead and rolled him over on his back, fearful he may recognize him. To his relief he did not.

Jack did the same with one of the other dead. The man's face was badly mauled. On his uniform was a patch he did not recognize. It was a circular patch with the figure of a Scorpion in its center. Directly beneath the patch were the letters LRDG.

"It's *Long Range Desert Group,*" Lawrence told him, flatly. He approached Jack from behind, looking at the patch.

"What on earth were they doing here?" an astonished raider asked.

Major Lawrence wished he knew. "Looks like they were bagged by enemy aircraft," he surmised.

He determined this by the fact that none of the equipment had been carted off by the enemy. After a surprise attack like this, it was common enough to gather as many useful weapons and equipment available.

"The Wogs haven't been here," another raider noted. "Otherwise they would've been stripped clean of boots, clothes, and watches."

This was true. Local tribes stumbling on such a scene made use of anything found. This did not necessarily make them scavengers for they regarded the desert as their home, and foreigners had come here uninvited. Thus goes the spoils of war, however they might be obtained.

Jack inhaled slowly to keep the awful stench from causing him to vomit. "Damn! I've never smelled anything so bad," he exclaimed. He mumbled through a handkerchief covering his mouth and nose.

Sergeant Davenport approached the major and asked, "Shall we arrange a burial detail, sir?"

Lawrence shook his head. "No," he answered, emphatically. "There's no time. Jerry may have ordered a ground patrol to this location and I want to be far away from here before that happens." Then he ordered, "Fill the Jerricans and vehicles with water and let's get a move on." He looked at the

LRDG dead. "Poor chaps," he solemnly added. "We'll stop for the night closer to our objective, far away from here."

Lawrence and Captain Hawkins took time to review their maps, discussing the route from the debriefing notes Jack provided. "How well can we rely on this Yank's report?" Hawkins asked, dubious.

Lawrence shrugged. "From reports made by LRDG and Bedouin tribes, not to forget aerial recces, I'd say they're reliable." He spread the map on the hood of a jeep, placing his Zeiss glasses and revolver on two corners to keep it from blowing away due to a slight breeze. "I still don't know how he could have single-handedly made it through the desert," he confessed.

"He didn't," Hawkins reminded him. "He said he came across a group of friendly Wogs who agreed to take him to our lines in exchange for rifles and cash. They only believed him because they'd never seen a Yank before, but knew there was talk of America joining the war on our side. They never crossed the Qattara Depression like we did, but went around it instead."

"That was wise of them," Lawrence noted. "If we weren't pressed for time, I'd have done same." He studied the map closely, reviewing areas marked as haven been scouted by LRDG and SAS. "This area here is our best bet," he said, pointing to a location on the map's center. "We have no reports this area has been scouted."

Hawkins appeared skeptical. "How in hell can they transport enough petrol from a base this far south in the desert to their tanks in the north," he challenged. "It makes no sense."

Lawrence did not agree. "Their Junkers-52 transports can ship the petrol from here to the front right before battle to fuel them," he replied, self-assuredly. "As of now, neither we nor Jerry have air superiority, so it's worth the risk."

Hawkins looked over his shoulder at Jack, who was helping filling cans with water. "I don't like him," he said, disdainfully. "He's not the sort we can trust."

Lawrence sighed. "We need him to identify the base. There could be areas out here he recognizes which might help us locate it, so it's necessary for him to participate on this trip."

Hawkins nodded. "I understand, sir. But I still don't like him."

Jack carried Jerrican after Jerrican to the vehicles, recalling how odd he thought the British adopted something made by Germans over their own design. He remembered the British chastising the Englishman who made their own flimsy water cans standard army issue. They fell apart and leaked easily. But when they captured a group of Germans and their equipment and saw how much better designed their water and petrol cans were, they adopted it on the spot.

*So much for enemy ingenuity,* Jack thought.

Major Lawrence called Jack over to his jeep. "Need you to have a look at the map," he told Jack. It was not a request, but an order.

Jack shrugged. "Okay."

The major used a pencil to denote their position and line of travel. "We're here," he said point of fact. "This entire area is some of the most desolate terrain in all of Africa." He moved his hand over the map denoting the area in question. "There are hills, ravines, sand dunes, and no water. Somewhere in this area here is where we believe you stumbled upon the fuel depot."

"I can't be sure," Jack interrupted.

"What do you mean?" Captain Hawkins demanded. His face flushed red with anger.

"I didn't have the privilege of utilizing a map during my escape," Jack explained.

"We know," Lawrence cut in. "Still, based on your report, this is the area Jerry must be."

"If that's the case, then why go to all this trouble?" Jack blurted. "Why not send your RAF to locate the base and bomb it?" He stood with his hands resting on his sides in a commanding position.

Lawrence looked at Hawkins, who shrugged as if to say, Why not? "I suppose there's no use keeping it secret any longer," he reasoned.

"What do you mean?" Jack asked. His brow furrowed from curiosity.

"We have no air superiority this far south," he started, carefully choosing his words. "It'd be too difficult for them to travel this far undetected. Enemy fighters would intercept them before they got halfway to target."

He sensed they were hiding something more. "What's the real reason?" he demanded.

Lawrence nodded for Hawkins to explain.

"GHQ wants us to locate the base and determine if there's a possibility for us to take control without destroying the petrol," the captain explained. "You see, we're planning an offensive of our own, and if there's any chance of our requisitioning the petrol for our own tanks, then we must simply look into it."

Jack was flabbergasted. "A base that size with hundreds of Germans? I know you guys believe you're super humans and all that, but I can't see a battalion of enemy troops surrendering to a group of British soldiers numbering less than twenty."

"Twenty-five," Lawrence corrected.

Jack laughed. "That base is too big to be overtaken by a force this size."

"You're probably right," Lawrence agreed. "In fact, I'm betting on it. The only reason why we're assessing if we can take it without destroying the petrol is because we're under orders to do so. In the end, it's my decision and I'm betting we'll be forced to blow up the entire base."

Jack shook his head, knowing they were in for the fight of his life. "Okay, so what do you want from me?" he asked, acquiescing to his situation.

"Is there any place on this map that indicates something familiar to you?" Lawrence asked, almost pleading.

"How many times must I explain?" Jack pleaded. "I didn't have maps during my escape."

"How about land markers?" Hawkins added. "Have you noticed anything remotely familiar about the territory we've traveled?"

"You must be joking? I was half out of my mind during my escape. I don't even remember the faces of the Bedouin tribesmen who found me."

Lawrence was satisfied as much as one could be. He folded up the map and ordered everyone to get ready to move; convinced they were on the right track despite Jack's lack of help.

They made good travel time on the desert plain for the next ten miles. Major Lawrence led the caravan in his jeep, and ordered the others to follow in single file. Private Brown, a tall, skinny red-headed man in his early twenties, sat in back of a Chevrolet lorry on a box of explosives and timing-pencils. Lieutenant Wilson drove their vehicle in the middle of the caravan when Brown heard it. A loud hissing sound generated directly beneath him. He needed no time guessing what it was for it was a sound he had grown well-accustomed with.

"*Blimey! A fuse has been lit!*" he screamed.

Wilson looked over his shoulder and saw Brown rising to leap out of the lorry.

Jack sat in the jeep directly behind them with Hemmings at the wheel. He thought it odd for the soldier to stand so carelessly in the lorry ahead of them and look as though he were going to jump clear while they travelled more than 48 km per hour. "What in hell does he think he's doing?" he asked, dumbfounded by the scene.

Suddenly a blinding flash appeared to their front, followed up an instant later by a tremendous explosion. The lorry had disintegrated!

Corporal Hemmings lost control of his vehicle and it overturned, rolling violently over and over. Jack was thrown clear. Other vehicles in the caravan were rocked by the force of the blast, and some men fell out, tumbling over rocks and sand.

Major Lawrence's lead jeep remained steady and he brought it to a halt, looking over his shoulder to see what happened. He knew from experience this was not an enemy attack, but an explosion from one of their vehicles.

*Not again!* he swore.

Men laid everywhere, some injured, some dead, and all of the vehicles were inflicted some type of damage from the explosion dispensing shrapnel. Equipment had fallen out of their vehicles, but nothing the raiders could not collect. Major Lawrence ordered those in fair enough condition to help the wounded.

"What the hell happened?" Jack asked, stumbling toward the major. "The truck in front of us just blew up!"

"Most likely one of the fuses accidently lit and set off a box of charges," Lawrence explained, shaking his head. "It's happened before."

"It's happened before?" Jack spat back, incredulous. "Why in hell would we be travelling with such junk if you knew it could blow us all to Kingdom-come?"

"That's enough of that," Lawrence said, calmly. He knew best to keep a cool head during a time like this. "We'll be on the move once we've gathered our equipment and bury our dead."

Jack remained clearly astounded and found it difficult to stand without swaying. Never in his wildest dreams had he witnessed such a debacle. Somehow, he knew in the coming days and nights he would likely see worse.

# Chapter 21

*With morale at an all-time low throughout British Army ranks, the need to bring the Desert War to swift end was all-important. Rommel proved time and again he possessed superior tactics and leadership on the battlefield. However, his inability to receive a steady stream of supplies convinced British HQ he could be defeated by depriving him of petrol for his panzers. Thus, SAS had responsibility of locating and destroying as much of Rommel's store of supplies as possible. Failure meant certain defeat.*

## October 16, 1942

Dusk cast a magnificent ray of orange light across the desert in one of the most picturesque scenes imagined. Every rock cast an eerie shadow when the sun continued its fall from the sky. Mountains to the west seemed to loom menacingly and then disappeared when the sun dropped from sight. But this was not the time to admire scenery.

Major Lawrence had ordered a halt an hour earlier to get away from the wreckage creating a stream of black, billowing smoke, thus giving away their location. If the Stukas investigated he wanted to be as far away from there as possible. When he took inventory over the accidental explosion which ripped his men apart, the news was not good. Eleven dead, two lorries and two jeeps out of action, nearly half his vehicle force. Some men suffered shock from the ordeal, and he knew it could be days before they recovered. All this added up to the major being in no happy mood.

Jack approached him. His left arm was bandaged from elbow to wrist. "Looks like we're dead in the water," he said, wearily. "Your force has been cut in half." He looked back from which they travelled. "We've got no radio either, so we have no way of getting help."

"We are still mobile and have the element of surprise on our side," Lawrence told him. The last thing he wanted to hear was defeatist talk.

"We can still push on, sir," Captain Guinness cut in quickly. He saw the Yank talking to the major and figured he might be hinting about returning to Kabrit, so he made it a point to encourage his CO to press on with the mission. "After all," he continued, "we've been in tighter spots than this."

Major Lawrence looked across the desert as if searching for something, and nodded slowly. "We have to press on no matter what the cost," he said, in a monotone which Guinness had never heard him speak. "Today is the Sixteenth. In seven days' time, Monty will be ready to attack Rommel and push him out of Egypt for good!" He paused for effect. "This secret base we're searching for is Rommel's only chance of supplying his tanks with enough petrol needed for a counter-attack. If we fail to destroy it…. the War in North Africa could be lost for good."

Jack stepped in front of the major so their eyes met. "How do you expect to accomplish that with less than half of what you began with?"

Major Lawrence ignored the question and motioned for Jack and Guinness to follow him to his jeep where a map of the desert laid on its hood. He marked the way they travelled from Kabrit to where they presently were with a pencil, and drew a line further south on the map, through a mountain range and to an open area he circled.

"My calculations indicate this is where the base is located," he said, tapping on the circle with the tip of the pencil.

Jack and Guinness leaned on the hood for a closer look. "How do you figure that?" Jack was as dubious as he sounded. "Since we started this joyride I haven't recognized a single sand dune, mountain, or rock, and I'm the guy you're relying on to find it."

Major Lawrence sighed like an exhausted teacher having to repeat himself to a student. "Your report coincides with reliable sources and our direction is based on theory where a base this sort would be strategically located to remain hidden."

"And how in hell are the Germans going to transport all that petrol to the front when they're this deep in the desert?" Jack was getting angry now. The heat and time in the desert was getting to him.

"Air lift," Guinness told him. "When Rommel makes his drive into Egypt he'll have his planes transport the petrol closer to the front for his tanks. That's why destroying those planes on this base is equally important as the petrol itself."

Still, Jack refused to believe he was needed on this mission. "I have no idea where this base is and I'm not SAS! Why in hell am I here?"

"There are things you saw which will prove helpful once we locate it," Major Lawrence answered, with patience. He witnessed this sort of delirium before, and knew it best to keep calm. *It's not his fault he's suffering in this heat,* he told himself. "The Germans have set up phony bases to throw us off before on similar missions. You're our insurance that won't happen."

Jack refused to back down. So far as he was concerned, the mission should be scrubbed. He knew the British were stubborn, but he persisted arguing. He took a deep breath to calm his nerves, but it was no use. He nearly trembled each time he spoke, and his body was drenched in perspiration so much that Lawrence and Guinness became worried. They took him by an arm each and sat him in the shade by one of the vehicles. Lawrence gave him a drink of water from a canteen.

"Drink slow," he warned. "You take this fast and you might pass out."

But Jack gulped down the water, forcing the major to withdraw the canteen. "How many men do you suppose are at this base?" Jack queried.

Lawrence shrugged. "I'd say three or four hundred men."

Jack laughed. "What the hell can a group fourteen strong do against a base fully staffed?" he bellowed. His laughter sounded like that of a madman.

Lawrence grinned. "Oh, you'd be surprised," he said, brimming with confidence.

"The fact is we are pushing on and that's the end of that," Guinness said, flatly. He wanted no further challenging on this point. "You're part of this team and will help us locate this base and destroy it." Guinness could not recall a time he spoke more sternly.

Lawrence placed a hand on Jack's shoulder. "Listen, Jack," he began, in a calm tone, "I understand how you feel about the army and the war. I thought for a moment back there I made you understand what this is all about, but I know now you don't." He paused, drawing a breath and wiping the sweat from his brow. "I'm growing tired of explaining things to you. Like it or not, *you* are an officer. You are expected to perform your duty and not jeopardize our mission in any way. We're going to locate this base and destroy it, and you're going to help us." He paused, glancing at Guinness, who supported his choice of words wholeheartedly. "This is the last time I expect to discuss this matter with you."

Before Jack could respond he passed out.

Lawrence used jeeps on runway attacks against enemy planes before, a tactic created by SAS founder, David Stirling. However, with only fourteen men, three jeeps, and two lorries at his current disposal his odds of completing this mission were not good. He concluded they had supplies enough for fourteen days, more than enough to keep them in the field. But the trick was how they were going to use what they had in the most efficient way. Travelling under pressure was something Lawrence was accustomed to, but to have suffered such a beating before going into action was something he had not accounted for. Thus, he decided they should locate the base first and only then determine how to best utilize his men and equipment.

By the time they reached the base of mountains everyone was exhausted. Not much conversation took place between anyone. The loss of so many men had a lasting effect on each man. SAS was a unit small enough for everyone to know each other quite well, and it was not uncommon for them to develop brotherly affection. To date it was the worst incident Lawrence suffered before having a go against the enemy. He had lost men in battle, but never by accident and before they reached their target.

In spite precautionary measures like posting guard duty, Lawrence gave permission to have dinner cooked by fire. Bully beef and biscuits were their rations, and were loathed by all men in the British Army. The heat of day had drained their appetite to the point it mattered little, but they ate their rations knowing they needed to maintain strength. After each man finished their meal they laid in their makeshift beds beneath or beside vehicles.

Jack sat on his blanket by the jeep looking up at the stars. *Magnificent!*

They shined so brightly in the desert. He glanced at the others bedding down for the evening and saw by their expressions their thoughts were miles away. He shook his head.

*What a waste,* he thought. *I can't believe I'm here! After all I've done to keep out of this war, only to find myself shanghaied and in the middle of the desert to fight the Krauts!*

"Are you all right?" It was Major Lawrence. He approached Jack unnoticed.

Jack turned his head quickly to see the major looking at him. "Geez, you always creep up on people like that?" he said, surprised.

Lawrence grinned. "Sorry about that. Force of habit, I suppose." Then he offered, "In our business silence is golden."

Jack rose to his feet. "My business is staying alive," he explained, curt and point of fact.

"So is ours," Lawrence replied quickly. "That's why we've learned to fight better than the enemy."

Jack nodded reluctantly. *Man has a point.*

Lawrence started walking away before stopping to say, "Oh, I almost forgot," he began, suavely; "your role has been changed to full-time status."

Jack stiffened. "What do you mean?" He looked fearful of the answer.

"It means I have to count on you to do more than simply identify the base," Lawrence explained. "In this outfit every man has a purpose. When one of us is killed or transferred out, the burden falls on the shoulders of those left standing." That said, he turned and walked away. He did not look to see Jack's expression, but was certain the man was wondering how far he would push him into being a fighting soldier.

# Chapter 22

*'Who Dares Wins' is SAS's motto. It represents their determination to do all necessary to defeat the enemy. They sometimes jokingly cry, "Who cares wins," but only members of the special unit dare speak that aloud.*

## October 17, 1942

When dawn broke the sudden wind howling across the desert awakened everyone. Major Lawrence shot upright like a lightning bolt. He looked north and saw the great cloud of dust fast approaching the mountains. The men sprang into action, everyone except Jack, who continued sleeping peacefully.

Lawrence kicked him in the rear. "Get off your behind!"

"What the hell!" Jack cried.

He needed no explanation upon seeing the giant sandstorm coming their way. That gruesome sight was all the encouragement he needed to help do what needed to be done.

Lawrence hoped to be quick enough to make a run around the mountains and escape the storm, but soon realized it was too late. Instead the men pulled canvas over each vehicle and secured them to the ground with stakes. They had no choice other than sit out the storm. Once finished securing their canvases each took refuge beneath the vehicles.

Jack took refuge beneath his jeep, lying beside Lawrence. "What kind of storm is that?" he asked, at last.

*"Khamsin,"* Lawrence replied, evenly. "It's Arabic for *hot wind."*

Lawrence and his raiders had been through enough of these before to know what to expect. *Khamsin* sandstorms were created by hot winds in the desert and raised temperatures by nearly forty degrees. Winds raged up to 100 miles per hour and were strong enough to overturn lorries and carry off any man unlucky enough not to be holding onto something secure. Visibility soon disappeared, and the fine desert sand found its way into every nook, cranny, and crevice. Your nostrils clogged with dust, making breathing extremely difficult. Your eyes swelled from soreness, and the quick change in temperature practically fried your brain.

When the sandstorm struck, its force pushed itself up hard against the rocks before reaching over the top of the mountain. Vehicles shuddered under gale force winds slamming against the base of the mountain as they knew it would. Their canvasses shook violently under the force, but held. Everyone strapped on desert goggles to protect their eyes and wrapped their faces with handkerchiefs. The storm was so thick vision dropped to zero and breathing became difficult. An additional precautionary measure was to tie their waist belts to bars beneath the vehicles, but this made breathing difficult due to the strain on their bodies.

Corporal Hemmings was tied beneath a lorry when he felt the bar loosen. He had barely enough visibility to see how over the course of time the weld had given way on one end, and now his safety was compromised. He kept cool and searched for another place to secure himself. He saw the axel to be inviting and decided to chance moving. Once he loosened his strap he felt the wind fighting to take him away, but he held on to the lorry for dear life, pulling himself closer to the axel. Hemmings positioned himself so the strap fit beneath his arms and around his upper back. Then he secured the buckle when it suddenly snapped and gave way.

Instantly, Corporal Hemmings found himself being pulled out from under the lorry as though a giant hand had taken hold of him. He did not bother screaming for help. He knew there was nothing anyone could do. Instead he held on to the bar with all his strength, so much that he could feel metal slicing through his fingers and peeling away flesh and bone. When he could stand the pain no longer he released his grip and was carted away, leaving no one the wiser.

Jack awakened from his deep sleep and could not move. It was as though he had been drained all strength and had difficulty focusing his vision, too. He inhaled deeply and his lungs felt like they would burst. He attempted to cry for help, but failed to muster enough energy. A few moments passed before he managed to lift an arm and push himself up. He knew then why he had so much trouble rising. He had been covered in a bed of sand from the storm and was left caked in it from head to toe.

Jack rolled over searching for signs of the SAS raiders. *Where are they?* No one was in sight. The vehicles were intact, heavily covered in sand. *They must be buried like I was.* "Hello," he cried, meekly. His throat felt scratchy and dry. *I need water.* He blinked rapidly, trying to focus on something—anything that could give him a sign where the others were.

Jack managed to sit upright, shaking his head to clear the cobwebs. "Hello?"

His cry was met with silence save for the trail end of the *Khamsin*, its strong winds now diminished. Jack managed to clumsily rise to his feet, leaning on the jeep. He looked up at the sky and guessed right it was late afternoon.

*In another hour it'll be dark.* Only then did he realize they weathered the storm nearly a full 24 hours!

"Is anyone here?!" he shouted, rubbing the back of his neck to get the stiffness out.

He managed to step forward with great effort and nearly tripped over a lump of sand. He looked down and was taken aback when he saw it was the body of a man covered in sand.

*"Hey, what in the—!"* He tried to jump back, but fell on his haunches.

It took Jack a few moments to pull himself together. Finally, he got up and reached down and rolled the man over.

"Major Lawrence!" Jack cried.

The man's face was wrapped in a handkerchief, but he recognized the major's uniform.

"Hang on," he told him. There was no hiding the surprise and desperation in his voice. He pulled the handkerchief away from the major's face and slapped him lightly on both cheeks.

"Come on, dammit! I know you're alive. You're too stubborn to die." He slapped him a few more times and this time he received the reaction he prayed for.

Major Lawrence coughed heavily, spitting out sand in the process.

Jack went to the jeep, reached under the canvas covering it and returned with a canteen of water. "Here," he said, opening its cap. "Drink up."

Major Lawrence felt water run down his dry throat and it proved to be more painful than relieving.

"Take it easy," Jack said, pulling away the canteen. He poured water on a handkerchief and wet the major's lips before allowing him another drink, then helped him to his feet.

Jack felt a bit embarrassed over the major's ability to quickly recover compared to his own. *I suppose that's why he's SAS*, he thought.

Major Lawrence scanned the area, taking in the scene. "Any sign of the others?" His voice sounded hoarse and exhausted.

Jack looked around too, uncertain and with no idea. "Still buried is my guess," he replied in a subdued voice. "I only just woke up myself."

The major coughed. "Come on," he said, moving around the jeep. "We've got to help them."

One by one they found each man buried in sand, but still breathing. Major Lawrence knew they were lucky the *Khamsin* rolled over them fairly soon. He experienced storms lasting for days before showing signs of letting up.

"Captain Guinness," he called, "let's get a head count."

A few moments later Guinness approached the major. "Corporal Hemmings is missing."

A cold feeling ran through Major Lawrence. He looked in all directions, hoping to catch a glimpse of where Hemmings might be. "Fan out," he said, sounding desperate. "He could be buried in the sand somewhere. Find him."

The raiders began their search, calling out Hemmings' name. They climbed up the side of the rocky mountain and poked around any deep sand dune where he might have been covered, but there was no sign of him. They continued searching for nearly an hour before the major reluctantly called off the search.

Jack stood beside Lieutenant Roberts when the major issued his orders. "That's it? We're pushing on without Hemmings?" He sounded as though he bit into sour grapes and looked like he would spit up his guts.

Roberts shrugged. "If he's not to be found, he's not to be found," he said, failing to be nonchalant in his disappointed tone. "We can't stay put forever." He turned to look straight at Jack. "The same could've happened to any of us, and Hemmings knew this." He paused before adding, "Besides, he wouldn't want us to risk being exposed to Jerry."

Jack had witnessed enough SAS behavior to realize they were a tight group, and Roberts was probably correct about how Hemmings would have felt same. Still, he could not help feeling they were being a bit cold-hearted toward their missing comrade.

Once night time came the full moon rose, illuminating the desert and the raiders went about digging out their vehicles. It proved to be a long, arduous job, and Jack slowly gained certain respect for what he was doing alongside such a tough group of soldiers. He had no idea men were capable of such a mission so far out in the middle of nowhere.

The jeeps were easy enough to recover. All it took was removing sand covering the wheels, allowing them to drive out from their sand pits. The lorries caught the brunt of the storm and took more time. They were heavily laden with equipment and it was necessary to use the grated sand channels for traction to drive them out of their 'grave.' It was midnight before the raiders were ready to move again.

"Lost a full day," Major Lawrence noted.

He looked at his watch and shook his head. A map of the desert lay on the hood of his jeep. Hawkins and Guinness stood on either side of Lawrence studying the map.

"We'll go around these mountains," he told them. "It might take us the rest of the night depending on what the terrain is like. None of our patrols have been out this way since the *Light Car Patrols* of the *Great War,* so this should be interesting."

"The men are ready, sir," Guinness said, doing his best to sound upbeat.

Lawrence was glad to hear it. "Good, let's get on the move."

Jack climbed into his jeep and saw a book lying on the passenger side. He picked it up and read the title aloud. "'*For Whom the Bell Tolls.*'" He turned to face Private Brown, his new designated jeep driver. "Yours?"

Brown shook his head. "Belonged to Corporal Hemmings," he answered, flatly. "I gave it to him, but I don't think he liked it much. Reminded him too close of what we do out here, fighting behind enemy lines and such. I'm reading a book titled '*The Virginians,*' which is a lot more relaxing."

Major Lawrence walked up to them right before they were about to move out. "I haven't asked if any of this terrain seems familiar to you," he said, hopeful Jack had something they could use about their location. "Remember, any information is helpful."

Jack took a moment to reflect, but it was useless. He had been half out of his mind for lack of food and water during his escape.

*The Bedouins who rescued me are the ones you should be asking,* he wanted to say.

This was true. The tribe he stumbled across helped him return to friendly lines.

Jack turned to face the major. "Look, I told you I didn't remember much about my journey through the desert," he protested. He looked around, taking in their surroundings. "I'm afraid I don't recall anything about this area," he added, hoping he would not have to say more.

"That's understandable," Major Lawrence replied. "Still, your memory may return if you keep your eyes open. Anything is possible. Also, in your report you mentioned the Bedouin chieftain we've been trying to identify. Once we locate this German base, he'll be your priority, identifying him."

"Well, what if this Bedouin isn't there?" I mean, why would he be there after all this time?"

This sounded reasonable enough to the major. "Intelligence reports indicate Rommel is planning a push toward Alexandria soon," he explained, "This Bedouin chief may be meeting to make more demands right before Jerry launches an attack. Makes sense if he does seeing how they need him now more than ever."

"What's the big deal about the Bedouin?" Jack challenged.

Major Lawrence shrugged. "They're a strange lot, these wogs," he said, coolly. "Win a battle; they come swarming to be friends. Lose; they can become your enemy in blink of an eye."

"I've learned not to trust them farther than I can spit," Guinness said, acidly.

Jack took an exasperated deep breath and searched their surroundings once more. Shaking his head, he said, "I don't remember going over mountains such as these, so we must've gone around them. Like I said, I stumbled upon a tribe of Bedouin who took me most of the way back to British lines. I was out of it most of the time."

"Catching up on much needed rest?" Major Lawrence said, flashing a crooked smile.

Jack shrugged off the remark and turned away.

Major Lawrence turned to Guinness. "We must be close," he said, with certainty. "It's not possible for the Yank to have wandered this far south in the desert alone, and there's no other reason for the Bedouin to travel this route if not to meet with Jerry."

"I quite agree, sir," Guinness said, nodding enthusiastically.

The major studied their surroundings. "We'll have to keep our wits on high alert. They'll have watching posts most likely, so make certain everyone maintains awareness."

That said, Major Lawrence ordered the group of raiders to get on the move, and they drove off into the desert night, hopeful they would come across the secret German base sooner than later.

# Chapter 23

*With the German offensive in full swing on the Russian Front, supplies were reduced to other areas including North Afrika. Thus, it was imperative all war material, in particular petrol, was saved and maintained for new offensives. More than ever, Rommel could not afford to lose a single barrel of petrol. This lack of steady supplies, he knew, might cost him victory in Afrika.*

## Camp *'Lili Marlene'*
## October 17, 1942

Privat Karl Mohr stood guard on the watch tower, pacing back and forth like a caged leopard. This duty seemed permanent, and he was grateful the platform provided enough room for movement so that he remained awake. It did not go well for a *soldat* to be caught sleeping while on guard.

A bright moon illuminated the terrain in all directions and Mohr had a most picturesque view, leaving him confident he could alert the post of any enemy approach well before an attack began. He was not about to allow a repeat at the previous base he had been assigned on the outskirts of Benghazi where they were attacked by English gangsters.

Privat Mohr's memory of that night remained vivid and filled him with shame. He recalled hearing distant sound of engines approaching, but failed to pinpoint their approach. Everyone who heard the jeeps reasoned them to be a German patrol on their return. Only after the crackling of gunfire erupting did Privat Mohr realize they were under enemy attack, and a well-coordinated one at that!

Mohr recalled grabbing hold of his machine gun and firing at the attackers in short bursts from the same type watch tower he walked this night. Seconds later he found himself facing a withering barrage of bullets tearing apart his post. Enemy return fire was so great the wooden stilts holding up the tower gave way and Mohr found himself crashing down and losing consciousness. He awakened next morning surprised he was lying on a cot inside a field hospital tent, his right arm and head wrapped in bandages. A doctor asked if he recalled what happened, but Mohr shook his head and told him he suffered severe headaches. To Mohr's surprise the doctor then informed him he had been awarded the Iron Cross First Class, an award seldom bestowed on low-ranking soldiers.

"Why, Herr Doktor?" Mohr asked, his eyes bulging from surprise.

"For bravery and action against the Britische gangsters," the doctor proudly told him. "Your quick reaction prevented them from destroying our fuel depot."

Shortly thereafter the base kommandant pinned the medal on the white bed shirt Privat Mohr wore and saluted him. "You have made us proud, Privat," the kommandant said, with pride. "The *Fatherland* salutes you."

Indeed, what made Privat Mohr equally proud was to have been awarded the same decoration *Der Fuhrer* received for his action during the First World War when he was seriously injured during a gas attack while performing duties as a messenger. From that moment on Privat Mohr became the most respected soldat in his platoon. Even his sergeants who teased him back on parade fields in Tunis now demonstrated respect and were proud to have him in their unit. Mohr wrote his father about his medal from the hospital bed in full detail, but omitted the part how the Britische still managed to destroy many precious planes.

When Mohr transferred to Camp Lili Marlene things seemed to brighten for him. This was an important base and only the best troops were assigned to such a post. Walking guard duty on the tower was not a problem for him, especially as the camp kommandant personally requested him for this post.

"I want a man like Privat Mohr on watch," the kommandant stated. "If we are attacked, I know he will perform his duty."

In the officer staff room, Base Kommandant, Sturmbannfuhrer Hans Mueller, debriefed his men of their current situation, and the face of things to come. Rommel's Quartermaster Chief of Staff, Oberst Otto Krieger attended this meeting on behalf of his superior. He wanted Krieger to supervise tactical dispense of supplies and material for their upcoming offensive. Although Krieger was senior to all present, Mueller remained in overall command of the base. This created resentment from Krieger, who still held a grudge from the coast road incident where Mueller challenged him at the fall of Tobruk.

Mueller stood over the table where a map of North Afrika covered most of it. He was flanked by Krieger on his right and Sturmbannfuhrer Wolfgang Klement on his left. Hauptmanns Konrad Diestl, Walther Kruger, and Leutnant Gunther Kleist also were in attendance. Other officers present were in command of infantry, supply, and administration posts. All fell under Mueller's command.

"Sturmbannfuhrer von Mellenthin briefed me on our situation from Field Marshal Rommel's headquarters," Mueller began, sounding somewhat cautious, "and I've been instructed to disclose information for those present. However, you may not discuss anything you are about to hear with anyone."

Everyone stiffened upon hearing this and had an idea what Mueller was about to tell them. In all branches of the military all over the world, rumors could never be prevented from spreading. The German Army was no exception despite its harsh penalties and strict regulations on maintaining tight communications. The officers before Mueller braced for what they suspected might be disappointing news.

"Our campaign in Russia is now in its second year and *not* going as planned," he continued, and made a face as though he'd eaten a handful of sour grapes. "Victory before winter sets in does not appear feasible. Our troops are bogged down, and Russian forces have been reinforced in greater numbers than expected. As a result, Der Fuhrer has increased army reserves to be transferred to the Eastern Front." He paused as officers glanced at one another, shrugging as if this were no surprise. "This also means we will receive no new troops and supplies until further notice," he warned.

Sturmbannfuhrer Klement reacted first. "They expect us to fight without reserves?" he protested, vehemently. All present knew he referred to German High Command.

"Rear-area staff will be utilized for reserves," Mueller replied, quickly. He observed more than a few present shake their heads and guffaw in disgust. "All troop and supply transfers from Sicily have been diverted to support the Russian offensive," he continued. "This means we must pillage for petrol, ammunition, and other supplies from captured Britische supplies."

"This should not raise concern," Krieger blurted. All heads turned facing him. "I am certain we will defeat the English before the year is out. Our supplies are sufficient enough to support our offensive. Our advantage is battlefield tactics and our victory in North Afrika will inspire our men on all fronts. The sooner we move onto Alexandria and Cairo, the sooner we will unite with forces in Russia through the Caucasus." He paused, staring directly at each officer to ensure he had their attention. "Victory is within our grasp," he arrogantly added.

An uneasy silence filled the room. Everyone glared at the boisterous Krieger. They respected his rank, but not the man. Krieger fell in their category of a *Hinterlaufhengst* (rear-echelon stallion). He was the sort seeking glory from behind a desk, not the battlefield. Of course his job was important, procuring supplies for troops. However, his arrogant manner earned him despise among the ranks.

*He behaves like an expert in field tactics,* Mueller thought with a sneer.

Had Krieger sought position in a combat unit he would have been granted such a request. His rank and social status authorized him privileges others were not accustomed to receiving. He was known however, for being superb in his field of quartermaster, and Rommel believed the Afrika Korps most fortunate to have his organizational skills on hand. Still, Krieger had less respect for the Britische than frontline soldiers. This was common among ranks. Men serving in rear units did not share common difficulties as those on the front lines, thus failing to understand mutual respect fighting men had for their enemy.

Mueller thought it necessary to remind Krieger of a long-learned history lesson. "Herr Oberst, we all have confidence in the field marshal, but let us not forget how the English have lost many battles throughout their history, but in the end won wars." He paused, gauging the Oberst's reaction. "That said," he continued in a tone a teacher might speak to a know-it-all student, "the logistics of supply and demand concerns me."

"How do you mean, Herr Sturmbannfuhrer?" Klement asked, intentionally drawing attention away from Krieger.

Mueller used a pencil to indicate positions of Britische forces. "The enemy controls the Mediterranean Sea by night while our Luftwaffe forces them to be cautious by day. This has not slowed their flow of supplies to ports in Alexandria and Cairo. They bring men and material from India through the Red Sea and Suez Canal unhindered. With unlimited supplies they can maintain a longer sustained battle than anticipated, forcing us to withdraw over due course."

Hauptmann Walther Kruger spoke up. "It is my understanding supplies on this base will sustain our next offensive through winter," he said, hopeful.

Mueller scoffed. "Our *Nazi* leaders in Berlin control what we hear," he began with contempt, "but we still control what we believe…. at least for the time being." His distaste for the Nazi Party did not go unnoticed, but that was their advantage fighting in a theatre far from High Command. Things could be thought and spoken without fear of retaliation.

Mueller continued. "We are ready to transport supplies to the front once orders are received. *Auntie Ju's* will be vulnerable to enemy fighters due to our failure to gain air superiority." He flashed a disappointing glance at Sturmbannfuhrer Klement for having boasted how the Luftwaffe is the best air force in the world, and yet failed to win the air battle over skies in England and North Afrika. "Still, I am confident we will manage to supply our forces adequately enough, at least for this offensive." He paused, lifting a canteen cup of water to his mouth for a much needed drink. In the desert, one's throat ran dry quickly.

"Von Mellenthin has pointed out this is our final moment achieving victory in the desert," he continued. "Every panzer lost is a panzer we cannot replace. The same goes for every soldier killed or captured. Every pint of petrol spent is a pint we must forage in order to replenish our supply." He looked each officer squarely to emphasize how dire their situation actually was. "Take my word, gentlemen," he went on, "our forces rely on our delivering supplies when most needed. Failure will mean defeat for the Afrika Korps."

Everyone shifted uneasily. For many this marked their first time a real sense they could lose the war. Up to this point all believed the German Army to be invincible. However, now after listening to Mueller's convincing point of view they sensed real doubt.

In midst of everyone stooped at the shoulders, wondering if they would be victorious, Wolfgang Klement spoke up. "We have enough fighters to ensure our supply transports will be protected for their journey to the front," he said, brimming with confidence. "My Stukas will attack enemy air bases before our offensive begins, knocking their planes out of action. Hauptmann Kruger will conduct reconnaissance sorties in his CR-42s and locate landing strips fitted for our planes. I am certain we will be successful with such precautions."

Klement's confidence was well-received. "How many JU-52s can we expect to arrive and airlift the supplies to the front once the offensive begins?" Hauptmann Diestl inquired, hopeful.

Krieger checked his notes. "We have one hundred and fifty transports arriving tomorrow evening and will be on standby for the offensive," he declared, beaming. Once Field Marshal Rommel attacks we will order them to depart and land at designated airfields prepared by engineers close to the battlefield, and secured by our forces." He turned facing Mueller. "I recommend we load the transports with petrol and other supplies upon their arrival immediately in order to be ready at a moment's notice."

Leutnant Joachim Model, an infantry officer in command of a detachment at Camp Lili Marlene, rose, snapping to attention. "Herr Sturmbannfuhrer, if I may be permitted to speak?" he asked, respectfully.

Mueller nodded. "Certainly, in my staff meetings I insist all speak their mind."

Model came from an aristocratic family. He stood 5'-9" tall, maintained his blonde hair plastered back with thick hair grease glistening in the light. He was close to rail-thin with a gaunt face emphasized by his narrow nose. Many believed he possessed the physical attributes associated with the *Aryan Race,* and his bright blue eyes did all the more to project this image.

*Der Fuhrer would be proud to have this man standing center stage,* Mueller muttered in silence.

Model cleared his throat. "Our bases are subject to attack by raiders under command of the *Phantom Major,*" he began, making a distasteful expression when mentioning their reference name for David Stirling. "Nothing attracts these desert raiders more than our JU-52 transports. I suggest we increase guards posted until our offensive begins."

Mueller and the others contemplated Model's point, eventually nodding agreement. "I believe you are right," he said, calmly.

His words caused Krieger to stiffen. "This is preposterous!" he blurted. Model snapped to attention when Krieger directed his address to him. "This *Phantom Major* is a war criminal, a pirate, nothing more! How can you determine extra precautions necessary?"

Mueller remained firm. Having been a frontline soldier, he bore witness to the devastation caused by Stirling's SAS. He knew this man should not be taken lightly and that High Command in Berlin was putting together a specially-trained unit to deal with them.

"Herr Oberst," Mueller began, respectfully, "these thugs you refer to are responsible for destroying more planes on the ground than the enemy has in the air. The threat of them destroying this base is very much real, and I intend to take every precaution necessary to prevent that."

Krieger balked. "Surely you do not believe the English are aware of this base," he asked, accusingly.

"No," he said, in his most respectful, but commanding tone to a superior-rank officer, "if it were, the English most certainly would have attacked by now. However, it would be inexcusable for us not to take every precaution." He paused, thinking things over a few seconds, and then said, "We'll do as Leutnant Model suggests."

Tank Sergeant Heinrich Priess walked around the base, making certain no one had fallen asleep on guard duty. He was a perfectionist and demanded unquestioning obedience, along with utmost professionalism. His tall, muscular frame and stern jaw commanded full attention from his men, too. His passion came from having been a scion of a military family. However, they were not of monetary wealth, and he could not afford a commission to officer school. Still, he took his non-commissioned rank serious and committed himself to superior performance.

Priess walked around the base inspecting his post and withdrew his cigarette case from his pocket. Since war's outbreak, smoking became his most recent favorite pastime. Before returning his case to his pocket he read the engraving. *'To Sergeant Heinrich, my most trusted soldat!'* The case was a gift from his previous commander who lost his life in the Battle of Tobruk three months earlier.

The leutnant always referred him as *Sergeant Heinrich* and his loss was a heavy blow. They had been through a lot beginning in 1939 when they invaded Poland, and again in France 1940, and then in Afrika since 1941. Right before Tobruk the leutnant said he would recommend Priess for Officer Candidate School, claiming he had a close friend at the academy that could help pull strings. That dream unfortunately ended during final days of fighting at Tobruk.

Continuing his inspection, he came across a corporal on guard by the foot of the tarmac at the airstrip. He expected him to turn and ask him to identify himself, but he did no such thing. Priess halted, his eyes shifting to and fro. It would not be unusual for the enemy to silently kill a guard and prop him up as though he were standing. Priess stopped that train of thought when he realized the guard had in fact fallen asleep while on his feet.

*My God, the man's asleep!* Priess could not believe his eyes.

The corporal used his rifle to lean on, but his drooped head, slackened back, and a slight snore gave him away.

In a fleeting moment, Priess faced temptation to lash out and deliver him a thrashing, but thought better. Instead he crept around the corporal and stood facing him. Slowly, cautiously, he drew his Luger P-08 automatic pistol from its holster on his belt. He held his arm straight, bringing the barrel of the pistol level with the corporal's head. Then, aiming right between the man's eyes, he flicked off the safety switch with his thumb, intentionally making a loud clicking sound.

The corporal opened his eyes immediately upon hearing the familiar sound. His eyes widened with shock and terror at the sight of the Luger. He remained frozen, uncertain what he should do. After what seemed an eternity the corporal spoke.

"Bitte!" (Please) he pleaded.

"Bitte was?" (Please what) Priess shot back angrily. A sly smile pursed the corners of his mouth. "Have you heard how Britische *gangsters* attack our bases at night?" he asked, still holding his pistol level at the man's head.

"Jawohl," the corporal said, nodding nervously.

"I suggest you take your duties serious." Priess' words were a statement, not a suggestion.

The corporal replied with a nod and lifted his rifle to port arms before marching along the airfield, eyes peeled for what might lay out there in the darkness.

Priess continued his inspection of the posts on guard duty, satisfied he taught the unassuming corporal a lesson he would not forget. When he approached the main gate a guard called out the alarm.

"STAND TO!"

A searchlight from a guard tower shot its ray in direction of something approaching. Priess ran to the front gate where a number of men gathered for action. Two more searchlights switched on, locking onto something moving fast toward their base. Upon closer inspection they saw men riding horses.

*El Karum*, Priess thought. *The Wogs aren't due here until tomorrow!*

He shook his head in disdain. Like so many Germans, he was offended on the idea of negotiating with Bedouins. They were regarded as savages, uncivilized, and thieves. If the proud German Army was reduced to having them join as allies, this meant the war was not going favorably. Still, orders were orders and the German Army was known for obeying them to the letter.

"Stand down," Priess ordered. He watched as the men cautiously lowered their weapons.

El Karum rode his horse up to the main gate with no fewer than fifty warriors in tow, all armed with German-made Gewehr 88 rifles, standard issue for German soldiers in World War 1, and not so much in use now, which accounted for why German Intelligence approved arming Bedouin with them. Bandoliers of ammunition with 7.92x57mm cartridges were strapped across their shoulders and chests. Each man dressed in the common black and white robes with Bedouin headdress.

"I am here to meet the man called Mueller," El Karum barked.

He spoke with authority, unafraid of the more powerfully armed Germans standing before him. Although they were allies, he possessed enough intelligence to know their relationship remained on shaky terms.

Priess sighed purposely and noticeably. Nor did he immediately answer. He looked up and down at the column of horsemen, taking his time before returning attention to El Karum.

"The man you ask for is *Sturmbannfuhrer* Mueller," he replied with emphasis on Mueller's rank. "He is currently in a staff meeting with his officers," he added with a grin, and shifted his eyes away from El Karum while speaking. He knew doing so was considered an insult, especially to an Arab chieftain. Bedouin custom required maintaining eye contact while speaking to one another.

This action did not go unnoticed by El Karum and his men, who glared with hatred at the rude sergeant. *You are a man I will be dealing with soon*, El Karum told himself. No one insulted him before his men without severe punishment.

"I have urgent business with your leader," El Karum shot back, in heavily-accented German. "I am expected."

"Of course you are," Priess said, returning their gaze with disdain. "You will wait for him in our supply tent and be notified when he is ready to see you."

El Karum was unaccustomed to wait for anyone. *Yes indeed! I will be dealing with you soon enough,* he promised himself.

For the time being his honor would wait. El Karum kicked into his horse's sides, making the animal march forward, and his men followed suit.

Before the Bedouin reached the supply tent, Sturmbannfuhrer Mueller and his staff exited the tent where he held his meeting. This was good for El Karum. It meant not being made to wait. He rode up to Mueller, who gave a half-hearted salute to the chieftain.

"I see you made it," Mueller said, forcing a smile.

El Karum scoffed. "I am a man of my word," he said, quickly. "When I choose to fight alongside someone, I do precisely that."

Mueller nodded and looked up and down the column of horsemen. "Not many men you have to carry out a war, don't you think?"

El Karum remained sitting on his horse ramrod straight. "These are my bodyguard. My main force is hidden in the mountains and will move on my command. When is the offensive to begin?"

Mueller started to answer, and then thought better of it. "Soon," he answered, calmly. A moment of silence between them passed before he asked, "Care to dine with us this evening?"

El Karum nodded and dismounted from his horse. "Thank you," he replied with little enthusiasm. "Do you have quarters for my men?"

"Yes," Mueller told him. "Leutnant, see to his men."

The leutnant and German guards looked on uneasy over the prospect of entertaining Bedouin. They remained prejudiced same as British. Clearing his throat, the young officer motioned for their guests to follow him to a group of designated tents while Mueller walked with El Karum to the dining tent. It was going to be a long evening, he knew, and he prayed enough wine and beer was available. He would need it if he were to sit side by side with an Arab, discussing politics and war.

# Chapter 24

*It soon became clear to the British they could not defeat Rommel with superior leadership. He was simply too great a military tactician. It also became clear that small, mobile units like the SAS inflicted greater damage on the Afrika Korps than units of equal strength. This created resentment between regular army officers and the Special Air Service.*

## October 17, 1942
## 2300 Hours
## Somewhere in the Desert

Major Lawrence sat in the lead jeep staring at the empty desert when something caught his attention. He raised his right arm, signaling the caravan to stop, and rose from his seat. Lifting his field glasses to his eyes, he searched the horizon carefully.

"What is it, Major?" Private Caine, his driver asked.

Major Lawrence studied the scene before answering. "Looks like a large body of something moving towards the mountains," he observed.

"Jerries?"

The major shook his head. "Too far to tell. I don't think so. Probably Bedouins on the move."

Captain Guinness walked up to Lawrence's jeep and heard his answer to Caine. "This could tie in with Captain Ruggero's report of a Bedouin tribe at this German base, sir," he pointed out.

Lawrence turned to face Guinness and nodded. "I have to give the *Fox* credit," he said, with admiration. "It's a cunning move placing a base this far south. With a score of JU-52s he could transport petrol and ammunition to his troops on the front rather easily."

Guinness and Caine nodded in agreement. "Better watch yourself, sir," Caine warned. "Remember Monty's standing order how we're *not* to mention Rommel's nickname."

This brought a laugh among the trio. When Montgomery took over 8th Army one of his first standing orders was having Rommel's name removed from any and all communiques, and staff briefings. The enemy would be referred to as *enemy force* or *German,* but Rommel's name would be omitted. Monty felt his men lionized the German general enough. After all, his popularity as *The Desert Fox* was world-renowned, and he had enough work on hand whipping 8th Army into shape for his upcoming offensive than to beat down Rommel's image of being a superior general.

Major Lawrence signaled the caravan to start moving again with a raised arm, making circles in the air with his hand, and then pointing forward. "Let's get on the move," he ordered to Caine.

## October 18, 1942
## 0430 Hours

The raiders reached the spot where Lawrence saw the large body of land shifting like a wave of sand flowing across the desert, much like a wave of water in the ocean. Lawrence's *sixth sense* told him to proceed with caution, and they disembarked their vehicles fully armed and ready for anything.

"Tracks are everywhere," one of the raiders noted. He was correct. Signs of horses were all over the area.

"What do you make of it, sir?" Lieutenant Roberts asked, while studying the tracks.

The major shook his head twice. "They're a larger group than expected this far south in the desert," he answered. He scratched the stubble of growth on his face. They had not enough spare water for a shave and each raider craved a bath. "Bring Captain Ruggero to me," he said to Roberts, who left to fetch him.

A moment later, Jack appeared. "What's up, Major?" he asked, wiping his eyes and slightly wobbling on his feet from exhaustion.

Lawrence pointed to the tracks in the sand and the surrounding mountains. "Do you recall this area?" he asked, hoping he would. "This appears to be a major staging area where Bedouins rest."

Jack took a step back, gathering in the sparse territory. His expression and body language indicated he was experiencing immense pressure.

Major Lawrence stepped closer and placed a calming hand on Jack's shoulder. "You survived this hell-hole because you have the will to survive," he said, speaking like an older brother. His men nearby nodded appreciatively. "Relax and do the best you can."

Jack recognized the sincerity in the major's words and for the first time on this journey relaxed some. "My plan during my escape was to move as far south possible and go around the Krauts' lines before heading northeast," he continued. "I foolishly believed I could find water holes along the way, not taking into account reasons why no one, not even the Bedouin, live this far south. I stumbled across a few streams and one oasis, but couldn't stay there long because the Krauts soon came. I came across a dead man and his camel, killed by the elements, and ate some camel meat that had not gone bad, and drank its belly water." He made a disgusting face. "Tasted and smelled like hell!" he cried. "It was days or weeks before I realized I walked too far south," he said, sounding like his memory returned. "I simply didn't want to fall into enemy hands again. I remember some German looking for me like he wanted to kill me for personal reasons rather than me being an enemy. It was the damnedest thing, too, and I'm sure I know him from somewhere, but can't put my finger on it."

"Why would you believe this German had it for you on a personal level?" Lawrence asked, curious.

Jack shrugged, still piecing together events. His mind suddenly took him back in time when he was alone in the desert, fighting for his life. Lawrence and his men saw this change in Jack, and remained quiet so he could concentrate without interruption.

"I remember mountains in the distance," he muttered. There was a drawn out period of silence before he continued. "I found palm trees, fruit, and water! I carried water in a satchel I found made of sheep or something. I didn't want to climb over the mountains, so I walked around them and that's when I saw it. A base—a military base! I waited until nightfall to see if it was British or German before moving closer. It got extremely dark and I was able to get within fifty yards of it when I heard horses on the move. They rode past me and I caught sight of a tall man at the front of the group. I took him for their leader. When they reached the gate to the base the soldier allowed them to pass. I remember they spoke in German. That's right, the Arab spoke perfect German!"

Major Lawrence grinned. "Sounds like we're on the right track. Let's get on the move," he said quickly.

Thirty minutes later the sound of an approaching plane caught the raiders' attention. Under cover of darkness they were assured not to be seen, but the plane was not so fortunate. The sound of its 830-horsepower engines was unmistakable.

"Hello, Auntie Ju!" Major Lawrence said, peering through his field glasses. "It's heading east," he declared, excited over this find.

He signaled the caravan to begin moving again by raising his right arm and rapidly pumping it up and down five times. In the back of his mind, Lawrence felt they were close to their objective. Once contact was made he reasoned they no longer needed the Yank, and thought about leaving him out of their attack. He asked Captain Hawkins his opinion.

"Why keep him once we locate the base, sir?" Hawkins wondered. "The man's not a soldier by any army's means."

Lawrence agreed with him on that point. "He'll simply have to tag along and keep low," he said, sourly.

Hawkins scratched his chin. "I can't figure out how a man like him got to be an officer," he said, puzzled.

Lawrence laughed. "Why would you say that? We have our share of people who bought their way into an assignment far from the battlefront," he said, admitting what every man in every army knew. "All it takes is the right connections. Sometimes it happens by pure chance, being at the right place at the right time, and all that."

Now it was Hawkins who laughed. "Looks like his timing is off now," he said, flashing a devilish smile.

Lawrence was not about to argue him on that point.

# Chapter 25

*The most admired song throughout the war was 'Lili Marlene.' Its popularity was so great the English made a version their own. Soldiers on both sides shared similar hardships in the desert with lack of water and unbearable heat. This created a bond between veterans of the Battle of North Africa not felt on any other front.*

## October 18, 1942
## 0630 Hours, German Base Camp *Lili Marlene*

Major Lawrence, Captains Hawkins, Guinness, and Jack looked through their field glasses in amazement at the size of the German base. It was utterly enormous! The base boasted an airfield, planes of all sorts, lorries, some panzers, kubelwagens, armoured cars, an aerodrome, buildings, but mostly large field tents.

"Blimey, they went all out, haven't they?!" Guinness exclaimed.

Hawkins guffawed. "Yeah, but we found them!" he retorted, triumphantly.

"How did they manage this so far in the middle of nowhere," Jack asked, awestruck.

Major Lawrence answered the question coolly, working hard not to express admiration for what the Germans achieved. "Jerry always had a knack for putting their best foot forward when taking on a project," he said, biting his lower lip while keeping his eyes glued to his field glasses. What struck him most was the airstrip. He could not help note how it had been constructed with great care, paving it with a hardtop layer. *They don't call him the 'Fox' for nothing,* he said, reflectively.

They continued observing activity on the base in silence, taking in everything. Finally, the major exhaled nauseously. "Blasted base is far bigger than Stirling dreamed," he said, hoarsely. "Guards are posted everywhere, like they have been forewarned about our presence."

"We'll manage, sir," Guinness said, hopefully. "After all, we've been in tight spots before."

The major shrugged. *True.* "Of course," he agreed. "I want each man to come here in groups of two for a look at the base and take in what we're up against. We'll begin our work at nightfall."

"Yes, sir," Guinness and Hawkins said in unison.

Nightfall seemed to take forever and the SAS raiders grew restless whilst taking in the scope of their mission. All agreed the base appeared to be a tougher nut to crack compared to other targets. With this in mind Major Lawrence thought it prudent to conduct a recce. He was joined by Captain Hawkins, Sergeant Davenport, and Jack, who wanted to object taking part, but decided not to press his luck.

They donned black fatigues, beanies for head cover, and covered their faces and hands with camouflage paint. They armed themselves with Smith-Wesson revolvers and stiletto daggers only, but if all went according to plan they would not need them. In fact, Major Lawrence instructed them to avoid shooting at all costs. To do otherwise would compromise their chance of a surprise attack.

"Our objective is to take mental notes to see what we're up against," he told them.

The base was alive with activity. Searchlights were perched on towers throughout the base, but not used so as not to give away their position. A roving kubelwagen with three soldiers patrolled the outer rim of the camp, and Major Lawrence and his team lay low when the vehicle stopped close by and a German soldier got out to relieve himself. The situation appeared tight when the German soldier appeared to sense something wrong and moved closer to where Major Lawrence lied face down in the sand and shrub.

"Was ist los?" (What is wrong?) One of the men in the car called out.

"I thought I heard something," the soldier replied, keeping his eyes on the terrain.

He held a Luger P-08 pistol in one hand, and removed a flashlight from his belt. Switching it on, he scanned the shrubs and sand. He did this for close to a full minute before one of the men back in the car called for him to return.

When they drove off Jack released a sigh of relief. Major Lawrence took in the scene and was quick to realize the fuel depot would be the priority target versus the planes. Panzers could not move on a sustained offensive without petrol, thus the planes, which were usually primary targets, would be secondary targets. Without fuel, he surmised, this base would be useless and eventually abandoned. They continued their recce and came across tents housing troops.

*There must be four or five hundred men here,* he thought. *That's not including the Wogs!*

Of course the base did not have such large numbers around the clock, but seeing how their offensive was about to begin, it stood to reason a maximum number would be needed to ensure the planes were loaded with petrol quickly when the time called for it.

The raiders continued their recce and stopped upon hearing music from a loudspeaker.

*That's a bit careless,* Major Lawrence thought. *They must believe they're so far from the front they have nothing to fear.*

Major Lawrence refrained venturing further. *No sense pressing our luck.* They circled the base once before making their way back to the base of the mountains where the rest of the raiders awaited their return. No one managed sleep, their adrenaline too high, and they anxiously wanted to hear the major's report.

Major Lawrence reached his command jeep and Captain Guinness handed him a canteen. Although thirsty beyond words, the major drank sparingly. *One cup a day* was their motto for running low on water could prove fatal to any mission, and the mission always had priority.

"How do things look, sir?" Guinness eagerly asked. Others approached them so they could hear it straight from their CO.

Major Lawrence still breathed heavily from hurrying back, and took a moment to catch his breath. He turned to his men looking all business. "Raiding the base with vehicles alone is not an option," he said, firmly. "This base is larger than we believed and we don't have the number of jeeps for our preferred assault. We'll send in teams on foot to place as many charges in the fuel dump and on as many planes possible. The remaining group will use the vehicles to head down the runway on a strafing run, which will confuse the Jerries into thinking our numbers are greater than we actually are." He paused for a look at his men to gauge their thoughts. "I know separating our numbers is risky, but I don't see any alternative."

Hawkins shrugged. "Who Dares Wins, sir," he said, beaming confidence.

Major Lawrence nodded. "Right, I'll take charge of one of the foot teams," he explained, "Guinness will lead the jeeps on the tarmac to strafe the planes, and Hawkins will take the lorries on east side of the base and attack the tents housing enemy troops. You'll only be able to make one run before the Jerries spring into action, so make it count. Any questions?"

There was only one person with a question, and it came no surprise to the raiders.

"Where will I be?" Jack asked, hoarsely.

All eyes shifted his direction, but Jack maintained eye contact with the major.

There was a drawn out period of silence before Major Lawrence answered, "You'll be with my team."

"When do we go?" Sergeant-Major Riley asked, anxious.

"Now," he said coolly.


## October 19, 1942
## Camp *Lili Marlene*

*What a waste of time,* Sturmbannfuhrer Mueller snarled. He reflected on his meeting with El Karum, which went far longer than planned. He checked his watch and saw it was 12:55 a.m.

The chieftain pushed Mueller's patience to its limit with constant requests for more of everything. First he wanted horses, then more rifles, then more automatic weapons, and then artillery. His demand then jumped to gold bullion, German chocolate (a delicious commodity in the desert), and more horses. The list was endless! Mueller knew dealing with Bedouin was an arduous chore, and they never seemed satisfied unless they believed they got the better part of a deal. This time, however, El Karum was way out of line. Mueller did not want his meeting with the chieftain to turn sour, but handing over more of everything was out of the question.

"You will have to make do with our original contract," the sturmbannfuhrer stated, frustrated. "Until we achieve total victory I cannot provide you more of anything."

El Karum remained adamant. "What I want guarantees my power over local tribes that will undoubtedly resist my rule. For me to maintain control I must be able to fight them, and I can only do this with superior weapons." He was practically snarling at the German officer.

Mueller was not falling for it. *Never trust an Arab when bargaining,* he had been told when first arriving in this theater of war. "You have been provided a rifle for every man who takes up arms against our enemy," he shot back, defiantly. "Your harassment of the English will not require additional weaponry. Your job will be to disrupt enemy supply lines behind the front. We will take care of the heavy fighting, which means you have no need for artillery. With this in mind I see no reason to alter our agreement. The Afrika Korps expects El Karum to honor this to the letter."

During their meeting Mueller spoke with finality and did not take his eyes away from El Karum. This confidence embarrassed the Bedouin chieftain, who sat with his chief lieutenants before their German allies.

*More humiliation,* El Karum thought. *First, the arrogant sergeant at the gate and now this officer! When will it ever end?*

Awkward moments passed before El Karum reached for his cup of tea and took a drink. He glared at Mueller while holding the cup to his mouth. Mueller reached in his tunic pocket and removed a silver-plated cigarette case. He removed one, tapped one end against the case before putting it to his lips and lighting it. He intentionally did not offer one to El Karum, who eyed the case before the major returned it to the pocket on his tunic. Taking a long drag from his cigarette, he inhaled deep and then blew smoke above their table where the dull, gray cloud hung luminously over them under the light bulbs hanging from the tent.

Mueller leaned forward, elbows on the table and looked El Karum squarely. "I suppose our meeting is concluded," he said, nonchalantly.

El Karum looked over his shoulder at his council. He did not appreciate being spoken to in such a manner before them. It was an attack on his dignity. Realizing more words only worsened his position; the chieftain rose from his chair and spat on the table. He then stormed from the tent with his council in tow, their fingers tickling the handles of their knives sheathed on their waste belts.

Mueller observed El Karum's exit with a mischievous grin. He shook his head. "Now I know what the English meant when they talked about dealing with Wogs," he confessed. "The deal never ends with a handshake."

The officers and enlisted men present broke into laughter.

"That was him! I'm sure of it!" Jack whispered to Major Lawrence. It was all he could do to keep his voice down. They had scurried their way to the German camp in haste, low-crawling on their bellies while keeping a watchful eye on the guard towers. The going had been rough, what with carrying explosives. They were a three-man team and the major knew he had to make do.

*What the hell! The Jerries took Eban Emael with three-man teams,* he told himself. Fort Eban Emael was the Belgian fort taken by a German airborne force of seventy paratroopers operating in three-man teams against 1,500 Belgian troops.

His team consisted of himself, Jack, and Lieutenant Roberts. Each was armed with a Sten automatic, a Smith-Wesson revolver, a stiletto blade, and a pack stuffed to its brim with *Lewis Bombs.* Jack questioned why he, too, had been armed to the teeth seeing how he had no intention of engaging the enemy face to face.

"We have to be prepared for everything," Major Lawrence told him, sternly.

Jack offered no argument this late in the game.

Reaching the base by foot had been relatively simple, however, the full moon illuminated their immediate area and they found it necessary to low-crawl once in eyesight of the guard towers. A score of Arabs on horseback had entered the base and were seen in conversation with persons who appeared to be in charge of German forces.

*The Kommandant,* Major Lawrence surmised.

Seeing the opportunity for Jack to identify the wog they needed to assassinate so they could prevent an Arab uprising, Major Lawrence handed him his field glasses and pointed in the direction of the group for him to observe. Jack crawled up so that he lay side by side with the major, and peered through the glasses. Enough light within the German camp permitted him a clear view and he was surprised how powerful the field glasses were.

"That was him!" he said in a low voice. "I'm sure of it!"

"Shush! Keep quiet," Major Lawrence told him, through gritted teeth and putting a finger to his lips to emphasize the importance of remaining unheard as well as unseen. He looked back at Lieutenant Roberts, who watched them through squinting eyes and shrugged as if to ask, "What's going on?"

The sound of horses stampeding out through the main gates captured the raiders' attention, and moments later the Bedouin riders disappeared in the night.

*Blast!* Major Lawrence swore, silently. *There goes our chance of getting the Wog!*

Jack stared hopefully at him. "I suppose this means you no longer need me for the rest of this mission?"

Major Lawrence shook his head.

Jack shrugged as if saying, "Can't blame me for trying."

Major Lawrence reached the fence and was relieved to find it had been poorly laid out. He could crawl his way through without having to use his wire cutters.

*They must be cocksure we wouldn't find this base,* he thought.

The major maneuvered through the wire and made his way to the back of a tent which he found to house a large number of personnel. He heard voices and laughter, and understood enough German to know they spoke of women while playing cards. He checked the immediate area for guards and soon realized their main threat was the guard towers, which had a clear view of the fuel depot, their main target.

He worked his way to the corner of a large field tent and took in the sight of the fuel depot. The night was well-illuminated by the brilliant moonlight and he saw barrels of fuel stacked four high in row after row. He fought temptation to toss a grenade at the target, knowing how one explosion would send the entire lot up in flame and smoke.

*Too risky,* he warned himself.

And he was correct! Doing so would have jeopardized their chances of escaping. Thus, they would plant bombs at key points in order for multiple explosions to ensure the fuel would be destroyed.

Major Lawrence moved forward to another tent and peaked around the corner facing north, then moved to the other side and made certain all was clear facing south. When he heard footsteps coming his way he dropped to the ground and flattened himself, knife in hand. A moment later he saw a German sergeant appear, who stopped at a group of dried bushes and unzipped his trousers to relieve himself. He appeared drunk by the way he swaggered, and held a cigarette between his lips, puffing and blowing out smoke.

The sergeant began talking aloud to himself as he stood there pissing in the wind, all the while unaware not more than three feet away laid Major Lawrence ready to pounce on him and slit his throat. The sergeant urinated for what seemed an awfully long time, leaving Major Lawrence to wonder if he would ever finish.

His patience thinning, the major began pushing himself to his feet with intention of taking down the sergeant when a voice called out from inside the tent. The sergeant looked over his shoulder and shouted an obscenity back at the person calling him. Laughter broke out from the group of soldiers inside the tent. Major Lawrence thought better of killing the sergeant, and remained lying still. Finally, the sergeant finished his business, zipped up his trousers, turned around and walked back inside the tent.

Major Lawrence took a knee position and signaled with a wave of the hand for Jack and Lieutenant Roberts to follow him. Jack was first to low-crawl through the barb-wired fence, and Lieutenant Roberts quickly followed. In a few moments they reached the major, taking a knee on either side of him.

German guards maintained roving positions on the outskirts of the camp and on the towers, but not inside the fuel depot, which the major knew worked well in their favor. By the looks of things, most of the Germans appeared to be celebrating with drink and music inside the comfort of their field tents.

*They're celebrating like they've already won the bloody war,* Major Lawrence thought. *Hope they haven't turned tables around on the front once again. At least they'll be preoccupied while we go to work.*

Privat Karl Mohr paced the watch-tower impatiently. He sensed something wrong. Ever since his first day of battle he gained a sixth sense allowing him to determine trouble. He never confessed this to his comrades though. They would have laughed themselves silly. He hated how he looked no older than a schoolboy. What bothered him most this night was how careless everyone seemed. Indeed, Sturmbannfuhrer Mueller had been consistent up to now when it came to security, always instructing officers and non-coms to beware the *Phantom Major*.

"He strikes in the middle of the night and shows no mercy," he warned.

Word of Rommel's next offensive would begin soon and with enough fuel for the panzers it would be only a matter of time before the Britische found themselves on the run and in full retreat. Morale in the Afrika Korps ran high. After nearly two years of seesaw battles the Germans were now poised for final victory. Then perhaps—home!

*It would be good to see father,* Mohr thought, reflecting on his family. *Mummy would be proud too.* Although she preferred her son go to school rather than join the military.

Mohr peered through his field glasses hanging around his neck and he carefully scanned the area. He saw El Karum and his men riding off the base before disappearing in the desert.

*Good, we don't need your kind,* he snarled in thought.

Mohr was no different than other Germans who believed dealing with such a degenerate race as Bedouin was a disgrace to the Fatherland's honor.

*What has become of the Aryan Race if we resolve ourselves to fighting alongside such people?* he reasoned.

Making their way to the fuel depot where barrels were stacked upon one another for as far as they could see in the middle of the night proved easier than the raiders believed. Guards walked their rounds, but appeared more interested in keeping safe distance so they could smoke cigarettes and talk about their women waiting for them back home.

Jack remained close to Major Lawrence, holding his Sten automatic loosely; wondering if he would have to use it.

*I certainly hope not*, he prayed.

He was not even certain he knew how to fire the damned thing. Lieutenant Roberts followed up the rear, moving stealthily and keeping eyes open for a guard who might appear. The major moved closer to Jack and removed his field pack. Next he opened it and pulled out a misshapen piece of plastique and timing pencils. He inserted the timing pencil and snapped one end with pliers. The explosive was now live.

*Thirty minutes!*

He placed the explosives in-between barrels full of petrol, comfortable knowing it could only be found with an intentional search. He looked at Jack to ensure he understood what was expected of him. Jack took a deep breath and nodded twice reluctantly. The major then moved off in the opposite direction where he would put his explosives in place, leaving Jack to go to work on his own.

Jack watched the major disappear in the maze of barrels and suddenly felt more frightened than ever. *How I got in this mess,* he wondered, cursing his misfortune. He had always considered himself a man of opportunity. Now it appeared his luck ran out. *I've got no choice other than playing soldier now.*

Jack resigned himself to doing what he had to do. He moved quietly along many rows of barrels, placing explosives and arming them as Major Lawrence had shown him back with the vehicles. His hands trembled at first, shoving the detonator into the plastique, praying the blasted thing did not blow up in his face. He snapped the end of the timing pencil; put the explosive in place and moved on to another section.

Captain Hawkins took the field glasses from his eyes and glanced at his watch. *It's nearly time to begin our attack.*

It was vital they reached the base in their vehicles right before the first explosive charges detonated. He checked his watch and looked over his shoulder. The raiders were preparing to move, completing their weapons and equipment check. He looked back at the German base through his field glasses and smiled evilly.

*In a few minutes I'm going to unleash a fury on Jerry unlike any other they've experienced. They won't know what hit them.*

# Chapter 26

*The SAS proved incredibly successful against German forces in North Africa.*
*A special unit was formed in Germany with instructions to capture or kill the*
*'Phantom Major.' His behind-the-lines actions created damage on German*
*forces beyond their wildest dreams. Every German soldier learned to respect*
*these daring men, and prayed they never fell victim to their tactics.*

## October 19, 1942
## 12:55 a.m.

Captain Guinness waited alongside Sergeant Davenport for the German guards to make their rounds by the planes before rising from their prone position in the darkness by the edge of the runway. Bent at the waist like crouching tigers, they darted onto the airfield, packs in hand, all the while keeping a close eye out for roving guards. Although it was middle of the night and they had plenty of darkness, there was enough illumination from the moon to give their position away if they got careless. Guard towers also were a threat, for they allowed soldiers a perfect view of the airfield and planes parked alongside the runway. Guinness checked his watch and saw time was not on their side if they were going to keep this a coordinated attack with the major's plan.

*Blast,* he cursed himself. *We've only thirty-five minutes to plant our bombs.*

His orders were to lead the jeeps with Captain Hawkins in the lorries following. However, he and Hawkins decided to risk exceeding orders by planting as many bombs on planes available to them in order to ensure they inflicted maximum damage.

"This would not be the first time orders were exceeded," Hawkins told Guinness. "After all, we don't have enough vehicles to make a proper jeep attack, and every SAS man is expected to improvise." He stared Guinness squarely. "How long do you think we'd last if we always obeyed orders," he added, with a wink.

Guinness reluctantly agreed, fearing Major Lawrence's wrath.

Upon getting closer to the airfield their first thought was how correct the major had been over the care Jerry had taken in setting up this base. The runway was nice and smooth. Each plane had a designated position on the side of the airstrip. Fuel trucks nearby had hangars of their own improvised out of large field tents, and guard towers were positioned in such a way they had a view of planes all along the runway. The raiders would have to calculate their movements as the guards on the towers paced back and forth in order to avoid detection.

Guinness and Davenport wanted to make most of their time and decided to stay close and work on a plane each all the way down the airfield. Splitting up would mean wasting precious seconds. The first planes they reached were Heinkel-111 H6 Bombers. These were beautiful finds for them, and were dreaded by British tank crews, which suffered harrowing losses by Luftwaffe air attacks. Fortunately for the British, the Germans had few numbers of this type aircraft at their disposal.

The raiders approached the planes with caution, keeping an eye out for any unseen guards lying in wait. The placement of explosives on a plane was extremely important in order to guarantee maximum effect upon detonation. There were four areas of choice when placing bombs on a plane. The first was the landing carriage. Placing explosive charges on the upper frame of the right or left wheel directly beneath the wing was like kicking the leg of a chair from under a man. The plane dropped on its side, damaging its wing, propeller, and engine, rendering it inoperable. Unless maintenance crews had a crane available to lift the plane off its side, it could be days before any attempts for repair were made. As it so happened, Captain Guinness checked to see if there were any vehicles fitted with cranes on the field, and much to his satisfaction there were none.

Another method used to destroy a plane was placing explosive charges on the base of the wing where it joined the fuselage. The lining on Heinkel-111s was extremely thin and snapped away easily once the charge detonated, sending the plane careening on its side. A third sabotage method was placing explosive charges on the engine. You did not have to fully destroy the engine. Parts were difficult to obtain, and a single part missing from maintenance shops prevented crews from working on the engine, thus keeping planes grounded for days, even weeks.

The final and most preferred sabotage method was placing explosive charges on the fuselage. Its body was highly flammable and burned to a crisp once the explosive detonated. A plane's fuel tanks added to its own destruction when intense heat from fire caused them to explode. One could always tell a blast from a blown fuel tank to that of plastique. A fuel tank went off with a dull thud, whereas plastique let out a very loud bang.

Captain Guinness and Sergeant Davenport carried enough explosives in two packs each to do a thorough job on a minimum of ten Heinkels each. They moved fast, placing charges on the fuselages before moving to the Messerschmitt ME-109 fighters. At war's outbreak the ME-109s were considered the best in the Luftwaffe. They outflew American-made P-40 Tomahawks and British Hurricanes and remained supreme in the Desert Air War until British Spitfires were introduced in North Africa.

The next plane type they came upon was the JU-52s. From their vantage point they could not destroy so many planes. Logistically it was impossible. They did not have the numbers in men, nor could they carry enough bombs. Shrugging, they knew they'd have to do the best they could. This sort of situation occurred before where they did not have enough men to do the job. They improvised by planting bombs on every other plane. With luck the explosions from each might damage the nearby planes with shrapnel making them inoperable. This worked well seeing how time was running out. Each raider kept a close eye on the guard towers when moving from plane to plane. When they placed their last bombs they nodded at each other and made their way back the way they came.

Lieutenant Roberts finished placing his explosives by the tents where German soldiers were billeted. He paid particular attention to the officers' mess tent. Taking out high-ranking officers would disrupt chain of command, creating confusion once fireworks began. SAS trained to know their enemy and they learned in the German Army a soldier was not trained to use initiative, but rather follow orders. This form of *iron discipline* was intentional in order for officers to have complete control of their men. Thus, common soldiers lacked ability for making critical decisions in absence of officers, which allowed British soldiers an advantage in the field where they were encouraged to use initiative.

The final area the raiders needed to pay attention was the maintenance shops. Depriving the enemy of repair facilities was as important as destroying planes and fuel. Major Lawrence, Jack, and Roberts met at the large machine shop where they would place their explosives. Upon entering the large field tent they were relieved to find it empty. Wasting no time, they placed plastique charges inside a locker filled with tools and shoved a box of nails in the locker too. Anyone nearby would be riddled with pieces of hot metal when the charges detonated. For good measure they placed cans of paint used for camouflaging equipment near the locker which would help start a fire.

"Let's get out of here," Major Lawrence whispered, once they finished.

They made their way back the way they came, which meant going through the fuel dump. Jack felt uncomfortable seeing how the whole lot was due to go up in smoke sooner than later, but offered no protest. He followed the major and Roberts closely. Things went smooth until he crept close to one of the barrels and the butt end of his Sten automatic banged against it. In the still of night a metallic sound was loud. The three raiders froze!

The music and cheering coming from tents where German soldiers celebrated continued, but the men on guard heard the sound within the fuel dump and stopped dead in their tracks. They waited for another sign to pinpoint its origination.

"Was ist das?" (What is that?) an alarmed guard asked his comrade.

His comrade shook his head.

Privat Karl Mohr heard the metallic noise ring out and tried focusing on where it originated. *Perhaps it's nothing,* he thought. *Then again...*

Mohr's sixth-sense roused him. He reached for his field glasses and lifted them to his eyes. It was too dark. Anyone could have sought cover in the shadows and he would have been none the wiser. This frustrated Mohr and he lowered the glasses, disappointed. He recalled times when Bedouin crept inside the base searching for supplies to steal. Sometimes their main intention was to get their hands on German beer and Schnapps, a favorite commodity with locals. Had they something to trade with they would have merely asked, but most times they resorted to thievery.

Mohr glanced at the field phone on the table nearby. *I should notify the sergeant-of-the-guard,* he told himself. He lifted the phone from its cradle, but did not turn the crank handle on the field box which would ring the phone in the command post. *What do I do?*

Jack remained frozen for what seemed an eternity. He screwed up and knew it. The clock was ticking and time was not on his side, he knew.

*I've gotta get outta here before this place goes up in smoke!*

He started to move when he thought he heard footsteps approaching. Jack froze. He held his breath. He heard it again! Someone was definitely coming towards him. He was certain of it!

Major Lawrence observed from a kneeling position what was going on. The fuel barrels had enough space between them for him to see Jack's position. A German sentry appeared suddenly and from nowhere.

*Probably sleeping on duty is why we never came across him,* he thought.

The noise the Yank made must have awakened him and now he was here to investigate. Lawrence assessed the situation and surmised he could sneak up to the sentry and kill him with his knife, but this risked exposing himself to the guard tower. In the end he decided to kill the sentry. He got to his feet and moved no further than two steps when all of a sudden the lights to the camp lit up. The raiders quickly dove to the ground, burying themselves in the dirt!

*What the hell is going on?* Lawrence wanted to know.

Searchlights!

The guard tower closest to their side of the fuel depot had switched on searchlights and began scanning the immediate area. Apparently more than one German sentry heard the noise from the Yank and was prepared to investigate. Major Lawrence looked up and saw the sentry making way toward Jack's position. The German was not on high-alert though, for he carried his weapon slung over his shoulder as though he did not really expect to find anything. The major gripped his knife tightly. If he got up and went for the roving sentry he would expose himself. The rows of barrels were aligned with the guard tower so that anyone moving between them would be seen.

Major Lawrence shook his head. *Sorry, Yank, you're on your own!*

Jack perspired profusely and uncontrollably. From his position behind the barrel he saw the guard tower and searchlight used to scan the area. It looked like a giant ray of light showering everything with sunshine as the soldier on the tower swept the light back and forth, sometimes slowly, other times quickly. Guards on opposite end of the base had been alerted by the activity and switched their lights on too, scanning the area over their sectors.

*What the hell have you done, Jack?!* he cursed himself. He looked behind him where the sentry had stood and was shocked to find him gone. *Where the hell have you gone?*

He was close to panicking and held his Sten automatic ready for action, but careful not to remove the safety switch. Jack knew he was no professional soldier, but had enough common sense to know firing his weapon would bring the entire camp to life. From the look of things it appeared only the roving guards in the fuel depot had been alerted something was amiss. The rest of the soldiers in their tents continued celebrating, singing, listening to music, and getting drunk.

*Wish I were doing same*, Jack thought.

Feldwebel Walther Prien relieved himself behind barrels of petrol in the fuel depot when he heard the metallic bang. It was not too loud, but enough for him to know it was man-made, and not a Bedouin with the habit of crossing through German camps as though he had no care in the world.

Prien had the nasty habit of hiding from his men during his watch, catching them napping whilst on guard duty. On many occasion he awakened them with a swift kick in the rump. Prien was not a large, threatening man, but trim and fit enough to take on anyone crossing his path. None of his men ever challenged him.

The guard on the tower observed Prien step out from the darkness and waved, acknowledging him. He wanted his sergeant to know he was on the ball and not sleeping. Prien went from the front of each row looking down each as carefully as he could. It was still too dark to see much, but he hoped he might find whoever was there. Every few feet he stopped and listened, taking in as much as he could. He heard nothing and continued moving from row to row. If the intruder was a Bedouin he would have a nasty surprise for him.

*I'll whip the skin off the man's back*, he said silently.

Then something came over him which he could not explain. He somehow knew the intruder was not Bedouin, but the enemy. He did not know how, but he simply knew. Perhaps it was because the intruder remained carefully out of sight, making a point not to give away his position with more sound. Perhaps it was his *sixth sense?* Prien did not know, but he felt he was right.

*This intruder is English!* Prien unsnapped the cover on his holster and withdrew his Luger P-08 pistol. He carried it low, but gripped the handle tightly. He knew on this night he needed it.

Captain Hawkins and his convoy were within one mile of the German base when they saw the searchlights spring to life. Hawkins drove in the lead jeep and quickly raised his right arm, signaling drivers in the vehicles behind him to halt.

*What the hell is going on?* he wondered. He prayed the Germans had not spotted them and prepared to repulse their attack.

"What do you suppose is going on, Captain?" Corporal Davis, his driver, asked.

Hawkins shook his head. "No idea," he replied, flatly.

The corporal looked at the captain expectantly. "What are your orders, sir?"

Captain Hawkins paused and looked at his watch. "We move in five minutes," he said with finality. "We'll hit the base in conjunction when the major's explosives are set to go off."

Jack had a poor memory when it came to faces, but there was something oddly familiar about the kraut nearest him. He had no idea why or how, but he was certain he had seen the man before. In any case, he had no intention of pondering the thought. He had to get out of there—fast! He took a second look at the guard tower, praying for the coast to be clear. When he turned around much to his surprise the kraut sergeant had disappeared. This sent Jack's heart racing.

*Where the hell did he go?* He looked to his right, then left, front, and rear, but found no sign of him. *My God, what's going on here?*

He checked his watch. He had to move now; otherwise he'd go up with the whole lot of petrol. He rose from his kneeling position and something heavy came down on him, knocking him to the ground. His Sten was wrenched free from his hands. Jack struggled to get the sack of potatoes, or whatever it was, off his back, but the weight was too much. Then he realized he had been jumped by the kraut sergeant. Jack was no fighter, never had been, but he had no intention of dying in the middle of the North African desert. He quickly brought up his elbow with strength he never knew he had, striking the man in the kidney. The kraut let out a howl and rolled off Jack, gasping in pain. Jack got to his feet right when the soldier on the guard tower shone the light on him.

Walther Prien lay on his back, writhing in pain, holding his left side where he had been struck. When the light illuminated the intruder, Prien's eyes widened with sheer surprise. *The man from Tobruk! The one from the downed plane!*

"*Sie!*" (You!) Prien shouted. He started to lift his right hand holding the Luger and leveled it on Jack. He squeezed the trigger, but the light from the guard tower caught his eyes, forcing him to turn his face. The shot went wide, missing Jack and giving him time to dash out of sight.

Prien jumped to his feet and took aim in the direction Jack ran. Before he had a chance to fire he found himself showered with sparks bouncing off the barrels of petrol around him. Someone was shooting at him and the bullets ricocheted off the barrels. He had to duck immediately, losing the opportunity of firing at the intruder.

*That's the man I swore I'd face before war's end*, he reminded himself.

Major Lawrence had hoped—*prayed even*—the Yank managed an escape, but the German sergeant had been better than he expected. He saw the German stealthily approach Jack from behind and strike him.

*Cunning bastard!* Major Lawrence swore.

He watched Jack fight back, but to no avail. He leveled his Sten in their direction and fired a three-burst barrage, striking the barrels of petrol nearby.

*Blast! How could I have missed?* The German had been his target, but in all the commotion he missed. *Amazing those shots and sparks didn't ignite the fuel!*

They had to move fast. Time was not on their side if they were to meet Captain Hawkins at the rendezvous. The camp suddenly came to life. An alarm sounded, piercing the night with its high-pitched shrill. Major Lawrence took aim at the guard tower nearest him and opened fire, spraying the sentry with two five-round bursts, shattering the light and striking the sentry, who cried out and fell flat on his back on the platform.

Jack ran like he never ran before. He had to get out of the fuel depot fast! The odd feeling swept over him about the German who pummeled him from behind.

*Why is that Kraut familiar?* he wondered.

Jack spotted Major Lawrence taking aim at German soldiers coming toward them. He fired three-second bursts and three of them fell dead.

"Keep running!" he shouted to Jack.

It was an order Jack found all too agreeable. When he reached the major he was practically out of breath. "We've gotta get outta here!" Jack cried. His chest heaved, sucking in much-needed air.

"I know," the major replied. "Keep your weapon ready and follow me."

Jack had lost his Sten in the fight with the sergeant, but still had his pistol. He pulled it from his holster and followed the major.

Sturmbannfuhrer Hans Mueller dashed from the officer's tent, Luger in hand. His tunic was unbuttoned at the collar from having enjoyed a relaxing game of cards with his men when shooting broke out. His expression was pure shock.

*"What in God's name is happening?!"* he cried.

One of the soldiers nearby told him he believed they were under attack from El Karum's tribe seeing how they were dissatisfied with their agreement, but the automatic gunfire told the sturmbannfuhrer otherwise. He knew the Wogs had few automatics on hand.

An alarm sounded and its high-pitched shrill reverberated throughout the camp.

Mueller barked commands to his officers and men, ordering them to deploy throughout the base. He had no intention of losing his camp to the enemy, not when Rommel relied on him to keep it intact for their coming offensive.

Sturmbannfuhrer Wolfgang Klement and Hauptmann Konrad Diestl had retired to their tents for much-needed sleep when the camp came to life with gunfire. Their first reaction was to throw on their clothes and get to their planes. With lightning speed, they jumped into the nearest kubelwagen and sped off to the runway. When they caught glimpse of moving vehicles approaching their path they recognized the vehicles belonged to the enemy.

"It's the *Phantom Major!*" Diestl cried, pointing in their direction.

"We have to hurry," Klement warned. He pressed down on the gas pedal, sending the vehicle down the road as fast as the little car managed.

Captain Hawkins saw the kubelwagen heading their way and swung the swivel-mounted, twin pair of Lewis guns in its direction, took aim, and fired a barrage of gunfire. The .303 caliber rounds tore into the German car, sending sparks over the men inside. Hawkins thought the car was going to split in two. He saw the driver lose control and the kubelwagen flipped over, rolling twice before coming to a stop on top of its occupants.

"Nice shooting, sir!" Corporal Davis shouted. His eyes bulged with excitement.

Being congratulated at this point was the furthest thing from Hawkins' mind. His primary concern was succeeding his part of the mission. *Now they know we are here, they are most likely getting ready for a fight.* He swore softly, wondering how Major Lawrence and his team were getting along.

"Drive hard and fast, Corporal," Hawkins demanded. "We've a lot of work ahead of us."

Privat Karl Mohr had been startled by the gunshots. When the sentry on the tower nearby switched on his searchlight he feared his *sixth-sense* had been correct. He witnessed the guard on the tower go down when he took gunfire coming from inside the fuel depot. The searchlight had been destroyed by gunfire, too.

*Someone wants us to remain blind,* he guessed, correctly.

Mohr felt fortunate for having been ordered to switch tower watch positions earlier that evening. The sergeant demanded each man be familiar with camp surroundings and ordered them to change positions regularly. Shortly after the raid began Mohr saw a kubelwagen dart out of the camp and head for the runway. He heard more shots fired from vehicles coming on the runway, and the next thing Mohr witnessed was the kubelwagen being torn apart before rolling over and coming to a crashing halt.

He saw muzzle flashes from the machine gun firing at them and he quickly manned his MG-34 machine gun mounted on the rail of the guard tower. He adjusted his eyes to the dark and the moonlight provided enough illumination for him to keep his bearings straight. Mohr took aim, held his breath, and squeezed the trigger.

Captain Hawkins saw the muzzle flash from the guard tower shoot out like a dragon breathing fire. His jeep was hit on its hood with a hail of bullets, tearing chunks of metal away and showering him and Corporal Davis with sparks. The men in the rear vehicles opened fire on the tower and their gunfire ripped into the wooden structure, forcing the German soldier to drop to the floor for cover.

"Keep driving!" Hawkins ordered. He knew they had to keep moving. Getting pinned down was not an option, and Hawkins was pleased to find no more shots coming from the tower.

Jack and Major Lawrence darted from one hiding spot to another. The camp was filled with Germans running everywhere, but it was clear they were completely confused. They all talked at once, no one listening to the other. When a German soldier ran in their direction, the major drew his knife and shoved it in the man's mid-section up to the blade's hilt. The soldier stared back wide-eyed in fear before dropping to his knees.

Jack noticed how Major Lawrence did this without so much as blinking an eye. A moment later Jack witnessed him shoot three Germans standing between them and the motor pool. The soldiers had seen them and raised their weapons to shoot, but the major was faster and cut them down in rapid succession. Major Lawrence had not slowed down his running during all this, and Jack had a tough time keeping up. In all this action, Jack could not help wonder how the major appeared to be so calm, like this was a natural evening for him. He admitted to himself he was impressed, but only for a moment. His primary concern was getting out of the camp before it went up in smoke.

Major Lawrence looked over his shoulder to see Jack was still with him. "This way," he shouted so he was heard over all the noise erupting throughout the camp.

To Jack, it seemed like Fourth of July in the middle of the North African Desert. Gunshots were fired in all directions, German soldiers hollered at one another in confusion, and no one seemed to notice them in spite running right past them, sometimes as close as a few feet. Major Lawrence led their way between tents on the edge of the camp where they faced a barrier of barbed-wire. He reached down and lifted the wire, signaling for Jack to crawl under first. Wasting no time, Jack got face down in the dirt and low-crawled on his belly through the wire barrier with the major close behind.

Sturmbannfuhrer Wolfgang Klement clawed his way from under the kubelwagen. When bullets riddled his vehicle he had lost control. The next thing he knew the little car was rolling over and over before coming to a halt on top of him and Hauptmann Diestl. Klement breathed heavily, his chest hurting with each inhale. He slowly rose to his feet.

*No broken bones? How's that possible.* He was grateful nonetheless. He took a step forward, but not without a limp. *Thank God that's all it is,* he prayed.

He looked for his friend despite all the gunfire and action taking place all over the base. When he walked around the other side of the kubelwagen he found his friend Konrad. The car had fallen on top of Diestl, crushing him. His tunic was stained dark crimson from his blood, and his eyes stared lifelessly toward the sky. The scene was grotesque, forcing Klement to turn away before he became sick. A feeling of sadness forced his eyes to water over loss of his longtime friend. They had fought together since the beginning of the war.

*So many battles and to die like this in a ditch in the middle of the Afrikan desert!* It was too unceremonious for Klement to fathom. *And so unfair!*

Klement shook his head to get his bearings and clear the cobwebs. *Pull yourself together! There's a war going on!* He knew the camp was under fire by the infamous jeep raiders. *Probably the Phantom Major himself,* he thought. A surge of anger overcame Klement and he found himself swearing to avenge his kameraden. Forgetting his injuries, Klement limped towards the airfield, determined to get to his plane.

Privat Karl Mohr opened his eyes, wondering why he laid on his back on top of the tower. He raised his torso, leaning on elbows and then remembered the jeep raiders firing at him. He had only been unconscious a matter of seconds, but it felt longer. He looked at his MG-34 machine gun lying next to him. It had been knocked off its mount from enemy gunfire and taken hits, making it inoperable.

*Damn!* he swore.

He got to his feet and saw the raiders driving down the runway firing at undefended planes lined up in neat rows along the airfield. Karl felt a surge of anger swell within. His helplessness made him equally angry for having been subdued so quickly. With no weapon to fight with, Karl climbed down the ladder and ran to one of the nearby tents to find a machine gun, a rifle, a pistol, anything with which to fight the *Phantom Major.*

Captain Hawkins knew they struck gold! In spite their presence being seen before their attack began, all his vehicles were intact. His jeep sustained hits, but the tough vehicle was still running strong. When they reached the runway Captain Hawkins looked over his shoulder at the rest of his team following, and grinned over their good fortune. With one hand still holding the pistol grip of his Lewis guns, he reached down and took hold of the Verey Light pistol. Pointing it skyward, he squeezed the trigger, sending the flare over the airfield.

The round shot out like a bolt of lightning and lit up the entire airfield when it burst.

"Let's go!" he shouted right before squeezing the triggers to his machine guns.

The vehicles fanned out to right and left of Hawkins' jeep, forming a small arrow-shaped group with Hawkins at point. All guns opened fire at planes sitting picture-perfect. The sheet-metal skin and engines tore up under a hail of bullets. Engines caught fire and exploded, sending flames on other planes next to them. In a matter of seconds, the airfield was lit up with burning planes.

Sturmbannfuhrer Hans Mueller saw the flare light up the airfield and his heart sank. *The Phantom Major again! How did he find us?*

His morale sagged further upon witnessing enemy vehicles dart down the middle of the runway, machine gunning precious planes. When a flare erupted the entire camp seemed to come to a halt. The shock of being attacked by the enemy had been far from a viable possibility, and yet it now happened.

Mueller saw how his men froze and knew it was up to him to snap them out of their momentary trance. "EVERYONE TO THE AIRFIELD!" he shouted at the top of his lungs. "FIRE TEAMS; BRING WATER TRUCKS! LEUTNANT MODEL, GET YOUR MEN MOUNTED IN VEHICLES AND GO AFTER THOSE GANGSTERS! SCHNELL, SCHNELL!"

Everyone scrambled into action upon hearing orders from their commandant. Mueller dashed to his kubelwagen when he was stopped by a bright light erupting from within the fuel depot. It was followed by an explosion powerful enough to knock everyone off their feet, including Mueller. The camp was showered with burning petrol, destroying tents, vehicles, and nearby supply buildings.

An explosion from far side of the camp erupted, and moments later vehicles showered by petrol caught fire and exploded along with planes going up in smoke one by one in rapid succession. Dull thuds from the fuel depot went off when barrel after barrel exploded in showers of flames. Fire teams hastily went into action, turning on water pumps operating hoses to douse them.

Sturmbannfuhrer Mueller scrambled to his feet with help of a sergeant who took him by the arm. He checked himself, grateful to be unhurt, but for the first time in his military career he felt defeated. Nearby soldiers did not notice his sorrowful expression. Mueller had always been the sort who succeeded in everything. In fact, he had never been in a battle he lost other than the *Battle of Britain*, which was downplayed by the Ministry of Propaganda. This was for all intent and purposes his first bloody nose since then—and he did not take this well.

This attack made Mueller feel he let his guard down, his men down, himself down, and most importantly he let Field Marshal Rommel down. He lowered his head in defeat when suddenly; Mueller felt a pair of hands shake the back of his shoulders. He turned and faced Leutnant Gunther Kleist. He was shouting at the top of his lungs.

"Herr Sturmbannfuhrer, we have to get every available—"

BOOM!

The blast blew everyone in the camp off their feet. Kleist was thrown into Mueller's arms, forcing him to fall on his back. Kleist rolled off him and got to his feet, shaking his head to clear the cobwebs.

"Are you all right, Herr Sturmbannfuhrer?"

Mueller did not reply, so Kleist repeated the question, pulling Mueller to his feet. Mueller looked around and immediately saw the hopelessness of combating fires as well as their attackers. He knew in the Wehrmacht to admit defeat was punishable by death, so he kept this opinion to himself.

"The petrol is gone, Herr Sturmbannfuhrer," Kleist cried, drawing Mueller close so that he could speak in his ear. "The airfield is under attack! We must send every available man to salvage what we can!"

Mueller's eyes remained transfixed on the destroyed fuel depot burning bright. Barrels of fuel continued exploding two to three seconds apart.

Kleist grabbed Mueller by the arms and shook him ferociously. "Herr Sturmbannfuhrer, we must act now!"

Disgusted with the condition of his commanding officer, Kleist drew his hand back and slapped Mueller hard across the face.

It worked! Mueller snapped back to the situation at hand.

Kleist saw he was now aware of what happened and said, "Forgive me, Herr Sturmbannfuhrer, but—"

"No need to explain," Mueller said, with a wave of his hand. "Come on. Let's get the men to the airfield before we have nothing left to save."

Jack and Major Lawrence scurried on outskirts of the camp, avoiding German soldiers who were in frenzy from the gunfire and explosions. They appeared in disarray, lacking direction from an officer, and this pleased Major Lawrence. Fires burned brightly everywhere and it soon appeared the Germans gave up trying to save the fuel depot.

When Jack and the major reached a dry riverbed they broke into a full sprint seeing how they were out of view of enemy soldiers. Another flare exploded in the sky and Major Lawrence saw Captain Hawkins and his team doing a good job of destroying enemy planes. He also noticed a large number of soldiers running towards the airfield.

The major stopped and pointed at them. "They're going to try and save the few planes they have left," he said, excitedly. His adrenaline ran high and his breathing was heavy from all their running.

Jack looked at the airfield, then back to the major. "So?" He had no idea what the major was leading to.

"We can't allow that," the major cried.

Jack looked incredulous. "Exactly what do you think the *two* of us can do?" he challenged.

Major Lawrence had no immediate solution. They were not armed to challenge a large group of enemy soldiers armed to the teeth. He scanned their surroundings, desperately trying to think what to do. He saw an abandoned gun post north of the runway. The soldiers manning it had left to help put out the fires. Had they remained in their position they would have been in perfect position to counter-attack the jeep raiders.

Major Lawrence tapped Jack's shoulder. "Follow me!" he ordered.

Jack did, but with great reluctance.

Privat Karl Mohr found an MP40 submachine pistol and raced across the base to join troops preparing to counter-attack the raiders. He was determined to get his pound of flesh, and saw the gangsters nearing the end of their first run down the runway and make their turn for a second run. German troops reached the edge of the runway and dropped to prone positions, weapons aimed downrange. They were lined perfectly to open fire on the raiders' flank when they approached. Mohr and his kameraden were ready for the slaughter!

The jeep raiders drove down the runway full speed. Each German soldier took careful aim and waited for the order to open fire. Surprise was on their side for it appeared the raiders were none the wiser as to what they were about to drive into. Mohr pulled back the firing bolt to his MP40 and chambered a round. He took aim on the first jeep and waited. He was unaware of the thin smile pursing his lips as his finger gently touched the trigger.

Captain Hawkins signaled the raiders to halt with a raised arm. He wanted to be certain they were in position before getting on the move once more. None of his men had been killed or wounded, and most of their targets were up in flames, but not all. He looked across the field toward the billets and saw how they were in complete chaos.

*Good for you, Major!* he thought, grinning.

He looked over his shoulder and shouted, "Okay, let's finish this!" He pumped his arm up and down several times, the signal for them to get on the move in a hurry, and off they went. The next events occurred too fast for him to realize what was happening.

Bullets came at them from beneath planes on their left flank, almost as though pilots were sitting in their cockpits firing away. The rounds tore up the raiders' vehicles, and the men automatically returned fire, but the counter-attack was brutally strong. Corporal Davis was hit in his left arm and leg, crying a high-pitched scream as pain ran through him like a lightning bolt. He kept his jeep under control, but felt like losing consciousness.

Captain Hawkins reached down and grabbed the steering wheel, keeping the vehicle in control. He handled this task best as possible, but his vision was impaired from a shower of sparks erupting from his vehicle as it took hits from enemy guns. The raiders continued to return fire, but had little effect. With his free hand, Hawkins reached for his Verey Light Pistol, aimed high in the general direction he believed enemy troops were positioned, and squeezed the trigger.

Right when the flare exploded overhead, lighting up the airfield, the vehicle bringing up their rear burst into flames, blowing apart its occupants like matchsticks. Captain Hawkins and the rest continued driving on, unable to stop at this point. A moment later his eyes widened in shock when he saw a plane running down the runway towards them full speed.

*A Stuka!* "What in the bloody—"

There was no time to finish his sentence. "Are you okay to drive?" he asked Corporal Davis. His tone was laced with desperation.

The corporal nodded and took control of the steering wheel.

Hawkins got to his feet and grabbed the pistol grips on the turret-mounted twin Lewis guns, took aim, and squeezed the triggers.

Sturmbannfuhrer Wolfgang Klement reached the runway well before the fighting went full swing. All around him destruction bathed the camp. He could not fathom how so much damage could be inflicted in so short a time.

*Not to Rommel's Afrika Korps!* he told himself, refusing to believe they could be attacked so effectively so far from the front lines.

Klement climbed into the cockpit of his Stuka Dive Bomber, quickly strapping himself into his seat and switched on the engines. His leg hurt beyond belief, but his adrenaline ran high and he ignored the pain, operating the pedals at his feet well enough to keep the plane under control. In a matter of moments the Stuka was on the move. Once on the runway Klement saw the raiders make a 180 degree turn at the end of the runway and race back in his direction. This was a do-or-die situation, and he quickly got his plane to full speed. The distance between Klement and the raiders closed. He was close to lift-off speed when he saw muzzle flashes erupt from the raiders' guns.

The Stuka's cockpit windshield spider-webbed, and took hits in the engine, propeller, and wings, too. Klement's face was cut from shards of glass, but he stoically pressed on. In his haste to get in the air he had not donned goggles and the wind rushing in the cockpit combined with blood from his face getting in his eyes blinded him.

*The throttle feels loose,* he noted.

The ailerons were disabled. Klement worked feverishly to keep his plane on the runway, but it swerved wildly, smashing into parked planes. Klement screamed in horror right when his Stuka's engine exploded in an orange ball of fire and black smoke. Flames engulfed him and in his final moments he experienced a pilot's worst nightmare—*being burned alive in his plane.*

Major Lawrence reached the gun post with Jack in tow. They watched the Stuka attempt takeoff before crashing into a group of planes and going up in smoke, and welcomed the diversion. Soldiers positioned on edge of the runway had stopped firing on the raiders when they witnessed the Stuka pilot taking his plane down the runway. The scene was incredible and stunned them, providing Major Lawrence and Jack an advantage.

Finding an unmanned MG34 gun post on the edge of the runway, Major Lawrence jumped in and took hold of the weapon. He lined his sights with the Germans who were completely exposed and vulnerable from his position. Taking aim, he squeezed the trigger and held it. The MG34 spat a bright, orange flame and its rounds traveled downrange on target. The machine gun was mounted on a tripod, which helped the major keep it under control, but its recoil remained violent.

One by one German soldiers dropped to the ground, rolling in agony from bullets tearing into flesh and bone. The pain was like a sharp knife tearing into them and their high-pitched screams nearly drowned the rat-a-tat-tat sound from the machine gun firing on them. Under normal conditions the major would have fired five to seven round bursts to ensure his rounds were on target, but the excitement of battle got the better of him and he maintained a steady staccato of gunfire.

Privat Karl Mohr knew something wrong had befallen his kameraden when he heard screams of pain down the line of defense. He was stunned upon seeing fellow soldiers cut down from a machinegun firing from one of their own gun posts. He saw Sturmbannfuhrer Mueller dive for cover and Leutnant Joachim Model follow suit. Others were not so lucky. Mohr raised his MP40 to shoulder level and lined his sights on the man firing on his kameraden.

Then he squeezed the trigger.

Major Lawrence and Jack dove for cover behind sandbags surrounding the gun post when bullets came zipping all around them. Sandbags provided good cover, but they were pinned down with no hope of leaving until the soldier took time and reloaded.

"Any more bright ideas," Jack hissed. He lay next to the major with his hands over his head.

"Get ready to move," the major replied, ignoring his sarcasm. "He'll have to reload any second now."

No sooner had he finished his sentence the firing stopped.

"Let's go!" he shouted, and took off running like a bat out of hell.

After running for what seemed a long time the major and Jack stopped, catching their breath. They looked back at the German camp and knew Rommel's plans to attack Alexandria and Cairo had effectively been compromised. Without petrol reserves the Desert Fox had no choice other than dig in and go on defensive. During this time British forces would mobilize and begin an attack of their own. With luck, the fortunes of war in the desert would turn in their favor.

# Chapter 27

*Special Air Service actions against Germans in North Africa inspired creation of many such units for behind-the-lines missions. Their success eventually turned negative opinions from General Headquarters staff to those of encouragement. Ironically, German success at Eban Emael in 1940 inspired British officers to create commando-style units. By the time Hitler recognized these units' effectiveness and pressed for creation of his own such units, the fortunes of war turned against the Axis.*

## Camp Lili Marlene

Feldwebel Walther Prien wanted vengeance. His pride was at stake and he was determined to kill the man from Tobruk. Taking in his surroundings, he looked on with dismay. Destruction in the camp was tenfold and fires burned everywhere. Soldiers ran in disarray. Prien heard footsteps approach from behind. With lightning speed he turned and raised his pistol to the man's head.

"Don't shoot, Sergeant!" cried the soldier standing before him. "It's me, Privat Mohr!"

Prien exhaled a sigh of relief. He saw Mohr was armed with an MP40. *Good,* he thought. *The boy might be of use after all.*

"The jeep raiders have succeeded in destroying the airfield," Mohr explained. He pointed behind him at the carnage. "Sturmbannfuhrer Mueller has ordered as many men possible to help put out the fires, but I'm afraid their efforts are in vain."

Prien nodded. "I know," he replied, displaying little emotion. "I want the men responsible for this," he hissed.

"I saw them make way into the desert," Mohr said, pointing in the last direction he had seen them.

"Do you have plenty of ammunition?"

"Jawohl!" Mohr quickly replied.

"Good. Follow me."

Major Lawrence and Jack cleared the ridge and were overjoyed to see Captain Hawkins and his remaining team waiting for them. "Good to see you," he said to Sergeant Davenport.

"And you too, sir," Davenport replied, with a weary smile.

Major Lawrence walked up to Captain Hawkins who leaned on his jeep while Lieutenant Roberts bandaged his injured arm. "Nothing serious I hope," he said, casually.

"I'll manage, sir," Hawkins replied, in an equally casual tone. Even the most minor wounds required immediate attention in order to avoid infection, which ran rampant in the desert. Learning basic field medication had been a necessity in the SAS seeing how they relied solely on each other.

It did not escape the major's attention one lorry and its crew was missing. He decided to discuss what happened with Hawkins later. The attack had drained all their strength, not to mention their close calls with death. But the first thing which came to mind was one of Stirling's adages.

*"The mission is not over until you bring your team safely home."*

Major Lawrence and Jack assisted bandaging the wounded. Fortunately no one had life-threatening injuries, but it was a long journey back to Kabrit and they would be in for a rough ride. Jack felt sick helping Private Caine wrap his arm with a field dressing. Caine had been shot in the left arm, and although it was only a flesh wound it bled profusely, soaking his shirt and trousers with blood.

"Thanks for the help, mate," Caine said, gritting his teeth while controlling the pain.

Jack felt sick in the stomach by the sight of so much blood, but managed to finish securing the dressing on the wound. "You're gonna be okay," he replied, grateful he did not vomit. "You need any salve?" He referred to an ointment used to help heal wounds. It proved quite effective in the desert.

*KA-POW!*

The shot rang out loud in the early morning darkness, the rifle's report echoing for miles across the desert. Instinctively, everyone dropped to the ground for cover, reaching for their weapons.

Jack saw Private Caine still standing, staring ahead like he was in some sort of trance. "Get down, you fool!" he growled.

Caine dropped face forward, hitting the ground like a sack of potatoes. Jack crawled to him and turned him over, and then quickly pulled back upon seeing a neat bullet hole in Caine's forehead. A small amount of blood trickled down his forehead, his eyes staring lifelessly at Jack. More shots rang out, and Jack crawled away from Caine and beneath a lorry for cover.

Muzzle flashes were seen at the top of a ridge. By the sound of shots fired, it appeared to be no more than a couple of men. Major Lawrence grabbed hold of a Sten automatic and fired in their direction. Others joined in and soon a loud cacophony of automatic gunfire stung their ears.

Walther Prien and Karl Mohr followed the raiders' tracks on a BMW R75 motorcycle with attached side car, making good time. They stopped at the base of a small hill and stealthily climbed it. When they reached the top they saw the raiders below tending to wounded.

*We found them! Perhaps the Phantom Major himself is among them! What an accomplishment this will be for a Wehrmacht Sergeant, to capture or even kill the most dangerous man in North Afrika.* It was all Prien could do to keep from crying with joy.

When they opened fire on the raiders below Prien had been caught by surprise when the raiders responded with lightning-quick return gunfire. Bullets kicked up rock and dirt, showering them and forcing them to duck for cover. They had no choice other than low-crawl back the way they came or risk being killed.

*I will live to fight another day,* he told himself before disappearing in the night.

When the shooting stopped, Major Lawrence and two SAS men stealthily worked their way up the hill where the gunfire originated. Upon reaching the top they found spent cartridges and tracks in the dirt where the enemy had been. After performing a quick recce of the immediate area they deduced the threat was over and returned to their vehicles.

"By dawn enemy planes will be scouting the desert for us," Major Lawrence told his men. "We have to get far from here right quick." He paused and stared toward the open desert they needed to cross. "It's a long and arduous ride to Kabrit," he added, solemnly. He turned and faced his men. "Let's move."

Everyone climbed aboard their vehicles, anxious to leave this place. Jack stopped and looked over his shoulder. In the distance he saw the dark sky illuminated by fires from the German camp. An occasional explosion erupted the still of night.

"A pretty sight," Captain Hawkins said.

Jack agreed and somehow felt proud being part of this team which played a critical role in changing the course of the war. Without petrol Rommel could not achieve a sustained offensive. This played into British favor for now Montgomery had time enough to build his forces and make good his own offensive and drive the Germans back to Tunisia.

"Yes, I couldn't agree more," Jack said with a smile and sense of pride.

"You handled yourself well," Hawkins added. "I think you have the makings of a top-notch soldier."

"Good Heavens, no!" Jack replied, defiantly.

# Chapter 28

*The fortunes of war changed hands many times throughout the Battle of North Africa. This was a period of uncertainty, fear, and determination. Sometimes having superior numbers in men and material was not enough. Sometimes having plain good luck made all the difference.*

## Rommel's Field Headquarters, October 19, 1942
## 10 miles south of Mersa Matruh

Sturmbannfuhrer Freiherr von Mellenthin disliked informing disturbing news to the field marshal, but he held title Chief Intelligence and this was his duty. Besides, he knew the field marshal expected answers from him soon enough. Von Mellenthin's face turned pale at the thought of Rommel's reaction and he needed a stiff glass of cognac to calm his nerves.

"Can I bring you something to eat, Herr Sturmbannfuhrer?" the clerk asked, standing at attention while von Mellenthin sat at his desk.

Everyone in his inner circle noted how the handsome aristocrat appeared leaner than when he first arrived in North Afrika. Then again, so did many men in the Afrika Korps. The hot weather destroyed one's hunger, not to mention the poor diet prepared by the quartermaster. Food was so distasteful they could not wait to grab hold of captured Britische supplies where they feasted on bully-beef, biscuits, and chocolate, which was ironically disliked by British troops.

"Nein," von Mellenthin replied.

The clerk clicked his heels, spun a 180 degree turn and left the tent.

Von Mellenthin reached for a glass of water on his desk and downed it, spilling some on his hand. He wiped his lips and then licked precious drops of water from his fingers. This was a habit all men in North Afrika performed to ensure not a single drop went to waste. Rommel, he knew, had been an early-bird riser, up by five o'clock each morning. With the coming offensive he thought better to catch an hour or two more sleep in order to be at his very best. Von Mellenthin snatched the single sheet of paper on his desk and hurried to Rommel's tent.

He knocked on the wooden pole before entering. "Herr Field Marshal, may I come in?" he asked, drawing a deep breath.

Rommel rolled over on his cot. "Yes, what is it?" he replied, rising to a sitting position. He swung his legs over the edge of the cot, rubbing his eyes right when von Mellenthin entered.

The field marshal's habits never ceased to amaze those close to him. His quarters were nearly as sparse as the common field soldier. By his cot stood a small end table where his marshal's baton rested beside a book. His uniform hung on a nail stuck in a pole inside his tent. On one side of the tent was a table and chair where he wrote daily letters to his wife. A single light bulb dangled from the ceiling. This was the extent of Rommel's personal luxuries.

Von Mellenthin cleared his throat. "I have disappointing news, Herr Field Marshal," he managed to say. He noted how Rommel stared back as if to say, get on with it. "Camp Lili Marlene was attacked early this morning."

The ensuing silence made von Mellenthin uncomfortable. Rommel's reputation for patience toward common foot soldiers was well-known and his impatience with subordinate officers was equally famous—especially when he received bad news! When von Mellenthin finished reading his damage report Rommel stared back in silence a painfully long time. Von Mellenthin could not determine if his silence was due to anger building up or being stunned by the news.

He took one step forward and said, "Herr Field Marshal?"

Rommel snapped out of his momentary trance. "What did you say?" he asked, puzzled.

Von Mellenthin read the report again and Rommel looked on in silence. He looked for his boots and found them beneath his cot. He pulled them on his feet one at a time in slow motion, as it appeared to von Mellenthin.

"How many planes did you say were lost?" Rommel demanded.

Von Mellenthin took a deep breath. "One hundred-sixty planes of all types destroyed or damaged to the point of being out of action," he began, unable to hide anxiety growing in his voice. "The camp kommandant is gathering numbers of those which may be repaired as we speak, but that does not appear hopeful as repair shops and equipment was destroyed too."

Rommel rose to his feet, straightening out the shirt he wore. "And the fuel depot?" he asked, his impatience growing.

Now it was von Mellenthin who paused. "We've lost the entire supply, Herr Field Marshal." His voice was tight and cautious.

The message was like a bomb for Rommel. He sat back down on his cot and then quickly rose to his feet, approaching his chief of intelligence so that no more than inches were between them. "All of it?" he asked, bitterly.

Von Mellenthin nodded.

More silence ensued before Rommel spoke after gathering his thoughts. "We have lost our ability to drive into Alexandria," he said, somberly.

General Georg Stumme, a fat veteran recently arrived from the Russian Front suddenly appeared in Rommel's tent. "Herr Field Marshal, I have just learned about Camp Lili Marlene. Tell me this is not so." He sounded like he begged for the information to be false.

Rommel swaggered on his feet. He reached for the chair by his desk. Von Mellenthin moved to assist, but the field marshal waved him away. He sat down heavily. It was known throughout the Afrika Korps and Britische High Command that Rommel had not been himself of late. Medical officers noted how he pushed himself to the brink of physical exhaustion. In late September he had been diagnosed with chronic stomach and intestinal catarrh and nasal diphtheria. It took an order from Colonel-General Alfred Jodl, Chief of the German Army High Command, to drag him from the sands of North Afrika to Austria for treatment. General Georg Stumme replaced him during his absence and Rommel requested he remain on his staff upon his return from Austria.

Stumme, who suffered from acute high blood pressure, walked to Rommel. "Why not lie down, Herr Field Marshal," he suggested, placing a gentle hand on Rommel's shoulder. "We've suffered difficult times before and will see our way through this," he added, meekly.

Rommel gave no response. Stumme looked at von Mellenthin, motioning with a nod of the head for him to leave. Von Mellenthin nodded compliance and left, closing the flaps to the front of the tent. Outside he was met with obvious stares from the staff waiting anxiously for news of their commander's health along with his reaction to the news. Von Mellenthin's body language indicated things were not well.

As if on cue the staff returned their focus to their duties, which mostly lay in shuffling the over-burdened job of paperwork needed to keep an army running smoothly. But their thoughts were far from their work, instead wondering what future lay for them in the ever changing fortunes of war in the desert.

When General Stumme exited Rommel's quarters he found von Mellenthin standing there to meet him. Stumme's expression was sorrowful, an indication to von Mellenthin their words they exchanged were not positive.

"The field marshal is returning to Semmering, Austria," Stumme said, wearily. "He feels the need for more treatment concerning his ailments."

Von Mellenthin bobbed his head. "I'm sure the loss of Camp Lili Marlene did not help his condition," he added, carefully.

"What do you think?" General Stumme shot back.

The staff in the HQ tent recognized the need for Stumme and von Mellenthin to have privacy, so they quietly left. Stumme waited for them to exit before continuing. "*You* are chief of intelligence!" he said, accusingly. "How could this have happened?"

Von Mellenthin did not like this verbal attack, but maintained his military bearing. "We took precautions deemed necessary to keep the base hidden," he started, trying to sound reasonable. "However, a base this size and of significant importance was bound to reach enemy attention." He paused, gathering his thoughts. "The Britische merely got lucky," he offered, feebly. "It goes against military logic they should have been able to locate and attack it."

General Stumme grunted. "It appears the Britische have once more managed the impossible," he snarled.

Von Mellenthin saw no point in arguing. "What are we to do now, Herr General?"

General Stumme did not answer immediately. He needed time to think. When he was ready he faced von Mellenthin. "The enemy is likely to attack in early November once they have completed construction on their waterline. Your reports indicate the attack will be in the south near the Qattara Depression." He moved to a map on a nearby table for references. "The Alamein Line is nearly sixty-five kilometers long and the enemy is within three thousand kilometers from our current position." He scratched his chin before adding, "This gives us time to continue strengthening our defenses."

While the general spoke a feeling of despair swept over von Mellenthin and his body language did not go unnoticed by him. "What is wrong with you?" he demanded.

There was a drawn out period of silence before von Mellenthin asked, "So there will be no offensive?"

The question left the general flabbergasted. "I would think *you* know answer to that feeble question. Reports indicate the enemy is receiving thousands of men, guns, equipment, and most importantly—tanks! We have no choice other than go on defensive until fortunes return in our favor."

Von Mellenthin nodded agreement half-heartedly. "Jawohl, Herr General," he said, sadly. A moment passed before he added, "I hate giving into the Britische."

General Stumme grunted. "Well, who in hell doesn't?"

# Chapter 29

*El Alamein was the key to Alexandria. Whichever army*
*was victorious here was most certain to win the war in North Afrika.*

## October 23, 1942
## 9:40 p.m.

When Lieutenant-General Bernard Law Montgomery took command of 8th Army he enjoyed the sight of reinforcements and supplies pouring in his lap in record numbers.

*All this to defend a small town called El Alamein,* he thought.

Yet he knew its importance. British prestige and future in the region lay at stake, and Churchill was determined not to lose to Hitler's Third Reich. Monty, as his troops referred to him, issued a simple order from his first day in command.

"The 8th Army shall not yield a single yard of ground from this day on! Troops will fight and die in positions they defend!"

Monty remained cocksure of himself based on his two-to-one advantage he obtained over the past two and a half months. During this time he received 41,000 new recruits, 800 guns, and over 1,000 tanks. Reports filtered to British HQ that Rommel's Afrika Korps could barely muster 500 serviceable tanks and only half the field guns they possessed. British troop numbers totaled 195,000 compared to the Germans' 100,000. Supplies flowed freely to Alexandria, only 60 miles from El Alamein. Whereas the Afrika Korps received supplies from Tobruk, which was 300 miles away and highly vulnerable to air attack. With such an advantage every man in the 8th Army now believed Rommel could be beaten for good. After two years of seesaw battle everyone from the lowliest private to general staff saw victory of war in the desert now within reach.

At 9:40 p.m. the order was given: *'Troop fire!'*

Every field gun at Monty's disposal opened fire on the German defensive line with a barrage of destruction unparalleled since start of the war. The roar of guns was so great that as far as Alexandria their thunder was heard. The attack caught the Germans by complete surprise. All along their forty mile defensive line confusion set in. The ferocity of the bombardment indicated this was beginning of a major enemy offensive, which they had been led to believe would not occur until mid-November. With Rommel in Austria, German morale sank by thoughts of fending off their enemy without their beloved leader to guide them.

All along trenches and dugouts Germans and Italians built, exploding shells showered Axis forces with rocks and sand. Hundreds of mines blew up, creating concussions so powerful that German and Italian troops were killed outright. General Stumme realized what was happening and attempted to contact key posts along their defensive lines, but the artillery barrage destroyed lines of communication. Acting on impulse, Stumme ordered his staff car driver to take him and Oberst Buchting to the main dugout where their tactical HQ for the entire German line was located.

They drove ferociously down the dirt road, bouncing along the way when suddenly from out of nowhere a machinegun fired on them. Seconds later more guns fired on them and soon the staff car was riddled with bullets from all sides. General Stumme thought they must have run smack into an enemy forward element—and they were defenseless!

General Stumme was about to instruct the driver to turn around when Colonel Buchting fell forward, his chest spurting blood from where he had been shot. The driver panicked and abruptly stopped the car. He put the gear in reverse and sped back the way they came, but bullets continued whizzing all around them. The windshield spider-webbed, but did not shatter and sparks erupted from the car like a roman candle.

In all this confusion the driver failed to see General Stumme was no longer in the car. Once they came under fire, Stumme leaped out onto the side footing of the car, hanging on the door as the driver attempted to evade enemy gunners. A pain in the general's chest caused him gasping for air. At first thought he believed he had been shot before realizing he was having a heart attack. Stumme's face distorted as he could not breathe and his grip on the door loosened. A moment later he felt himself sailing through the air, tumbling and rolling before coming to a stop on the side of the road. The driver sped away, none the wiser and for the time being the Afrika Korps was now leaderless.

Lieutenant-General Oliver Leese had been assigned commander of British XXX Corps and it was his responsibility to break through an immense minefield which lay before tanks of Lieutenant-General Herbert Lumsden's X Corps. However, this task proved more difficult than expected.

Along the forty mile Axis line, which Rommel dubbed this no-man's-land zone as *'The Devil's Gardens,'* his men spent much time between August and October laying half a thousand mines stretching from the Mediterranean Sea to the northern tip of the Qattara Depression. Only Rommel himself knew how to maneuver the field and planned on beating the Britische to the punch by attacking El Alamein first.

This changed with the loss of Camp Lili Marlene, which had been Afrika Korps' lifeline for future offensives. The long supply route from Tripoli and Tobruk was dangerous for vehicles under constant harassment from enemy planes. Much of Afrika Korps' supplies by ship had been sent to the bottom of the sea by the Royal Air Force and Navy. At best Rommel's forces received barely six thousand tons of supplies compared to the thirty thousand tons required for his sustained offensive. Rommel's hope on fuel supplies had been with his reserves at Camp Lili Marlene, now destroyed.

British soldiers remained under cover in trenches, weapons in hand, each silently praying for all the best when a lone soldier climbed atop the embankment holding a Smith-Wesson revolver with a string of thin leather rope attached to the butt of his revolver, the other end attached to his pistol belt. Bringing a whistle from his free hand to his lips he drew a deep breath and blew hard as humanly possible. Despite 900 field guns firing round after round in a deadly cacophony making many turn deaf, all soldiers reacted to the signal. By the hundreds, soldiers scurried from trenches and pressed forward. Backpacks worn were marked with a white *St. Andrews* cross to guide persons behind them. They moved slowly forward, walking, not running, at a steady pace with rifles held high port and bayonets attached.

Sappers moved stealthily, searching for enemy machine gun posts while hundreds of men carrying mine detectors scoured for deadly mines. When one was located a sharp ping was heard in the earphones they wore. A small lamp was then placed on the spot as a marker. Soldiers managed to maintain a steady pace for the first hour of their attack before terror struck them—*S-Mines!*

S-Mines were small cans which showered shrapnel in a 360 degree radius. Its sole purpose was created to maim or kill troops. In one section the Germans ingeniously planted a 200 lbs. Luftwaffe bomb the mine detectors missed. A young Tommy tripped a wire and a thunderous explosion went skyward, tearing apart four dozen men. Everyone in the immediate vicinity dove for cover. This went on for the rest of the night and into early morning hours of next day.

The number of injured and dead grew. Scenes were horrific for young British soldiers newly arrived to the front. There were dead German and Italian soldiers everywhere, victims of field gun bombardment. Bodies were torn and mangled into twisted heaps of flesh. Walking over a severed arm or leg became commonplace. One British soldier found an enemy helmet lying before him and kicked it aside, and nearly fainted upon finding the head of a dead German soldier still strapped inside the helmet.

By midday of October 24, 1942 British advances came to a stall. Montgomery fumed over the delay and demanded to know what caused the holdup. It turned out Germans managed to keep their line of defense largely intact and displayed fine valor keeping English forces at bay. British sappers were unable to keep pace at beginning of zero hour and now crawled inch by inch instead of yard by yard.

Montgomery ordered General Lumsden to throw in the bulk of his tanks into the fight, but Lumsden balked. "Our tanks will be cut piecemeal attempting to run through minefields!" he replied, defiantly.

By nightfall Montgomery stood in his command post and ordered his tanks to move forward in spite British soldiers' inability to clear the minefield. Then the worst happened. Luftwaffe planes joined in the fight, dropping bombs on British supply columns, destroying a number of vehicles carrying vital munitions. British vehicles drove in such tight formation that other vehicles caught fire and went up in flames, too. With fires burning brightly in the night, German field gunners trained their sights on the flames and fired a barrage of deadly 88mm anti-aircraft guns, tearing through British tanks like a knife through butter. Fighting was so fierce a single column of tanks lost two-thirds of its force in less than half an hour.

Lieutenant-Colonel James Eadie in the Staffordshire Yeomanry Regiment literally broke down over loss of his command. There was nothing he could do under the murderous 88mm gunfire, and as destruction of British tanks continued Major John Lakin noted, "Those eighty-eight's lit our tanks like someone lighting candles on a birthday cake!"

By 3:30 am on October 25, 1942 Monty met with Generals Lumsden and Guingand, whom Monty noted, had the look of defeat written all over them.

Lumsden wanted to call off the attack. "It's not going the way we expected, sir," he said, sounding more like a young lieutenant rather than commanding officer of fifty thousand men. "Our boys have been unable to clear a path for our tanks to maneuver the minefield and the Germans are throwing everything they've got into the fight. The Luftwaffe has also joined the fight and their bombs are tearing apart column after column of our tanks."

Guingand next took up argument. "At this point of battle we have nearly several thousand casualties," he said, despondently. "Field hospitals are overflowing with wounded and our doctors are nearing exhaustion. Few tanks have breached the minefield, but without infantry support their efforts are fruitless. If we don't pull back before dawn we risk losing them to enemy field artillery."

Their conversation dragged on with Monty attentively listening, and his silence was all too obvious. When they finished he remained seated and stared at both his generals with his usual calm, self-assuredness.

"There will be no change in my battle plans," he said, firmly. "Any type of withdrawal is strictly forbidden. Our tanks and men are to continue advancing. We fight and die where we stand, gentlemen!"

The generals were about to argue, but stopped when Monty raised a halting hand. "We've lost over one hundred tanks, I know," Monty confessed, "but we still have nearly nine hundred serviceable tanks capable of turning tables on Jerry."

"Not if enemy field artillery remains intact!" Lumsden shot back. "Tanks are not designed to take on field guns as you know, sir!"

"Any tank is expendable if it brings us closer to victory, gentlemen," Monty replied coolly. He saw the shock in his field commanders' eyes and sternly added, "If either of you are incapable of carrying out my orders, tell me now so I can replace you forthwith."

Lumsden and de Guingand were stunned into silence. They watched as Monty rose from his chair and told them, "I suggest you return to your posts." Next he turned his back on them and said, "I'm going back to bed."

Earlier the same day Rommel returned to North Afrika and resumed command from General Stumme, whose death was still unknown. General

Ritter von Thoma had taken over command of Panzer Army Afrika in absence of Stumme and greeted Rommel on the airfield when his plane landed. They shuffled Rommel to his command tent and saw he still suffered from exhaustion. His face was pale and he wore his uniform disheveled. He looked like he needed help to remain standing, but no one dared assist. He kept a handkerchief in his hand, blowing his nose whenever it ran.

Rommel removed his greatcoat and peaked cap, handing them to a lieutenant standing nearby. To those having served a long time with the field marshal, he appeared like he lost ten pounds, causing his uniform to hang loosely on him. Rommel took a nearby chair and sat heavily down.

"Well, Ritter," he began, sounding tired from the long flight from Austria, "what is our situation?"

General von Thoma, a tall, slender man with Aryan features admired by Nazi enthusiasts, stared back in silence as though waiting for further permission to speak. He appeared exhausted like many officers in the Afrika Korps. His cheekbones were sunken in his face, leaving one to believe he was malnourished. When he did speak he did so with a voice commanding respect, and von Thoma knew Rommel well enough to be concise when discussing matters of utmost urgency.

"Herr Field Marshal, our situation is critical!" he screeched. He waited for Rommel to respond, who displayed no emotion.

Von Thoma used a map on the table near Rommel for reference. "Britische are moving on three points," he explained, using a pencil to mark on the map. "They have pushed through our minefield here," he stopped to circle the location on the map, "and are now attempting to take the coastal road north. In the south they have large numbers of tanks and infantry poised to attack our forces here. They haven't achieved much success due to the bulk of their forces being pinned down by our air raids and field artillery, however, our fuel situation is dangerously low. With this in mind, Herr Field Marshal, if the Britische break through any point in force we will be unable to move our panzers to meet the threat."

Rommel shook his head in sour reflection. *This cannot be happening.* "Had Camp Lili Marlene not been destroyed we would have fuel enough," he lamented.

Von Mellenthin stood off to the side and clicked his heels before speaking. "Herr Field Marshal, the kommandant of Camp Lili Marlene is outside and available to report on what happened," he said, offering him opportunity to hear from the man most responsible himself.

Rommel rubbed his face with the palms of both hands. In the background the sound of big artillery pounding their fury reached their ears. Despite their HQ being located nearly two kilometers away, explosions shook the ground beneath their feet. Lamps hanging inside the tent swayed, and the worry of a Britische breakthrough became evermore apparent. Rommel nodded and motioned with his hand to have Mueller report.

Sturmbannfuhrer Hans Mueller entered the tent and felt the eyes of all present focus on him. He appeared visibly troubled, but maintained his bearing. He was after all a German officer and prepared to take whatever was in store for him. He wore signs of battle all over him. His uniform was dust-covered as was his face, save for large circles around his eyes having been protected by desert goggles. Like many he had not eaten a good meal since the start of the Britische attack, causing him to appear like he was going to fall down exhausted. He removed his cap, tucking it under his arm, and clicked his heels while standing ramrod straight before Rommel.

Mueller maintained eye contact with Rommel while the field marshal studied him. During this time Mueller sensed the presence of someone staring much deeper at him. It was a disturbing feeling because he had the deep sense that this person had it in for him for personal reasons rather than professional ones. He slowly shifted his eyes to members in the tent, whose hardened gaze was meant to frighten those standing under scrutiny. Then he saw him.

Oberst Otto Krieger, the quartermaster chief, stood amongst the staff. He thrust his chest out best he could while straining to suck in his large stomach. Mueller recalled their row regarding treatment of prisoners after they had taken Tobruk, and he could tell he enjoyed seeing him now placed under scrutiny. An evil smile pursed Krieger's fat lips and if it was not for the stern discipline instilled in him from years of military training; Mueller would have reached out and slapped Krieger regardless of his superior rank.

Finally Rommel spoke. "How did this happen?" he sternly challenged.

Mueller stiffened and explained in detail about the enemy attack destroying his base. When finished he drew a deep breath and concluded with, "I was then ordered to bring the remnants of my command here and assist in defending our positions against enemy attack."

Von Thoma then spoke. "You do realize, Sturmbannfuhrer, the loss of petrol at your base has cost us not only the drive to Alexandria," he barked, "but the ability to maneuver our tanks all along the front to meet any enemy breakthrough and repel it?"

The words cut through Mueller like a hot knife through butter. "As kommandant I assume full responsibility for loss of my command, Herr Field Marshal," he said, turning attention back to Rommel.

Krieger saw his moment to crush Mueller and stepped forward to obtain center stage. "I regret, Herr Field Marshal, this loss of petrol cannot be replaced," he lied. Krieger knew the Wehrmacht fighting in Russia had priority, but all it took was a report to German High Command of their dire situation for reserves to be directed to the North Afrikan theatre. After all, Hitler could not afford his favorite general to fail. Still, he made his point.

Silence engulfed the tent. Attention swayed in Rommel's direction as he blew his nose hard. He looked at General von Thoma with resignation. "For the time being Mueller needs to be with his men on the front," he said, sounding all business. He directed his attention to Mueller and said, "There'll be time to sort out responsibility later."

Mueller looked astonished and relieved. "Danke, Herr Field Marshal," he managed to reply in a choked voice.

Rommel waved a dismissive hand. "There are no more laurels to be earned in Afrika," he said, sourly. "No guarantees can be made in war gentlemen, other than someone wins and someone loses. The English have received greater numbers of men and material than Panzer Army Afrika. Reports state Americans will attempt a landing in the east, presumably Morocco. The last thing we need is a two-front war in the desert. Once this happens all here will be lost."

Officers present grew uncomfortable hearing the field marshal speak in such a defeatist manner. This sort of bold talk was strictly forbidden in the German Army and could lead to court-martial and dismissal—even for someone of Rommel's stature!

Von Thoma stepped forward. "We are not surrendering, Herr Field Marshal?" he asked, cautiously.

Rommel coughed, shaking his head. "Goodness, no!" he snarled. "I merely state a victory in the desert for us is no longer a reality." He let his words sink in a few moments before continuing. "The Fuhrer had promised enough fuel for us to take Alexandria, and the latest rocket launchers and Tiger tanks to arm our troops with. Another two panzer and three infantry divisions were to be shipped to us, but that never happened." Rommel coughed hard, desperately catching his breath. "Our reality is all too obvious," he added, resigned to their fate. He looked the staff members in the eye from one man to the next. "We must retreat to Tunisia and set up defense positions strong enough to hold back the enemy in order for us to withdraw as many of our troops and material to Sicily."

Rommel noted the pained expression on staff members and nodded in empathy. "Our men are fighting and dying over rocks and sand not even the Bedouin would think twice for," he explained. "Each tank destroyed is a tank which cannot be replaced. Our men have fought valiantly keeping the enemy at bay, but they have nearly one thousand tanks to our three hundred. We have lost by attrition, gentlemen. The most we can hope for is stalling the enemy long enough so we may begin a gradual withdrawal."

## October 26, 1942

Morale among German soldiers sunk to an all-time low. Men abandoned positions when troops of the British 1st Armoured Division, Australian 9th Division, and the 2nd New Zealand Division poured through German defenses in numbers never before seen. British troops cheered by the sight of once proud men of the Afrika Korps now taking flight. For the first time in battle they were equipped with superior tanks such as the American-made Grant and Sherman tanks, powerful enough to defeat German Panzer IV and III tanks on an even playing field.

Sergeant Heinrich Priess and all able-bodied men at Camp Lili Marlene were transferred to the front to participate in the Battle of El Alamein. He commanded a 25-ton Panzer IV and was one of the few able to make a difference on the battlefield. He expertly commandeered his tank over terrain while handling the main 75mm turret gun himself. Priess sought targets and fired round after round, working the gun-loader harder than ever. At the start of the war in the desert the panzers were the finest built. Now tables had turned. Their 30mm armor was easily pierced by American and British tanks, destroying them completely.

By this stage of war victory depended on efficiency of tank crews. Rommel may have thought the war in the desert was lost, but this never entered the mind of Sergeant Priess and others. He sped circles around enemy tanks putting good use to the longer firing range his 75mm turret gun offered. He had been schooled on how to knock out enemy tanks. The secret was aiming for the treads. If you destroyed a tank's ability to maneuver you were most certain to destroy it with the second shot.

Despite Priess and a few other tank commanders' good fortune it was not enough to save the day. British troops pressed forward, tossing grenades while following closely behind their own tanks. If a column got pinned down they called up artillery to join in the barrage of fire, pushing back German panzers and troops in droves. Tanks shook violently from artillery explosions erupting all around them. German infantry was showered with hot metal fragments, some even buried alive by walls of dirt pouring over them as enemy artillery distorted terrain from numerous explosions.

Finally all German troops were ordered to retreat. Priess' tank travelled no further than one kilometer before receiving a direct hit! His tank burst into flames and the air inside turned black with smoke, making the crew sick in the stomach. To make matters worse, each man caught fire and they scrambled to get out before they were burnt alive. Priess clawed his way through the hatch and jumped clear from his burning tank. He rolled over and over in the sand, furiously putting out the flames on his uniform.

When he managed to put them out he looked for his crew. Some were not fortunate. Flames enveloped them completely and Priess witnessed them running and rolling like chickens with heads chopped off before finally lying still as their bodies smoldered. The stench of human flesh mixed with black powder and diesel fuel was appalling, and this caused Priess to vomit what little food he had eaten earlier in the day. He saw other tank crews face similar fate and grew weak with depression as he realized there was nothing he could do to help anyone other than himself. The price of fighting hours on end and nearly having the skin off his back burned had completely drained him of all strength.

Walther Prien fared no better. He had long ago sworn he would never be taken prisoner and had no intention of surrender. The Afrika Korps had withdrawn before only to go on the offensive when time was right, and he intended to be part of the next offensive with Rommel once more leading them to victory.

Prien fought long and hard with his platoon, firing rifles and machine guns until they had no more ammunition. However, the Britische juggernaut was too great and their line of defense was heavily bombarded by tank and artillery fire. His entire platoon had been wiped out and he had no idea how he managed to survive. When an artillery shell exploded near him, knocking him unconscious, the last thing he recalled was telling his mother how proud he was to serve the Fatherland.

When he awakened he struggled to his feet. He found it a chore simply to breathe. In the distance he saw wave after wave of Britische Tommies running through minefields they breached and assume control of German positions. These were the same positions he fought long and hard to keep them from breaking through.

Prien stumbled toward the rear lines and came across a German soldier lying face down. An MP40 submachine gun was beneath the body and Prien needed the weapon. He knelt beside the body and rolled him over and was taken aback when he found the man alive and numb from shock!

*Something familiar about this man,* Prien thought. He moved in for a closer look. "Privat Mohr—what on earth has happened to you?"

Karl Mohr was overcome with shell-shock from enemy bombardment tearing up the entire German defensive line, and could not speak. Prien helped him to his feet.

"What do we do, Herr Feldwebel?" Mohr finally managed to ask. His tone was that of a desperate man.

Without saying a word, Prien led the way toward their lines. Artillery shells continued to rain all over the desert, making their march rough. It would prove to be a long, arduous retreat, but necessary if they were to keep from being captured. In the back of Prien's mind he could not shake the thought of having another opportunity of coming face to face with the man from Tobruk.

*I did not survive this battle in vain,* he told himself. *Our paths have crossed before, and they will again. The next time will be our last.* "Tommy, I shall return," he said aloud.

Privat Mohr marched beside the sergeant and heard him, curious why he would make such a statement when it became all too obvious the Britische were winning the Desert War.

"Yimkin," Mohr said, in a hushed tone.

This was the local Arab term for 'perhaps,' and the same response the Britische often wrote whenever finding the statement, 'Tommy, we shall return,' scrawled on buildings or destroyed vehicles by retreating Germans.

# Chapter 30

*"This is not the end. This is not even the beginning of the end.*
*It is, however, the end of the beginning."*

— *Winston Churchill*

## Alexandria, Egypt
## November 5, 1942

Major Lawrence drove his jeep to the row of beach houses and came to a stop at the bungalow he knew Jack Ruggero resided in. He stepped out of his pristine-clean vehicle, quite a change from the one he used on his most recent mission, and took in the beauty of the early morning hour. The sun rose brilliantly and the waves of the Mediterranean Sea lapped on the beach breaking the calm and quiet. A slight breeze rustled through the palm trees and here and there were military couples walking hand in hand.

He walked up to the beach house, stopping on the porch and knocking on the screen door.

"Hello major, how good it is to see you again," Valerie said, flashing a radiant smile. "Please, come in." She did not seem bothered to be seen wearing a rather skimpy nightgown. "Jack is sitting outside on the veranda reading the paper. Go and join him while I get us some tea."

"It's good to see you, my dear," he replied, taking her hand and kissing it before heading out to the veranda.

"Oh," she said, stopping, "thank you for bringing him back to me in one piece. I know how rough you desert raiders have it in the field, so you have my thanks." With that said she took her leave to the kitchen to fetch tea.

Major Lawrence stepped outside and found Jack reading a newspaper. "Anything interesting?" he asked, grinning.

Jack put the paper down and got to his feet. "Hello, major! What brings you here?"

"I thought I'd stop by before heading on to the front."

They shook hands vigorously, pleased to see one another. Jack motioned for him to take a seat at the table. "The papers are full of good news for the British Army," Jack said. "It looks like your new guy, Monty, has the Desert Fox on the run."

Major Lawrence nodded. "Yes, well he had a bit of help, if you know my meaning," he said with a wink.

Jack nodded with a smile. "He turned the Afrika Korps into a shadow of its former self," he added, jubilantly.

Major Lawrence pondered that. "Yes, well when you outnumber your enemy two to one in every field, it's easy to see why."

Jack leaned back in his chair. "I never thought I'd say this," he confessed, "but I'm actually proud of having played a part in all this."

"You should be," the major told him, coolly. "Had Jerry been able to make use of the petrol we destroyed, our offensive might very well have turned up with different results."

Jack nodded in reflection. "Yes, but I understand Rommel's still not finished," he said, indicating what the newspapers wrote about the war in the desert. "States here the Germans are in full retreat and if he makes it to Tunisia he'll be in position to evacuate his army to Sicily." Jack showed him the newspaper article. "Do you think they'll make it?"

Major Lawrence shrugged. "Driving rains have slowed his retreat, but it's also slowed Monty's advance. Our boys are licking their heels, but it's still up in the air if we'll catch them before they make it."

Valerie appeared carrying a tray with a pot of hot tea, cups, and biscuits. She poured them each a cup and excused herself to change.

Jack offered the major some milk with his tea. "I know how you limey's like it with your tea. I prefer mine with sugar, but no milk."

Major Lawrence sipped his tea. "I've some good news," he said, jubilant.

Jack looked up, curious.

"Monty heard of our job in the desert, no doubt in a report from Stirling, and wants to decorate you personally for your efforts."

Jack's mouth dropped open. "You're joking?" His voice rose in a pitch.

Major Lawrence took another sip before setting his cup down. "Not at all," he said, shaking his head. "Makes for good relations with you Yanks seeing how you're about to join in the fight. Besides, Colonel Stirling enjoys seeing our boys receive attention. You see, there are those at GHQ who'd like to see us disbanded. Stirling believes showering our boys with glory will convince them our line of work is a necessity, and not some fluke."

Jack sank heavily in his chair.

"What's wrong?" the major asked, noticing the gloom on Jack's face.

Jack looked up at him. "Doesn't seem fair," he explained, distraught. He paused to gather the right words. "I mean, you boys did all the work. I was simply along for the ride and not by choice if I may point out."

Major Lawrence shrugged. "This is the way Monty wants it," he said, with finality. He saw how uncomfortable Jack appeared and sought to soothe him. "Look, you did more than your share," he continued. "You fought well when the time came. Remember the German you ran into in the middle of the petrol dump?"

Jack shuddered. "How can I forget," he sneered. He paused, looking as though he thought hard about something.

"What is it?" Major Lawrence asked, curious.

Jack lit up like he made a major discovery. "The man who knocked me off my feet back in the middle of the fuel depot... I know where I saw him," he boasted. "He was the kraut who chased me on the beach. The son-of-a-bitch machine-gunned my heels before I made it inside Tobruk right before it fell. The next time I saw him I was standing among a bunch of POWs while he rode in a kubelwagen. I could've sworn he was looking for me."

Major Lawrence looked stunned by Jack's revelation. "Pretty impressive, but not uncommon," he admitted. "That sort of thing happens a lot, where you come across an enemy soldier you faced at one time or another. Well, at least you don't have to worry about him for some time." He leaned back in his chair, grinning. "It appears as though your luck at the card table follows you on the battlefield, too. Guess you're a regular *Jack of Spades*. That's what I believe you chaps refer to a lucky card, right?"

Jack nodded and looked over his shoulder, staring at Valerie who was busy in the kitchenette. He turned back facing the major. "I prefer *Jack of Hearts!*" he said, beaming mischievously.

## November 5, 1942

Rommel stood in the back of his command car parked along the coast road near Tobruk. He watched in silence while his men trudged eastward. The remnants of his army resembled that of a defeated one. Men sat in vehicles wrapped in bandages. German soldiers had hastily grabbed any working vehicle they found and now sat atop lorries, armoured cars, kubelwagens, and tanks. They drove past broken down English and German vehicles, burnt out and damaged beyond use, the scars of seesaw battles fought over the previous two years.

The driving rain let up and rays of sunshine cracked through dark, gray clouds. Weather forced their retreat to maintain a slow pace, but with clear skies the main threat would be harassment by enemy planes. Sturmbannfuhrer von Mellenthin sat in Rommel's car, advising him on latest intelligence reports.

"Herr Field Marshal, we must keep moving," he warned. "Enemy planes will soon fill the sky, making our drive to the Sollum and Halfaya Passes more difficult than bad weather."

Rommel nodded. He noticed his driver held a camera used for taking numerous photographs of Rommel on many occasions during his campaign in North Afrika. Rommel had every intention of using the photographs for a biography he planned to write at war's end. When the driver offered the camera to him he shook his head. "I never photograph my retreat," he said, solemnly.

Embarrassed for making the offer, the driver put the camera away and focused on the road.

Von Mellenthin rose so that he stood in the vehicle beside Rommel. "Herr Field Marshal, I implore you—we *must* leave!"

Rommel ignored the demand from his intelligence officer and stared blankly at his defeated army. His men looked at him as they passed, showing their sorrowful eyes for having let down their favorite commanding officer. This made Rommel feel more dejected in spirit. So far as he was concerned it was their Fuhrer who failed them by not supplying him with material and reinforcements so that he could meet the Britische on the field of battle on equal terms.

"Look at them, Freiherr," Rommel said, with tears welling in his eyes. "They believe they have failed me, when in fact it is our Fuhrer at fault."

Von Mellenthin glanced at the men in the car, praying they were trustworthy and loyal to Rommel. The Gestapo secretly placed informers close to commanding officers of an army to keep Berlin informed and ensure loyalty to the Fuhrer. Defeatist talk was not tolerated in the German Army and von Mellenthin did not want Rommel to say anything which could be used against him.

"Had I been given permission to retreat on the third of this month more of our army might have been spared," Rommel fumed. "But no, the Fuhrer commanded us to achieve victory or death at all costs!" He paused again, trembling with anger. "I find it ironic only after I disobeyed his order did he authorize me a withdrawal." He shook his head. "This is madness!"

Rommel stepped down from his command car and walked across the road through the line of vehicles and men as they headed west. In the distance he saw Tobruk, the port city which marked his greatest triumph over the English. Now it was nothing more than a memory.

"If only I had supplies enough to fight with," he hissed. He started to turn back toward his car when he saw a soldier scrawling words on the side of a destroyed panzer. It read, *'Tommy, we shall return!'*

"Yimkin," Rommel said, softly. He finished with, "But not likely."

## November 5, 1942
## El Alamein, Montgomery's Field HQ

Jack Ruggero and Major Lawrence arrived at Monty's HQ close to noon right when the general was about to have tea. Upon hearing of their arrival Monty invited them to join him. The command tent was bustling with activity, but the mood was casual, calm, and above all confident. The threat of a German counter-attack proved no longer feasible, and in the background of the tent a radio loudspeaker had been switched on to broadcast a speech by Prime Minister Winston Churchill.

Jack and Major Lawrence were escorted to the place in the tent reserved for Monty. He sat alone by a table and read a newspaper. Upon seeing his guests he rose to his feet. "Ah, Major Lawrence, good of you to come!" he said, pleasingly. Monty returned the salute from the major and Jack and shook their hands. "This must be the Yank who helped keep

Rommel from putting to use all that fuel he planned for his offensive. We're most grateful, young man. Had Rommel received enough fuel for his tanks he might have struck first, thus putting our plans for an offensive on the back-burner."

Monty motioned for his guests to sit down on chairs beside the table. "I must say, Churchill has let up now that Jerry is on the run. The old man had been chewing my ear off with questions, constantly demanding to know when I was going to launch my attack. 'Rommel! Rommel! Rommel! What else is more important than defeating Rommel?!'" he said, mimicking the PM's rant. He stopped long enough to listen closely to Churchill's victory speech come to a close, and he motioned with a raised hand for all personnel nearby to quiet down.

*"This is not the end,"* Churchill's speech concluded. *"This is not even the beginning of the end. It is perhaps, the end of the beginning."*

The men in the tent erupted with applause over this incredible victory.

Monty shook his head, reflecting his relationship with the prime minister. "When he pushed me for an attack in September I told him he'd have to find someone else to lead it. I had no intention of attacking until we were ready. I also knew he had no one in line to replace me and my ruse worked, because he left me alone after that episode."

Monty continued telling them his story not holding back anything. During this time Jack found him to be a charming fellow. He was a lot shorter than Jack thought he would be, and rail-thin. His face was narrow and his skin pink-white. His hair was thinning on top and there was little physically imposing about him. He did, however, possess enough spirit for ten men, or even twenty. Energy poured from his fiber as he spoke and there was no questioning his ability to command attention. He spoke of details of the battle, indicating his ability to keep a close handle of things in a personal nature, and Jack was thoroughly impressed. When Jack asked about his background, Monty was more than willing to go over his whole life story.

Jack and Major Lawrence sat sipping their tea and listening to Monty talk about topics like where he was born and how he got to where he was today. He did not come from aristocracy, but certainly carried himself like he had. While the conversation came to a close an orderly approached with a small box in hand.

"Oh, I almost forgot," Monty said, and took the velvet-covered box in hand.

Everyone got to their feet as Monty opened the box and removed a medal. He pinned it on Jack's uniform and said, "By order of the King, I present you with the *King's Medal.*" Next he saluted Jack and shook hands vigorously with him. "I can't thank you enough, young man," he continued. He turned facing westward in the direction of the German retreat. "I can honestly say our victory is complete and absolute," he boasted. He turned and faced Jack again. "The *Jerries* are kaput, as the saying goes."

## The End

# About the Author

David Lucero lives in San Diego, CA with his family. He is an 82nd Airborne Division veteran and has been writing since the age of fourteen. He loves to travel, exercise, spend time with family and friends, and write books. "I get so much fulfillment when I'm reading and writing. To put words in a story, create characters, to take readers to another time and place, nothing is more satisfying.... Well, almost."

## Books by the Author

*THE SANDMAN*

*Who's Minding the Store?*

*BIG JIM*